Queen of Shifting Sands

Kaitlyn Carter Brown

Whimsical
Publishing & Illustration

Edited by Micheline Ryckman and Deborah O'Carroll
Cover art by Salome Totladze
Cover design by Micheline Ryckman
Map by Hunter Ryckman

To those who have known grief,
To those who have grown weary of life,
To those who want to see new sunrises,
Look to the stars.

KAITLYN CARTER BROWN

QUEEN OF SHIFTING SANDS

SANCEN DESERT

INSTANOLDE

PALACE

TEMPLE

DOCKS

THE GUNGOLE

DELTA LANDS

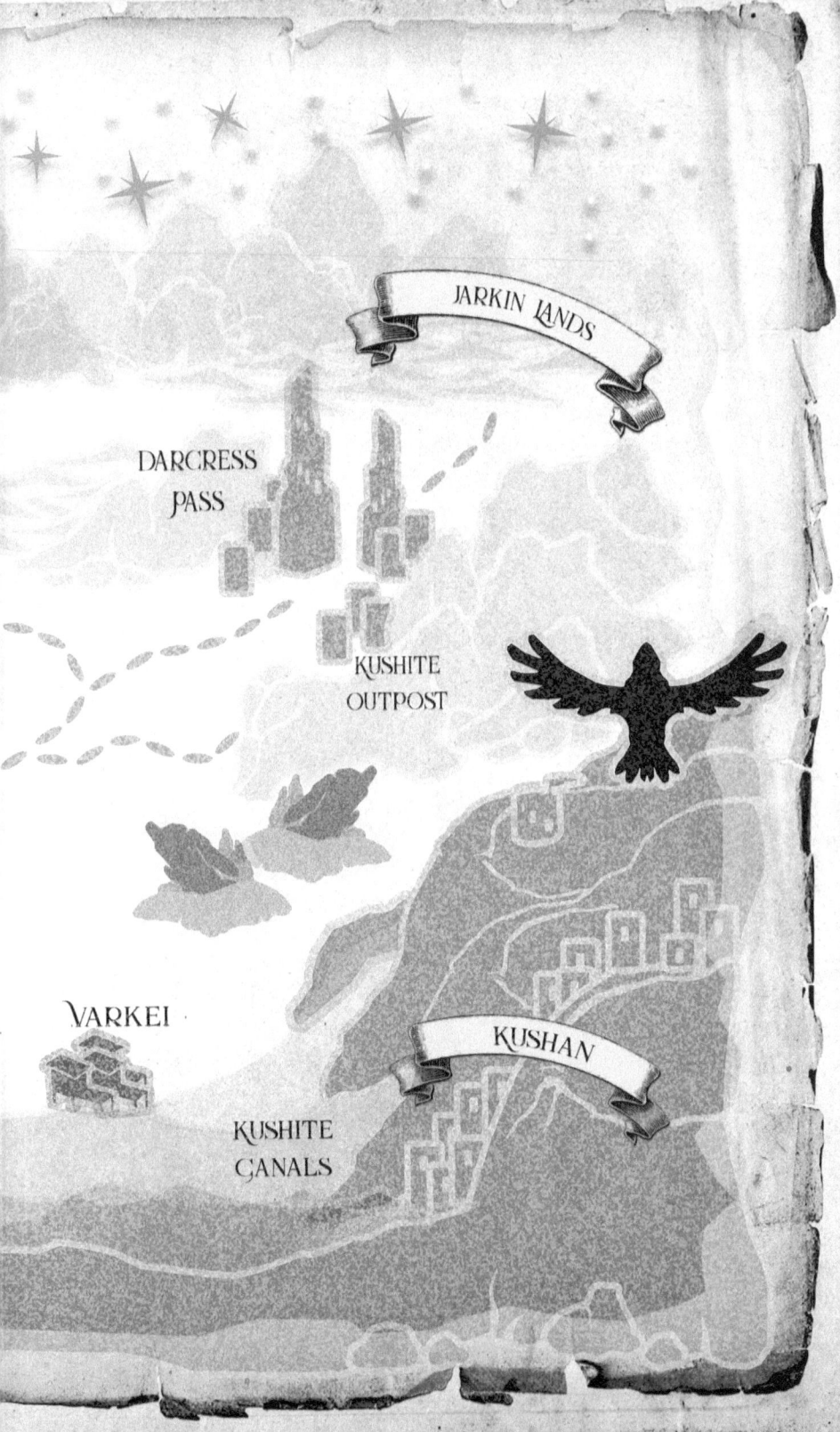

Chapter 1

Elerek

The great gates of Instanolde's palace rumbled back with a stone-shattering *thud*. The sound startled Prince Elerek, upsetting the open book in his lap, the tome tumbling beneath the wheels on his chair. He leaned down to retrieve it, his hand outstretched, when a tingling chill that had no place during high summer took hold of his fingers—a numbness that felt like death.

Something dreadful had happened, he knew it, and the deep, resounding blast of rams' horns confirmed it. One long note strained across the palace's stonework and up to the highest golden spire, announcing the arrival of royalty, of the *king*.

The king who ought not to be there.

Lifting his eyes, Elerek looked across the library, its gallery gilded in elegant arches, toward the window. Sunlight cast a pattern of equal parts light and darkness through the wood lattice. A second note, a third, and a fourth followed, their bellows ringing urgency.

A lump emerged in his throat, strangling his voice. "No, they can't be back."

Only four days, long and hot, had passed. Not nearly enough time to travel across the vast Sancen Desert with a company of soldiers.

Elerek had watched them leave in a clamor of chain mail and belts strapped with scimitars. Men in polished hauberks, with bright orange turbans encircling their sallet helmets. Formidable soldiers of Instanolde, the strength of a people bold enough to make a life here among the sands at the edge of the desert.

And none stood taller than King Cormek, fierce in his countenance and bold in his young rule.

"Alert the prince—now!" A guard's cry echoed.

Elerek's heartbeat droned in his ears, one pensive beat after another. He gripped the rims of his wheeled chair, avoiding the fallen tome and wheeling himself out of the library and into the corridors beyond. Many of the passages he took belonged to servants and soldiers, and he'd memorized the routes where the floors were smoother and his chair rolled freely.

Before the steps of the palace, beneath the relentless noonday sun, a handful of men assembled alongside three cardants. The sides of the great lizards heaved from exertion beneath their leather saddles and they lowered their heads, encircled with long horns, to the sun-scorched stones.

Three—out of the fifty cardants and their riders that had ridden with the king.

Elerek caught his breath, searching the Sancen-scorched faces of the men. Sand, grime, and blood streaked their clothes.

Cormek. "Wh-where is my brother?" His hands trembled.

Two of the soldiers turned to the cardant at the back of their company. With tentative, almost reverent motions, they lifted a wrapped bundle from the saddle, blood soaking through the fabric, and laid it on the mosaic stonework before Elerek's feet.

Silence fell across the courtyard.

Elerek blinked, tears falling down his face. A cold, dark void consumed him. An echo rattled in his ears of raised voices and harsh words. What had now become their *last* words.

An assembly gathered, pouring down the steps of the palace. Guards in stern severity, wide-eyed servants, and robed advisers with stunned expressions. Whispers of an ambush, an attack, buzzed through the air like insects.

"Were there no other survivors?" someone asked, desperate sorrow in their voice.

"Only Torra Lystra. We escorted her to her family home."

Lystra of House Arghan. Cormek's betrothed, the future queen of Instanolde.

She survived. Elerek closed his eyes, releasing a long exhale.

She'd ridden with Cormek to the desert, her skill with the cardants and knowledge of the Sancen enough to rival any soldier's. Elerek remembered seeing her on the glittering morning of their departure, watching as she flung herself into Cormek's waiting arms, her long ebony hair flying behind her. The ring of Cormek's laughter as he swept her off her feet filled the courtyard. When they kissed, the intensity of their passion rivaled the dawn.

And now, Cormek was dead.

The soldiers who had laid out the body dropped to their knees, heads bowed. One by one, the rest of the crowd mirrored their motions.

A shiver crept up Elerek's spine, his head elevated above the entire assembly.

"Your Highness." A soldier spoke. "Gem of the Gungole."

"Fire of the Sancen." Another took up the refrain.

"Fierce as the dawn."

"Mighty as the constellations."

Elerek couldn't breathe. Couldn't think. It wasn't supposed to be like this.

As one voice, the chant filled the air. "Long may you reign —king of Instanolde."

I can't.

Chapter 2

Lystra

Lystra wore orange. The color of kings, and of the flames that would soon light the funeral pyre. She moved a trembling hand to the wide belt of her kaftan, adorned with obsidian beads, and cinched it tighter to compensate for the emptiness consuming her.

Three days had passed since her return from the desert. The priests of the city temple ruled that they could wait no longer to burn the body. Cormek. Her betrothed.

She shuddered, sinking onto a cushioned stool behind her dressing screen. A sob caught in her throat as thoughts of the king—*her* king—regal and beautiful, overwhelmed her mind. Of his strong arms pulling her close, the glow of sunlight in his eyes, the taste of his lips on hers . . .

Lystra dug her nails into her palm, gritting her teeth, holding back her grief.

She could devote an endless number of sun-scorched days to mourning her beloved, but not this night. This night demanded duty, the honor that Cormek was owed. Not as the girl he fell in love with, but the queen he meant to crown. Now, she was neither.

The details surrounding the journey back hazed her mind like a sandstorm on the horizon. An Instan soldier had sat behind her, his body a shield as they rode for their lives. How many had taken arrows in the name of her protection? The battle, the ambush, screamed in her ears with the song of scimitars loosed from their sheaths, the cries of warriors, and the shrieks of cardants and their riders being hacked to death by enemy axes.

The thought of the cardants provoked fresh tears. The immense reptiles with their long, serpentine necks and proud, horned heads possessed no equal for magnificence in Lystra's eyes. All mercilessly slaughtered.

The door to her chamber opened. "Lystra? Are you in here?"

Smearing away her tears, Lystra stepped around the dressing screen. At once, the arms of her cousin wrapped about her neck, filling Lystra's nostrils with the smell of rosewater.

"Oh." Corsha stepped back from their embrace and laid a hand on Lystra's cheek, her jewelry jangling on her arms. Her eyes, the color of smooth-cut jade, glowed with sympathy. "Oh, *vianni.*" Precious one. A whisper of mothers to daughters.

Lystra closed her eyes, a dam against another onslaught of tears.

"Come, let me do your hair." Corsha led her to an ornate vanity carved of dark wood.

Seating herself, Lystra stared into the mirror. Dark circles encased dull eyes that had done an abundance of weeping. Her skin, gaunt and dry from her time in the desert, looked as if it belonged to the wraiths said to haunt the gullies and canyons. Behind her, the warm tones of her gold-painted furniture, embroidered cushions, and the silken curtains enshrouding her balcony seemed far too bright, a cheerful sacrilege.

Corsha took a brush and combed Lystra's hair, the motion soothing.

"Thank you," she whispered.

Her cousin offered a weak smile. "Will you stand at the pyre? In the circle?"

Lystra's gaze dropped to her hands. "It is my place."

Those who stood closest to a pyre were marked as most beloved, most intimate. Cormek's charm had certainly captivated their kingdom, but this honor fell to her, his betrothed.

"Besides." Lystra squared her shoulders, sitting poised before the vanity. "Grandmother would want nothing less."

Corsha didn't reply.

As if summoned, the chamber door opened again and in swept a figure shrouded in black silk. Dalmah, matriarch of House Arghan and proclaimed countess. Her cold eyes, as old as the desert itself, sent a prickling up Lystra's spine.

"Stars, you're not ready yet?"

That voice cut like a knife. Lystra watched her grandmother in the mirror, marveling that someone could look both beautiful and ugly at the same time. Every movement summoned an aloof elegance, her clothes, silver-striped hair, and jewels bowing to her every whim. But Lystra saw only a woman who would do anything to get what she wanted.

"She's nearly there," Corsha purred. She clipped a string of beads into Lystra's hair, the gems dangling over her forehead like a diadem.

Dalmah scowled. "I didn't ask you, girl."

Corsha cowered, blending into the room's splendor.

"Lystra will walk at the head of the procession. Every eye will see her, their rightful queen."

Not anymore. Lystra drew a hollow breath. No matter how fiercely the desire burned in her bosom—to rule and reign—that destiny would also burn to ash tonight alongside the body of the man she loved.

Standing, Lystra smoothed her gown. "Corsha was only trying to help, Grandmother."

"Hmph." Dalmah stepped closer and adjusted the beads across Lystra's forehead, hanging them in a delicate swag pattern. "You will paint your face with mourning stripes."

Behind her, Lystra's maid appeared holding a tray of jars with paints of harsh blacks, burnt oranges, and red the deep hue of blood.

"Must we?" Lystra's heart sank. "It's an old tradition, Grandmother. I'm sure I'll be the only one wearing stripes."

A triumphant smirk twisted Dalmah's ruby lips. "Precisely." She took Lystra by the shoulders and sat her down before the mirror again.

Balancing the tray on the edge of the vanity, the maid removed the lid from the jar of black paint. She lifted Lystra's chin, using a brush to paint thick strokes down her cheeks, masking her weariness and her grief.

No longer Lystra of House Arghan, the kingdom would now see an image, an icon to mark this tragedy. The queen that her grandmother had spent her life cultivating—and now would never be.

"Faster, girl. We haven't all night."

Lystra closed her eyes as the maid painted her eyelids with shaky fingers. Surely her maid, young in years, had never participated in such an ancient tradition. If her grandmother cared so much, she ought to have done it herself. But Dalmah would never get her hands dirty—not when someone else could do the work for her.

Crash!

Lystra opened her eyes. The tray lay overturned, the paints spilling across the patterned wood floor. The maid gave a yelp, scurrying to upturn the jars.

A string of curses flew from Dalmah's lips. She took the maid by the arm and sent a swift slap across her cheek.

"Stop!" Lystra rose to her full height. "Grandmother, leave her alone."

Perhaps some power of command had been retained from her grandmother's lessons. Dalmah grew still, a pillar of black silk, and then stepped away from the maid. The girl sniffled and sank back to the floor to clean up the mess.

Lystra knelt beside her and took up a brush. She dragged it across a puddle of blood-red paint and handed it to her maid with a kind smile. "Please, continue."

"Th-thank you, Torra."

Lystra shifted her gown, assuming a more comfortable position on the floor. Torra, a noblewoman's title, all that she would now ever be.

The maid worked quickly, blinking away her tears and focusing on the task with a newfound resolve. Alternating stripes of red and orange ran down Lystra's cheeks and neck. Black edged the orange in harsh outlines, the color of death side by side with the color of royalty.

"There, Torra. I think you're ready."

Lystra reached out to touch the girl's arm. "Thank you. You've done well."

A smile flickered across the maid's lips as she returned to the task of cleaning the spill.

The smallest of embers lit in Lystra's soul, a candle in the endless night. She rose to her feet. "Shall we depart?"

Dalmah marched her gaze over the length of Lystra's figure. No approval brightened her expression, but she gave a single nod.

Lystra's eyes darted toward her cousin, visible relief softening Corsha's posture. Unfortunately, they both knew, it wasn't only the servants that suffered Dalmah's wrath.

Next, the pyre waited. To burn Cormek, and bid goodbye to the beautiful life she had almost lived.

Chapter 3

Lystra

L onely desert air dried the paint on Lystra's face. She stepped through the gilded iron gates surrounding the estate of House Arghan. Before her, the kingdom of Instanolde lay smothered in darkness, veiled even from the starlight. Her kingdom.

On any other night, the streets would resound with the music of performers, the hawking of vendors selling their wares, and the callers announcing a dance. Their world— Cormek's world—set aflame by the vibrant and brilliant life they'd cultivated from the desert sands.

Without him, Instanolde shared the emptiness that cleaved to Lystra's soul.

Dalmah pushed a small oil lamp into her hand, its flame feeble against the weight of the starless expanse. The rest of Lystra's family—House Arghan—followed suit. Lystra tried to meet the eyes of her father, Jethro, but his usual warmth had turned severe, admonishing Kimzi, Corsha's elder brother, to stand up straight.

Lystra's heart sank. Grandmother's stringency would rule tonight.

"Lead the way, Lystra," Dalmah commanded, as if in answer to her thoughts.

Swallowing, she lifted her head high and stepped into the streets. One by one, her family followed, but they were not alone in the darkness. Silent figures, veiled and robed, formed a long procession, moving like a slow, mournful river toward the temple. Toward the pyre.

Cormek's people. Our people. Lystra lowered her eyelids, her gaze skimming the hem of her gown. Together, she and Cormek had wanted to give them so much more.

Before long, the silence gave way to whispers, slipping through the air like the soft ripples skirting across the sand dunes.

"She survived the desert, the attack."

"The true fire of the Sancen."

"Our queen comes to the pyre to rise from its ashes."

I am not your queen. The king was dead and her wedding and coronation would never come to pass. Lystra sent a frantic expression to her grandmother, but the makings of a smile played on Dalmah's lips. Only her grandmother could orchestrate even death to suit her whims.

When they reached the gates of the temple, they laid their lamps along the edge of the street, forming a line of flames that bled into the city in every direction. Lystra entered the courtyard, craning her neck to glimpse the apex of the temple tower. Each step up the seemingly endless staircase brought her closer to the heavens, for the dead were to be burned near to the stars.

Reaching the edge of the half-moon dais, Lystra's lungs heaved, breathless from the climb. Unseen players were scattered upon the ramparts, strumming ouds, the twang of their strings drifting down from the skies. Their mournful song seemed too tame against the frantic clamor of her heart.

And there, the pyre lay. Priests, clad in yellow robes with deep crimson tassels, stood ready. Waiting for her.

Lystra stiffened, the image of Cormek filling her mind. Standing tall, rallying his men to fight with the signal of his silver scimitar curving a delicate arc up toward the sky. His white burnous draped from his shoulders, flying behind him like a cape.

Did that same man now lie here prepared and anointed to be consumed by flame?

Lystra's head grew light and dizzy.

Her grandmother touched the small of her back, nudging her forward.

She didn't dare look, thankful for the darkness. Each step filled her nostrils with the sharp scent of incense—and the rot of flesh. King's flesh.

Blinking back tears, she looked to the nearest priest and gave a timid nod.

With a *whoosh* of oil, they set fire to the pyre. The flesh caught, for it seemed that kings burned as well as anyone, and a rush of heat bathed Lystra's skin. The paint immediately began to streak from her face, down her shoulders, and onto her gown. It itched, but she didn't dare move. Between the dancing tongues of flame, she could just make out Cormek's outline, his features marred by time. Velvet lips that once danced with hers now cracked with ash.

The king had swept into her life with a melodious laugh and a smile that made her heart melt. Cormek lived life to the full—and he had extended a hand, asked her to dance, and invited her to be a part of it. Chosen her. Crowned her as his betrothed, the future queen.

A sob welled up in her throat. Lystra clenched her hands.

13

Her body trembled. She wanted nothing more than to collapse before the pyre, her orange silks pooling about her, and weep until she could weep no more.

"Stand tall. Shoulders back." Even now, at the end of everything, would Dalmah's commands not give her peace? Behind her, whispers mixed with the incense in the air, her name among them. No doubt the image of the almost-queen would be one that Grandmother wouldn't permit anyone to forget. After all, a decade of lessons in protocol and politics had prepared her for this, the glory of the throne.

But Cormek had been the true reward, the culmination of everything. He had not only been her chance to be free, but to be loved and cherished for all that she was and all that she could be.

And his body lay before her. Burning.

"Make way." The shout of a guard broke through the heavy atmosphere.

By now, she knew most of the noble houses would have gathered behind her along with notable members of the royal household.

Lystra drew a sharp breath and looked over her shoulder, the beads draped across her brow swaying. Voices murmured. The sea of silk parted, clearing a path. The creak of wood wheels joined with the crackle of the burning body as a wheeled chair came into view, flanked by two guards in palace orange.

In the chair sat a man—a man crafted in the likeness of Cormek. His brother.

Prince Elerek.

Shame rose hot in her cheeks beneath the painted stripes. The prince never attended galas or festivals and kept to himself. She couldn't recall having exchanged more than a handful of words with him. Even Cormek had hardly mentioned him.

The prince held his head high as he wheeled across the dais. Toward the pyre.

Directly beside her.

Lystra's lungs burned. Air became scarce, shared with the flames consuming Cormek's flesh *and* this man who emerged from the darkness wearing her betrothed's face.

Her hands slowly clenched. This was her place, her honor.

The prince stared into the flames with a deep, dark fury. The firelight flickered on the gold trim on his jabador tunic and painted his face a red harsh enough to compete with the paint dripping down Lystra's cheeks.

And then, he looked at *her*, his emerald gaze burning with an intensity identical to Cormek's. "Torra Lystra."

Lystra swallowed. Her throat felt like sand.

"You survived the desert, the attack." His voice clipped like ice.

"I . . ." She could hardly speak.

"Our kingdom needs survivors." Elerek's eyes returned to the fire, his features as dark as the smoke rising from his brother's body.

He was the heir, and he would take the throne, the throne meant to be hers.

The embers in her hollowed-out soul began to pulse, stoked by a heat even her grief could not smother. It forged her into steel, sharp as a scimitar and wielding the strength of the mountains cutting across the eastern horizon. A warrior wholly unwilling to surrender, to let go of all that she had stood to gain.

Grandmother's words filled her mind. *"To your kingdom, to your subjects, you are immortal, born of starfire. You are a queen —resilient."*

Lystra lifted her chin, hoping she possessed an ounce of the decorum that Dalmah desired. "I loved Cormek, as I love Instanolde, and its people."

"And Cormek loved you." The prince's gaze turned towards her again, but this time they were not ice. No, they had melted, turning as deep as the river. "Are you hurt?"

Lystra barely heard this question over the pounding rage of her own heart. It caught her off guard, this simple, rudimentary question set against the horror and sorrow of watching the man she loved burn. A kindness from the prince, but still, she found herself scowling. "No, I wasn't hurt."

The prince squared his shoulders, his jabador taut against his broad, muscled build. "I'm glad," he whispered. "The people see you as starlight, when we haven't a right to any."

"Starlight?" Lystra blinked. What was this strange conversation she was having with the man who ought to be her rival?

Then, the prince's face turned a deep scarlet. He began to stutter, staring down at the flames. "I . . . uh . . . *hope*. Th-that is, I refer to hope as starlight."

Lystra sniffed, casting a glance skyward. The smoke ebbing from Cormek's body obscured any sign of the constellations.

She didn't want this soft sentimentalism. No, she wanted to burn with the severity of the sun itself—and she did not want the prince's pity. Though, perhaps he deserved some of his own, the prince who spun hope into starlight and now burned with embarrassment.

"Instanolde must be ready." The prince swiftly recovered, all at once turning hard and cold again, a newfound fury smoldering in his gaze. "The attack was just the beginning."

Lystra ran her fingers across her bare arms, her skin prickling with a chill that the fire couldn't chase away.

"Instanolde won't survive the summer. We lost the Darcress Kasbah to the Jarkins—the mountain men."

"I know who they are." Lystra clenched her jaw. She had

watched them kill Cormek. Shoot him down with a black-fletched arrow and shatter his chest with an axe.

The prince kept talking. "Without it, only the desert stands to defend us. Once the oppression of summer lessens, they'll come for us." He shook his head. "Perhaps it's mercy that Cormek won't see his kingdom fall."

No. Her grief had blinded her. Losing Cormek already lay beyond her ability to bear. She couldn't think past this moment, this cruel moment where all that she'd lost burned to ash. Their expedition was meant to be safe, a routine inspection of Darcress. No one ever attacked on the eve of high summer.

But the Jarkins did, and now, Instanolde would fall.

Lystra's gaze hazed with tears, her cultivated image crumbling. Turning away from the prince, she put the pyre at her back and swept through the assembly. Glittering nobles and officials stared, passing whispers behind their hands.

"Lystra." Dalmah's claw-like hand grasped her wrist. "You must stand. Until the end."

Lystra wrenched her hand out of her grandmother's grip, leaving a streak of royal orange along Dalmah's palm. "I won't."

"You will."

"I can't."

Then, Lystra turned and fled down the stairs and into the shadows of the temple courtyard. The emptiness welcomed her, the silence wrapping her in its embrace, and there, she sank to her knees and wept. Her tears ran red, mingling with the mourning paint—red like the Instan blood that would be spilled at summer's end.

Chapter 4

Elerek

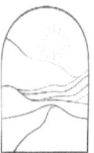

As the last of the pyre's flames gave way to the chill of the night, leaving only smoldering tendrils of smoke, Elerek expelled his held breath. It was done.

Lifting his gaze toward the skies, clear, unobstructed, and salted with stars, he let the sight comfort him—as much as he could be comforted. Directly above, the river rower constellation charted its voyage across the inky sea, the stars spinning and shifting in a delicate dance unique to its grouping.

Perhaps the rower had come to ferry Cormek's soul among the stars. To take him to his rest in the heavens, into the presence of the Starkindler himself. Far, far beyond the shattered world he'd left behind.

Elerek hung his head, his shoulders hunched to keep from shaking. Cormek was meant to rule, to reign, and to leave him behind in the shadows. *I wasn't meant to outlive you.*

No, it was Elerek who was meant to die.

"Your Highness." A priest approached. He bowed at the waist.

Tensing, Elerek's hands moved to the rims of his chair's

wheels. One of his guards stepped forward, taking a protective stance.

He drew a deep inhale, forcing his muscles to relax against the rising, familiar panic that came whenever anyone got too close. "Yes?"

The priest bowed again. In his hands, he carried a small white jar, ornately decorated in azure. "With your permission, the king's remains will be guarded here for the remainder of the night and taken for burial in the morning. In the family crypt of House Karim?"

With *his* permission? Elerek swallowed. "Alongside our parents. There is nowhere else more appropriate."

The last two days had been filled with questions from soldiers, servants, nobles, courtiers, anyone and everyone. After being ignored for most of his life, he could hardly see why he might possess the answers now.

Only he remained of House Karim, and there would be none after him, regardless of the Jarkins' imminent invasion at summer's end. A savage sunrise that Instanolde would not survive.

The priest dipped his chin. "We have gathered some of the king's ashes for you, Your Highness." He extended the small jar. "May your future reign be illuminated by starlight, honored by the memory of your brother."

His reign. It would be short, even shorter than Cormek's near year upon the throne. Elerek's hand moved to his chair's wheel rim again, rolling it back half an inch. "Hand them to my captain."

The priest hesitated, his brow furrowing, but obeyed. The captain, his hand encased in a thick glove, then carefully passed the jar to Elerek.

Let the rumors begin. Elerek stared at the jar with its labyrinthine swirls and painted floral accents, lovely and yet filled with death. The cursed prince of Instanolde who could not be touched and carried death in his hands.

"We all have one life, Elerek."

A shuddered breath quivered in Elerek's lungs. Those words, sharp as the edge of a curved scimitar, cut through his mind. The voice of the brother he would never hear again. Only his words remained, words that outlived the charred remains on the pyre before him and the ashes gathered in their pretty jar in his hands.

One life, Cormek had said. A mighty gift from the Maker of the stars, the chance to *live*. Yes, he was right, but Elerek had never viewed his sorry existence as a gift. Not when he had been marked for death since his infancy.

When he'd been cursed.

When the long list of sins of his warmongering father had finally caught up with him. King Lorkin had been many things, arrogant, ruthless, a man bent upon conquest of all the outlying tribes of the river delta who severely chastened those who refused his rule. His name was whispered with hatred. Such a man would be difficult to punish, and curses were the most profane weapon beneath the desert sky.

But the curse was not for him. No, it was given to his child, for anyone who touched the prince. That was when the deaths began.

Elerek glanced at the priest, and then at his captain. "May I have a moment, please?"

By now, the dais lay mostly deserted. Only the temple guards stood sentinel over the pyre, and the shadows were deep and dark. The captain and the priest both bowed and stepped back, giving him space.

Elerek wheeled his chair forward, still cradling the ashes. He passed the pyre, putting the remains of his brother at his back, and stared out over the edge of the dais and across the darkened kingdom. Beyond, the sky glimmered with stars.

A pair of tears marked a trail down his face. He bowed his head, holding the jar in both hands, and his breath shuddered in his lungs.

"I . . ." The words he needed to say all jumbled together inside him. They weren't harsh or angry, no, those he'd already unleashed to his brother's face on the morning that Cormek had left for the desert. Everything that remained was riddled with guilt and drowning in sorrow. "I'm sorry, Cormek."

Elerek inhaled, his eyes turning skyward again, where he hoped his brother's soul rested among the pure, white lights. "You told me, Cormek, that you wanted to build a new world. One where Instanolde and its tribes could live in peace while being protected from her enemies." A dream that had died in the desert, slain alongside a king who had ruled with such hope, such optimism. "You asked me to be a part of that new world. And stars above, you tried. You tried to let me in, even when Father only wanted me shunned. And I gave you nothing, no chance to be my little brother."

His little brother who had everything. The love of the kingdom, the title meant to be his, the freedom to love the girl of his choosing, all crafted into an image of glorious perfection. Cormek held the radiance of gold and meanwhile, Elerek had only tarnished.

"You told me"—the words came easier now, faster, loosed from the place where he'd kept them bottled up inside—"that we could choose what sort of men we could become, and you would not be like Father. My brother, you were never anything like him. You were kind, compassionate, courageous . . ." A sob lodged itself in his throat. "And you were right—I've let my curse consume me. Lived as a man already as good as dead."

An easy path. Smooth, like the routes he chose for his

wheelchair, avoiding the uneven flagstones and gravel. How many days had he spent wallowing, imagining what might have been if the curse had never fallen on him, and waiting for the death that had haunted him every waking moment of his life? After all, when the curse had run its course, taking with it his life, no one else would suffer. No one else would die from a curse that couldn't be broken.

"No one knows the number of their days."

No, but he knew the number of Cormek's days, and they were fewer than his own.

"Our days weren't equal," Elerek whispered. He wiped his eyes and looked down at the jar of ashes with a new resolve. "You chastised me for acting as if I were different, something less, something broken—*cursed*—and I made you pay dearly for that."

Elerek could still hear his own harsh words echoing back to him twenty times over. *"Don't you dare assume that you understand an inkling of what I've suffered. You can't know, you're not like me."*

"I was wrong," he whispered. "In that moment, we were so divided, but maybe for the first and only times in our lives, we were the same. We both lived beneath death's shadow."

And now Cormek was dead. Never to rule the kingdom he loved so dearly. Never to marry his bride. Never to build a lasting peace for Instanolde and its tribes.

Elerek bowed his head, wiping a sheen of tears from his eyes. His chest ached with yearning, wishing with all his heart for one more chance to speak to Cormek. To look into features carved in his own likeness face-to-face, born of the same blood.

"I'm sorry, Cormek. I'm so sorry."

The wind picked up, a breeze heated by the impending advancement of high summer. It ruffled his curls and swept a bit of ash from the pyre to fly over the edge of the dais and out over the city, as if blanketing all Instanolde in death's shadow. Suffocating it. With Darcress beneath Jarkin control, nothing would stop them from laying waste to Instanolde at summer's end.

One summer to live.

Elerek's days were already numbered, a fate he never wanted Instanolde to share. But now, it seemed that they would face death together, and he intended to give her the hope he never had—a fighting chance at survival.

He sat up straighter, squaring his shoulders against the back of his chair. Resolve pounded in his chest as he stared out at the kingdom his brother had loved so much, the kingdom he died defending.

"I swear to you, brother, I'll try." The words tasted strange, seasoned with starlight—with hope. "For you, for Instanolde, for all that you held so dear. I'll try to live."

Chapter 5

Elerek

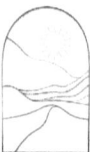

With a jolt, the guards lowered Elerek's chair, its wheels resting on the ground level of the temple courtyard. Still clutching the jar of Cormek's ashes, he sent a glance of contempt toward the tower stairwell.

Most of the time, he thought little of his physical limitations and even regarded his chair with fondness. The skeetos plague had struck in his infancy, only mere months after the curse had been cast against him. His parents could no longer come near him, and already several nursemaids had died. The plague stole the strength from his legs and left scars along his hands. No healer could intervene on account of the curse, thus he'd been left crippled.

"They're just stairs, El. You don't have to scowl."

Elerek continued to scowl as he watched the tall figure hop down from the carriage, the tail of his emerald turban flying behind him. "Razhar, didn't I leave you at home?"

"You did." Razhar flashed a winning smile, the kind that turned the entire world into one expectant adventure. "I chose not to pay attention."

"Course not." As always, Razhar was his utter opposite. Shaking his head, Elerek eyed his friend's ensemble, a garish combination of green, scarlet, and gold. Matched with Razhar's bronzed skin and hair the color of strong coffee, he looked more suited to a riverfront gala. In fact, Elerek doubted that he owned anything appropriate for a pyre.

Razhar ran a hand along the well-trimmed beard shadowing his cheek. "Right, let's go home."

Home. The palace. A monstrosity of marble that, without Cormek, felt cold, dead, and empty.

The carriage had been modified to accommodate Elerek's chair, but he still found the space cramped and stifling. He held tightly to the rims of the wheels, keeping his chair steady as Razhar and his captain boarded, taking the seat across from him.

Before sliding the door shut, the captain took a long glance up and down the street, his gloved hand moving to the hilt of his scimitar.

"Really, Norbah, I think we're quite safe." Razhar folded his arms.

Elerek shuddered. No one was safe. One way or another, danger lay one step away.

The captain didn't reply, signaling the driver and shutting the door.

Elerek appreciated his dedication, the years of service Norbah had given Instanolde's armies and the palace guards. Especially after becoming cursed, and continuing to watch over him.

"Norbah, I'm promoting you to general of Instanolde's armed forces."

The captain looked at Elerek with astonishment. "My lord, are you sure?"

"I can think of no one better."

Removing his helmet, wrapped with an orange turban, Norbah bowed his head. "Thank you, Your Highness."

Razhar raised a wry eyebrow. "What about me?"

Elerek winced as the carriage hit a rut in the road. "I thought responsibility didn't suit you, Razhar?"

He laughed. "That was before my best friend became prince-heir. Surely a profitable position. Visibility with the people, at least. I'm sure I'll be very popular."

Elerek rolled his eyes, but deep, deep down, he didn't know where he would be without Razhar and his cheeky humor.

Norbah cleared his throat. "On the subject of visibility, it's good that you were seen at the pyre. The people recognized you as their future king."

"The people are obsessed with Torra Lystra," Elerek muttered. He could hardly blame them. The image of the beautiful queen who had survived a Jarkin attack and returned with her betrothed's body burned into his mind with the heat of the funeral pyre.

He knew her, or rather, knew *of* her. One could fill a tome of Nathool epics with the praises Cormek sang of her, recounting her charms, her graces, and her extraordinary skill with cardants and the races.

But he hadn't expected her to make such a statement, to stand in *his* place at the pyre, declaring her grief to the entire kingdom. Nor had he expected the kingdom to respond, to declare her as their queen with such unbridled devotion.

And, of course, he'd stuttered like an idiot in front of her. Even now, the memory of the heat of her eyes was enough to cause his face to warm. Maybe she'd forget? No, she'd remember the prince who stuttered about starlight. Elerek resisted a sigh.

Razhar cocked his head to one side. "She was there?"

26

Norbah nodded. "She stood closest; her face painted with mourning stripes."

Wrinkling his nose, Razhar made a face. He'd never been one for traditions.

"Her grandmother also stood in attendance," Norbah continued, a dark scowl beneath his full beard. "The former Arghan queen."

Former. House Arghan had held the throne before Lorkin began his conquest. Elerek began drumming his fingers on the arm of his chair. "Torra Lystra's influence could divide Instanolde. Overthrow me." Justice of a sort, since his father had overthrown her grandmother.

"Perhaps you ought to let her." A sly smile broke free of Razhar's features. "I'm sure she'd do it in spectacular fashion."

The general shook his head. "Unity is crucial. We cannot afford to let Instanolde fray. The tribes and great houses must align like a constellation poised in its dance."

Cold terror, like a draught of ice, shot through Elerek. "Many wouldn't even swear fealty to Cormek." His gaze drifted down to the jar in his hands, and he wished that his brother could have proven himself to the kingdom. Proven that he was different. "Why should they swear to me?"

"Because they need you." Urgency resonated in Norbah's deep baritone. "Once word spreads of Jarkin's conquest at Darcress, they'll shrivel in fear. You must become a symbol of strength, the very heartbeat of Instanolde."

Elerek looked up, his attention drawn to the symbol embossed on Norbah's leather hauberk. A range of sharp mountains cut by a jagged gap through which ran a river, a force of change witnessed by a sky full of stars. Rivers didn't last long in the desert, and he didn't suppose that he would either.

"Tell me that the fight is worth it." His whisper barely overpowered the rumbling of the carriage. The resolve he felt at his brother's pyre was quickly melting in the face of the insurmountable odds, of the path that lay before him. The fight to save Instanolde.

Across from him, Norbah and Razhar exchanged sorrowful glances. This time, Razhar spoke first. "It's worth it, El. Don't you dare give up."

Elerek hunched his shoulders. "I need to hear it," he whispered.

The general's face grew rigid. "For however long or however short, *you* are the king of Instanolde. Nonnegotiable. All else falls to choice—your choice. I beg you to be wise, shrewd, to rule with honor and integrity."

"We're here to remind you, El." Razhar smiled.

Dying stars shone out all the brighter knowing their end had come. Closing his eyes, Elerek prayed that he could become all that Norbah had asked and all that Cormek had hoped.

Elerek both admired and despised the palace. A monument of grandeur, it towered over the city like a glittering gemstone set in an exquisite diadem. But everywhere he looked, in every curved, mosaic archway, ghosts hung about like servers at a festival, their trays bearing bitter memories rather than sweet palm dates and maamoul cookies.

Cormek had wanted him to be a part of it all. The parties.

The politics. The world which they were both destined to join. And Elerek had pushed him away.

Elerek wheeled himself past the marble steps leading to the gold-painted doors, instead taking a servants' passage, one without stairs. He knew all the halls and corridors well, because he did anything possible to keep to himself and limit his contact with others. But all passages led to the throne room eventually.

The creak of his wheels and the footsteps of his friends were swallowed by the great domed ceilings. At the end of the room, two bowls of fire burned bright. Their deep orange glow on the marble pillars reminded Elerek far too much of his brother's pyre, as if the room itself were a testament of his death.

Between the bowls of fire, the throne stood. A sharp, angular thing carved from a monolith of stone that flickered obsidian in the firelight. Built to impress. To intimidate. The ploy shouldn't have worked on him—but it did. The thought of his crippled body sitting there was ridiculous.

"Norbah." Elerek glanced at him. "Place this up there." He held out the jar of ashes.

The general bowed, his orange cape sweeping about his figure as he obeyed, setting the jar reverently upon the throne.

Elerek closed his eyes. Fatigue, like a heavy blanket of incense, settled over his shoulders, sinking into his bones.

Frantic, raised voices echoed through the palace, waking him from his vigil. And then, someone began to sob.

Elerek looked over his shoulder, dread prickling up his spine. The voices came from the kitchens, and only one group of individuals took to the hearths at this time of night.

Razhar sighed. "I'll handle this, El. It's been a long night for you."

"No." Elerek pivoted, turning away from the throne and

taking another corridor. This one familiar and scented with the smell of fresh baked karahz bread. "They're my family."

The cursed.

Nothing, not even becoming king, would keep him from caring for them, fighting for them, and seeing that their last days were not spent alone.

True to tradition, Elerek found a small feast ongoing. A fowl roasted on a spit above the flames and the low table was piled high with bread, heaping bowls of couscous, and dates. But nobody partook.

"You just *let* her go?" A bearded man, built of muscle, slammed his fist to the table.

"Come now." A man in scribe's robes sat cross-legged with his back to the fire. "We couldn't have stopped her."

At the table's corner, a young woman bowed her head and wept.

"Your Highness!" One of the men turning the spit at the fire, a soldier still in uniform, snapped to attention and clasped a fist to his chest.

Elerek's skin prickled as the room erupted, the men and women rising from the cushions encircling the table only to drop to one knee.

"Don't, please." He wheeled his chair closer. "You'll burn your dinner."

The soldier returned to the spit. Anxious eyes and nervous fidgeting spread like the plague among them.

"What happened?" Elerek's eyes roved from face to face, counting their number. Who was missing? "Oh . . . stars, not—?"

"Azraa." Driss, the scribe, bent over the table and took a silver cup to the samovar standing sentinel over the food. The cup filled with the pungent scent of the strong, spiced brew of coffee. "It happened so fast." He then took another cup and filled it as well.

"Here, I'll help you." Ishtal, the big, bearded stonemason took the steaming cups and began to pass them around. "El? Coffee?"

Azraa. Elerek nodded, rubbing the sore place on his forehead where his circlet pressed into his skin. He didn't even curse her.

Sometimes it spread secondhand, and sometimes it didn't. They hadn't any idea why, but it all began with him. Each of these souls were gathered here because they'd touched him. An accident, a stray brush, an offer of aid—and a price was paid.

As the coffees were passed, he watched as their hands cradled the cups. He wondered if they could still feel the warmth in the silver cups, or the same unfeeling numbness that the curse inflicted in waves that ebbed and flowed like the banks of the river. There were times that Elerek wanted to scream, the very air around him a void, the cold deadness all consuming.

And then it would return, the feel of clothing, the taste of food, the warmth of the sun, reminding him that the curse wasn't through with him yet.

"Myra tried to stop her." Ishtal frowned, glancing at the end of the table, where the weeping girl sat with her head in her hands, her narrow frame trembling.

Elerek wheeled his chair beside her, the sound of her sobs pelting at his soul like the drive of springtime rains. He reached with timid fingers, brushing her shoulder.

She lowered her hands. The haunted look in her dark eyes, brimming with tears, pierced his soul like an arrow fired by a superior archer. "I—I'm sorry, El." Myra spoke quietly. "I tried to stop her."

His heart dropped. "Stop her?"

"Sh-she left the palace . . ."

"She *what?*" Elerek's eyes widened.

A low growl emitted from Norbah, the sound worthy of some desert predator. "When the curse reaches its final stages, *no one* is to leave the palace."

"They know the rules, Norbah." Elerek spoke sternly, tugging at the collar of his jabador. "It's all right to mourn. It hasn't been the first time and won't be the last. Razhar." He watched as his friend sauntered into the room and procured a handful of dates from the table. "Would you go look for her?"

"I . . . I might not be able to find her." Razhar spoke with his mouth full, the light leaving his eyes.

But the whole room had turned to Elerek, staring at him with expectant, hopeful gazes made of starlight. "Please, Razhar?"

No more arguments were made. Razhar bowed and swept from the room in a flurry of emerald.

Elerek raked a hand through his hair, pushing his curls back from his forehead. He supposed, with all that had been lost, he should be thankful. Though Razhar counted many companions among the cursed, he'd managed to keep his distance and thus avoided the curse.

Bushra, a baker, took an empty cup and filled it with coffee. Circling the table, she set it before Elerek. "Myra, coffee?"

"Tea, please."

A moment later, the older woman set a cup of steaming water and a tin before her. "Dear Azraa. I'll miss her singing as we shaped pitas."

"She always repaired my ripped tunics," Cole, the soldier at the spit, added.

Myra drew a shuddered breath. "I loved her as a sister." She took the tin, spooning tea into her cup. "I'm glad she won't suffer any longer."

Elerek watched her hands as she prepared the tea. He thought of the leaves, grown upriver and imported to Instanolde, like most luxurious delicacies. They'd endured such a journey, and yet were only considered valuable because they were dried out and dead. As the others chimed in, reciting memories of Azraa, Elerek's hands clenched. It wasn't fair. The curse was meant for *him*. Why did others have to suffer too? Their lives were valued, precious. Many had forsaken family and friends, accepting noble positions in his household. Elerek ensured that they were given comfortable lives as they waited for their turn to die.

He wished it were over. For him, and for them. But now his duty was to live. For Cormek. For the kingdom.

A hand touched his arm. Panic, like lightning from a spring thunderstorm, bolted through his heart and nearly caused him to spill his coffee. Then, he remembered; there were none here left for him to curse.

Myra's fingers ran along the embroidery on his jabador. Free of tears, her face held the noble beauty of the marble statues that lined the scholar's avenue. His heart beat faster.

"Elerek, have you ever loved anyone?" Cormek's voice, so innocent and secretive. His infatuation with Torra Lystra had just begun to blossom. Elerek listened and nodded politely, but his thoughts strayed to Myra, to her smile, full of kindness, and her gentle voice, like the sound of doves. The touch of her skin beneath his fingertips as she leaned in to kiss him, and the bitter knowledge that even loving someone could result in heartache.

"The burning—are you all right?"

He gave a small shrug. "It's over now."

"You ought to rest."

He entwined his scarred fingers with hers, her skin cool to the deadness in his own. "I'll try." He looked around the table. The conversation had turned to simpler topics. A building project. A new recipe. Gentle speech from simple people. Living. This was what he had to fight for and, he swore before all the stars in the heavens, he would see it done.

"Goodnight." Elerek backed his chair away from the table. "If Razhar brings news, please, wake me."

Norbah brought his fist to his chest, the soldiers mirroring his motions. A sign of honor. "My *king*."

A reverent silence laid claim to the room. Elerek's face warmed as their eyes turned toward him with a sense of awe and wonder. He quickly wheeled himself into the darkened corridor, away from the light of the hearth and the smell of coffee.

Behind him, soft footfalls followed. He stopped, glancing over his shoulder. A faint glow of firelight escaped from the kitchen, outlining Myra in the shadows.

His heart rose in his throat. "Yes?"

She drew close. Her hands cupped his face, and her lips brushed his.

The smell of her hair filled his nostrils. He slid his hand along her neck, pulling her toward him, drinking deep of her lips.

Myra's breath shuddered as they separated. "Do you want me to stay with you tonight?"

The question hung in the air. Guilt burned in his soul hotter than the funeral pyre. Elerek looked away, his face turned to the darkness again. He'd spent his life trying not to drown in it.

"No," he whispered to the emptiness.

And not just tonight . . . Stars, he had to be strong. In a world full of cold and cruelty and curses, what Myra offered seemed too lovely to refuse.

"Please, El." She sniffled. "I don't want to be alone."

She had chosen the curse. Chosen to love him, the

untouchable, the unlovable. Declared her love to him with courage, fear as far-flung from her as the dancing stars above. After a lifetime of separation, cut off from the touch of another human being, from even the possibility of love, once they'd begun to close the distance between them, it had been difficult to stop.

But there came a cost, and every time she came to his bed, every night they spent together, he remembered the terrible truth. That no matter how lonely he'd been, how much he loved her, *he* had doomed her to death.

Elerek closed his eyes. "Neither do I, but . . . I can't."

"Because you are to be king?" Myra sniffed. "You really believe that you'd be the first king to have a mistress? More likely the first without."

Mistress. He despised that word. It had been whispered enough about the palace, mostly in connection to the many that had passed through his father's chambers after his mother died, and more than once, the temple priests had spoken out against such relationships.

He thought again of Cormek's resolve to not follow the paths of their father. Elerek wished he could aspire to merely a shimmer of his brother's brilliance.

Yes, he had failed in many, many things. But right now, today, he could make a choice. Even if that choice hurt, and proved a costly, difficult thing.

"I don't know what these days will hold," Elerek whispered. "But yes, if I am to be king, we cannot be together."

Myra took a step back, her face pale. "El, I love you." She unwrapped the scarf from about her shoulders. "I chose you."

In the faint light, he could just see it trailing down her upper arm.

The mark of the curse.

Where skin ought to have been, a pale, transparent film

covered sinewy muscle and white bone. Flesh vanishing. Slowly turning to water. Eventually, she would drown. They would all drown.

Perhaps Myra and he would flow in the same current.

"I love you." Stars, he didn't realize how much this would hurt. Elerek squared his shoulders. "But this is best—for both of us."

"Is it?" Myra settled the scarf about her shoulders again, hiding the mark.

Elerek felt as if the desert sands shifted beneath his chair, threatening to swallow him whole. He wheeled himself farther into the darkness, the space between them growing. "Please, Myra, don't make this harder than it must be."

Then, he left her alone in the corridor.

Chapter 6

Lystra

L ystra lost any concept of time as the shadows deepened. The stars rotated in their dance above. Eventually, smoke ceased to plume from the tower, marking the end of the burning. Those in attendance filed down the stairs and departed, but none took notice of her.

Chills crept up her arms. Her tears had long since receded, leaving her empty. Her dress, stained with ash and the mourning paint, felt threadbare with the stone wall of the temple at her back.

She couldn't go home, not with Dalmah. No, to step into that house would be to step into a cage. And now, she feared she might never escape.

If Instanolde fell at summer's end, then what point remained in living? How could she rise from the ancient stones of her city and hold her head high? All her years spent at her grandmother's tutelage, preparing to rule, and now her kingdom lay ready to crumble to dust. She'd promised all her days to Cormek; how could she walk on without him standing at her side?

A wail that was not hers pierced the night.

Lystra jerked her head up, eyes searching the courtyard.

The shadows surrounding the fountain shifted. The marble masterpiece portrayed blooms and leaves, its waters running with silver starlight. And near its edge, a girl stumbled with another wail.

All at once, Lystra found herself on her feet, striding toward the fountain. Then she stalled. Did it matter if she helped the girl or not? If the Jarkins came? If Instanolde fell?

No. She drew a deep breath. It had to matter. She'd lost much these past hours. If she lost herself—the desire to show kindness and help others, even against the impossible—she couldn't fathom it.

Lystra cleared her throat. "Hello."

The girl started and turned—and a greenish skull with bulging, watery eyes stared back at her.

Lystra shrieked, covering her mouth with her hands.

The girl's skin was gone. Every organ, vein, and bone stood on display. Water ran down the girl's body, dripping from the hem of her thin kaftan.

"Please—" The skull's jaw worked, more water spilling from the transparent film that served as lips. Dripping, skeletal fingers reached forward, for *her*. "Help me . . ."

Lystra stumbled backwards, her hands shaking.

"Stay back!" a voice called, accompanied by the swish of silks and slippered feet.

Priests. Their yellow robes stood out, even in the darkness.

"No one touch her." An older priest in a turban held out his hands in warning, stepping closer to the girl than any other dared. "Torra, tell us how to help you?"

The bulging eyeballs in their watery sockets turned to the priest. She wailed again. "Please, please, *break it!*"

Break what? Lystra found the temple wall at her back again

as she watched the horrible display.

Then, the girl *burst*. Whatever humanity remained transformed into crystal clear liquid. With nothing to hold it, the water that was the girl splashed across the flagstone and pooled at the priest's feet.

A horrified gasp died on Lystra's lips.

Several priests dropped to their knees, uttering prayers of peace for the deceased's soul to find its way to the heavens.

The turbaned priest slowly backed out of the puddle, the water that was once human. His eyes turned to her. "Oh, Torra Lystra."

Was he one of the priests who stood at the pyre? Lystra didn't know. She could only stare at the dampened flagstone.

"Wh-what happened to her?" Her voice sounded as if it belonged to the jerboa mice that roamed the Sancen.

The priest shook his head, the light glinting on the silver hoops rimming his ears. "It's a curse, Torra. One more horrible than any I've ever beheld."

A curse. Lystra knew of them only by myth, stories crafted around fires. Vile manipulations of the natural world, curses were known to be powerful, dread works of darkness. Curse binders, those who practiced the dark art, had been notoriously hunted and executed by Lorkin, Cormek's father.

Lystra wrapped her arms around herself, shivers crawling over her skin. "Wh-who was she?"

"She arrived earlier this evening. Her name was Azraa. She came seeking peace, knowing that her time was short."

Peace. Lystra gazed down at the water again, already seeping into the rock's crevices and draining away. She hoped that the girl found it, and that there remained some left for her.

Her legs began to tremble, as if they too might succumb to liquid. She leaned against the wall for support.

"The hour is late, Torra." The priest spoke gently. "Would

you have us escort you home?"

She sniffled. She hardly dared to tell them, who knew her as the brave queen who stood at the pyre of her beloved, that she feared to return home.

Her hesitance provoked further pity. "We have rooms here, for those who need them."

She gave a timid nod. Another priest spread a wool scarf over her shoulders and led her toward the temple's entrance. Inside, candles illuminated the space and the air felt heavy with incense. Beneath her feet, the mosaic floors blurred. She wanted to sleep. To forget. To imagine that none of this had happened. That Cormek hadn't burned away. That Elerek hadn't revealed the Jarkins' threat. That she hadn't just seen a young girl perish from a deadly curse.

The priest led her to a humble room and lit a lamp.

"You'll find blankets and spare clothing in the cupboard." The priest bowed. "Sleep in peace, Torra."

That was all she wanted.

Lystra woke in an unfamiliar room wrapped in coarse wool and plain linen. Such a contrast to her lavish room at home.

Lifting her head, she grimaced. Smears of red, black, and orange covered the pillow. The horrid mourning paint. Her eyes darted to the corner, where she'd left her silks in a heap. If only grief were so easily discarded.

A temple servant arrived to inform her that a wash awaited. Lystra whispered her thanks, grateful for their kindness.

Once the last of the mourning paint had been scrubbed from her body and the smell of smoke left her hair, Lystra dressed in a simple linen kaftan and set out to find the priests.

The long corridors took her back to the sanctuary. Though she'd entered this space many times before, it still took her breath away. A rainbow of colors dazzled the eyes—from the deepest midnight blues to the brightest yellows.

Lystra craned her neck, drawn to the twisting carvings of vines and blooms as they crept round the pillars and stretched up to the great domes, painted with magnificent skyscapes.

A crude representation of the real sky and the dancing constellations. Still, Lystra stared. True beauty never stopped man from attempting an imitation, thus the attempt became beautiful in its own right.

"Good morning, Torra Lystra."

She tore her gaze away from the ceiling's expanse, offering the young priest a smile. "I want to thank the temple for its hospitality. Might I speak to the priest who offered me sanctuary?"

"High Priest Orzak?" The man's eyes dimmed. "He is overseeing the burial preparations. Please, wait here."

Burial. Cormek's remains. The incense in the air threatened to choke her.

While she waited, she kept near the pillared arches rimming the sanctuary, for fear that even her shadow might desecrate the lovely colors of the inner sanctum. In the center, an altar burned with incense, decorated with multicolored candles. Several priests tended the candles as one might cultivate a garden.

A mite of shame took root in Lystra's heart. Like many, she held the rites more out of tradition than true piety. As the centuries turned, so did the functions of their religion. Priests came and went like monarchs, each bringing their own dynasty with its features, and no one seemed to know what remained true or false.

At one time, they had worshiped the stars, each dancing constellation a deity with its attributes and blessings to bestow. The riverbanks flooded and watered their crops because Bushun, the plough constellation, rose in the western hemisphere and took pleasure in their sacrifices.

During another era, they set aside worship of the stars, claiming one deity held all in his command. He desired fealty and did not sway with the whims of their priests or the quality of their sacrifice. They celebrated seasonal festivals in adoration of the holy affection between the people and their god. The Starkindler, they called him, Maker of the stars.

Lystra lowered her gaze. If one could make the very stars, couldn't they undo a curse? Couldn't he have saved Cormek?

Entire decades had passed with no religious affiliation at all. Where the seasons came and went without the prompting of priests or sacrifices. Their people endured with no great calamity, seemingly faring no better than the times they had a system of worship.

"Torra Lystra." The aged priest with the rings in his ears appeared. He bowed at the waist, as one would do to royalty, his yellow robes flaring about his figure.

Lystra's skin prickled, undeserving of this formality, her future as queen lost. "Thank you for your hospitality, High Priest."

"It is the least we can do."

"And." A lump rose in her throat. "For seeing to the . . . preparations."

Grief filled the old man's eyes. "So young in years, you and our departed king. Such sorrow. You were strong to stand at the pyre. You honored His Highness's legacy—and the prince-heir."

Her stomach turned bitter, as if churning with yirro root. No one knew this prince, the one who hid in the shadows. And now, he would become king? How could he possibly know Instanolde's life, soul, and vibrantly beating heart? Could he capture the loyalty of the people?

Surely he doesn't love Instanolde as I do.

And the people loved *her*. Did that not count for something?

Not if the Jarkins destroyed them all.

"Do you know the prince-heir?" Lystra inquired. "For all the time I spent at the palace, I hardly saw him."

The priest nodded. "Elerek was brought here as an infant when he contracted *skeetos*. Poor child, the plague malformed his legs beyond repair. Stricken, the king wouldn't permit us to hold and pray for him."

"He mentioned something." Lystra reached up to rub her shoulder. "That Instanolde lies in a vulnerable position . . . with the Jarkins."

Orzak bowed his head. "I feared that such news would prove true. We wait for official word from the palace and its generals. I don't think the people have realized this yet, too grieved by the loss of their king."

"As was I." Lystra shook her head. "The desert, the attack, I'd rather not think of it."

The priest's eyes radiated kindness. "Unless one is acquainted with grief, one cannot possibly understand its ways. Its taste is subtle, like the finest tea leaves, yet as strong as any wine."

Lowering her gaze to the tips of her silk slippers, Lystra drew a steadying breath. "Are you saying . . . I'll always feel like this?"

"Each of us traverses our own journey, Torra. I can hardly say, but you will learn. Joy still resides among the living."

Could they really live while knowing they would die? When anyone could be taken away in the blink of an eye?

If she could return to that moment, just before the attack, she would have frozen it forever. The touch of the sun on her shoulders. The rush of riding atop the back of a cardant. The sweeping vista of the desert, pinnacled by the sight of the mighty Darcress Kasbah with its towers built of redstone. Cormek alive, his white burnous flying behind him. He looked over his shoulder and smiled at her with all the love in the world.

In that moment, she had no idea what lay before her.

Lystra hastily wiped the tears from her eyes. "Thank you, Orzak."

The priest gave a small smile. "Even if the end draws near, it is not yet. If I may venture, I do not believe that your story ends here. Lean into the support of your house. Lift your eyes to the stars. Do not forget to hope."

Lystra stiffened. The support of her house would have her bend only to Grandmother's demands. The pyre, the mourning paint; she wondered what Dalmah was scheming next. "I should go." She shoved her hair over her shoulder. "Again, thank you."

"Of course. I will light a candle in remembrance of your grief."

"Will you light one for the girl? The one who perished from the curse?"

Orzak nodded. "A terrible thing. I must keep a lookout. Curses rarely strike in isolation."

Lystra shuddered, taking a step back. "We need no more death in Instanolde."

Despite her words, her heart gave an agonized twist. Death, it seemed, wished to make her kingdom its home.

Chapter 7

Lystra

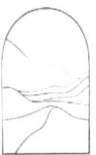

Lystra wore a scarf up over her head as she took to the city streets with long strides. Unlike last night, nobody recognized her as the tragic queen of the desert. The sobriety of the pyre had passed. Life pulsed in Instanolde again.

"Dates! Fresh dates from the Karim lands."

"Loccan pottery, perfect for your summer stores, yah?"

"Oranges! Pistachios! Moon fruit! Blink and you'll miss 'em!"

Lystra heard it, even in the echoing hails from the merchants. The cadence of a heartbeat, but one that sounded as if it beat in someone else's chest. A world that went on. Simple tasks for simple lives, oblivious to her sorrow. No one could know, unless it happened to them.

"Make way!"

As one, the crowd paused. Shoulders pressed in around her. They huddled against the red wall of a potter's shop as several cardants lumbered down the street, carrying guards sporting palace orange. Their hauberks gleamed, polished to perfection. Lystra searched their faces but didn't know these men.

She would be a stranger at the palace now. The palace that was meant to be her home. Her refuge to grow with her husband. Her escape from Grandmother.

When she arrived at her avenue, she slipped into the alley behind the estate of House Arghan, out of sight from her father's guards. There, a haphazard stack of melon crates served as her path up and over the wall. She typically didn't make the attempt in a kaftan and had to hitch her skirt up over her knees to clear the top.

Lystra dropped down behind the stables, the pungent, lingering odor of reptile filling her nostrils—and a fresh gust of grief slammed against her soul.

Pens fanned out on either side of her, half cast in shadow and half in bright sunlight. All of them empty. The only sign of the magnificent creatures lay in curling shreds of old scales.

Ghira, Qual, Adum . . . they're all dead.

Cardants she'd hatched from ebony-hued eggs. She'd selected their parentage, raised them with tender care, and trained them for greatness. Cormek had been delighted by her vision for a stable at Darcress. She could imagine the cardants, riding free among the red-toned rocks with their mounts.

Instead, they'd been butchered. The Jarkins cared no more for the reptiles than they did people. She wondered if their corpses still lingered near Darcress, their bones picked clean by vultures.

Lystra ran her hand along the pen's smooth wood railing. *This . . . this is freedom.*

Here, Grandmother's influence lay afar off. Here, Cormek recognized and valued her strengths. Here, she was at peace.

Somehow, she couldn't bring herself to cry. The desolation

hollowed her out, as if a piece of herself had died with each cardant.

The sound of scratching woke her from her grief. Lystra turned to the last pen.

This one, at least, held an occupant. Sama, a gentle, older cardant, lay with her spiked tail, thick as a tree, in the sun and her head in the shade.

"Good morning, old girl." Lystra opened the stall and stepped inside. Thick, scaly lids parted, revealing sharp yellow eyes.

Kneeling in the hay, she took the reptile's head—the size of an ox's and studded with horns—in her small hands. The cardant's eyes drifted closed. "Fancy some sunshine?"

The lizards could be horribly sluggish in the mornings. They needed the heat, the pulse of the desert, to survive.

Really, so did the humanity that chose to call it home.

Lystra didn't wait for confirmation, ducking into the tack-room and opening a drawer where she had stashed spare clothing. Discarding the kaftan, she dressed in black pants and a flowing tunic of crimson. She twisted her hair up in a knot and covered it with her scarf.

Lystra liked to think that the warmth of her hands prompted Sama up, but most trained cardants grew eager with the anticipation of a ride. She mounted Sama outside the stalls, her leather saddle wedged between two great spines, and took the long leather reins in her hands.

Sama snaked forward through the estate's gate, her side-rock gait smooth and level as she took back roads through the city, weaving around and between dwellings, avoiding the highways crowded with merchants and wagons.

Lystra tilted her head back as they passed beneath the portcullis of the southern city gate, its shadow a marker between worlds. Instanolde's mighty walls, wide and golden, fanned out on either side of them, but it was the desert that stole Lystra's breath.

She leaned into Sama's gait, hot wind whipping about her hair and clothing. A stream of dust trailed behind them, stirred by the pounding cardant limbs.

"*Questa!*" At the command of Lystra's voice, Sama left the road, taking a trail that snaked between great mountains of sand shaped by the wind.

Keeping her eyes ahead, Lystra's gaze filled with the mighty eastern mountains, a haze of blue on the horizon. And in between, the whole of the Sancen spread out like a map.

Nothing provoked terror and awe like the Sancen. Nothing else could be so beautiful and deadly. Wide enough to stretch from south to the north, long enough to make the cliffs and canyons stretch for miles and miles, warping all sense of distance to the naked eye.

Miles and miles . . . Lystra gasped. Tugging on Sama's reins, she brought the cardant to a halt. Dust settled about her and the reptile, glittering like gold. Sagebrush and lonely tamarisk fluttered in the wind, filling her ears with a desolate, lonely sound.

The whole of the desert erupted, morphing in her mind's eye. Ghosts of men and cardants overran her vision. She could hear their screams—and worse, the silence that followed. Days of hard riding, hearing nothing but the pounding of cardant claws over rock and sand. Cormek's body slung across the cardant behind her.

Lystra found tears streaking down her cheeks.

A healthy fear of the Sancen fed their will to survive. But this, this felt like panic—as if the Sancen were lying in wait to destroy her. Waiting to try again.

Breathe in. Breathe out. She was safe now, but deep down, she wondered if they'd ever be safe again.

She guided Sama around, taking a trail that wound close to the city walls. While the inner panic remained, her hands kept steady on the reins. A measure of control, while all else shifted like the desert sands.

When she reentered the city, she bade Sama halt as she took a long draught from her waterskin. Out here, water defined the difference between life and death, just as the Gungole River delta made their bustling kingdom possible.

As she wiped a few stray droplets from her chin, she bowed her head. Why did she feel so exhausted? It was only a short ride, hardly strenuous, atop an older cardant. She loved riding and she loved the reptiles. Nothing had changed, and yet everything had.

Tears filled her eyes. Was all that she loved and held dear to be thus tainted? This felt like losing a piece of herself. A piece that she wasn't so sure she could reclaim.

When she returned to House Arghan's estate, she used a servant's passage to sneak into her chambers. Her maid had put the room in order and no sign of the paint spill lingered on the floors. Lystra slipped from her riding clothes into jeweled slippers and a sky-blue kaftan embroidered with flowers.

"A queen makes statements with whatever means available. A bold outfit is never wasted." Lystra huffed, putting a hand to her stomach to dispel the restlessness growing there. In this scenario, she figured that her grandmother's instruction might

hold some wisdom. She owed her family an explanation for her absence last night.

She followed the sound of chatter to the rooftop. There, her family gathered, lounging on cushions and low couches around a table set with a small feast. Iced mint tea glistened invitingly in a glass pitcher, tantalizing her parched throat.

Corsha reclined beside her brother, her cheeks rosy from laughter. Kimzi, the apparent object of her mirth, continued in the telling of a story with long-limbed gestures.

Across the table, Dalmah sat with her spine arrow straight upon one of the couches. Her sharp eyes immediately fell on Lystra, watching from beneath the shadow of her purple scarf.

However, Jethro spoke first, rising to his feet with a scowl on his lips. "Lystra. Where have you been?"

She lifted her chin, settling herself on a cushion beside Corsha. "The temple offered me sanctuary. I took it."

Visible relief cascaded over Jethro, making the silver striping his beard all the more prominent. He shook his head and seated himself again, resting his hands on a girth grown from a contented life. "I'm glad you're safe."

Kimzi broke a round slab of karahz bread in half. "Ah, Lystra's dependable, uncle. I told you. I bet she even went riding this morning."

With a slight *humph*, Dalmah sipped from a silver cup of tea. "Has she any cardants left to ride?"

Lystra's face grew hot, but she kept her countenance. With smooth, delicate movements, she poured herself a cup of tea, as if to remind her grandmother that she still remembered every facet of her training. "I rode Sama. She's a gentle soul."

"Which, it seems, spared her." Jethro spoke quietly. He shared Lystra's affection for the cardants, a point that won Lystra an edge against her grandmother.

She didn't reply, her thoughts returning to the desert—and

the cardants that perished there. Though House Arghan possessed riches in abundance, it had taken a fair amount of her own allotment to establish such a fine stable. To build suitable pens, hire helping hands, successfully pair, breed, and raise fine lines and racers worthy of the desert.

All dead.

It could easily take the better portion of ten years to regain all that she'd lost. And they might not outlive the summer.

"Vianni, how are you feeling? Since last night?" Corsha refilled her own cup with tea, eyeing her with a shrewd and caring gaze.

Those were thoughts better spoken in private. However, after her escapade, Lystra knew that she ought to display some form of strength before her father and grandmother.

"The sun rose this morning. I suspect my own journey will take time."

Corsha reached over, giving her hand a squeeze. But the makings of a storm began to brew on Dalmah's brow, like the first haze of a sandstorm kicked up across the plain.

"Good, good." Jethro adjusted the collar of his deep red robe. "I intend for us to present ourselves to the palace first thing tomorrow."

Lystra held her breath. To see those halls in all their splendor, the glory meant to be her future home, without the light of Cormek's presence, would be just as difficult as standing at his pyre.

"I spoke with Timon last night." Kimzi sat up straight, asserting himself, always trying to fashion himself into a budding lord. "He doesn't believe that House Yissal will swear fealty to the prince-heir. What do you intend to do?"

House Yissal was no small house. Lystra's stomach clenched. It may prove that the prince-heir wouldn't earn anyone's support. Perhaps it was possible for the throne to be removed from House Karim. There were no other heirs. Only Elerek and the threat of the Jarkins at summer's end.

"House Arghan will support the prince-heir," Jethro declared. "If Instanolde is indeed facing a superior threat, House Arghan can give aid and strength to the throne. Our new king will need allies and Instanolde requires a strong leader."

A leader to ride out and meet the Jarkins—to defend Instanolde to the last. Lystra wrinkled her nose, having a difficult time imagining Elerek accomplishing such a task. In contrast, Lystra's own childhood had been filled with her grandmother's teachings in diplomacy, decorum, city law, etiquette—all tools at a queen's disposal.

If she had to ride out to meet the Jarkins, could she? For her kingdom? For her people?

Doubt crept in. Her grief had stolen the desert from her, even the freedom of riding cardants—her greatest joy. After years of craving the throne, and the liberation it bought, she wondered if she was strong enough for it. Cormek had supplied a lovely illusion, granting her all the freedom, all the power, and little of the actual responsibility. His shoulders had been enough. Alone, Lystra seemed insufficient to the throne's demands.

She couldn't do it alone, and that would mean relying upon her grandmother's expertise. The same cage but a much bigger prison.

"A mistake." Dalmah spoke in a low tone. She leaned forward, eyeing her son with a shrewd gaze, ready to challenge him. "One by one, you'll watch the other houses and tribes refuse fealty. Then, House Arghan will look foolish standing with a less than capable king."

Jethro's face darkened. While he was technically the head

of their household, it was difficult to sway a former queen's authority. "Well, what do you suggest, Mother?"

"We elect the prince's abdication and put Lystra forward as a worthy candidate."

Lystra forced herself to swallow her tea. Dalmah's next scheme. A scheme that used her but didn't involve her opinion. But if it got her the throne, would it be worth it?

"Any tribe or house that does not support the prince ought to be counted as an ally. They will support Lystra." Dalmah's voice rang with confidence, like the clear blast of silver trumpets at the western gate. "The people rest in the palms of her capable hands. She is loved and adored."

A gift. Lystra slowly breathed in. Such a gift from her people couldn't be ignored.

Jethro narrowed his eyes. "Would it not be better for the people of Instanolde to be united? To stand strong in the loss of their king and a brutal Jarkin attack?"

Tilting her head, Dalmah's hair cascaded over her shoulder, revealing soft rivers of silver amid the ebony. "You think this prince capable of unifying them?"

Jethro's gaze turned to Lystra. "I'd like to hear what my daughter thinks."

All eyes fell on her. Watching. Waiting.

Lystra lifted her chin. Grandmother's voice drilled in her head. *"A queen is bold. She speaks with authority. She ordains with power."* "I want to do what is best for my people. I do believe Instanolde requires unity and stability to meet whatever the Jarkins plan next. And . . ." She looked at her grandmother, matching her fierce gaze. "I desire to rule, to take the role that I've spent my life preparing for."

"But?" Corsha looked doubtful.

Lystra gave a slow exhale. "I agree with Grandmother's

distrust of the prince. If there exists a way to establish me on the throne, I will take it."

The prince who called her starlight—hope. Even he could see she was made for this.

Pride radiated from Dalmah's face. "You are already a queen. You only need the people to give you the crown."

Warmth spread across Lystra's face. These words should have been a compliment. But from Dalmah, they sounded more like orders given to a soldier.

A long sigh escaped Jethro. He rubbed the side of his face and opened his mouth to speak, but the air filled with a high-pitched screech. For a moment, the sun became eclipsed.

Lystra lifted her eyes just in time to watch three great birds fly overhead, their black feathers flecked with tips of white. Atop their backs, men in vibrant yellow tunics stood bright against the sky.

They flew toward the palace.

"A delegation," Kimzi breathed. "From Kushan."

The canal tribe. The Kushites dwelt upriver, where the Gungole split into three, carving its way through deep canals. There, nestled within deep canyons and verdant pockets of earth, the Kushan made their home. They guarded the canals, overseeing all trade from the lands beyond the desert, and kept watch from atop their condors. No other tribe held as much influence over Instanolde, being the source of wealth and imported goods. No other had the advantage of the skies. No other pledge of fealty held so much weight.

"If Kushan doesn't swear . . ." Dalmah's voice sounded like a threat. "The prince hasn't a chance."

Lystra feared that she was right—and that fear gave way to a terrifying, desperate hope. But how much did such a hope cost?

Chapter 8

Elerek

As Elerek positioned his chair at the front of the dais, he stole a glimpse over his shoulder. The harsh angles of the throne filled his peripheral and sent a shudder down his spine. His gaze fell on the small jar of Cormek's ashes.

I'm trying, Cormek. I'm trying.

"They're here." Norbah swept into the throne room, his orange cape billowing behind him like the wingspan of some great bird.

Elerek drew a deep breath and held his head high, the weight of the gold circlet heavy on his brow. "Not wasting any time, are they?"

Taking his place at the foot of the dais, the general shook his head. "That's worrisome, Your Highness. Kushan is our best shot against the Jarkins."

Elerek swallowed against the rising panic in his stomach. This one moment could break his rule.

Kushan had soldiers. Archers mounted on the backs of

swift condors. Commanders of the skies, able to turn the tide of battle, to cross the Sancen, and able to launch a counterattack.

"Why should they swear fealty to me?" Elerek adjusted the ornamental sash draped across his shoulder, its labyrinth of gold stitching complementing the pattern running from the throat of his collar and down his chest. "They wouldn't even swear to Cormek."

Kushan had declared a preliminary period, electing to watch the new king's reign with wary eyes for one year's time. Trade still flowed as freely as the Gungole, to their relief, but Elerek knew that change could sift them like sand whenever it pleased—and often not at their convenience.

Norbah huffed, taking a soldier's stance as the rest of the palace guard filed into the throne room, standing between the marbled pillars. "If they don't swear, others will follow." He turned his head, meeting Elerek's eye across the dais. "You'll have to convince them."

The houses and tribes could elect their own candidates for the throne, and such measures typically resulted in skirmishes. More violence. More bloodshed. Instanolde divided and ripe for the Jarkins' invasion.

Elerek felt sick. If he couldn't hold Instanolde together, who would? *Well, Torra Lystra could . . .*

"El." Norbah's mouth lifted in what might have been the sternest of smiles. "You look like a king."

The king Cormek would want him to be. The thought tugged a small smile from his lips.

A guard's voice rang out loud and clear. "The Kushite emissaries, Your Highness."

The great doors of the throne room were pushed back. Elerek squared his shoulders and made his wheeled chair his throne. He hoped that they couldn't see how his scarred hands trembled.

The trio of emissaries wore yellow tunics that draped dramatically past their knees, and tightly wrapped turbans, also of yellow. Their dark complexions, neatly trimmed beards, and pointed features reminded him of Razhar—whose veins ran with Kushite blood.

"My lord, prince and heir." They bowed at the waist.

Elerek dipped his chin. "Welcome."

One of the emissaries stepped forward. He bore a staff and a striped outer robe that identified him as a scribe. "My name is Timos. It is with grief that we acknowledge the passing of your brother. Please, accept the offering of our mourning."

"Thank you." Elerek swallowed the lump rising in his throat, wishing for the millionth time that Cormek was still alive. "Our kingdom finds comfort in the grief of its sisters along the river."

Timos bowed again. "We bear the will of our chief, Wuhaz, born beneath the constellation of the river vessel." His eyes narrowed. "We have looked at the dance of the skies beneath which you were born and found it ill. Kushan will not swear fealty to you, prince-heir."

Elerek forced himself still, upholding his display of regality. Out of the corner of his eye, he saw Norbah's head sharply turn, desperation in his gaze.

"I am disheartened." Elerek turned down his lips to show mild disapproval, a royal façade. "Not two seasons ago, Kushan offered my brother the span of a year to prove his merit. Surely, I might petition for the remainder of that year, the last two seasons? Any of us would be hard pressed to find a manner by which we may choose the stars of our birth."

Rather than rely on house or family names, the Kushan identified each other by the constellations present at the time of their birth. A tradition as ancient as the stars themselves. Elerek's mind fled to his books, the charts that wrought beautiful illustrations of the stars, trying to remember his own constellations—Sealin, the horse; the north maiden; and the wrathgiver.

Nothing ill or unusual, all three were major constellations. Nothing obvious to contribute to this, the losing battle he waged here before his throne.

The emissary bowed again. "Kushan drew a deep breath when your brother ascended to the throne. Our prayers were seasoned with hope. We sought a king not yet embittered by war. Kushan suffered greatly at the hands of your father, Lorkin. You would do well to remember the wrongs done unto the river tribes."

His father. Not Cormek and not him. Elerek folded his hands in his lap, his fingers lacing together. His eyes briefly lifted to the soaring, domed ceiling of the throne room with its marble pillars and multi-colored glass windows. His hands hadn't built this palace. But just as he inherited something so enormous and weighty as a kingdom, so had he inherited the sorrows and wrongs of those who came before.

"It is for the dead Kushite children"—Timos' voice was tainted with bitterness—"whose blood ran into the Gungole— the source of our life—that we withhold our fealty."

Elerek thought of Razhar, an orphan from those same wars. A Kushite child spared from bleeding into the Gungole. That mighty river, the flow of life through the desert, the keeper of the delta wetlands, their world depended on it. The delicate dance of alliances forged and struck along its banks were capable of life and prosperity, or starvation and bloodshed.

All too often, Lorkin had chosen the latter.

Elerek clenched his jaw. His father made his choices without any thought of the world after. No care for what he would leave behind. The curse binder had done the opposite, inflicting a cruel punishment only on the world after. If the curse was meant as revenge, to make Lorkin suffer for his wrongdoings, it wasn't enough. Lorkin gave up on him, replaced him with Cormek and merely moved on.

"Is it true, prince-heir, that the Jarkins hold the Darcress Kasbah?"

He gave a grim nod. "It is."

"Then, they will come at the end of summer. With your men and cardants slain alongside your brother, who will you send out to meet the barbarians?"

Norbah's head turned again, but Elerek saw the steps of the dance the Kushites led. He leaned forward, drawing his hands into fists. Rage pumped in his heart. If this was a fight he must lose, he wouldn't waste a single breath. He owed it. Not to himself, but to Instanolde.

"Only a unified Instanolde can stand against the Jarkins, from whom we've experienced generations of savagery and butchery. Darcress failed us. We cannot fail one another."

The emissary shook his head. "You will send Kushite archers and condors. You would have us fight and die for you. It is the way of Instanolde's kings, and we will not bleed for you again."

"I would send loyal warriors who would fight with courage and dignity." Elerek deepened his voice, nearly a growl. "Those who would see our lands kept safe, our children protected. Such devotion might be our only chance to survive."

But Timos only sighed, unmoved, like a boulder not even the canals could dislodge. "If doom should come to Instanolde, so be it. The canals will grant Kushan protection. We will watch." He looked up, and his eyes seemed to pierce Elerek's soul. "You would do well, prince-heir, to remember that death comes to us all. Some sooner. Some later. Some as the result of justice."

Elerek stared at the emissaries, his gaze unblinking. If only they knew that his curse had doomed him to drown like one tossed into their canals.

"While you watch . . ." Fury stoked his soul, burning embers from the hottest fires. He fought to keep his voice level. "Know that my duty is to protect my people. I swear to you, until my dying day, I will seek to defend Instanolde—and that includes Kushan—from whatever threats come her way." He paused. "Tell your chief that I wish him no ill will, but I would have the remainder of the year promised to my brother."

The emissaries exchanged glances. Elerek looked at Norbah, but the general only tightened his gloved hand around the hilt of his scimitar.

"We will confer and bring your petition to our chief."

Elerek released a short exhale. "I am honored."

The emissaries bowed and two took several steps back, but Timos remained.

"Yes?"

Timos bowed a second time. "An inquiry, prince-heir. As we searched our archives and libraries, seeking the rotation of the heavens at the time of Your Highness's birth, we found a discrepancy. The stars seemed to indicate that you, not Cormek, are the elder of Lorkin's sons. A year separates you in age."

An uncomfortable knot lodged itself in Elerek's stomach. He regretted the small breakfast of couscous and moon fruit. "It is not a discrepancy."

"You are indeed the elder?"

Elerek nodded. A root of bitterness planted between him and Cormek. It wasn't his brother's fault. To their father, there was only one choice of an heir, and it wasn't the son who was cursed to drown.

Timos frowned. "That is a strange thing, Your Highness."

They can't know, can they? About my curse? Elerek drew a

shallow breath. If anyone discovered his curse, his reign would end. They would only see a man who doomed those he touched to turn to water in the desert.

As to the man standing before him, Elerek's mind spun. His responses were limited. For a moment, he thought to blame skeetos, the plague that caused his hands to scar, his legs to wither. But he'd never seen his limitation as a hindrance before and saw no reason to begin now.

"Well," he finally replied. "A year can change a great many things. A king can choose to name a son born a year after his first as his heir and a tribe can choose to give a king their fealty. Time will tell whether these decisions held any wisdom."

Timos narrowed his eyes, appearing unsatisfied by this answer. He bowed again. "Thank you, Your Highness."

Chapter 9

Lystra

Lystra left the rooftop as soon as she could. She knew her father would send his guards to confer with those associates he had at the palace. They would know soon enough if Kushan had sworn to the prince-heir or not.

Descending the stone steps, she paused in the majaz, a deep, floral aroma sweeping her senses. The threshold, carved of pale stone, had transformed into a forest of pink. Woven baskets covered every inch of the marble floors, bursting with boughs of tamarisk covered in row after row of tiny pink flowers. It smelled like the flower merchant's shop when she chose the arrangements for her wedding.

Several servants shuffled the baskets along, making their way toward the kitchens. Lystra caught sight of her maid among them.

"What is all this?"

The maid gave a small bow. "It's for you, Torra."

"Me?"

"For healing. For grief."

Well, yes. Lystra knew the boughs were often gifted to

those who were sick as a sign of hope and healing. Tamarisk blooms were used to cure a host of maladies. But for her?

"Who sent them? And why so much?"

The maid offered a small smile. "From all over. People have been bringing them all day. They wish you well, Torra." A blush crept over her amber cheeks. "Many called you the *Malikaa*. Their queen."

The room seemed to spin in a haze of pink and tamarisk. Lystra swallowed and reached a hand to the polished wood of the staircase. She wondered if the palace was filled with boughs and baskets. If the prince-heir shared this honor and adoration.

The people's queen. A shiver shot through her body. Suddenly, her grandmother's schemes seemed tangible.

"Would you suffer me to say that I told you so?"

Lystra turned, lifting her eyes. Dalmah descended the staircase in a vision of grace and elegance. Her wrinkled hand touched the railing lightly, gemstones glittering from her many rings.

"We play a delicate game, granddaughter. Its moves are subtle, but the results are quite poignant—much like the tamarisk."

The mourning paint. The pyre. Lystra's lungs shuddered. "Cormek's death isn't a game, Grandmother. I loved him."

Dalmah's eyes softened, but only for a moment. "I know, granddaughter. But he is dead. Sitting here in mourning won't accomplish anything."

"There are moments that it's all I can do," she whispered.

"Well, then you ought to be thankful to have me." Her grandmother stopped three steps from the floor, towering over her. "You see that your people love you. Their breathtaking queen who rode out into the Sancen in glory and returned with nothing. Tell me." She cocked her head to one side. "Did you mean what you said? That you want what's best for your people?"

Lystra thought of Kimzi. Her cousin once kept a parrot who loved to talk. It sang in the evenings when the musicians strummed their ouds. But each time Kimzi took an excursion with his friends, the parrot had to be caged. The cage stood in the courtyard, right in the center of the house's activity. Still, it hated the cage. It refused to sing. Finally, it succumbed and perished.

She knew exactly how that parrot felt.

"I raised a queen." Dalmah looked down upon her with sharp eyes. "When I begin a task, I see it through. Now, it is true, you've suffered a loss. A great loss. Still, last night, beside the pyre, I saw a queen forged by fire and girded in perseverance. I ask, Lystra, that you trust me. Work with me. And we will see this task through, together."

Lystra swallowed. The look in her grandmother's eyes was ruthless. Surely the prince-heir would be easy prey to her formidable grandmother. She could almost believe that Dalmah could take on the kingdom—and win.

It would be her victory—but on Dalmah's terms. Her conditions. The parrot must learn to sing despite the cage.

"Father will have us all at the palace in the morning. To swear fealty."

A smile curled over Dalmah's lips. "You leave your father to me. I will take care of everything."

Lystra tensed. These words didn't fill her with starlight—hope—rather, they filled her with fear. But the kingdom would be hers to protect. Her beloved people beneath her care. And the Jarkins would be hers to fight because, after all, Cormek was hers to avenge. That was worth the fear. This arrangement would secure her future, perhaps for good.

Lystra took a step back, putting room to breathe between her and Dalmah. "All right," she said simply.

Her grandmother smiled.

Lystra spent the afternoon in isolation. Under normal circumstances, she might venture a visit to the palace, confer with the stables, or train with her cardants. But now, all that was gone.

Escaping the heat of the long afternoon, she slipped into her father's study. Built of stone and enforced with wood bookshelves, the room kept cool even in high summer. Lystra pushed back the lattice of the two narrow windows, letting light spread across the plush, crimson rug.

Aside from the histories and treaties her grandmother selected for her edification, Lystra had never been much for reading. Not when the call of endless sands and brilliant skies gave cry to her name. The study smelled of stale parchment and traditions, reminding her far too much of Grandmother.

But it was amid such histories that curse binders walked like the wraiths of the deserts. Lystra hadn't forgotten the horrid display of the girl bursting into a shower of droplets. She could imagine the scorn she'd receive if she dared to ask her father or grandmother about such things—things the kingdom had shed much blood to be rid of. Taking a thick tome from the shelf, her fingers fluttered through the pages.

An hour passed. And then two.

Only scant mentions of the hunts Lorkin had decreed were

scattered throughout the tomes. Anyone accused of association with the binding of a curse was put to death. Immediately.

Casters shared this fate—that is, one who has received the curse and performs the required rites and rituals. Often, the curse is sold from the binder, who then remains guiltless of the curse's actions. This dark transaction complicated the hunting and executing of those involved in the heinous practice.

Note: curses, being dark and vile and vengeful in nature, come with hidden "costs" to those who practice them. A divine punishment. Some say—

Lystra turned the page. A ripple of ripped parchment met her fingers. The page had been torn out. She sniffed.

The girl was dead; she couldn't ask who cursed her. Perhaps she didn't even know. Still, she wondered if others were cursed—or if the binder still lived. That seemed the last thing that Instanolde needed when the world was falling apart.

Sighing, she shut the book. She'd had enough of the study and needed an escape.

Hurrying down the corridor, she arrived at Corsha's chambers. Her cousin appeared and beckoned her inside.

"We are going on an excursion," Lystra declared.

Corsha's eyes narrowed skeptically. "To where? Not on a dusty cardant ride?"

Lystra cocked her head to one side, her hair cascading over her shoulder. "The night market."

That caught her cousin's attention. Smiling a secretive smile, Corsha sauntered toward her wardrobe, flinging back its doors. "Surely you're not going in that?"

Flinching, even Lystra had to admit that she needed something more elaborate for the Instan streets after dark.

She backed toward the door. "I'll meet you in five minutes. I do hope you'll wear shoes suitable for dancing."

"You're sure about this?" Corsha glanced over her shoulder, her eyes as scrutinizing as those of the physician that inspected Lystra upon her return from the desert. She had no wounds, at least, none that could be treated.

Lystra stilled, her hand on the doorknob. Should she venture to the market? Blend in amongst the crowd seeking to enjoy the evening? Part of her wanted to say no, dismiss the idea as silly and acknowledge the deep loss still cleaving her heart. But the other part wanted to simply shove it out of sight, forget that it existed, and try to feel like herself again.

Besides, if she were to have any sort of future serving her people—and saving them from the Jarkins—she couldn't do it crippled by grief. Lystra lifted her chin and gave her cousin an affirmative nod.

Corsha acknowledged her with a hopeful smile and began digging through her clothing. "Wear a veil." Her command echoed against the interior of her wardrobe. She leaned back, eyeing Lystra with a sharp gaze. "Considering . . . it just might be simpler."

A knot wedged itself into Lystra's stomach, reminded that her home was filled with tamarisk and the whisperers all called her queen. "I will."

Chapter 10

Elerek

The emissaries didn't linger long, for which Elerek was thankful. He deferred to Norbah to show them back to the courtyard where their condors waited. Then, wheeling his chair down stone corridors cast in filtered sunlight, he barricaded himself in a small parlor. Curtains of silk hung at each window, swaying gently in the afternoon breeze.

Yanking the gold circlet from his head, he let it fall to the table with a clatter. Not yet a king, and without Kushan, he felt as if failure were a weight sinking onto his shoulders.

Surely Kushan would swear to Torra Lystra. She could probably convince them with the blazing heat of her eyes alone. Maybe it would be better if she overthrew him.

His hands grew cold and clammy, as if death itself were creeping into his skin. The sunlight lost its warmth, and the movement of the wind faded away, leaving him in a cold, dark void. Elerek gulped a shallow breath. His fingers moved to his collar. Unfastening the intricate lacing, he pulled back his tunic. Beneath his breast, along his ribcage, transparent skin enveloped his side.

The mark of his curse. Unchanged.

But soon, it would spread. Turn his skin to water. Drown him from the inside out. Like Azraa—of whom Razhar found no trace—and so many others. How long had he wished for death? Now, he wished for days—days to avenge his brother and save his kingdom.

"Goodness, all your soldiers gawking about. You'd think a lovely woman had walked by, not an old, ugly condor."

Elerek quickly refastened his tunic as Razhar swept in and flung himself onto a cushion with a dramatic sigh.

"Have you ever ridden one?" Even the thought of mounting the broad, feathered backs of the great birds made Elerek's heart race with terror. Nothing beneath the summer sun would convince or coerce him into such a thing. He couldn't even ride a cardant.

"Sure I have." Razhar stretched his muscled arms over his head. "Kushites are taught to fly condors before they learn to walk." He blinked, looking directly at Elerek for the first time, his infectious smile fading like the dancing stars in the predawn murk. "What's wrong now, El?"

Elerek gave a small shrug.

Pulling himself up from the cushion, Razhar leaned forward. His vest hung loose from his sculpted shoulders, the edge of the tattoo on his chest appearing at his collar. A constellation. "Kushan didn't swear, did they?"

Elerek shook his head.

His friend waved a dismissive hand. "Stupid stuffy lot, they'll regret it eventually."

Razhar had never been keen on his own tribe. While he shared their skin of polished bronze and amber eyes—great assets for Razhar's many admirers—Elerek suspected that he found them dull. A definite damper in his adventurous lifestyle.

"Others will follow their lead." Elerek glared down at his hands. "My reign will end before it's begun."

"Now, don't say that."

"One summer to decide Instanolde's fate," Elerek growled. "That is, if the curse doesn't take me first."

Razhar huffed and reached into the inner pocket of his vest, pulling out a roll of velvet and a small pouch. "Well, then, we'll just have to make the most of it." Spreading the velvet on the table between them, a delicate pattern of gold embroidery in the shape of a spiral glimmered in the midmorning light.

Sometimes, he wished he could punch him. "Will that be before or after the Jarkins kill us?"

"Now, now." Razhar dumped the contents of the pouch onto the velvet and began lining up a series of tiny gold figures. "We both know you're the one with a mind for strategy. If anyone can outsmart the Jarkins and preserve Instanolde, it's you." He pushed the rest of the pieces, tiny shells from the Gungole river snails, toward Elerek and looked up with expectant eyes. "You go first."

"I don't want to play." Elerek sighed, but still he gathered the *barjee* shells into his palm, tossing them across the velvet board.

Razhar's face lit up with a grin. "Ah, come now. I'll let you win."

Cocking an eyebrow, Elerek moved his pieces, one by one, across the embroidered path and his heart felt a bit lighter. "You have *never* let me win, Razhar."

"Hence the 'mind for strategy,' right?" Moving the shells to his side of the board, Razhar gave them another toss, their subtle rattle an echo of familiarity, of comfort. His voice grew soft, like a whisper riding the wind. "That's what your brother would've wanted, yes? To fight for Instanolde?"

Elerek leaned back, comforted by the wood at his back. Sometimes, it seemed his chair was made of stronger stuff than he was. "I fought with him, Razhar. Hours before he rode out. Told him that he didn't know me and could never understand my pain. I yelled at him to go, and to leave me. Now . . ." He sighed, watching Razhar march his figurines like an army, forming a barricade. "I'll never have the chance to ask for his forgiveness."

Silence settled over the room. Only the soft wind, blown across the Sancen, stirred. A bit of feeling returned to his awareness, bringing with it the smell of heat, of wildness. A freedom none within the palace walls would dare taste.

Finally, Razhar inhaled. "You and Cormek fought often."

Elerek gathered the shells into his hand but didn't toss them.

"He kept trying to get under your skin. Like sand in our shoes. You know what that means?" Razhar smiled. "He didn't give up. Not on you."

Hot tears filled Elerek's eyes.

Razhar reclined, cocking his hands behind his head again. "Cormek forgave you for your insensitive, disgruntled attitude time after time. What makes you think this would be any different?" He released one hand to gesture toward the game. "It's your turn."

This time, Cormek was dead. Elerek scattered the shells across the board and set to work outflanking his opponent without a word.

"See?" Razhar leaned forward to survey the game. "I can insult you without fear of a grudge. I know that you care—deep down in that insensitive, disgruntled mess of yours." He clicked his tongue. "Stars above, how do you always do it?"

"Mind for strategy." Elerek kept his finger on his last figure, taking one last stock of his arsenal. Razhar was right; he never stayed angry at Cormek for long. Partially right. "I'm *not* insensitive."

"No, El, sometimes you are. You put up walls that don't need to be there and shut us all out. But when you care, you care *fiercely.*"

Elerek pushed the shells across the table to Razhar's side of the board. "Well, I was shut out first."

Razhar rolled his eyes. "By the wrong kind of people. There are plenty of us who care about you, so maybe try to remember that. You can't take on the world alone, El."

Now that, Elerek had to admit, might have a bit of truth to it.

Razhar shook his head, muttering beneath his breath. "Oi, rubbish game." The light in his eyes took on a mischievous gleam. "Don't forget, there's a birthday celebration for Ishtal at noon. Bushra is baking m'hanncha and the entire kitchen smells like oranges."

Oranges. A delicacy the kingdom would surely lose if trade ceased functioning through the Kushite canals. Elerek closed his eyes, feeling as if he were drowning already. The tasks too numerous, too enormous.

"I'll try to stop by." He recovered, refocusing his attention on the game. "I haven't any idea how many houses or tribes will come today. I ought to find Norbah and form some sort of plan to win them over."

"Has House Arghan come yet?"

Something cinched inside his stomach. Elerek shook his head. Aside from Kushan, they were the house he dreaded the most. Not only did he fear what they might do, but Torra Lystra would be among them. The girl his brother loved. The girl his kingdom called queen.

The numbness returned to his hands.

"May I offer a suggestion?" A sly smirk emerged in the corner of Razhar's mouth. His figures formed a new blockade. "Why don't you—?"

"Please, Razhar—"

"Oi, let me finish my sentences, El."

Elerek tilted his head back against his chair, staring at the ceiling. "I don't want to get married."

Razhar threw up his hands. "How did you—?"

Leveling his gaze at his friend, Elerek leaned forward. "You were just praising my ability to strategize, weren't you? This is a painfully obvious one. If I align myself with one of the houses, the throne will be secure after I've drowned. No house war to further divide this kingdom."

Razhar sniffed and folded his arms, his pout reminiscent of a child's. "So, since you've so thoroughly thought this through, do you have anyone in mind?"

Elerek busied himself evaluating the gaming board. The thought of proposing marriage—even as a political advantage—made him sick. Add to that the process of explaining his curse, that he couldn't touch his bride. He had loved one girl, and she would die on account of it.

Another girl, however, had the power to unite the kingdom.

No, I could never . . . The chill returned to his skin, sinking straight to his heart.

Razhar looked back at the velvet gameboard, absently moving his pieces about. "Maybe I'll tell Norbah and the rest of the lot. They'd have the palace decorated for a wedding within the hour. Properly motivate you."

"I'm motivated to save Instanolde," Elerek muttered. He wondered why becoming king had to be so complicated.

"Well." Razhar finished his turn at the game with a huff. "*Your Highness*, I've an evening of dancing in the night market ahead of me. I suppose I'll scour the land for the perfect queen for you while I'm at it."

Now that the time of mourning had passed, Elerek supposed that the streets would again come to life with light and music. The world went on. Did the people know their own danger, the countdown to summer's end? If they did, would they continue as they did now? Was the death of their king only a changing of the seasons like the rising and receding of the floodlands? Would they live differently if they knew the end drew nigh?

His thoughts turned to his own cursed family. They knew their days were numbered, watching their skin slowly transform to water, and still they celebrated birthdays, shared meals together, and baked m'hanncha with imported oranges.

Elerek exhaled, the tension in his body departing. He let the shells slip from his fingers and began to move his pieces again. "What would I do without you, Razhar?"

Then, and only then, a shadow crossed Razhar's brow. But it was fleeting, like the morning fog beneath the Sancen's heat. "Really, El, I do not know."

Chapter 11

Lystra

S lipping the gate shut behind her, Lystra drew a deep draught into her lungs. Even here, among the avenues of estates, she could imagine that the market already scented the cooling air with faint traces of smoke and spice. It smelled like a promise, full of all the thrill and vibrancy of Instanolde after dark. The city stirred to life.

Corsha sighed with contentment, her auburn hair rippling behind her like liquid gold. Practically blooming in shades of fuchsia and orange, a perfect cactus blossom, she'd opted for a beaded bodice with sheer sleeves that hung off her shoulders and loose, silken sirwal pants. As fading sunlight fell in horizontal shafts between the narrow set dwellings, the two girls glittered like gemstones set amid the sand. "Oh, let's hurry. It's been so long."

Too long. Lystra ventured a smile beneath the shimmer of her veil.

Yes. She could do this. Push aside the curtain of grief, even just for a moment. Lystra relished the swish of silk about her calves, her kaftan the color of deepest midnight. Gold embroidery embellished the neckline and down the front and a matching gold scarf wrapped about her shoulders and over her hair. With her eyelids painted ebony and a veil hanging over the lower half of her face, she looked like any other young woman venturing out to market. Another set of flashing eyes. The perfect mural of the normalcy her soul yearned to feel again.

But not a queen, and not a bride.

Emotions surged into her chest. Shadows of another night danced across her mind like the constellations above. The first night of a journey, a series of steps that sent her down a collision course with the king of Instanolde. She had accepted an invitation to the palace, to a gala, with the promise of music and the company of all the nobles and houses.

Somewhere, in the glow of torches, the strum of ouds, and the perfume of the evell blossoms, the young king, hale, tall, and striking with his pale Karim skin and dark curls, looked across the room and his eyes found hers. Lystra remembered wearing red and regretted it, a deep blush warming her face.

Some magic worked that night. They had danced till the constellations joined them, the heavens one glorious ballroom. And when they parted, among the blooms of the palace gardens, the king kissed her.

Lystra drew a sharp breath. Beneath her veil and painted face, a chill swept over her skin. Her feet felt as if they were made of stone, weighed down to the flagstone avenue.

Cormek was dead. Never to dance with her again. Never to kiss her. Never to become her husband.

Corsha turned, glancing over her shoulder. "Lystra? Are you all right?"

Lystra closed her eyes, waiting for her heart to calm. Would she really carry this grief, Cormek's death, forever?

"Oh, vianni." Corsha's hand slid into hers. A small gesture, but the feeling of touch, of skin on skin, brought a balm. "Do you want to go home?"

"No." Lystra spoke quickly. She couldn't be like this forever. She had to find a way in this world in which Cormek died and she lived. The world where his people—her people—needed her to give them hope.

Starlight. She wondered if the prince-heir's stutter would ever leave her head.

"Take all the time you need." Corsha squeezed her hand.

When she took her next step, it seemed a league of a journey all its own.

The closer they drew to the night market, the brighter the streets became. Torches tinted with mineral powder flashed in bright hues of green, deep purples, and vibrant scarlets. Lystra caught her breath, her eyes moving from one booth fashioned of colored fabrics to the next. No wagons or beasts of burden crowded the traffic, leaving plenty of room for shoppers, wanderers, and entertainers.

Corsha clapped her hands as a minstrel and his ensemble strode past, filling the air with the strums of their instruments. Grabbing her cousin's arm, Lystra swept along with the crowd, clearing the street as a troupe of dancers in beaded anklets filed past, following the music's hypnotic draw. Around the next corner, a juggler laughed as he moved through his routine, adding one item after another.

"I'm *famished*," Corsha exclaimed as they approached the baker's booth. Stacks of flatbreads adorned with cheeses, spices, and seeds glowed in the torchlight.

Such smells. Lystra would swear to the stars themselves that no other city boasted such wonders. Spices lay in mountainous piles, their color as varied as the women's dress. Goat and lamb roasted, wild pheasants simmered in pots of stew, both fruit and vegetables steamed on long skewers. Tiny cakes of almond and imported cherries baked on stone hearths.

They purchased a honey bread loaf and retreated to a fountain set on a street corner, perching on its ledge to share the treat.

Lystra swept her veil to the side just enough to taste the morsel of honeyed cream and flaky dough. Her eyes lingered over the square. Everywhere she looked she saw life, vibrant in the flicker of colored fire and intoxicating as the strongest of wines. Laughter rang from swarthy faces clad in curled beards while painted eyes gleamed like starlight above veils.

And yet Lystra could imagine a second veil covering her face. For everywhere she looked, she also saw death. The Jarkins marching with spears and axes in hand, hewing down the dancers, overturning the spreads of spices, and smashing musical instruments. The fierce men of the mountain knew no limits to their savagery. Diplomacy was conducted with javelin, axe, and scimitar. Innocents ravaged and enslaved. Soldiers left to die in their own blood.

She turned her eyes to the dancing constellations. Tiny specks of light amid a sea of blackness. *Starkindler, if you are real, I beg of you . . . show us mercy.*

"It will pass, vianni." Corsha's whisper permeated her consciousness, gentle and sweet.

Lystra looked at her cousin.

"You will heal. You will feel whole again."

Grief had shown itself to Corsha too. Both her parents had died—her father in a tribal skirmish and her mother of the plague. And still, Corsha laughed, smiled, *lived.*

"You give me hope," Lystra whispered, a small smile appearing behind her veil.

Corsha returned the smile and popped the last bit of the bread into her mouth. "Lystra, speak truthfully. Have you really sided with Grandmother? Will you make a bid for the throne?"

The whirl and wonder of the night market faded away. Lystra heard only the pounding of her chest, the heart that went whole into the desert and returned broken into shards.

"It seems . . . a desperate act. Are you so?" Corsha sighed, her eyes rising to meet the stars. "I can't help but wonder, would Cormek have wanted you to do this? Unseat his brother?"

Lystra closed her eyes. The darkness behind her eyelids reminded her of the void, that shadowed obscurity where the crippled prince lingered. "I'd forgotten that he even had a brother."

"You never met him? Not even at the palace?"

She thought of the prince's eyes, how one moment they had been sharp enough to shape stone and then soft the next. "Once or twice. He seemed . . . distant."

"Cormek didn't talk about him?"

Frowning, Lystra picked at a memory, one where her betrothed's eyes matched the coldness in his brother's face. "Only when they argued," she said quietly.

Lystra had never pried. Whatever battles had come between the brothers was no concern of hers and Cormek shoved them swiftly aside. But now, in the light of all that had happened, she had no idea what Cormek would think. "I want to take care of my people."

Corsha tilted her head, her jeweled earrings glittering. "Is being queen truly the only way to help Instanolde?"

No, probably not. But considering the time left before the Jarkins returned, it seemed the best route.

"All I can do is my best with what I've been given." Lystra opened her eyes and stared down at her hands. Callouses from gripping the reins of cardants lined her palms. Soft underneath, but the exterior hardened. "And Grandmother raised me to be queen."

"And you've spent your life trying to escape Grandmother." Corsha sighed. "Now's your chance."

Lystra ran her fingers along the gold beadwork on her belt. "Not if the Jarkins attack at summer's end."

Corsha made no reply.

The music of the minstrels slowed their tempo, strumming their ouds in a deliberate cadence. A man in multicolored robes emerged, spread a mat, and seated himself cross-legged. A crafter of tales, a spinner of legends. Already the dancers had turned to soldiers, standing at attention with eager ears.

"Behold, an account!" The man's voice, rich as wine and strong as the Gungole at springtime, resounded off each redstone edifice. "The hunter, the warrior, the spear who claims men's souls—Gaudab Batu-Khasar of the Jarkins, man of the mountains."

Lystra stiffened. The magic of the night shattered. A shadow emerged in her mind. Flesh and blood emerging from the mirage of the desert. One who wielded a longbow with black-fletched arrows and carried two axes strapped to his back.

I saw him.

"Fierce in name and in deed, Gaudab Batu-Khasar stands higher than any man. Thick are his arms. Like fire are his eyes. Large are the hands that twist men's necks. In the high, green country he was born. They fend themselves from snow and cold, clothing themselves in the strength and skins of wild beasts. When Gaudab was young, he slew a mountain cat that prowled through their encampment. Though the cat scarred his neck, he prevailed. He led a company to the southern riverfront. His arrows fired upon the vessels there. Ships taken for Jarkins who have no canals. He preyed upon the tribes, the forces gathered along the river. Fear followed his name. A shadow to haunt river, mountain, and sand. Now his footsteps stalk ever closer, leaving Instan blood in his prints."

Some of that blood belonged to their king.

The crowd grew denser about the crafter, captivated. Lystra rose to her feet, watching in horror. Were her own people really so blind? Didn't they realize that this man had killed Cormek? The cream of the honey bread churned like curd in Lystra's stomach.

Two quick claps rang across the square. "Enough, old man. Take these heresies elsewhere. Terror doesn't befit a night as lovely as this. Minstrels, begin again and let us dance till the sun rises!"

In a flash of deep emerald, a tall young man swept into the square. He held his head high, his ruddy complexion a deep, glistening bronze.

"Hmph." The crafter's nose wrinkled, unwilling to relinquish his moment in the crowd's attention. "Then perhaps a tale of mystery, of counter curses and—"

The young man laughed. "Ha, there's no such thing. Now." He huffed, adjusting the collar of his verdant vest. "Shameful, really. To utter tales so foul in a place so merry. Come now, a dance!"

Lystra startled as the minstrels struck up their music again, the sound jarring her from her astonishment. The dancers pulsed to their rhythm, causing the onlookers to appear out of place, standing like statutes, but the young man had a plan. One by one, he took them by the hand, whoever was willing, and led them in the steps. These were common dances, traditional, and it didn't take long before the square was a swirl of color, movement, and smiles.

Corsha laughed with glee, needing no prompting, and joined the fray. Lystra hesitated. Could her feet recite the steps? Her body flow with the tandem of the ouds beneath the weight of her grief? But in that moment, that indecision, the young man approached her, flashed a smile, and held out his hand.

"Come, Torra, won't you join us?"

She held her breath—and took his hand.

He swept her into the crowd. The music rose in volume, as if to reach the stars themselves. The dancers filled her with an energy that burned bold and bright. A kinship of the life they loved. Lystra lost herself, given away to the joy of her people below and the stars above.

Then, she realized that she still held the young man's hand.

His amber eyes watched her with a sparkle of admiration. "You're glorious." His lips parted in a wide smile, his teeth white against his dark skin.

Lystra smiled beneath her veil. Dancing was an art practiced by every Instan daughter, no matter the tribe or house. Many celebrations and galas had filled the gardens and courtyards at the palace, for the king had loved to dance.

He dances just like Cormek. The same precision in his footwork, the same elegance and flourish. He tossed his head of dark hair upward, starlight dancing in his eyes. Life pulsed through his being, a spirit wrought of joy and elation.

This. The thrill, the joy, the love of the life her people lived among the sands. This was why she had to save her people, so they could dance like this young man, with blissful abandon.

The song came to an end with a shout of exultation from one of the minstrels. Laughter and clapping broke out.

Dropping Lystra's hand, the man bowed. "Thank you, Torra. You have brightened this night."

Lystra never imagined that she would dance again, particularly with anyone that sparked the memory of Cormek. An intoxicating sensation, a cup from which she wanted to drink again.

"Another, if you please!" Corsha's voice rang across the square.

As another song began, the young man eyed her with a hint of mischief.

She extended her hand. "Please, do me the honor?"

He dipped his chin and loosened the silken scarf about his neck. His tunic lay open at the chest, revealing a tattoo across his breast, something like a constellation. Lystra tried not to stare, but soon realized that she wasn't alone. Several ladies eyed him from among the dancers. If he noticed, he performed a splendid job of pretending that he didn't.

"Forgive me, Torra. I'm quite out of breath." He brushed away the sheen of sweat on his brow. "I've never met a dancer like you."

She who had danced with kings. To say such a thing would give her away and she rather enjoyed the disconnectedness, the intentional amnesia. Forget oneself and the world's griefs and burn like starfire. To imprint Cormek's form and face onto this handsome stranger and believe the illusion.

When she did speak, she held her chin high. "I've only danced with one other like you." Her voice painted it as a challenge.

"Ah." The young man took her hand and guided her into the first series of steps. "High expectations. I'm glad to measure up."

She laughed, and her body quivered with the sound of it after so long a fast. Perhaps Corsha was right. Grief's night would end, and the dawn would come again.

The young man moved closer as the music slowed. His hand went to her waist. As he spun her, the world melted. Deep crimsons, flashy purples, dark indigos, and fiery oranges. When her vision focused again, she only saw the man's amber eyes.

"Tell me your name," he whispered as she circled about him, her skirts swishing in time with the oud's strings.

She replied in a laugh. If she said it, the spell would break. She would become the almost queen again, the weeping maiden, the dying ember for a doomed city.

Starlight spoken by a prince-heir with cold, cold eyes.

The young man gave a cheeky grin. "Do you venture to the night market often?"

This was a game she could play. "Only when it's worth it."

"Right, high expectations." His fingers trailed along her jawline, beneath her veil. The air grew warm, electrified, as if a storm were brewing over the mountains. Perhaps there was. "It hardly seems fair to hide. Where I come from, the young ladies don't go about veiled."

A tradition held upriver. "You're from the river tribes?" That explained his bronze skin, several shades darker than her own.

He nodded but didn't elaborate.

Lystra blinked, flashing her painted eyes. "You would do well to uphold tradition, wherever you find yourself."

He gave a small shrug. "Tradition never suited me. I have this moment—this thrill, excitement, this passion—and that is enough. I shan't be expected to grow weary of it."

The pure embodiment of her deepest desires. To flee, to ride on a cardant's back until the Sancen fell away, liberated of all sorrow forever. To laugh and dream and dance into eternity.

Such things could never exist. But they could wish. They could try.

Then, with the music filling the air, the dancers spinning in their delirious abandon, he drew her veil away like a curtain and leaned in to—

Heat covered her skin. He was going to kiss her.

Reality with its weights and its sorrow slammed against

Lystra's soul. Such frivolities weren't meant for her. She was born and bred for responsibility—and her kingdom had only months to survive.

Lystra pulled her veil away, facing the young man with the countenance of a queen. Unbreakable, a monolith of surety, a model of grace that would never be swayed by the charm of a handsome man.

"Thank you for the dance. I enjoyed every moment." She bowed her head. "The present may change in an instant. Never take it for granted."

The young man stared, slightly stunned. Then, realization dawned on his face like the sun in the east. "Oh, Torra . . ." All pretenses, like her veil, fell. He saw her for who she truly was—the queen that was meant to rule Instanolde.

Then Lystra turned and hurried into the night.

Chapter 12

Lystra

House Arghan marched with the dawn.

Lystra's grip on Sama's reins tightened as the great, gold domes of the palace came into view, rising above the city skyline. Soldiers in orange turbans rallied to open the gates. Ahead of her, Jethro rode his own cardant, while behind, a horse-drawn carriage bore Dalmah, Kimzi, and Corsha.

Here, today, she would make her bid for the throne. The people would rally to her side while Grandmother's schemes cleared the path ahead. Lystra breathed deep, wishing the air in her lungs would transform to confidence and seep into her blood. She knew she'd need it.

Whatever reckless abandon had seduced her last night had run dry. She'd slept fitfully, dreaming of dancing. Sometimes her partner was Cormek, alive and well, but he always caught fire at the end of the dance. Sometimes it was the young man. He never caught fire.

She hadn't any idea of his name, but he knew her. The look of wonder upon his face mirrored the awe that had blanketed the entire kingdom. He had danced with the girl who would be queen. The thought of his almost kiss made her heart pound.

She briefly closed her eyes, thinking of Cormek's kisses. She would trade the stars themselves for the chance to draw him close, stand on tiptoe, and kiss him one last time.

Everywhere she looked, she saw him. His footsteps haunted the mosaic stonework. The hem of his robes sweeping the steps. The feel of him, girded in strength as he led her through the immense, carved doors. It didn't matter the activity, whether tending cardants from the royal stables or attending galas in gowns made of dreams, she felt alive with Cormek. He made the palace a home—her home.

Now, the soldiers held stoic expressions as they bowed to House Arghan. The welcome of rams' horns didn't sound. No one offered her the welcome and hospitality owed the future queen of Instanolde.

Dread, deep and dank, bore down upon her shoulders like a weight. Had she so soon become the enemy? Her popularity as the people's *Malikaa* had only grown. Did the prince-heir fear her? The girl that he himself had declared as hope bathed in starlight?

"Daughter?" Jethro handed off the reins of his cardant to a waiting page and offered her his hand. "Take courage."

She avoided his eyes but accepted his hand, wondering how many of Grandmother's schemes were written on her face. Yes, Cormek was gone, but this palace would once again become her home.

Dismounting Sama, she arranged her skirts. She'd chosen a dress of pale rose, its skirt split down the front, under which she wore navy pants tucked into polished riding boots. The collar gathered at her neck, secured with a gold ring, leaving her shoulders and back bare. Bangles covered her arms and a string of gold beads draped across her forehead. Today, she would be everything that her grandmother desired.

A queen come to claim her throne, riding a mighty cardant of the Sancen. She arrived as herself, without heraldry, born of Instanolde with sand in her blood, prepared to fight till her last breath for her kingdom.

As they passed beneath the palace's double arched entrance, external stonework gave way to luxurious marble. A shiver crept up Lystra's spine. Few windows were open and even fewer torches were lit. The grandeur and glory of the palace remained, and yet an unfamiliar shroud had dulled its colors and cooled its warmth, as if Cormek's pyre had burned away all the light.

Death had been brought to Instanolde, found its abode at the palace, and had come to linger.

Behind her, Lystra heard Dalmah inhale a long breath. *She has memories here—and ghosts too.*

She stole a glance over her shoulder. Her grandmother sparkled, her kaftan trimmed in gold and studded with beaded embroidery. But nothing in high summer could possibly rival the cold in her eyes. For a moment, Lystra glimpsed the queen that Dalmah had been. A stone-cold ruler who lost her throne with the dawn of House Karim's rule.

Now, Lystra would become what she did not.

A servant escorted them down marbled corridors. Corsha shot Lystra a sideways glance. Lystra held her head higher, hoping to dispel the doubt clouding her cousin's gaze.

They entered a council chamber. Gold lattice covered the windows, sending mosaic patterns of light across the stone floor and the large, octagonal table.

And there sat the prince-heir.

Of all the ghosts haunting the palace, this one held the most power. A specter without a crown, his head of curls, glossy as ink, lay bare. He waited behind the table with his plague-scarred hands folded, dressed in a qamis the color of rust.

And his gaze fell upon her, watching with the falcon eyes of a hunter waiting for prey. No hint of the softness he'd accidentally exhibited at the pyre was visible in his features, leaving no doubt in her mind that he did indeed see her as a rival.

Let him stare. Lystra lifted her chin. Assertive. Perhaps, as she rose like the summer sun, her dawn would outshine him, and leave him blinded.

"House Arghan." Behind the prince's chair stood a soldier, draped in the orange cape of a ranking officer. "Welcome."

Jethro stepped forward, laced his fingers together, and bowed at the waist, the customary greeting before royalty. "May your reign always be illuminated by starlight."

Lystra clenched her jaw. Pleasantries to prelude her grandmother's plans.

"Would Cormek have wanted you to do this? Unseat his brother?" Corsha's voice returned to her from the night before.

A stab of empathy pricked her heart, but she quickly deflected the blade. Cormek had been declared heir very young; surely this prince wasn't ready to rule. *She* had waited her entire life for the throne. *She* had trained and studied. *She* was ready.

Elerek dipped his chin. "And starlight guide you. Be seated."

They obeyed, settling in the chairs before them. Silence fell over the chamber as servants passed through, pouring tea from a silver samovar with a herd of silver cups flanking it as goats would their shepherd. But nobody drank.

"You may speak."

Lystra noticed the way his shoulders tensed, as if bracing himself. The news had flown as swiftly as Kushite condors, declaring that the river tribe had denied him. A bitter blow; this prince would be desperate now.

Jethro cleared his throat. "Your heirship, allow me to introduce the members of my house. My mother, the Countess Dalmah. The children of my brother, may starlight guide him forevermore, Lord Kimzi and Torra Corsha. And my daughter, Torra Lystra."

When the prince's eyes turned again toward her, Lystra met his stare, melding her posture into the regal demeanor taught by Dalmah. She let her eyelids relax, her mouth firm, and she kept her arms tight against her sides.

He blinked once, and Lystra thought she saw something else flicker there. Curiosity, like the feeble flame of a candle. Did he wonder about her? What she might do?

"This is Norbah, whom I have appointed general of my armed forces." Elerek gestured to the officer. "He has served faithfully in the Instan army and as chief of my personal guard."

The officer smiled, the likes of which Lystra rarely saw from a soldier. "I am honored to continue my service to Instanolde."

Elerek's gaze shifted back toward them, his chest expanding with a deep inhale. "I have eagerly anticipated this meeting. House Arghan stands as a monument of strength and integrity among the great houses. I acknowledge the undeniable loss you have suffered with my brother's passing, a testament to the loyalty you showed toward Cormek's rule."

A test, a challenge, like that of two cardants standing with muscles coiled at the starting line. Lystra wondered what he might do when the trumpet blew.

Dalmah cocked her head to one side, causing her earrings to jingle. "You are not your brother."

Lystra inhaled slowly as the tension rose like the simmering mirages of heat rising from the desert floor.

But Elerek didn't flinch. "Obviously." A sort of smile came over his lips. "But the crown passes to me, and I am the *only* choice—unless the kingdom fixates itself on some other plot."

Searching for deceptions. A common tactic. Lystra looked at her grandmother, wondering how she would spring the trap —corner this prince and leave him no choice but to stand aside.

"The *kingdom* has given its say." Dalmah spoke slowly, letting the intrigue she'd woven like a spider amid its webs fill the prince's mind.

Lystra looked at her father, but gauging his reaction was akin to assessing the slow-rising Gungole.

"We've come to speak in favor of the reign of House Karim, swearing devotion and fealty to the throne." Jethro spoke quickly, sealing their fate. "Instanolde stands vulnerable in the tragedy that took your brother which begs for unification and stalwart resolve if we are to emerge the victor over the Jarkins."

Across the table, Elerek's severity broke with a graceful raise of his eyebrows.

Dalmah remained cool and composed, her lack of reaction a frightening thing. Lystra found it difficult to breathe in the stifling chamber and her regal clothes uncomfortable. Making her bid for the throne was meant to give her control and now, she'd never felt more out of control.

"I'm pleased to hear that." Elerek betrayed no relief, remaining tense and rigid.

"You will have more than that." The countess lifted her head, her eyes gleaming like the sharpest of knives.

Panic rose in Lystra's throat. What was she doing?

"As House Arghan has stated, disunity begets nothing in these trying times." She stood, towering over the assembly, placing her jeweled knuckles on the table. "I propose a marriage alliance. Between House Arghan and House Karim. If you would accept my granddaughter Torra Lystra's hand and allow her to stand at your side as your queen." The countess leaned forward, looking rather like a bejeweled bird ready to peck. "It would be our highest honor."

At your side.

As your queen.

Our highest honor.

The words' resonance held a hollow sound as all oxygen fled the room. Lystra's vision swam before her eyes, the chamber spinning as if she still danced at the night market. The eyes of her family members stared dazedly, unfortunate spectators in this spiral.

And there, across the table, Elerek sat in his wheeled chair, still and somber. He narrowed his gaze, as if deep in contemplation, studying her with shrewd eyes. A buyer inspecting wares.

Lystra opened her mouth but found she could not speak, silenced like a captive awaiting judgment. Her grandmother had spoken for House Arghan. No contradiction could come from her lips. Not now. Not here. Not with her hands so shackled and her promised freedom manipulated and twisted. Corsha was right. She'd been played a fool.

Worst of all, Lystra had let her do it. Trusted her. And she bartered her off to be married to a stranger. Dalmah's cold, calculated logic knew no bounds, but still, not even a week had passed since Cormek's death. Surely she could have prepared her, but how would she have reacted?

Lystra looked at Elerek—the perfect broken image of Cormek—and found her heart callus and cold.

"A gracious offer . . ." The prince's features hardened. "One that I'm inclined to accept."

Please . . . Lystra's breath hitched, her countenance stitched together by the thinnest of threads. No longer would the prince look upon her and see a queen. No, instead he'd see a frantic girl who had fallen to superb players. Now Grandmother could play him too.

Worst of all, she could see no sensible reason for Elerek to refuse. If the great houses and tribes wouldn't support him, taking the betrothed of his brother could win him the kingdom.

Lystra tore her gaze to her father. She let her guise fall, exposing her terror. But Jethro looked on with an expression carved of stone. He also wouldn't speak, not here, unable to contradict Dalmah's declaration.

Meanwhile, Dalmah smiled a greedy smile. "Marvelous."

Lystra felt as if a thick snake coiled about her neck, choking her.

"However, before I consent." A bit of warmth bloomed on the prince's face, revealing again the boy she'd seen at the pyre, the one who spoke of starlight. "I wish to speak to Torra Lystra alone."

Once again, every eye in the room turned on her. It reminded her of the moment she rode out with her riders to the starting line of a cardant race, spectators rising from their seats, craning their necks, waiting for a spectacle. Lystra dipped her chin, ignoring all except the prince as her family filed from the room, escorted by the officer. She would not walk into this cage —to be his queen—blind. Her people deserved a leader who would not manipulate for power, whether that was her grandmother or this prince.

Alone, the prince leaned forward. He rested his hands on the table, fingers laced together. His gaze leveled with hers, his eyes cut like polished jade. "Are you well, Torra?"

She blinked. She dared not tremble, lest her jewelry give her away. One deep inhale later, and she donned the mask of the strong, stoic queen. "Quite." She hoped she sounded bold.

"I . . ." His throat worked as he swallowed. "I wish to

extend my condolences. Instanolde lost a king, but I know that he was more than just a king to you."

Lystra narrowed her gaze. Was this the soft side of him that she'd glimpsed, or simply a façade meant to convince her? Well, she wouldn't be taken. Her grandmother knew how to play these games too and right now, Lystra knew she never wanted to lose again.

"Cormek was the king that Instanolde deserved, and I know that he loved you." Elerek raked a hand through his hair. Beneath his curls, a sheen of sweat shimmered on his forehead. "I do not wish that this proposal be an insult to his memory or an offense to you."

Oh, she indeed took it as an offense. Lystra's hands clenched about her skirt. Her grief swirled into a rage that would've caused even Dalmah to shrivel. "I beg you to decline my grandmother's offer."

Silence filled the chamber. Elerek narrowed his eyes and squared his shoulders, severe as the eastern mountains. When he spoke, his voice was smooth, like melted chocolate heated for sipping and spiced with turmeric. "You came today to be queen, did you not?"

Lystra swallowed, choosing words to challenge. "I came to make my own bid for the throne built upon the devotion of my people."

"Ah." Elerek shifted in his chair, as if trying to make himself comfortable. "I anticipated as much. The love of Instanolde's people is quite a gift. But if I may, our circumstances leave us . . . few choices."

Her face burned hot.

"Torra, you were there . . . in the desert." His voice dropped to a whisper. "You understand the threats mounting against Instanolde. We have three months before the Jarkins return. I will see that Batu-Khasar and his ilk pay for the death of my brother. If we're to stand any chance at all, we need a united Instanolde. That is something that you can accomplish."

A queen to stand where he could not. The lump in her throat seemed to thicken, depriving her of oxygen and tensing her spine. "So, an alliance. Logical. Strategical. The love of our most cherished kingdom at its center." The words tasted sour. They reeked of Grandmother. "A canary to sit in a cage until you have use of it."

Elerek stared at her, head tilted, the slightest of wrinkles furrowing his brow. A war seemed to wage in his eyes. "Torra, we do not live in days that permit our own selfishness. *Our* kingdom will rise or fall on our actions."

She scoffed. "I'm not being selfish. I'm sure there are plenty of pretty girls from noble houses who would love to be your wife."

But he was right, and deep down, she knew she was being selfish. Rage clouded her reason, like a sandstorm stirring upon the dunes.

The prince didn't flinch. "I'm not looking for a wife. I need a queen to take care of my kingdom." His voice softened. "I ask you to consider that we might make better allies than enemies?"

Lystra shook her head, unable to speak.

"I'm not saying that it's easy." A calculated expression seduced Elerek's face, pushing away the desperation of a young lord in need of friends in high places. The look of a strategist. "We weren't dealt simple days. Yes, I know that you've suffered—"

"*You know?*" Lystra leapt to her feet, her silks flaring like flames about her form. In that moment, she hated him. "How can you possibly know what I've lost? What I've suffered? To have a lifetime of days stolen from under you? To watch those whom you love murdered in a fury of blood and hatred?"

As if her outburst of fury wasn't horrid enough, hot tears

filled her eyes. Sobs, raw and unhinged, clawed at her throat. Any thought of controlling herself and her emotions fled.

And there, across the table, Elerek transformed. No longer the cold and calculated prince nor the man who spoke of starlight in the face of disaster. Agony smoldered in his face. The people of the Karim tribe were pale and burned easily in the sun, but now, the prince had turned an ashen pallor—like a corpse.

Lystra blinked, her pent-up tears running free, stunned by the sight before her. No, he did know. She stared at her own grief in the face of another.

But, like a mirage upon the sands, it vanished.

"I watched at the pyre too, Torra." The cold edge returned to Elerek's voice. "Your grandmother, the countess and former queen, is regarded as the head of the Arghan household. She has put forth this offer and I have accepted. Now." He waved his hand toward the door. "I have arrangements to make—for a coronation, and a wedding."

This cold rebuttal told Lystra all that she needed to know about this prince. For all his talk of starlight, hope, he was simply another jailer to hold the keys to her cage. She stepped away from the table with a huff. "We will see."

He lifted his chin. "I suppose we will."

Chapter 13

Elerek

lerek didn't move, watching the dust dance in the shafts of golden light across the empty council chamber. Emotions, clashing like armies upon the battlefield of his mind, waged war with his grief and intentions. And he was not alone.

Torra Lystra's outburst rattled in his skull, each syllable rending his soul to shreds. Her voice overlapped with another argument, another attempt at reconciliation, another sort of alliance. Looking into her teary gaze was like staring into a twisted mirror. All his wretchedness painted across her face like the mourning paint she wore to the pyre.

Lystra was wrong. He knew, knew better than anyone.

Her ambition had blinded him. The girl who stood at *his* place at the pyre, the uncrowned queen who captured the allegiance of the people, another stunning jewel on Cormek's crown—a perfect queen for the perfect king. But she wasn't the opposition.

He needed House Arghan. Their support, their power. He needed a queen, and Lystra was the most perfect candidate.

She could keep Instanolde from falling apart, shine as the glorious sun across the scorching desert while he faded like starlight.

Bowing his head, Elerek closed his eyes. *He* was the piece that didn't fit. The villain in the fairytale of Lystra and Cormek's romance, an evil monster who'd taken the princess to be imprisoned in some remote fortress.

And there was no greater imprisonment than that of the curse. Lystra had no idea what marriage to him meant. He must tell her the truth. All of it.

Doubt crawled into his mind like some unwanted maggot. Lystra possessed a strong will. What if she outright rejected him? Then again, the Countess Dalmah held that same strong will—and she had spoken for House Arghan.

The sound of Norbah's boots broke the silence. As he reentered the chamber, astonishment drew his eyebrows up into the folds of his turban.

"El . . . did you accept?"

Elerek's jaw tensed. "I'd be a fool not to, wouldn't I?"

Agreement pulled a small smile from the general's lips. "It's a fortuitous move. The status of a powerful house like House Arghan matched by the people's love for Torra Lystra."

Elerek rubbed his forehead, suddenly feeling exhausted. "She's ardently against the arrangement and . . . still grieving my brother."

"Hmm." Norbah's broad shoulders dropped ever so slightly. "The Jarkins won't spare us on account of our grief. Torra Lystra will come to recognize her duty. Raised by a former queen, prepared to rule alongside a king."

More preparation than he had. Still, Elerek wondered if he'd asked too much of her, knowing well what grief could do.

"Stars above, I leave you alone for an hour . . ." Razhar flew into the chamber looking rather like a flustered peacock. No less dashing, he wore a purple vest, trimmed in gold, that left his dark chest gleaming in the morning sunlight. "I strongly dislike the idea of you two conspiring without me." He folded his arms. "El, you *actually* found a queen?"

"Skies, man." Norbah rolled his eyes. "As if anyone would take you seriously dressed like *that*."

Razhar pretended not to hear, tossing the tasseled tail of his turban over his shoulder.

Elerek cleared his throat. "Don't sound so surprised, Razhar. I did not initiate the discussion, but yes. I have the fealty of a powerful house and have secured a queen to rule long after the curse has claimed me." How quaint it sounded coming out of his own mouth.

Razhar's eyebrows lifted. "Well? Who is it?"

"Torra Lystra of House Arghan." The queen of Instanolde, as she was always meant to be, but never had the thought crossed his mind that she could be *his* queen.

Instead of the gleeful reaction Elerek anticipated, Razhar's smile faded, his face turning rather purple. "Torra *Lystra?*"

Elerek leaned back in his chair with a huff. "You're the one who wanted to watch her overthrow me. This seemed the better option. Do you object?"

"No, not at all." Then, Razhar smiled. "I'm gobsmacked. House Arghan made the proposal?"

"Yes, however . . ." Elerek squirmed, sliding clammy hands along his pants. The curse's numbness had overtaken his limbs again. "She reacted . . . poorly. The whole thing is awkward."

Norbah squared his shoulders and gripped his scimitar, taking his soldier's stance again. "Like I said, El. We've a duty to complete. Instanolde beckons us to strength."

"Come now, Norbah." Razhar shook his head. "The girl just lost the love of her life and is settling to arranged matrimony with this grumpy, insensitive lout."

Elerek propped up his elbow and leaned his head on his fist, quite finished with Razhar's obsession with the word "insensitive." "She'll be queen. Nothing more."

"Ah, a tragic tale of love and loss." Razhar sighed dramatically. Catching himself, he frowned and cocked his head. "Hold on, she knows about the curse, yes? From your brother?"

A nauseating rolling began in his stomach. Elerek wondered if he were going to be sick. "No, Cormek swore he'd never tell a soul."

"Mm." Razhar ran a hand along the back of his neck. "You ought to tell her, El. Especially before she hears it from someone else—or catches it."

"*I touched you. And now, you will die.*" Elerek had done his fair share of stuttered explanations to those he'd accidentally bumped or brushed, watching their faces shrivel with the realization that their days were numbered. Every time, it broke his heart and shattered his soul into a thousand tiny shards.

"If I tell her, this alliance will fall through. Snubbing House Arghan on the eve of my coronation won't help matters. We need stability, unity, especially since . . ." The Jarkins would return, and they had to be ready when they did.

A faraway look entered Razhar's eyes, the expression of an explorer eager to begin a journey. "I had the pleasure of meeting Torra Lystra last night, at the night market." He cleared his throat. "I think you will find her both bold and dynamic."

Elerek eyed his friend. Razhar's adventures typically involved lengthy retellings, and the last time Razhar had met a girl out in the city, he wouldn't stop talking about her. It was rather odd of him to keep mum about the company he kept now. "Why was she at the market?"

"Even in disaster, we must live. So, you'd better tell her the truth, El." Razhar raised an eyebrow. "What was that you were saying about unity?"

Norbah gave a low chortle while Elerek shook his head. "Why do I keep you around?"

Another glorious smile spread across Razhar's face, but his eyes went dark. "Well, eventually, I think you'll find that you need me."

I do. The words were so difficult to give air and sound. But he needed them. All of them. Those who saw the darkness, the brokenness, and stood by with a loyalty he never deserved.

And Lystra knew the darkness, the brokenness, too. Elerek tugged at his gold-lined collar, weary of stiff, royal clothes. What would Lystra say when he told her about the curse? How would she react to the knowledge that she would watch a second king die?

There would be no pyre for him. No, he would drown. Would she make a show of grief for the kingdom—paint her face with mourning stripes?

Elerek breathed in deep, steadying his soul. Their duty and devotion lay with Instanolde and despite how they—both he and Lystra—felt, they owed it to their kingdom. It would affect everything, everything they said, everything they did, and everyone they had ever loved.

So yes, he would marry. Lystra of House Arghan would be his queen, his heir. If he could give the kingdom his devotion, then he could also give it to her. She had survived the desert, the attack, and she would survive him and his curse too.

Chapter 14

Lystra

Lystra stormed outside the palace. Hot wind gusted at her clothing, her hair, with the ferocity of a sandstorm. Leaping astride Sama's saddle, she paid no attention to her family, wheeled the cardant round, and whispered speed.

The cardant did as she asked. The desert-dwelling reptile seemed to be the only presence intuitive to her needs. Dust streamed behind them in a long trail, like a signal from a smoldering fire. The rush, paired with the storm swirling in her soul, returned her to the desert, to the moments she never wanted to live again. The Jarkins emerging from the desert like beetles from beneath a rock, dressed in leathers and animal skins. A brutality gleamed in their eyes, something wild and untamed, and as savage as their weapons.

When Cormek drew his scimitar, his cardant restless in the sounds of battle and chaos, he'd looked back. Straight at her.

"Lystra, ride for Instanolde. Ride hard. Don't look back."

She remembered freezing, even there in the desert, her hands quivering on the reins of a cardant that would fall to the

Jarkins only minutes later. Uncertainty wavered in his voice. Just a ripple, but enough to strike a deadly fear in her heart.

She had wanted to reach out. To touch him. To kiss him. One last time. But a void emerged between them. Deep as the Sancen, wide as the Gungole.

That void remained in her heart, even now. She'd carried it back as she fled the desert and survived the attack—back to *this*.

Her life had one direction—the throne of Instanolde. She'd loved one man—Cormek. Nothing would ever replace what she'd lost. Nothing.

With one effective push, Dalmah campaigned like an army to seize her fate, the future of the prince-heir, and whatever came next. Lystra sat amid the ruins, grasping at pieces like broken pottery. But the damage was done. There would be no taking control of her future, piecing her destiny back together.

Winding Sama through the city streets, dodging wagons, she didn't care who stared. The sound of her jewelry filled her ears. Dust gathered about her skirt, streaming behind her. She could bless the kiss of the afternoon sun on her bare shoulders, the only comfort she could receive. *You belong in the wilds.*

Without tether. Without hands guiding her future. She knew how to ride when there were no paths. Straight. Forward. Bold.

With a hiss, she pulled Sama sharply to a halt. Here, at the edge of the market, cardants were simply too large for the narrow streets. Vendors had just begun to erect their booths in preparation for the evening market. Memories of the night before swept through her mind—the rush, the thrill of dancing in the square.

Now, she felt trapped. She belonged to Instanolde as much as the wilds. Her people needed her. Sobs clawed at her throat. Cormek stood with duty and honor, fighting till the last breath left his lungs.

Didn't she owe it to Cormek? To also fight with duty and honor against whatever may come? Ensure the survival of her people? But like the narrow road before her, an impossibility for the reptile she rode, she'd hit an obstacle too great. One she couldn't conquer.

She let her tears fall. *I will not marry Elerek.*

"Move aside!" a driver called from a lumbering wagon filled with rolls of rich carpets.

Lystra jerked the reins and Sama sidestepped, brushing against the wall of a low-roofed dwelling. The reptile blinked its orbish eyes, watching the donkeys drawing the wagon with an interested expression. Lystra tightened her grip.

She must look a sight. A noble daughter dressed in silks riding a cardant through the city. She sighed, turning Sama down the road that would take her home.

To her family.

To House Arghan.

To Grandmother.

Her father's guards waited in the courtyard. At any other estate, they might have taken the reins of her cardant and offered her a hand. Not here. Lystra swung herself down with ease, looping the reins over Sama's head and loosening the harness about her snout.

"You're a good girl," she whispered, patting her scaled neck.

Sama only blinked.

Then, the door to the estate burst open, her family spilling into the courtyard.

Lystra turned, handing the reins off to a guard, and stalked across the flagstone, determined to speak first and fast. "My departure was abrupt. I apologize for any anguish I've caused." She narrowed her eyes at her grandmother. "I've been dealt enough anguish of my own."

Dalmah looked on, her velvet lips verging on smug.

"Daughter, what did the prince say?" Jethro demanded, a storm gathering across his brow. "What have you done to House Arghan?"

"Nothing." Lystra's eyes darted between her father and grandmother. "I am certain that the prince will welcome the strength and support of House Arghan." She narrowed her eyes. "With or without a queen."

The smug curve of her grandmother's lips deepened.

"You turned him down?" Corsha's eyebrows shot up her forehead.

Lystra opened her mouth, but Dalmah's tongue moved faster. "She cannot turn him down. House Arghan will not suffer the shame of such an act—particularly one so foolish."

Heat flooded Lystra's face.

"Mother," Jethro growled, a lion on the prowl. "My daughter will not be forced into anything—particularly not into a marriage of political alliance. Such an arrangement wasn't discussed or agreed upon. I'll not have such conniving beneath my own roof. Is that understood?" Then, and only then, his gaze softened as his eyes returned to Lystra. "Is this truly your desire? I don't wish to see you suffer."

Lystra smoothed back her windswept hair, his words too little too late. "I want what I am owed. I have the people's support, their love. I would continue Cormek's legacy, rule as he would have. Save his—*our*—people from the Jarkins."

And I will have no one cage me. I will be free.

Dalmah clicked her tongue. "You will have all this—and more."

"At what cost?" Lystra bit back. "I've spent enough of my life being used by you. I won't let that prince use me too."

Her grandmother's eyes narrowed, black slits beneath her curtain of dark hair. "That, my dear, is up to you."

Lystra felt the snake at her neck again. Constricting slowly.

"Jethro." Dalmah turned to her son. "Do you not see the merit in this plan? The people deserve their queen, do they not? And surely engagement to the prince is far better than forcing his abdication."

He folded his arms. "Yes, I can agree with that. But Lystra—"

"Lystra will do as her kingdom requires," Dalmah trilled, smooth and strong, like a wine of the deepest ruby. "If she does indeed wish to serve *them*—and not herself."

The prince's voice rang in her mind, harmonizing to her grandmother's tune. *"Torra, we do not live in days that permit our own selfishness."*

Lystra's heart plummeted. To deny would be her undoing. Her people wouldn't see a queen intent on preserving her people, just a simple, selfish, foolish girl. If she lost the throne, she would be nothing. If she took the throne and Elerek's hand, she would still be nothing. Dalmah had laid the path before her, but it was a path hedged with thorns. She couldn't escape without consequences—not without being scathed.

And Instanolde, would her people be better off with her, Elerek, or both? Well, if the Jarkins had their way, it wouldn't matter at summer's end.

Jethro heaved a deep sigh. "We cannot back out now."

A gasp slipped from Corsha's lips. She grabbed Jethro's arm. "Uncle, please, Lystra can't—"

"As your grandmother said, Lystra will do as the kingdom requires." Jethro patted Corsha's arm, removed her hand, and turned back toward the house. "I don't want to hear any more about it." He disappeared inside. Out of reach. Deaf to all pleas.

Lystra's eyes drifted down to her dirty slippers. Here, in her own home, she felt herself an island. Marooned on the sands. Only Corsha stood on her side, and her cousin was as helpless as she.

A familiar ache wrecked her heart. Cormek knew. He'd seen beyond the wild girl who raced cardants, the Torra trained by her grandmother's tutelage, the future queen the kingdom revered. He'd treasured her heart, the kindness she labored to give, and the hope and the wonder she dared not lose. He wouldn't recognize her now.

Gathering a fistful of her dirtied skirt, Lystra marched up the steps and into the majaz. The scent of tamarisk hit her senses. Pale petals lay strewn across the marble as the boughs dried and wrinkled, waiting to be gathered and re-purposed. She knew the feeling.

"A word, Lystra."

She stopped in her tracks. Dalmah's shadow darkened the doorway. Behind her, Corsha edged inside, her eyes wide.

Dalmah scowled at her younger granddaughter as she swept toward the stairs. "Alone. In my chambers."

Lystra sighed, tossing her cousin an expression of hopelessness, and then followed her grandmother.

Chapter 15

Lystra

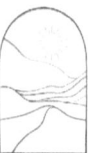

The rooms belonging to Dalmah held nothing but painful memories for Lystra. Hours upon hours of lessons. Strict instruction to produce soft movements. Harsh words to deliver eloquent speeches. How to give the appropriate bow to a specific official. How to step gracefully on marble tile, instead of clanking about in her riding boots. All things that supposedly cultivated a queen.

But nothing about protecting a kingdom, fighting Jarkins, or saving their people. Lystra shook her head. In comparison, everything else seemed utterly futile.

Sweeping the curtains back, Dalmah slid the wood lattice from the western window. Lystra blinked as light streamed across a circle of cushions and a low table. Silks draped from the ceiling and an ornate copper lamp hung above the table. Shelves, lined up like soldiers, covered most of the walls, filled with books, decorated pottery, and small carved chests housing relics and trinkets of another era.

Lystra folded her arms. An obstinate posture, but it suited her messy hair and dusty clothing. "You betrayed me. You said you'd put me on the throne, that you'd take care of everything."

With an air of graceful elegance, Dalmah alighted upon a low couch. The way she drew her legs up and laid her hand delicately on its arm reminded Lystra of a lioness at ease. Always watchful, always ready to prowl. Dominate. "Have I not done all that?"

Lystra shook her head. "You said nothing of marriage. Do you not care that I lost Cormek? The man I loved? Now, in less than a week, you've bartered me off to a man I don't even know. A desperate man who is already holding the throne by a mere thread."

Her grandmother smiled, and it seemed that her eyes were full of poison. "But this is neater, isn't it? That *boy* is desperate and, my granddaughter, *you* are what is holding him to the throne. Now, it is wholly within your power to be rid of him." Her gaze darkened, presenting a challenge. "However you see fit."

What did she mean? Lystra drew a shuddered breath. Her emotions were beginning to gather, swirling like incense burned in the temple. She'd already cried in front of the prince. She hardly wanted to cry now.

"Do you not believe that you are the queen Instanolde deserves?" Dalmah cocked her head to one side. "Or are you so narrow-minded? Is this what I've raised? A foolish girl who only looks after her own heart?"

Each insult, fired like arrows, found its mark. Only her grandmother, the only mother she'd ever known, could wound her like this. Fortitude she possessed in plenty, but here, before Dalmah, every part of her felt wholly insufficient.

"As you know, House Arghan held the throne once. I was its queen." Her gaze began to smolder, like the dying embers of a funeral fire.

Yes, and now you'll tell the story again. Lystra huffed and sank in an unceremonious heap onto a cushion.

"A severe drought had come upon the land. Crops failed. Many starved. My father, king of Instanolde, reached out to the Nathool tribe for an alliance, for they commanded the fertile fields of the west. As heir of House Arghan, I married the Nathool prince, your grandfather, Tanark. An alignment for the sake of Instanolde's future, for food to fill the bellies of starving children. But between Instanolde and the Nathool lay the Karim tribe. They too were starving, but rather than negotiate or broker for peace, Karim revolted. They destroyed the Nathool, taking their fields for themselves. Next, Karim set their sights on Kushan, seeking to control not only the fertile fields but the canals through which flow our trade. Instanolde came to their aid, but at great cost—both to us and Kushan. The fight was lost and there, my husband lost his life. Karim took control beneath Lorkin. Though I remained the rightful queen of Instanolde, Lorkin shunned me, turned the people against me, and forced me out."

Lystra's stomach churned, her fingers absently twirling the tassel at the corner of the cushion. Another beloved lost to the shifting sands of war and strife. Did her grandmother not realize the similarities? Could she not show mercy? Kindness?

"We all can agree that Lorkin proved a terrible, bloody ruler. Cormek showed the signs of being a different sort and his fate is truly tragic. The tribes are weak, particularly after the discord sown by Lorkin. This boy, a spare cur raised in the shadows, bears none of Cormek's attributes. He cannot bring unity, not on his own."

Lystra leaned forward. "Then why didn't we call for his abdication? I *can* unite the tribes. I can bring peace."

But she wasn't enough to save Instanolde from the Jarkins.

She pushed this thought aside. Her intent lay in the throne, in the hope of freedom that she craved with her whole soul.

Dalmah didn't speak. A light that didn't come from the window entered her gaze. This spark burned with something darker. Lystra's spine began to tingle with a chill that shouldn't have existed in the summer heat. There was more to her plan. The marriage was just the beginning.

Rising gracefully, Dalmah moved to a chest standing in the corner. Lifting its lid, edged in gold filigree, she rummaged through its contents.

"When I lost the throne, I hated House Karim. Because of them, my husband was dead and my crown forfeit. When Lorkin continued, time after time, to paint the sands with blood, I cursed my own weakness. I should've fought. I should've turned the tide of Instanolde. I will not have you pass up this chance." From the chest's depths, she pulled a case wrought in ivory. "We must be brave, yes, and bold. Innovative. Fierce. Your best chance against the Jarkins lies in Kushan. Only they have the defenses and resources to combat them and they've already sworn to oppose the boy."

Her grandmother stepped closer, holding the case out in her extended arms.

Lystra removed its lid. There, lying in satin, the cold steel of a dagger gleamed. Its blade was curved and etched with intricate designs. Its handle was set with ebony and amber. A lethal and beautiful work of art.

She caught her breath. *Does she mean—?*

"I implore you, granddaughter. You are strong. You are the hope of House Arghan, the heartbeat of Instanolde. We need not a king. Not a Karim one. Destroy this mongrel. No one will mourn the crippled boy. Endure the preparations, the ceremony, go into his chambers—and drive this blade into his heart."

Kill the prince. The heir. The king.

The last person standing between her and the throne.

Her heart beat loudly, pulsing blood through her ears. The Sancen showed no mercy, a harsh world where all life fought for survival. Perhaps, as people of the desert, the time had come to embrace this ferocity. Survive.

She'd taken blades to cardants before, those suffering from severe injuries or illness, giving them the grace of a quick end. It took much to muster her nerve and brace herself against the smell of blood, but she'd owned the reptiles long enough to know when such drastic action was necessary.

She imagined the dagger, plunged to the hilt into Elerek's chest. Blood dripping down his front. The last Karim. Finality.

The image of Cormek hazed across her mind, an arrow through his back. He wavered. The axe cleaved his chest. He toppled. The surviving soldiers had taken his body, wrapped it in a bloodstained robe, slung it astride a cardant, and took it back to Instanolde.

Death seemed to follow her everywhere, no matter how hard she rode or how far she ran.

Ride hard. Don't look back.

"No."

Dalmah's eyes narrowed.

Lystra shut the case and pushed her grandmother's hands away. "No. There's been enough death. I won't become the cause of it."

The heated air turned oppressive, intensified by the embers in Dalmah's eyes. A soft curse escaped her breath. "You fickle, foolish girl."

Lystra's cheeks burned.

"To think you once showed promise, strength. Now your kingdom teeters in the balance and you lack the courage to accomplish what is necessary."

"The prince's death isn't *necessary*, Grandmother."

Dalmah narrowed her eyes again. "Then, you'll marry him."

Another sort of death. Another sort of cage. Were these truly the only options for her future? A future once glorious and bright, now reduced to an endless, starless night.

"As you said"—Lystra's voice dripped with venom—"I can't back out now."

Her grandmother drew the dagger and its case to her chest, but her hands shook with rage. Huffing, she shoved the ivory case back into the chest beneath a pile of silks. "Get out of my sight."

Lystra spun on her heels. She sought solace in her own chamber, locking the door behind her. Planting her back against the door, she closed her eyes, craving the stillness, the silence. And then, she sank to her knees and wept. For the world she lost, and the one that remained.

Perhaps it was no use. Let them perish at summer's end. What else could they do? She'd never wished for death before or contemplated that it would be a blessing.

But she couldn't end. No, she must endure.

Enduring meant marrying the prince, becoming queen, unifying Instanolde. Enormous, impossible tasks. Perhaps she might have been strong, once, but grief had stolen her power, her endurance, and left the fickle, foolish girl that Dalmah thought her.

"I'll prove you wrong, Grandmother," she whispered. She didn't know how. Not yet. Well, besides taking a knife and ending Elerek's life.

No. She couldn't consider it. Not even for a moment. Not even if it would rid her of another manipulator, loose her from the chains holding her back.

Thoughts of her cardants filled her mind, the noble reptiles riding across the desert sands, climbing rocks and buttes. They knew how to respond to their rider's movements, to read each distinct cue from hand, knee, and tug of rein. Trained to form a distinct partnership, one where neither rested above the other.

Lystra had only experienced one such relationship. Cormek—and he was dead. Even her cardants now lay slaughtered in the desert.

What was one more death? Surely it couldn't matter. The Jarkins would come for them all, slaughter them upon the shores of the coveted Gungole. Did it matter whether Elerek died then—or now?

Yes. Their lives had to matter. When summer ended, their lives might be all that they had left to forge some sort of difference in this cruel world.

Hours later, a knock tapped lightly on her door. Rising from the floor, Lystra sniffled and wiped her eyes. To her surprise, Kimzi stood at the door, his checkered turban unraveling in a way that gave him a roguish appearance.

"So sorry to bother you, cousin." A softness eased into his tone, like the sweet filling inside a crumbly pastry. "But I have a proposition, if you're up for it."

Lystra stumbled forward and wrapped her arms around him.

"Oi, you haven't even heard it." He gingerly patted her shoulder.

"I'm listening." She squeezed him tighter, finding him altogether comforting. Something between a younger brother to boss about and an older one with which to pull pranks.

"Well, my friends from House Quilam purchased a set of cardants they're considering putting forward as racers. I saw the reptiles this afternoon and I think they ought to talk to you."

Lystra stepped back, frowning. "They haven't been trained or bonded with a rider?"

Kimzi shrugged. "Ah, you know the Quilam boys, they're as impatient as vultures."

"Impatience will make unpredictable and sometimes violent cardants." She scoffed. "A racer takes time, and lots of it."

A smirk appeared on her cousin's face. "Now, now, I'm not the one in need of a lecture. I suppose you might talk them into allowing you to train them yourself."

Lifting her chin in a posture of primness, Lystra sniffed. "I suppose I might."

The work with the unruly cardants and their impatient counterparts did her soul good. When the sun set and constellations began their dance across the night sky, she returned to House Arghan's estate covered in sweat and dust. Almost at once, a messenger from the palace arrived bearing a letter. Lystra's name was written in an elegant script across the front of the rolled parchment, tied with an orange ribbon.

. . .

Torra Lystra,

With your acquiescence, I have arranged for our anointing to take place at the temple in three days' time. A fortnight shall pass, and then we will wed and hold our coronation. Our kingdom needs starlight.

— Elerek

No heraldry. No titles. A few lines of scrawled ink to change everything.

Much like a dagger, Lystra mused, though her eyes trailed on the word starlight. The ink smudged a bit, as if the prince had hesitated to pen it. Perhaps he wondered if she would remember. She inhaled deep and wrote a reply.

Your Highness,

I acquiesce and consent to this arrangement, to give Instanolde starlight.

— Lystra

Chapter 16

Elerek

Elerek despised the narrow hall that led to the baker's courtyard. The uneven stonework, its grout long worn away, sent his bones jarring and caused his chair to rattle unmercifully. Equally infuriating, the passage was nearly too narrow and Elerek had often chafed his knuckles against the stucco walls.

Once, he'd knocked one of his chair's wheels clean off and toppled to the stones in a most ungraceful manner. The chair's axle had cracked and required extensive repairs. Being moored to a single chair or couch left him feeling like a ship anchored along the riverside.

Elerek clenched his teeth as he heaved his chair over a large rut in the stonework. If they survived the summer, he'd remodel the entire palace. No more slim corridors and blasted stairs. His chair had become an extension of himself, an advantage over his ill-formed legs and weak muscles.

Carefully maneuvering through the remainder of the corridor, he arrived in the courtyard. Most of the time, the scents were enough to lure one in—medallions of batbout, flute-shaped briouats filled with spiced lamb and onions, and plenty of garlic karahz—though this morning, Elerek followed the sound of chatter.

A gathering of his cursed tribe stood in a circle, a basket of seeded karahz between them. Driss bent over the table, a long scroll in hand. Bushra looked over his shoulder, occasionally making corrections to his work. But as the chair's creaking wheels touted Elerek's approach, they snapped to attention with stunned expressions.

"El!" Driss gasped. "What are you doing here?"

Fin, a stable hand hardly more than a boy, softly cleared his throat. "Ought we to call him 'Your Highness'?"

The scribe's face turned red. "Yes, you're right. Your Highness." He made a grand bow and hastily rolled up the scroll.

Elerek smiled and gave a small wave of dismissal. "All this heraldry before breakfast is tiresome and wholly unnecessary."

"Isn't the anointing today?" Ishtal folded his arms. "You ought to be preparing."

His smile faded. He still had to figure out a method of receiving the anointing customary before a coronation *without* the priest touching him.

And he wasn't particularly thrilled at the prospect of seeing Torra Lystra again. Had her fury simmered? She'd responded to his mention of starlight in his letter; did she remember that it meant hope? Did she realize that he meant for *her* to be that hope?

"Yes, yes, it is." Huffing, Bushra took a woven plate and heaped several karahz loaves onto it. She circled the group and pushed it into his hands. "So, off you go."

Balancing the plate on his knees, Elerek steeled his grip on his wheel. "What's going on?"

Sheepish glances passed among them.

"Out with it."

Once more, their eyes shifted, a circle of nerves and secrets.

Elerek huffed. "You all spend far too much time with Razhar."

"It was Bushra's idea . . ." Driss began.

"It's quite the occasion," Ishtal continued. "One is only crowned once."

"One would think." Elerek gave an encouraging nod. "And?"

"And, well," Fin sputtered. "You're getting *married.*"

The youth spoke the word as if it were some lofty, mythical thing. Perhaps it was, among the cursed. Elerek thought of Norbah, who hadn't seen his wife and son since becoming cursed and couldn't bear the thought of endangering them. He thought of Hassam and Yazmine, two cursed who were among those who had already passed. They'd fallen in love and wed quickly, much to the delight of their tiny tribe. They drowned one month apart.

Elerek bowed his head. Around that time, he'd begun to draw close to Myra.

"And every wedding requires a proper feast." Bushra snatched the scroll from Driss's fingers and tapped it on the table. "So, we intend to give you one."

Elerek gave a knowing nod. "I see."

"Think of it as our gift." Bushra folded her arms, well-muscled from years of baking. "After your coronation, you might not have as much time for us. And Starkindler knows, you've done so much." A slight quiver entered her voice, an echo of affection.

I've killed you. Every one of you. Elerek's breath quaked, and he felt certain his sorrow was written in bold ink across his face.

Sure enough, anguish blanketed the faces of his cursed

tribe like the sand-strewn hazes that veiled the eastern mountains.

"You'd rather we didn't?" Driss asked slowly.

"No, I'm . . . I'm honored." Elerek uncurled his clenched hands, trying to loosen the tension mounting in his shoulders. "I just don't believe that I'm worthy."

"Let us be the judge of that, El." Bushra waved a dismissive hand. "Now, eat your breakfast and let us work. We've a wedding to prepare for."

Crash!

Shards of pottery scattered like fragments of starlight across a darkened horizon. Flour, oil, and mixed seeds spilled and crept into the flagstone's crevices. And in the center, Myra knelt and scrambled for the pieces.

Winding down to her elbow, a snake-like tendril of liquid stretched across her skin.

The curse mark—spreading. Elerek's insides seized.

The others noticed, making a grand show of looking the other direction. Bushra and Driss stooped to assist in the cleanup. Fin brought a rag and began to sop up the spilled oil, much like the spill of cursed water they would become when they drowned. Elerek prayed that Myra wouldn't be next.

"Does it hurt?" Fin whispered.

"Quiet," Ishtal growled.

Myra shook her head. "No, not really. It just startled me." The quiver in her voice spoke a different truth. She lifted her head, pushing a length of dark hair over her shoulder. "What's this about preparations?"

Silence met her question. Another set of nervous glances and averted eyes.

Elerek cleared his throat, wondering if they could hear his heart, pounding furiously in his ears. "The coronation." Surely she'd heard the news by now.

Her eyes turned to his, her gaze dark and void of stars. She didn't speak, merely wiped the flour from her hands and rose to her feet. "El, may I speak with you? Alone?"

The air thickened, tightening in Elerek's lungs. He couldn't look her in the eye, those soft, gentle eyes. A flame caught in his heart, a fire that wasn't permitted to burn. The rest of the cursed, the unintentional spectators, all pretended not to notice.

They knew, of course, that a prince and a cursed servant girl loved one another. But not everything, not the secrets that haunted the dark. At least, if they did, they didn't speak of it. Did they pity Myra? Now, even as they prepared for his wedding?

"Is it necessary?" Elerek didn't want to be cold, insensitive. But he also didn't want to burn, and the distance between him and Myra would keep them from catching fire.

"It won't take long." Myra's voice lowered. "I know you're busy."

He nodded. The hours had hardly given him time to breathe. Meetings with city officials, enduring the houses swearing feeble fealty or scorning his crown, and the soldiers. Always meeting with the soldiers. All the while suffocating beneath the weight of his future—and the pomp and ceremony of a coronation and a wedding.

The narrow corridors forced them single file. Elerek didn't want to see the pain upon her face. He wheeled his chair through smoother passages, the edge of the palace gardens overtaking the warm tones of the palace, bathing the world in green.

Myra stopped along one of the arches, its curve accented with hanging vines, her gaze turning out to the gardens. Somewhere, a fountain babbled its endless melody.

"I heard what you've done." She adjusted her scarf, letting it cover her curse mark.

"Are you surprised?" Elerek's jaw tightened. The numbness took root in his limbs again, slowly spreading, stealing away the sun's warmth on his shoulders. In times where it became unbearable, Myra would wrap her arms around him, hold him until the feeling returned.

No more.

Myra stared down at her slippers. Her eyes grew glassy with unshed tears. "No," she whispered. "I just don't want to lose you."

"There isn't a place for us." Stars, he didn't want to have this conversation. "We can't be together. Not anymore."

Drip. One of her tears stained the front of her dress.

Elerek looked away. Better a tear from a broken heart than a drop of cursed water for a victim doomed to drown. "I shouldn't have permitted you to choose the curse."

"The hearsay claims"—Myra's voice cut like the sharpest of scimitars—"that your queen isn't pleased with this arrangement. Are you permitting her to choose this?"

"She is surety for Instanolde, beloved by its people. We both have a duty to this kingdom." And Lystra would see it through, of that, he had no doubts.

She drew near to his chair, reaching for his hand. Her thumb traced the plague scars along his knuckles. Cold, cursed skin, like his. "I chose *you*, El. I'm not afraid of the curse, I never have been. I only fear the pain it causes you."

He could feel her touch, the caress of her fingers, breaking through the numbness. It felt like a rope, a rope by which he desperately dangled, his only link to some sort of connection with the rest of humanity. Without it, he had only the slow pull of life ebbing from his bones and dulling his senses, whispering of his impending death.

He moved his hand to his chair's wheel, breaking the connection. "This won't do any good, Myra." His whisper hung in the air, like dust caught in a sunbeam. He pivoted his chair away, back toward the palace and its responsibilities. "It has to be like this."

Cormek's last charge, his last words to the brother he would never see again, pounded in his mind like the march of disciplined soldiers. The charge to live—and it mattered *how* he lived. The last of his days poured out for a future he would never see.

A sob caught in Myra's throat. "Was it real, El? Did you—" She caught herself. "*Do* you, love me?"

Stars. Elerek's hands clenched, his wheels grounded. His heart strived against his ribcage, like a prisoner in torturous agony. "Yes, Myra, it was real." He shifted in his chair, glancing over his shoulder. Her love was a precious gem, one he had never been worthy of, one that he had tarnished, much the same way his curse destroyed all that it touched. "I love you— but I also failed you. I'm sorry."

Tears fell from Myra's eyes again. She circled his chair, facing him, and then leaned forward, the dark curtain of her hair falling around her face. "Then don't push me away." Her lips brushed his, but he could not feel them.

He rolled his chair back, the cold, empty void wrapping about him in its numb embrace. He ignored it, setting his face like flint. "In two weeks," he ground out through gritted teeth. "I'm required to take vows. Before the throne, before the priests, before the kingdom. My heart must yield its loyalty to Instanolde. I must put its needs first and I owe it to Torra Lystra to keep those vows. I cannot betray that sacredness and cheapen its meaning."

Myra stared at him, her face pale.

"I need you to understand that and respond accordingly. Take care of our people, my family. Bushra was right, I won't have as much time to spare. Will you do that, for me?"

Myra folded her arms. "Razhar and I have done all that we can."

Razhar? Elerek frowned. What did she mean?

Her eyes caught fire, burning with a heated passion. "Once Torra Lystra finds out about you, do you think she will keep those same vows? Will she cherish you as I have? What do you know of her, other than that she was betrothed to your brother? Your intentions may be noble, but she's using you, El, to take the throne."

He moved his hand to his chair's armrest, and his fingertips began their anxious tapping on the polished wood. He didn't look at Myra, afraid that she might see the truth in his eyes, the hidden glimpse into Lystra's secrets he'd seen the day the marriage was proposed.

The girl who knew grief, who had been shattered and asked to bear too many burdens. That he and her were more alike than he wanted to admit—and that made him afraid. Grief had taken its toll, the weight of the curse a load great enough to crush him. In his desperation, his loneliness, he had done things that he had regretted.

Lystra couldn't break, couldn't fail. He needed to strengthen her, to make her a queen, to—to give her starlight.

Still, Myra's words stung. The thought that the woman he would marry would never think of him as anything more than an advantageous arrangement bled with sorrow, even though he didn't want her affection. No, even as he drew lines between him and Myra, their memories as distant as the constellations in the sky, he knew that she loved him.

Feeling cold and numb, even now with the summer sunlight dancing across his shoulders, Elerek lifted his gaze. "Then she can take the throne. I was never meant to have it anyways. Now, I have things to do. Goodbye."

Chapter 17

Lystra

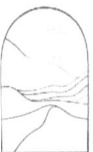

Lystra wished she could have gone by cardant to the temple instead of by carriage, but the ceremonial gown of a deep emerald lavishly adorned with beaded gold sunbursts wouldn't have arrived in the pristine state required. The scent of myrrh and aloe rose from her skin and deep ebony lined her eyes.

Adorning herself externally had somehow steeled her internally. Each bath, perfume, and paint transformed the grieving girl into the somber queen that stepped off the carriage and into the temple courtyard.

Behind her, Dalmah and Jethro emerged from the carriage. They also wore emerald, the color of intended royalty.

Lystra adjusted the draping lengths of the sheer sleeves. When her betrothal to Cormek was announced, she had worn emerald then as well. She drew a deep breath. There would be no thoughts of Cormek today, or the day after.

Soldiers already filled the courtyard, lined up in bright uniforms and polished helmets. The sight made Lystra shiver.

All too soon, they would be required for war. To defend their kingdom and shed blood for their survival.

She passed the fountain, her sandals treading the stones where the girl had spilled to her watery death. Azraa. Her name deserved to be remembered.

Ahead, in the shadow of the temple doorway, the priests waited. Orzak, draped in yellow, stood flanked by two acolytes with midnight-blue turbans. They bowed at the waist, welcoming the prince-heir at the temple door.

Lystra stood a little taller.

Elerek was also adorned in emerald and wore a thin gold circlet upon his brow. He bore his countenance in a cold, stern severity. No one would think him anything less than the brother of Cormek, the prince-heir of Instanolde, and future reigning king.

He caught her eye.

Grandmother asked me to kill him. Her spine tingled. She wanted to look away, afraid that Elerek would see right into her soul, into the murderous intentions stewing within House Arghan.

Lystra blinked. No, what happened in Dalmah's chamber would hide in darkness, a secret among secrets.

As she approached him, she bowed, her jewelry twinkling. "Your Highness."

Elerek nodded his head. "Torra."

Once the anointing was complete, she could also bear the title "Your Highness." The thought lit the embers of her heart, the fires stoked by Dalmah, the queen her grandmother raised.

Orzak also bowed. "Torra Lystra." But as he rose, Lystra caught a shadow in his gaze. She wondered what he thought of this arrangement.

The sound of music drifted over the temple's walls. A

joyous sound, life pulsing in each beat of rawhide drum, in perfect sync with Lystra's heart.

Elerek's eyes turned skyward, golden spires reflecting in his irises. "The announcement went out with the morning heralds —of our betrothal." He gave a small smile. "They celebrate you —*Malikaa.*"

Queen of Instanolde. Her destiny, sure as the stars themselves. Except, this vision included a king, not the one she imagined, and sorrow returned to her heart.

Steeling herself, Lystra only nodded, determined that her every word and move today would mirror perfection. No one, neither her grandmother nor the prince-heir, would have any reason to criticize.

Before she entered the darkened doorway of the temple, Lystra glanced just once over her shoulder. House Arghan would remain outside the temple, her family the first to welcome her after her blessing. Her father wore a grim expression, the lines about his face stern. As for Dalmah, she may as well have been carved from salt, pure and hard.

Then, Lystra gathered her skirts and followed the sound of Elerek's wheelchair inside. The scent of incense burned in her nostrils. It swirled in a cloud above the altar, thick and heavy like a stormfront. Around it, bowls contained green-tinted flames, casting an odd glow across their skin.

Squaring her shoulders, Lystra drew a shallow breath, dizzy with the incense. Her nerves frayed, like a candle's wick before it took to light. Suddenly, she wished the entire ordeal could be over, and quickly.

Beside her, Elerek shifted in his chair, his fingers adjusting the cuffs of his robe. Perhaps he was just as uncomfortable.

Orzak stopped before the altar. On a short table draped in tapestries, three unlit candles waited. The priest set a small jar of oil beside them. "With your permission, we will begin."

"One request." Elerek cleared his throat. "That my general stands in ceremony with us—and performs my anointing."

Lystra frowned.

"As you wish, Your Highness." Orzak blinked. "This request is . . . unusual."

"The custom of anointing may be deferred to the role of soldier when no temple officiant is present, on a battlefield, or when a kingdom is at war." Elerek spoke in a strong, calm tone, like that of a scholar orating on the avenue. "Vaana's writings. And we are to be at war . . . soon."

Sorrow lingered in the priest's gaze at the mention of their impending future. "Vaana's treatises are highly honored. Your Highness must be well-read."

"I am." Elerek gestured to his entourage. The general stepped forward, solemn and stark, the *chink* of his armor filling the silence.

Orzak bowed his head. "In this moment, we honor and stand in remembrance of the fallen. Though the life of Cormek of House Karim—and those of his men who fought in sure devotion to king and kingdom—was cut short, we honor the days he was given and the life that he lived. We choose to measure a life not by its length of seasons, but its fullness, its love, hope, and service to those who remain. May Cormek dwell always among the starlight, in the presence of the Starkindler, the Maker of the stars."

Lystra held her breath, the weight of the darkness, the incense, and the memories of the man she loved constricting her chest.

Out of the corner of her eye, she saw Elerek bow his head.

"Your grief will wax and wane like the seasons, but do not fear it. Grief is a companion to us all." He nodded to the acolytes. One took up a long, thin match and lit the end from the bowl of uncolored flame atop the altar. The other took the jar of oil and handed it to the general.

Orzak gave the blessing. "Elerek of House Karim, eldest son of Lorkin and Crianna, by the will of Instanolde, we bestow blessing upon you as heir of Instanolde. May the stars dance over your reign. May your face turn with grace and justice upon your subjects. Hope with the strength of the eastern mountains, endure with the relentlessness of the Sancen. May the Maker of the skies, the Starkindler, light your way and illuminate your soul forevermore."

Eldest? Lystra blinked. Surely she had misheard. Cormek had been the elder, the heir, hadn't he?

The general stood before Elerek. He took the jar of oil in one hand—heavily gloved, Lystra noticed—and dipped his bare fingers in the oil. Squeezed from rare vasma plants, the oil held a burnt, reddish tint. He spread it across Elerek's forehead and the dark oil dripped down his brow like an inverted crown. Lystra thought it looked rather too much like blood.

One candle was lit.

Handing the jar off with his gloved hand, the general stepped back.

The acolyte approached Lystra and Orzak began again. "Lystra of House Arghan, eldest daughter of Jethro and Vasha, by the will of Instanolde . . ." He recited the same blessing and the acolyte's fingers drew across her forehead. The oil's scent overwhelmed her senses, sending a fire down her throat.

The second candle was lit.

"We bless your reign." Orzak stood behind the table, pushed his sleeves up to his elbows, and took the two candles, using them both to light the third.

"*No.*" The word cut through the air.

Lystra startled at the voice, wrought with fury and wound

tight with desperation—and it had come from the lips of the prince-heir.

Elerek had gone pale, the stripe of oil bold and bright against his skin. He stared at the priest, at Orzak lighting the candle meant to symbolize the union of their rule. Had he changed his mind about marrying her?

Then, Lystra saw what he saw.

Orzak's hand had transformed, a skeletal structure held by transparent skin that dripped water onto the table, threatening to snuff the candle out.

Cursed.

Now it was Lystra's turn to gasp. "The other night, after the burning."

Lowering the candles, Orzak pulled his sleeve down over his hand. "Yes, unfortunate."

"The girl . . . the girl who died . . ."

Elerek's gaze swept the room. "High Priest, we must speak alone. *Now.*" His eyes fell on her, their embers scorching straight to her soul. "You as well, Torra."

The priest led them to a small alcove at the back of the temple, where only the crypts of the dead might hear their voices. Lystra shuddered and fought the urge to brush the itchy oil from her forehead.

If Orzak was cursed, the girl must have given it to him, but how did it transfer? Furthermore, Elerek knew about it. And that made her wonder.

"How long have you been cursed, High Priest?" Elerek demanded, his growl rumbling through the alcove of stone and bone.

Orzak's gaze skimmed the floor. "Since the night of your brother's burning."

Elerek muttered a string of words far too foul for the temple. "She *touched* you." The veins along the prince's neck grew taut. "That's all it takes. High Priest, do you have family?"

Lystra stifled a gasp. One touch?

"No, Your Highness. At this level of my order, we remain celibate."

Elerek began to tap his fingers on his chair's armrest in a nervous, frantic rhythm. "It is absolutely vital that you *never* touch anyone *ever* again. It may or may not be within your capabilities to pass on the curse as Azraa passed it to you."

Lystra scowled. No one had mentioned the girl's name— and Elerek knew it.

"You saw what happened to her." The fire left the prince's voice. Now, darkness dripped from every word like the trails of blood-red oil down his face. "That . . . that is what will happen to you."

The priest closed his eyes. "As the Starkindler wills. I understand. My days are numbered."

Lystra's eyes filled with tears. The priest had given her such comfort after Cormek's burning. *He told me that my story wasn't over.*

"I . . . I'm sorry." Elerek's face darkened with anguish. "I truly am. Now." His gaze shot briefly to Lystra. "It's imperative that this remains secret. Tell. No. One. Not now, not with a host of threats on our doorstep. Is that understood?"

Word of a curse that spread through touch would cause panic. Lystra's support from the people would vanish in an instant. Unification would become impossible. There might be nothing left for the Jarkins to conquer, only water, spilled on the edge of the desert. They all breathed on borrowed time.

"How do you know about this curse?" Lystra watched his face carefully.

Elerek scowled. "I've seen its results firsthand. No one should suffer like that." He quickly looked away. "High Priest, what remains of the ceremony?"

"We've done all that is required, Your Highness."

"Thank you. I've preparations to attend." Elerek turned his chair to leave the alcove.

"Wait a moment, Your Highness." She summoned strength to her voice.

Elerek stopped, his gaze cool. "We're equal rank now, Lystra." He bade the priest depart.

Her name upon his lips sent a shiver down her spine, the sound of stones moving in the desert. Great, immense things that could shape the world—but also crush her.

Once alone, Lystra glared. *"Elerek."* Even his name tasted bitter. "How did you know that the girl's name was Azraa?"

He blinked.

"She told Orzak that she worked at the palace. Did you know that she was cursed? That she would die like that?"

Elerek's jaw tightened. "As I said, I've seen it before."

He wouldn't tell her. The thought terrified her. In two weeks, she would be bound to this man. Queen to a king full of secrets. She folded her arms and took a steadying breath. "How do we stop the curse?"

Elerek lowered his gaze, shielding his features. This prince had lived his entire life in the palace's shadows, and yet the throne hadn't pulled him toward the light. "I don't know." There was a hollowness to his voice, a deep, deep void. Then, he grabbed the wheels on either side of his chair. "I will see you at our wedding."

Chapter 18

Elerek

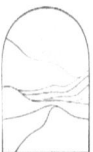

A temple priest was cursed.

Elerek couldn't wait to escape the dark temple, the heavy incense, and the burn of Lystra's gaze as she uttered his name.

The carriage was no better; the air that passed through the lattice windows was capable of baking bread. Elerek pulled at the collar of his embroidered tunic. Today, the curse gave him no favors in the sweltering desert. He could feel every thread rubbing against his sweating skin, and he wished that he could rip the thing to shreds.

Seated across from him, Norbah cleared his throat. "El, you should—"

"Not now."

The general's face tightened. Elerek watched him, waiting for the protests—for Norbah to assert himself as the closest thing to a father he'd ever possessed.

But he didn't. Norbah only turned his steely gaze to the window.

Elerek closed his eyes, pushing out the jostle of the carriage and the sound of mule's hooves and wooden wheels. It didn't matter that he isolated himself. He didn't curse Azraa. He didn't curse Orzak. He didn't know how to stop this ruination. Could the kingdom really mean to crown him in a fortnight?

The carriage rumbled to a halt. Opening his eyes only a sliver, he watched the dust dance in the shafts of sunlight that spilled across the carriage as Norbah opened the door. Aimless and drifting, untethered to any concern or care.

A pair of soldiers bearing his curse lowered his chair back to level ground. Blinking, Elerek let his gaze skim the stark line of the palace walls, dark against the sun's intensity. Stationed with soldiers, the thick, immense walls might have belonged to a palace or a prison. Perhaps both.

He wanted to flee, somewhere where he couldn't cause any more turmoil. A place to hide, where even the curse couldn't remind him of death's ever-present shadow.

And yet he didn't want to be alone. Not completely. No, he couldn't be alone. Elerek's hand moved to his forearm, the rich silk and gold-laced thread covering the ragged flesh beneath.

He tried. Once.

For one moment, everything had made perfect sense. End it. Escape the drowning, bleed blood instead of water, and die by his own hand instead of the curse's design.

Razhar had found him that day. Called for aid, for Cormek to come running. Saw that his wounds were bound, and the life kept in him. When Elerek awoke, the pain of living hadn't ceased, but Razhar, Norbah, Myra, and the rest of his friends were there, waiting for him without shame, only concern. The pain reminded him of what was true. That he needed them, his family.

"Ah, the prince has returned!" A clear voice rang like the

bells atop the guard's keep. "Or might we simply forgo the next fortnight and call you king?"

Waking from his heavy thoughts, Elerek lifted his eyes and scowled. Lounging against the palace steps as if it were a luxurious couch in his own quarters, Razhar glittered like a ruby in a scarlet tunic terribly paired with a yellow sash, orange scarf, and his favorite emerald turban.

Elerek wheeled his chair closer to the palace steps. "You hardly treated me like a prince, I didn't expect that to change when I'm king."

Heaving himself up with a sigh, Razhar sauntered down the steps. "Ah, but when you're king, you might actually have to follow through on your threats to exile me."

"Dressed like *that*, I certainly would. Where are you going?" Pushing his curls off his forehead, Elerek's fingers came back slick with oil from the temple. He'd forgotten about it.

Razhar shrugged. "Nowhere. This scarf used to be Cole's. He's a very terrible *chemis* player but you were delayed at the temple."

Norbah grunted and pulled a handkerchief from his pocket and offered it to him. Elerek could still smell the stench of the temple as he wiped the oil from his forehead.

"I'm actually here to rescue you. There's a dreadful line of officials and servants inside waiting for your approval on various aspects of the coronation—and your wedding." Razhar cocked his head to one side, causing his turban to perch precariously on his head. "I trust your second encounter with your intended bride went well?"

"Disaster." Elerek resisted the urge to give a cold laugh at the irony. Perhaps Razhar couldn't always be there to rescue him.

"The high priest has been cursed." Norbah hunched his

shoulders. "It seems that Azraa went to pray before she passed."

"Oh." Razhar's brow wrinkled.

"A highly ranked man who is revered and cherished by the people." Elerek shook his head. "I can't just relocate him here to hide."

"But you explained it to him?"

"Of course I did." Rage, heated and bitter like spiced coffee, rose in his soul. Handling the curse's newly claimed victims had never been an easy thing, but he couldn't help but think that things could have gone better at the temple. "And Torra Lystra was there for everything."

"Ah." Razhar's features brightened. "Then she knows about it, and you explained it to her."

"No."

"El . . ." Razhar groaned, covering his face with his hands. "Could you possibly be any more insensitive? You're marrying her in a fortnight!"

I am not insensitive. "She saw Azraa *die*. The night of Cormek's burning. If she knew the curse came from me, do you really think she'll still wed me?" Elerek shook his head. He'd shaken off the barbs of Myra's words when she'd taken aim at Lystra, but it seemed a few of their wounds remained. Would Lystra hate him, when she knew the truth?

Norbah huffed. "We've been over this. She hasn't a choice."

The fact that Norbah was correct brought him solace, but it also made him feel monstrous.

"Well . . ." Razhar spoke slowly, far more rational than his outlandish character warranted. "What if I spoke to the priest? I'll explain the whole thing. If he possesses any mite of honor, which I would hope considering his rank, perhaps he might see that our focus is better served defending ourselves against the Jarkins? Either he fulfills his duties and keeps his distance, or we let him retire and you appoint a new high priest upon the eve of your coronation."

A smile cracked at the edge of Norbah's lips, softening his stonelike demeanor. "Stars, there's something in that head after all."

Razhar only sniffed and made an exaggerated attempt to straighten his turban.

Someone would know. Someone outside. Elerek's stomach felt sick with dread. "The moment word gets out—tracing the curse back to me . . ." He gestured to the palace. "Everything falls apart. I become the enemy."

"Orzak is a noble man," Norbah countered. "I don't believe that he would do that. Since he is cursed, I would assume that he was brave enough to offer Azraa some comfort in her final hours."

Elerek bowed his head. He could give no one comfort.

"El." Razhar's voice grew soft. "Do remember that you may *be* cursed, but you are not *the* curse. There is a substantial difference, much the size of the Sancen."

"Such faith," Elerek whispered.

But it was all they had—and no one could take it from them.

With a great creak and rumble, the massive double gate of the interior courtyard drew back. Immediately, the stonework resounded with the high-pitched screech of reptiles as three cardants burst through the gates and into the main courtyard.

Norbah drew his scimitar with the clear ring of steel, planting himself in front of Elerek. "Hold them back!" he roared. "Protect the king!"

Elerek's chair skidded backwards, his hands shaking. The air froze inside his lungs as the cardants thrashed their mighty, horned heads, revealing rows of pale teeth made for tearing flesh. Bridles of leather that appeared much too thin looped about their heads, slipping treacherously through the hands of two young men.

They weren't stable hands, their clothes too fine for that. No, the boys of the stable kept their distance, whips and rope clutched in pale knuckles.

At the word "king," alarm flashed through their eyes. As one, every hand reached for the cardants' harnesses, pulling their heads low, as if the reptiles too owed him honor.

Elerek's wheels stopped, run up against the carriage behind him. Nowhere to escape. Cardants wouldn't care for the circlet on his brow, content to snag an easy meal.

He almost preferred his destined drowning.

"What is the meaning of this?" Norbah demanded, stalking forward, still with his scimitar drawn.

Abdul, the palace stable master, circled the reptiles in a wide orbit. He dropped to his knees. "My lord general, forgive me. These cardants—and their young owners—are leaving."

"What are they doing here?" Norbah pressed, his tone a deep growl.

One of the young men handed the reins off to his companion and stumbled forward with a clumsy bow. "My lord, I am Birark of House Quilam. Our house has recently acquired these reptiles and we'd hoped to seek the counsel of your stable master."

Abdul shook his head, his great beard wagging with the motion. "Atrocities, General. These cardants can barely suffer a bridle and I haven't the time to waste on them. If I'm to train any cardants, it'll be for soldiers."

As if to punctuate his point, one cardant—the largest of the three—reared up on her hind legs and screeched a cry of attack that froze the blood in Elerek's veins. Grabbing at the reins, the second young man swore and struggled. Birark joined him, but even their conjoined efforts weren't enough.

Elerek caught his breath. He'd seen plenty of cardants—from a safe and extended distance—but he'd never seen anything like this one.

Bright streaks of green and orange lined the cardant's horns and scales. A dragon of the desert. She fought, screamed, and strained for release—for freedom.

He caught something familiar in its eyes. A fierce fire, bold enough to consume. He'd seen that look before, that swift and certain determination.

In the eyes of the girl he would wed.

"We've no use for them," Norbah barked. "Stable Master, see these boys out."

The second young man shook his head, pulling the cardant's reins tighter. "I *told* you."

Birark snarled. "Your cousin won't have time to help us. Not anymore."

Wait. Elerek narrowed his eyes, studying the young man with his proud brow and blazing eyes. Gripping his wheels to keep his hands from trembling, he drew himself to Norbah's side. "You belong to House Arghan."

The young man stepped forward, bowing at the waist. "Yes, Your Highness." He lifted his face. "My name is Kimzi. Torra Lystra is my cousin."

"I have heard of her wisdom and devotion to these creatures." Elerek glanced at Abdul.

The old stable master nodded. "I've worked with her myself, Your Highness. There is no one better in all of Instanolde."

Elerek turned his gaze back to the large cardant. Subdued by the ropes, the reptile clenched its jaw, growling softly. He would rather it live in the desert, not his palace. "Lord Birark, name your price for that one."

"Your Highness?" Birark's eyebrows vanished beneath his lopsided turban.

"I will pay top price, have no fear." Elerek narrowed his eyes. "Not one word of this to your cousin, Lord Kimzi."

The young man bowed, but he couldn't hide his smile from Elerek.

Chapter 19

Lystra

Something gnawed at Lystra's mind the way cardants tore at the bones of their prey, their sharp teeth rending chunks of sinew and muscle from pale bone.

Elerek knew. He'd seen. He assigned suffering to the curse's victims.

She slept fitfully, haunted by nightmares of leering skulls dripping with water. Every vision ended the same, waking in the dark, her sheets damp with sweat—the cold eyes of the prince-heir piercing her mind, taunting her.

A frightening curse threatened her kingdom, but that didn't unnerve her. No, it was his eyes that gave a shudder to her skin, filled with a darkness so deep she feared it might consume her too. The similarities he bore to Cormek fell away, lost amid the sands' mirages, and she wondered what had made him into this sort of creature.

Morning gave her little time for contemplation. Precious hours remained before her coronation, her wedding, and everything changed.

When the sun was not yet high in the sky, Lystra was

paraded through the city streets in an open-air carriage, decked in jewels and silks. The perfect image of the perfect queen. Crowds gathered along the avenues, waving branches of tamarisk and tossing evell petals. They cheered and chanted her name. *Malikaa.* The desert air filled with adoration.

The journey ended at the henna shop, where the artists ushered Lystra, Corsha, and others of her maiden entourage inside. They scrubbed her nails, rubbed oils into her skin, and perfumed her hair. With ink dark as chocolate, the women took slender brushes and delicately applied long swirls and ornate patterns to Lystra's arms, ankles, and shoulders.

"Such beautiful hands, lovely skin," one of the artists cooed, creating a star-like pattern across the back of Lystra's hand.

"Thank you," she replied in a whisper, thinking of Dalmah's insistence on the care of her hands, especially with the callouses left from her work with the cardants.

They held her hands gently, as if she were some fragile thing. Lystra bit her lip as the girls twittered away like swallows in nesting season, talking of bridal silks and jewels and the latest method of styling one's hair. Still, the touch of the artisans, painstakingly transforming her into a bride, brought her a small measure of comfort.

One touch. *"That's all it takes."*

All at once, Lystra couldn't breathe. How could Elerek have possibly—? The realization struck her like a thunderclap.

Is . . . is Elerek cursed?

Would the artisan girls notice if her hands began to shake as they painted tiny flowers upon her knuckles? She forced a slow exhale, holding back her terror. Her companions laughed and giggled and Lystra feigned smiles and blushed like the maiden awaiting marriage and her royal husband that they imagined her to be. Her husband who quite possibly carried a curse in his hands—in his *touch.* Never in a million years of dancing constellations had she imagined wedding a cursed prince.

No. Lystra exhaled, steadying her shoulders. She didn't know for sure. She couldn't jump to conclusions. She couldn't be wrong, especially on something like this.

But if she was right . . .

The pieces fell together in her mind and she assembled them into the most perfect and terrible mosaic. The mystery of Elerek's birthright being passed on to his brother. His outburst of terror at seeing cursed flesh contrasted so heavily against the cold, calculated demeanor with which he spoke to Orzak. Lystra had never seen him touch another person, save for the general's anointing—the general that he kept close by. And he knew that the curse caused not only death—but suffering.

If she were right, and he were a man whose touch could kill, her people—and the kingdom she swore to defend until her last breath—prepared even now to give him all the power of the throne. The prince to whom she would speak vows, bind herself to, could kill *her*.

With hands that could only destroy, what sort of future could Elerek possibly build?

Lystra pinched her eyes shut. The henna girls had moved behind her, sweeping her hair away to bare her shoulders, and the tiny reed brushes sent a tingle across her skin. She tried to reconcile, to pair the determination to see their kingdom survive burning in Elerek's eyes like embers lit by starfire with the water-filled sockets of the girl she'd seen drown.

No, she couldn't know for certain. But she knew one thing, one pulsing desperation beating in her heart. Elerek wasn't the only one resolute to save their kingdom.

Perhaps that was her grandmother's lesson, the scheme that ended with a dagger plunged to the hilt in Elerek's chest. If Lystra were to take the crown for the sake of saving her kingdom, the responsibility of standing in the brink against its threats fell to her.

Maybe Elerek was cursed, and maybe he wasn't, but if this curse were another evil with which she must do battle for the sake of Instanolde, then she was responsible to stop it.

And she would discover the truth—on her wedding night.

Chapter 20

Elerek

Throwing open the lattice, Elerek closed his eyes as the light of a new day fell across his face. A day he could feel, its warmth dancing lightly upon his cold and cursed skin. The day he became king.

The sun had still risen over Instanolde, glittering with radiance across towers of stone, domes overlaid in gold, and mosaic arches bursting with color. Elerek gazed out over his kingdom, a kingdom between the life of the Gungole River and the death of the Sancen Desert, built of survival and hardened like sun-baked clay. How he hoped it would, like him, survive a little while longer.

One summer to live.

And they would live it. Elerek released his held breath in a slow exhale. He'd hardly been up an hour and already this day seemed an eternity of apprehension. He'd bathed and been clothed in magnificent robes of pale gold, woven with elaborate patterns that draped dramatically from his shoulders and about his chair.

A thin circlet of gold sat on his brow, a princely adornment ready to be replaced by the formal ceremonial crown wrought with gold and fire opals.

The ring of silver trumpets resounded beyond his window. Elerek peered down into the courtyard. The gates parted, and a carriage passed through flying flags of orange, announcing royalty.

"She's here." Razhar's cheery voice filled the chamber.

Just like that, the tension flooded Elerek's shoulders again. Today, Torra Lystra of House Arghan became queen.

Down below, a page opened the carriage door and Lystra stepped out in a pale linen dress. Her hair, not yet styled for the wedding, hung free, rippling softly down to her waist. Even from here, he could see the henna patterns marking the golden skin of her arms.

Razhar joined him at the window, dressed for the occasion in a sky-blue kaftan that draped to his knees, adorned with gold tassels. "Stars above. Admit it, El, your bride is quite lovely. A perfect evell blossom."

A burst of wind swept over her, catching in her hair and molding her loose dress against the soft curves of her figure. Elerek blinked and looked away. Now *that* was something he'd never admit—out loud at least.

The light caught in Razhar's eyes as he gave him a sidelong glance. "And you told her, yes? About the curse?"

Another knot lodged itself in his stomach. "Not yet."

Razhar groaned and dragged his hands down his face.

"I'll tell her *tonight*, I promise." He prayed that she would understand and see what he was trying to do.

"You'll tell your bride that you're cursed and cannot touch her on your wedding night?" The scorn fled Razhar's features, leaving ample room for a cheeky smirk.

"That remark isn't even worthy of acknowledgment."

"Ah, but you did anyways."

Shaking his head, Elerek turned his chair away from the window. "Come along, now that she's here, we're bound to begin."

"You've no idea how long women take to prepare for such events, El. We have hours."

Perhaps so, but Elerek knew he'd go crazy if he spent one more minute cooped up in his chambers. Perhaps his friends lingered in the bakers' courtyard. The cursed had all received permission to attend the day's events, and he hoped that they would—as long as they were careful.

Razhar followed him down the sloped corridors, the tassels on his kaftan swaying with every step. "I spoke to Myra this morning."

Elerek's hands clenched, bringing his chair to an abrupt halt. "How is she?"

Only days had passed since they'd last spoken, but it felt like years. A full rotation of the heavens and each glittering constellation.

"I took it that she'd spent the morning weeping her eyes out." Razhar's gaze grew soft. "She told me a sad story."

A story doomed from the beginning. Elerek closed his eyes. "The whole kingdom will be watching us—Lystra and I. Rumors are just another way to crack a foundation."

"You love her, El."

Razhar, always the romantic. "I do," he whispered. "But if I'm to be king, for however short a time, I cannot permit myself such an impropriety."

"I understand." Razhar sighed. "You're stronger than most people give you credit for."

But the strong could fall, Elerek thought morosely. Even kings.

When Elerek entered the throne room, the entire chamber seemed constructed of light. Gone were the shadows that had hung over the palace since Cormek's death, each pane of stained glass burning brighter than any tinted torch, sending a cascade of dazzling color over the marble. He caught his breath, blinking in the spectacle.

A terrible thrill rose in his soul, belonging to a moment in a forgotten dream. The birthright that was taken from him—taken by the curse. And now, after living his life in the darkness, every eye in the room was fixated on him, from the soldiers lining the hall to the nobles in their grand array.

The crowd mostly consisted of strangers. All the great houses and nobles had come with their families as well as delegations from the tribes that thought it worth the journey. Elerek caught sight of his own household, their faces beaming.

He tried not to lean forward as he wheeled his chair down the length of the throne room. Pushing his shoulders back, he held his head high, hoping to appear regal. Soldiers raised fists in salute at his passing.

Memories of Cormek's coronation fluttered through his mind. His brother had stood head and shoulders above the crowd, the perfect image of a monarch that even Instanolde herself couldn't possibly deserve.

Starkindler, I know not how this fate has come to me, but it has. He hoped he could be worthy of it.

Near the front of the assembly, House Arghan stood. The men were stern, proud, and wore brightly colored turbans. The women glittered in golds—except the Countess Dalmah. Bold, black mourning attire hung from her rigid figure. Even a shroud-like veil of black covered her face. Elerek watched her from the corner of his eye, a slight shudder tingling down his spine. Who had she come to mourn? She proposed this alliance.

Beside the throne, a small ramp had been installed, allowing his chair access to the dais. There, Orzak stood alongside two acolytes, bearing candles and hanging autums filled with smoking incense. They spoke in low tones, evoking blessings and whispering prayers.

Elerek hoped with all his heart and soul that their prayers would be heeded.

The high priest approached him, bowing at the waist. As he straightened, the brilliance of the room catching in his eyes, Elerek saw no loathing or anger in his aged face. Only kindness. He wondered what Razhar had told him.

The priests began a slow orbit around his chair, moving like shadows on a sundial. The smoke from the autums swirled around him, morphing the palace colors. They began to chant, the soldiers joining in the refrain.

"Gem of the Gungole."

"Fire of the Sancen."

"Fierce as the dawn."

"Mighty as the constellations."

"Long may you reign."

Traditional titles. Elerek thought of them as adornments, like jewelry, pretty to admire but rather useless. The deeds of a man produced his worth. Maybe he hadn't always been a perfect man, a mile of failures stretching behind him, but today he would try.

Then, their eyes lifted. Elerek turned his chair.

Lystra had entered the throne room.

For one moment, the whole of the room fell completely still. Silent and reverent. Elerek heard only the pounding of his own heart, the breath stolen from his unmoving lungs.

Not Lystra. The queen of Instanolde.

Grace imbued her every movement, each deliberate step toward the throne. *Her* throne. A destiny as sure as the stars themselves. Her wedding kaftan seemed to float from her figure in ethereal elegance, the white silk spun from starlight itself and trimmed in gold. Its sleeves were sheer, the intricate henna bold beneath. She carried herself with strength, a fierceness as radiant as the burning summer sun.

Elerek satisfied his burning lungs. No other would ever be worthy of the throne. He knew this as truth, and it seemed that Cormek had known it too. Stars, Cormek should be here.

At that moment, when every eye in the room looked to its queen, Lystra's gaze shifted, her eyes blazing like fire opals, to *him*.

Chapter 21

Lystra

A s the morning of her wedding dawned in the east, Lystra rose and stole into her grandmother's chambers.

Dalmah had also risen early and was nowhere to be seen. Lystra moved swiftly, treaded softly, and opened the chest. She took the dagger and its sheath from the ivory case and tucked it into the folds of her dress. She didn't intend to use it, not yet anyways, but if she were to become the wife of a man whose touch could kill, she wanted to be ready.

When she slipped back into the hall, her heart thrashed against her ribs so loud that she could hear nothing else.

Now, the dagger lay stowed away among her belongings, taken to the chamber she was meant to share with the man who knew of the mysterious curse, and she moved through the pillared hall toward the throne meant to be hers.

In her hands, a bouquet of white blossoms perfumed the air. Her feet made no sound on the marble. Her kaftan shimmered with her movement, its silk light as air. How many weeks had this gown hung in her closet, awaiting her marriage to Cormek? Now, its rich gold beadwork served only as a testament of her devotion to her kingdom.

Courage. She had to think only of courage. She hadn't imagined the difficulty, the weight of each footstep. To think not of the sorrow that cleaved her heart from her chest and replaced it with stone, the gaping void left by the only man she had ever loved.

He should be there.

Waiting at the end of the aisle like a tower, mighty and tall, to welcome her home in his arms. His eyes would shine like gemstones, glittering with all the love in the world.

But he wasn't.

There, before the throne, another king waited for her.

Elerek sat rigid in his chair—regal, powerful, and draped in robes of pale gold. Behind him, the throne stood grave and empty. For all his faults, his scarred hands and misshapen legs, he looked the part of a king—his jaw set like stone, his shoulders squared, his eyes smoldering with intensity.

Their gazes met.

Lystra didn't look away, didn't blink. She steeled her soul, but the questions burned beneath her tongue. Was he cursed? Would his touch doom her to drown? Would the dagger she stole be required of her tonight—on her wedding night?

She mounted the dais, a calculated action in her kaftan. Elerek pivoted his chair and together, they faced the throne, side by side. Only the throne. Not each other.

Lystra inhaled deeply. She wasn't marrying him, but Instanolde.

In that respect, Elerek remained a means to an end.

A short ceremony followed, full of customary vows and lofty concepts. The priest's speech of entering a sacred covenant, of a man and woman pledging themselves mind, body, and soul to one another filled Lystra with a dark, vile guilt. In this abuse of a most sacred order, both she and Elerek were condemned, willingly sacrificing such a covenant to preserve their kingdom.

And if he was cursed, she'd have no choice. Her kingdom demanded freedom from every evil. She would become its shield, its salvation.

"Do you give this vow, before the burning heavens themselves, the starfire of the Starkindler, this pledge with the deepest recesses of your soul?" Orzak asked. "To one another? To your kingdom?"

"I do," Elerek replied without hesitation.

"I do." Lystra hoped her voice sounded just as strong.

Orzak stepped back. Now would come the crowning. The general—not the priest, Lystra noted—approached the throne, upon which two chests sat beside a small jar of white-and-blue pottery. An urn for ashes, she realized, and something twisted inside her heart.

Setting the chest's lid aside, the general lifted the crown—wrought of gold filigree with stars bursting with sapphires and fire opals.

He approached the new king.

"With this crown, I crown you, Elerek, son of Lorkin, may he forever dance among the skies, heir of House Karim, as king of Instanolde. May you blaze with the light of the Starkindler, who lights all eternal fires. May you reign over your people with mercy, justice, and a hand steady as the rising sun."

As the crown came to rest on his brow, Elerek's eyes closed briefly. Lystra noted the slight clench of his jaw. She wondered what he was thinking in this moment, this great, monumental moment.

The queen's tiara had been created to match the king's,

likewise alight with fire opals. Not Orzak, but one of the acolytes, lifted it from its case, holding it delicately.

"With this crown, I crown you, Lystra, daughter of House Arghan, queen of Instanolde. May you reign with grace, honor, and a strength as sure as the dancing stars above."

The tiara came to rest upon her brow. Small and delicate, but its weight was heavy.

It was done. Their choices had been made. This fate had fallen upon their shoulders. King and queen.

No feast or celebration followed the ceremony. All the proper acknowledgments and greetings were given to the noble houses who came to stand witness to their union. Even those who hadn't sworn fealty—of which there were many—were greeted with grace.

One notable absence, Lystra took note, was Kushan—without whom the Jarkins could level them. She wondered if her presence might change that. Perhaps she could convince them to reconsider, to give them another chance.

When the time came to bid their guests goodbye, Lystra craved each word, each touch from her family. Corsha's embrace, her father's kiss, even the clasping of her grandmother's hand in hers. Dalmah's eyes spoke of boldness, a spark of vengeful fire.

Her grandmother leaned forward, her whisper hot on Lystra's ear. "Remember the queen I raised. Don't let the foolish girl win."

Lystra's chest fluttered. Perhaps she ought to have told Dalmah about the curse, and the stolen dagger. Would that have changed anything?

No, she didn't need her. She'd freed herself and after tonight, no one would cage her again.

Chapter 22

Elerek

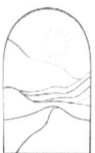

One by one, the strangers departed, dispelling the noise of voices he didn't recognize. An empty silence stretched to the golden palace domes, one that Elerek didn't know how to fill. Even the anxious tapping of his fingertips on his chair's armrest did little to settle the tension tightening in his core.

King of Instanolde. The birthright he craved. The nightmare he feared. Its weight fell upon him like the burden of the heavy crown on his brow.

"I think you're doing splendidly." Razhar stood just to the left of his chair, hovering like a sapphire jewel in his peripheral. "But as far as celebrations go, this one is dull."

The smiles and congratulations of his own household brought him comfort, their faces pinnacle landmarks among the dwindling crowd. Just a few more guests, greetings, and names he would never remember, and the evening would be over.

Elerek glanced up at him, lifting an eyebrow. "Once the Jarkins are routed, I'll permit you to throw the celebration of your choosing—as long as I'm not invited."

Laughing, Razhar smiled. "I'll hold you to that, Your Highness."

It amused Elerek to think of how different they were—star-strewn night and scorching desert day—yet their friendship had endured, constant and sure.

"I'm pleased to see our family here," Razhar added, his gaze drifting about the room. "They certainly didn't want to miss this."

Elerek managed a smile. Their strange little tribe of cursed soldiers, bakers, and scribes had adopted them both.

Only Myra hadn't come to congratulate him, avoiding him as one who was cursed ought to be avoided. He saw her, standing among her companions, her eyes glistening in the lamplight. Necessary distance lay between them, a canyon like those where the Kushite condors soared, and they'd have to become accustomed to it.

And Lystra? Elerek's gaze trailed after her, moving like a gossamer dream as she gave gracious smiles to their guests. Even the fire opals glittering on her brow dulled in comparison to the burning embers of her eyes. Even on Cormek's arm, she'd hardly seemed real, certainly too exquisite for a kingdom on the verge of ruin.

The distance between them held a no less noble purpose. As his brother's queen, she had survived the desert and the brutal attack. As his queen, she must survive all—the ruin of the curse, the end of his reign, and the trial of Instanolde as they faced the impossible.

One summer to live.

House Arghan departed last. Lystra's cousins embraced her, her father kissed her forehead, and her grandmother, made of the shadows themselves, clasped her hands. Touch. One human reaching for another. Elerek dismissed the thoughts of sorrow, of the void surrounding him, firing across his mind like rogue arrows. His was a family not linked by blood, but a bond of cursed waters.

"Razhar." He turned to his friend again. "Would you retrieve the urn from the throne? My brother's ashes?"

Razhar's turban bobbed as he nodded and spun on his ankles to obey.

Once House Arghan departed, the throne room grew dark as servants began pulling the lattice over the windows and putting out the lamps. An attendant asked for their crowns, to be polished and put under lock and key until the proper occasions.

Without it, Elerek felt more like himself. Lystra, however, still looked like a queen.

"Your Highness." His eyes lifted to hers as she approached him, her steps slow and deliberate.

Lystra lowered her gaze, shadows falling over her brow like her grandmother's veil.

He had to tell her. Elerek rubbed his hands together, his palms growing clammy.

"Instanolde lies within our care." Lystra's chest rose with a deep inhale. "I pray we honor her as she deserves."

"Well said." A lump rose in his throat.

"Ah, Your Highness." Razhar returned, the jar of ashes held carefully in both hands. He bowed, his kaftan sweeping in extravagant flourish. "It seems we were destined to meet again."

Lystra's marble countenance shattered as a sharp gasp fled her lips. She raised a hand to her mouth, as if embarrassed that the sound had come from her. "You!"

"Lystra." It felt strange to say her name without preface or title. His queen—and his wife. "May I introduce my oldest friend and closest confidant, Razhar Emblino. I hope he wasn't too insufferable at the market."

The shadows were long in the darkened throne room, but

not long enough to obscure the crimson blush blooming on Lystra's face. Razhar shuffled a bit on his feet, his slippers noiseless. Elerek frowned. Something hung in the air, a strange tension that made him feel like an outsider looking in.

Recovering, Lystra squared her shoulders. "You should teach your friend better manners, Your Highness. I didn't get his name in the market."

"Surely it's not always the custom to give away one's name to a dance partner." Razhar chuckled. "I found myself rather stunned to be in the presence of future royalty."

Elerek relaxed. There was dancing involved. Another of Razhar's talents. "Do you dance, Lystra?"

She kept her eyes fixed on Razhar, studying him from beneath her painted lids. "Well enough. I'm more suited to cardants."

Elerek's thoughts strayed to the monster in the stable. House Quilam had put forward a hefty sum, but he'd paid it with a smile. "My brother spoke often and highly of your talents."

The mention of Cormek sent a forlorn chill through the air. Lystra pushed a stray hair behind her ear, dislodging one of the blossoms. It floated to the marble stonework below. Grief, raw and familiar, appeared in her eyes, but she gave reply anyways.

"I typically rise early. Cardants love the dawn."

Razhar tossed the tail of his turban behind him. "Mornings make me quite disagreeable. But one must rise early for grand days." He looked at Elerek with a silly grin. "Now, cardants. Might be a good hobby for you, El. I'm sure your queen will show you the ropes."

Like the sun rising gently over the horizon, Lystra's face immediately brightened and—was that a smile?

"You may laugh." Elerek rubbed the back of his neck. "The concept is utterly absurd."

She fluttered her eyelashes. "If you can manage that chair, you could manage a cardant."

"My *chair* isn't going to trample or tear me to shreds." Stars. He wasn't talking to Razhar, but the *queen*. Cold. Regal. Severe as the sunrise.

And yet. Lystra lifted her chin, regarding him with an aloof, almost smug smile. "Ah, I see you know so little of cardants. Perhaps a trample or two might set you straight."

Razhar sputtered, choking on his own laughter. Elerek scowled, glaring him into composure.

"Well." Razhar straightened his collar. "The hour is late. I shan't take up any more of the newlyweds' time." He handed the jar to Elerek, giving care to not touch him, and then bowed to Lystra. "My congratulations, to you both."

Elerek shook his head as his friend hurried away. "Perhaps we might agree to permit the cardants to trample him instead?"

A bit of pink returned to the queen's cheeks. "I find it's not a crime to laugh. Some of us survive on smiles."

Right, his promise to not be insensitive. To seed the darkness with starlight, with hope. His queen was owed all the hope she could get. "Then smile we shall." Elerek drew a deep breath, glancing down at the jar in his hand, reluctant to return to grave matters. "I'd hoped that you would care for these." He extended it to her, keeping his fingers on its base and wishing that he'd kept Razhar around to hand it to her.

Lystra stepped closer. Panic surged through him, screaming at him with the sound of ringing ears and a frantic heartbeat. How he prayed she couldn't see his terror. But she took the jar without calamity, her fingers avoiding his own.

"These are his ashes, aren't they?" she whispered.

Elerek nodded.

Bowing her head, her shoulders quivered. She held the jar

against her chest, her fingers tenderly stroking the painted pottery. "Razhar was right. The hour is late."

"I'll show you to our chambers," Elerek whispered, his heart still furiously beating.

The halls lay empty, silent save for the slight creak of his chair's wheels. Lamps burned low, creating circles of warm light against the deep shadows. Elerek stole a sideways glance at Lystra's face. His bride was gilded in white and gold, blossoms in her hair, henna caressing her skin, and ebony glistened at her eyes. Her features were carved of stone, weathered by the winds of all that she had lost.

The royal chambers lay behind a tall set of doors with a scene of mountains, dunes, and blossoming shrubs carved across its width. Inside, candlelight illuminated a parlor worthy of a queen.

Elerek watched as the expression of stunned surprise subdued Lystra's features. "I hope it's to your liking." He gestured to the silk curtains draping across the left side of the room. "You'll find your chambers beyond."

Lystra moved farther into the room, her wedding gown trailing on the richly patterned rugs. She parted the curtains. A soft smile appeared on her lips. "My old room also had a balcony that looked out to the west. I can watch the same constellations dance."

Glancing toward the identical curtains on the right, behind which his own new chambers lay, Elerek's stomach twisted. He felt like a trespasser. The ornate room with its paneled walls and lavish couches was meant for royalty. Certainly not for him. Likewise, the bride, in her cold and noble beauty, didn't belong to him.

Lystra ought to have arrived in this chamber rejoicing, blushing with love for her husband. Not holding his ashes.

I'm sorry, Cormek. His brother had died in an age when the sun rose strong but not deadly. He hadn't lived in times where enemies and curses threatened to crush the life that they loved.

"Lystra . . ." The ease with which they smiled and spoke of trampling cardants fled. Here, in a room embellished for lovers, even breathing was difficult.

She glanced over her shoulder. Her eyes were glassy in the candlelight, shining with unshed tears. He saw the slight shudder of her shoulders as she drew in air.

"You . . ." Elerek swallowed, shifting in his chair. "You looked lovely tonight."

Her hand, still on the curtain, slowly clenched, squeezing a fistful of fabric.

Just talk. He could do this. "I hope that, now, we won't be enemies?"

Releasing the strangled silk, Lystra circled the couch and seated herself, her every movement graceful in her gown. She lowered the jar of ashes to the table and then reclined, staring silently down at the henna adorning her hands.

Now. Tell her. Elerek leaned forward and cleared his throat. "Lystra, I . . . I have something to—"

The door to their chamber opened. A slight figure slipped inside without waiting for invitation, bearing a tray.

"I've brought tea, Your Highnesses."

Myra. She strode inside with her head held high. Her gaze, sharp as Norbah's scimitar, fell on Lystra, brazenly studying her.

Not to be outdone, Lystra stared right on back.

Elerek sat up, pushing his shoulders back. "Leave the tea." He spoke through clenched teeth, unleashing a wrathful glare. "You are dismissed."

Myra lowered the tea tray to the table. She'd changed into a kaftan of scarlet, far richer than that of a palace servant. The collar had been left unlaced, exposing a deep neckline. Too deep. "As you wish, my lord." She then turned her burning gaze toward him. "Is there anything more I can do for you?"

Don't do this to me. His hands clenched, skin stretched white over his knuckles. Rage riled in his chest. Perhaps he deserved this humiliation one-hundredfold, but did it have to be *now*? Before the woman he'd married, lifted to the most powerful position in the kingdom?

"You are dismissed." He ground out the words.

She lowered her eyes and faded back toward the door. Silence, thick and heavy, fell over the chamber, but all Elerek could hear was the blood pounding in his ears.

Stars. Why was he so angry? He expelled a long breath and unclenched his hands, wiping clammy palms along the edge of his robe. Myra would be reprimanded later. No permanent damage had been done, but his heart thundered like mad— furious as a storm.

Drip. He glanced down at his hand. A droplet, crystalline in the candlelight, rolled from beneath his cuff, traveled down his finger, and fell onto the wood of his chair's armrest. Followed by another, and another . . .

The curse.

He quickly clenched his hand again, tucking it against his side, where, beneath layers upon layers of golden thread, lay the mark of his untimely death. Not yet. He couldn't die yet. An awful cold, far beyond the curse's usual numbness, froze the fury in his heart.

"Who is she?"

Lystra's voice brought him back, reminded him that he sat in the chambers of Instanolde's king and queen, and that it was his wedding night.

Almost fearful to turn his attention back to Lystra, he steeled himself, but found only a curious frown on the queen's features.

"Um . . . I believe she works in the kitchens."

"Dressed like *that?*" Lystra raised an eyebrow. He could see the tension building in her face.

"I apologize." He could think of nothing else to say. He moved his hand away from his ribs. This time, no droplets fell from his fingers. But had the mark changed? Had it grown?

Lystra looked away, smoothing the skirt of her wedding gown with henna-painted fingers. The air grew stifled. Unbearable.

"You had something to tell me?"

Yes. Elerek clenched his jaw. But how could he? Certainly not after that lurid display. If he explained the curse, would the discussion lead to those he had touched—including Myra? How would Lystra react? Would she see that he'd given her, his queen, his loyalty wholly and completely?

And what of the curse? Was it changing? Getting worse? All at once, he could no longer breathe.

"It can wait till tomorrow." He rolled his chair backwards.

How forlorn the queen looked, perched like a white dove amid the lavish furniture. Her words regarding a caged canary returned to him, their stench vile and rotting.

She didn't deserve to be left like that. She hadn't chosen these terrible days any more than he had chosen his curse. Starlight; he needed to give her starlight.

"Goodnight, Your Highness." The smile felt strange upon

his lips, but he did it anyways. "I meant what I said, you were beautiful tonight."

Lystra bowed her head, her features lost to the shadows. "Goodnight, Your Highness." Her voice remained a ghost of a whisper.

Behind the curtain, Elerek's bedchamber had been sparsely arranged, leaving room to navigate his chair. The exquisite canopy bed, wardrobe, and dressing screen looked far too opulent for someone like him. Even kings go to sleep as mere men, alone with their thoughts.

A single window turned north. Above the black line of the distant mountains, the constellations appeared. Somehow, the starlight gave him comfort and calmed the fury stoking his soul. He closed his eyes, raked a hand through his hair, and drew a deep, steadying breath.

Piece by piece, he stripped off his royal robes, feeling less like a king and more a mortal man again. Pulling the thin, linen undershirt over his head, his hand dropped to his side. Despite the droplets, the strange flow of water, the curse mark lay unchanged along his ribs, reminding him that this was temporary, that he wouldn't be king for long. Still, the familiar sight dispelled relief across his shoulders.

When he finally parked his chair at his bedside and half-crawled, half-dragged himself into bed and cast a light blanket over his useless legs, he hoped that sleep would come quickly.

Instead, his thoughts turned to his new queen. He wondered if, across their rooms, she too couldn't sleep.

Elerek shifted onto his back, staring up at the bed's canopy, and sighed. He'd asked so much of Lystra—was it too much? If she knew—no, *when* she knew—the entire story, would she hate him? She couldn't hate him. No, they had to work together. Two halves of a strange union, a necessary whole. What could he do to prove himself? To be worthy of her?

Tell her the truth, you idiot. Guilt tightened his chest. He turned his eyes to the open window. A wind swept up by the desert flirted with the silk curtains and ruffled his curls. The night stalker constellation moved higher in the hemisphere, followed by the lion constellation lowering itself into a crouch, ready to pounce. The stars were familiar, predictable, steady and stalwart. His eyes drifted closed, comforted by these thoughts.

A clatter shattered the night. The hair on the back of his neck prickled. His eyes shot open. Then he saw it.

Starlight on the glint of a knife.

Chapter 23

Lystra

It seemed too horrid a thing to pair a dagger meant for the cursed with a wedding gown. Lystra wore black when she slipped through the curtains of her chamber, allowing the shadows to swallow her whole.

Her fingers tightened around the dagger's hilt, slick with sweat. A lump lurched into her throat. One drop of doubt.

How she hoped—how she prayed—that Elerek wasn't cursed. That he would be only a man, one who shared her nerves, her fears, the enormity of the task before them.

But what if he is?

The alternative visualized before her. Her grandmother's dagger, clenched in hands adorned with delicate bridal henna, and plunged into his chest. The dry, deliciously cool air of the desert poisoned with the sound of his final, sputtered gasps. The sheets stained with his blood.

She swallowed. Her soul turned molten and then cooled hard as forged steel. A crown now belonged to her. She'd sworn to defend her people. If it came to it, she would stand between

Instanolde and a curse that could kill maidens, priests, and generals with a mere touch.

As she crossed the parlor, her eyes caught on the jar of Cormek's ashes. What would he think of her? Murdering his brother on their wedding night?

A second drop of doubt.

If Elerek were cursed, surely Cormek would have known it. Would he have kept such a thing a secret? She knew Cormek better than most. The young king's kindness often yielded to mercy. Perhaps he might have kept the secret out of affection for his brother. If that were so, how many had died—drowned and perished—out of mercy?

No, Instanolde didn't need a king like Cormek in days such as these. She needed resolve, strength, a wrath able to summon the stars themselves and defend these sands to the last.

Could Lystra be that resolve, that wrath? A third drop of doubt.

She held her breath as she slipped behind the curtain of Elerek's chamber. A window lay open, gently fluttering the silk and teasing her skin. Here, bathed in scant starlight, the furniture seemed smaller, the room larger. The wheeled chair sat empty beside the bed.

And Elerek. He lay on his back, eyes softly closed. His chest and shoulders were bare, sculpted tight with muscle from managing his chair, skin as pale as the alabaster of a perfect statue in the starlight.

Lystra blinked. He could be any man, king or damned.

But there. A shimmer of silver, cast in starlight, gleamed across his body. It followed the curve of his lowest rib, a rope that hadn't yet tightened. Its likeness matched the one upon the priest's hand and promised the terrible fate of the girl in the courtyard. A drowning that hadn't yet delivered Instanolde's new king over to death.

No. A ragged breath tore from Lystra's lips. She trembled, panic and horror clashing like enemy armies in her mind. The entirety of her fears, her nightmares, all lay exposed by starlight. The king of Instanolde, to whom she had pledged her life and loyalty, was cursed.

Only one option remained.

Step by stilted step, she approached the bed. She raised the dagger, her fingers tight about the hilt. She fixed her eyes upon his breast, where she knew beneath his heart beat. Her mark had to be true, it had to be swift.

As fast as the axe had shattered Cormek's heart.

Lystra stopped. Her eyes turned the dagger with its lavish, golden hilt and silver blade. A weapon far finer than that of the Jarkin who had murdered her betrothed. Was this her fate? To lose the man she loved only to live to murder her husband?

"You cannot be weak." Grandmother's voice screamed in her ears. *"Pity makes queens weak."*

So be it. She was weak. Curse or no, Elerek would live until he drowned. Lystra would not take his life.

Drawing a deep breath, she satisfied her aching lungs, but the air tasted tainted. This was wrong, all wrong. Now this terrible knowledge lay between them, like the parlor separating their bedchambers. The king carried this secret—and had married her anyways? Stars, what was she doing here? She had to flee. She had to think.

She backed away from the bed—and tripped over Elerek's wheelchair.

Starlight caught on the blade, still clenched in her fist.

Elerek shot up in bed, eyes wide.

The whole of time fell still as they stared at one another, a mural painted on the palace walls. The air, that tainted breath, lay captive within her chest.

"Lystra . . ." Elerek lifted a hand, as if to defend himself. "What . . . what are you doing?"

Blood pulsed in her ears. She righted her stance, holding the blade out in front of her, as if to defend herself. Its hilt felt hot, iron in the smith's forge, smoldering with her guilt.

Elerek's eyes darted to the blade, and then back to her. "Lystra, wait." His voice deepened, raw and terrible. "You don't understand—"

"I do." Her voice sounded as if it came from someone else. "I touch you, and I'll die."

"I won't let that happen."

The desert wind fell silent. Even the stars seemed to pause in their dance, called to attention by the resolve of the king.

Lystra looked at him—*really* looked at him.

The face that stared back at her was Cormek's. Here, in the darkness and the starlight, she saw the man that she loved. The deep intensity of his stare, framed by the rise of his cheekbones and a cascade of dark curls. Memories from the desert stabbed her soul afresh. In her mind's eye, Cormek toppled before the Jarkin warrior, the light leaving his gaze.

She lowered the dagger.

Death had changed her. Fear had paralyzed her. Grandmother had twisted her.

Elerek's breath escaped in a long shudder, his shoulders dropping. "Who told you?" he demanded. "About the curse?"

"No one." Lystra swallowed.

He stared at her, eyes set ablaze.

"You knew Azraa. You knew that she died. If what the priest said is true—that you are your father's firstborn—you lost your birthright to Cormek on account of it." She narrowed her eyes. "You knew that it takes only one touch, and you don't let anyone near you."

The blaze in his eyes smoldered, turning to ashes as grim as a funeral pyre. "It's what I must do. Everyone I touch . . . just like Azraa. They drown." His hand moved to his side, to the ribbon of transparent skin slashing his body. "I meant to tell you." The weight of his mournful voice was enough to sink a whole fleet of river vessels, damning their sailors.

Yes, he should have. Before the coronation. Before their wedding. But these critical remarks fell silent on Lystra's tongue. Unable to draw her eyes from the mark, her hardened heart began to crack, like baked desert clay. "How did it happen? What did you do?"

The embers in his eyes caught, blazing with agonized flames. "If curses were only dealt to sinners, then none would be spared. I only know that it happened when I was scarcely a year. Cormek had just been born." He shook his head. "I suppose it was some plot of revenge against my father's bloody rule. Starkindler knows he created enemies. Death begets death. Always."

Scarcely a year. Elerek had been cursed nearly his entire life. Lystra blinked at this realization, at the pain he'd carried through all those years. "Cormek knew, didn't he?"

Elerek's shoulders hunched, his muscles tight. "Yes. He swore to keep my secret. Everything was better, easier, if I simply faded away." He huffed. "He wanted more for me than a cursed life of obscurity."

"That sounds like him." The image of Cormek came easy, full of life and compassion, reaching out to the brother who couldn't reach back. Cormek had everything meant to be Elerek's. She could hardly bear to think of it.

Elerek's jaw drew taut, as if it were made of stone. Defenses against the sorrow. "I loved my brother, and I took him for granted."

Shame drenched Lystra's soul. Hadn't she and Elerek both stood at the pyre, closer than anyone? Death had brought them here, to this moment, where a curse lay claim to a king and his queen came armed with a dagger.

"Lystra." As he spoke her name, severe and somehow gentle at the same time, the heat returned to his eyes. "Give me the dagger ... please?"

She bowed her head, looking to the weapon in her hand. The tool of a cutthroat, an assassin. Everything that she wasn't. She extended it to him. "Forgive me."

"Don't let the foolish girl win." Dalmah had asked for violence, equating it with strength. Lystra's vision perceived the opposite.

What had she won, then?

Elerek took the dagger in his plague-scarred hands, but he kept his gaze fixed on her. "You must understand. Curses aren't so easily broken. And something like murder—it taints and infects." Only then did his eyes soften. "I do not think it a wrongdoing to be tempted, but our duty is to protect our people, isn't it?"

For once, Lystra found herself unable to hold his stare. She turned to the open window, the ink-black mountains and star-strewn horizon blurring through a veil of hot tears. She wished that she'd stayed in her chambers. Yet she needed him to share his story. She was married to a cursed man; how would this strange arrangement work?

"Including those who bear this curse?" She folded her arms.

"Yes." Elerek shifted on the bed, leaning forward. "Thirty men and women serve in my household and bear its mark, their days numbered."

A gasp fled Lystra's lips. She shot him a horrified expression. "Thirty? You *cursed*—"

"No!" For a moment, his face twisted into a snarl, but then he withdrew it, forcing his features to soften. "As I told the high priest, sometimes it passes secondhand, but not always. Most of it was accidental. It can kill in a week or take years. Norbah, my general, taught me archery when I was twelve. A momentary lapse of thought and he corrected my posture." Agony wrote cruel lines across his forehead. "I'm not a monster. Those whom I have cursed I've kept close, giving them employment and shelter here. They're my family."

Lystra marveled at the devotion in his eyes, the loyalty of a soldier to a beloved commander—much like that which she'd seen the general give his king. No, not a monster. "And what would happen to them if . . ." She looked down at the dagger in his hands.

Elerek hung his head, the shadows laying claim to his face. A slight tremor worked through his shoulders and down his arms, almost as if Lystra's question had caused him physical pain. "I tried, Lystra. Once. I tried to die." He lifted his left arm, exposing pale skin to the starlight.

Lystra held her breath, staring at the ragged scar, running like a range of mountains on a map from his elbow down to his wrist.

"In perfect unison, every one of the cursed became ill to the point of death. Razhar—obviously he isn't cursed—found me. When I recovered, so did they."

Thirty. A slaughter. Blood on her hands. She blinked, and twin tears fell hot down her face. Circling the bed, her slippers moved noiselessly on the floors.

Lifting a trembling hand, she pushed her hair back from her face, studying him. The whole of him. Cormek had been Instanolde's warrior king, but he wasn't the only king who had fought battles. Tenacious eyes and scarred flesh. Pale and beautiful in the glow of the night, and yet broken by the weight of a lifetime lived in sorrows.

"You lived . . ." she whispered.

Elerek nodded. "I lived."

Now he was king, and she was his queen.

Lystra sank onto the edge of his bed. The sharp intake of his breath echoed in her ears. This time, he couldn't flee. For better or ill, their paths had overlaid, a trail through the wilderness. One they were to traverse *together*.

She'd known that alone, she'd never manage the burden of the throne. But she never thought to find an ally in Elerek, to forge a future in which they—together—preserved Instanolde.

"Lystra, I'd like you to know . . ." The muscles tightened along his jaw, his eyes shifting through the shadows lurking in the room's corners. "I would never do anything to hurt you."

A shudder ran down her spine. A deadly curse lay trapped in his skin. She could never touch him, never draw close, and still, she believed him.

"Instanolde has never needed me. I was never meant for the throne. But now, here, with one summer to live . . ." His throat bobbed as he swallowed, as if he struggled to summon the words. His eyes found hers again, sharp as spears. "Do you see . . . I . . . *I need you?*"

The silk at the window stirred. The desert breathed upon them, its air caressing Lystra's skin and ruffling Elerek's hair. In it, Lystra tasted all the wildness of their desert desolation. This impossible land where they had chosen to survive, to live.

He will die.

Lystra felt as if shackles of the coldest iron were bound about her heart. One way or another, the curse would take Elerek. He didn't need her to come to his chambers to take his life; it would be taken from him anyways. Instanolde would ask her to mourn another king, to stand at another pyre. But there would be no body to burn. Death had come to stay.

"You . . . you wanted me to be queen?" Not a canary. Not a channel to the people's affection. Not a power upon which to boost his own. No, quite the opposite. Lystra's chest shuddered with a suppressed sob. Another flood of tears streamed down her face, which she hastily wiped away. "Why must I always cry in your presence?"

Instead of scorn, Elerek gave her a gentle smile. "Tears are not weakness. But yes, House Karim and its bloody history ends with me. Placing Instanolde in the hands of House Arghan is the best and most responsible thing that I can do. *You* are my heir, the hope of Instanolde's salvation."

A dying star's last brilliance.

Lystra sniffled, pulling the sleeves of her robe down over her hands, suddenly chilled.

"Can you forgive me?" Elerek drew a deep breath, his bare chest expanding. "I've asked much of you—for the sake of our kingdom."

Her entire life had been fixated on this one thought, becoming queen. The sum of all she had ever wanted. Well, she'd achieved it, but it hadn't quite come with the freedom she'd envisioned. She had forsaken much, lost much, and this path, joined with a cursed king, promised more loss still.

If she could not give of herself to save Instanolde, she wasn't worthy of her crown. Lystra drew herself up, as if her place seated on his bed were her throne and he her kingdom. "I wouldn't be here if I didn't wish for the wellbeing of Instanolde."

"I counted on it."

A tingle of heat blazed across her skin, the scattered embers of a devouring flame. "Elerek, if we are to do this, you must promise me one thing."

He watched her, his gaze severe.

Lystra turned toward him, her chin held high. "These were not secrets to keep from me. I've been shamefully manipulated by those who ought to have had my best interests at heart before and I refuse to let that happen again. No secrets, no matter how dire. Swear to me that I will have nothing but the truth from your lips."

Silence fell over the chamber, heavy as smoke. It hazed the clarity of his gaze, like the solid stare of a marble likeness.

Be different, Elerek. Her husband. Lystra held her breath. Different from Grandmother.

Then, the king gave a firm nod. "I swear it. Together, we'll find a way to save Instanolde."

Together. The word seemed heavy enough to crush them.

Elerek dropped his gaze, his hand brushing the dagger's hilt. "Curious."

"Hmm?"

He lifted the weapon, starlight catching on its steel. "There's a constellation etched into this blade—the wrathgiver constellation."

There. Lystra could see it, the mark of stars. "Is that significant?"

Elerek narrowed his eyes. "The wrathgiver was a vengeful assassin. Each murder, one after another, caused his heart to turn to stone."

Shame flushed her cheeks. Lystra gathered her hair, pulling it over one shoulder. "I suppose that's appropriate," she whispered. "You know the stars well."

He placed the dagger on the table beside his bed, well out of reach. "The Starkindler gave us the constellations to discern the times, mark the eras, and to remember his statutes. Stories are capable vessels of profound truths."

"Ah, I'd forgotten you were well-read." She managed a small smile. "I'm afraid it's been years since I've heard the stories. But you do believe in the Starkindler?"

Elerek gave a slow nod. "I have to believe in something

good. Something greater. Otherwise, I'm only a cursed wretch waiting to die."

Something greater. Something beyond them. Beyond kingdoms and enemies, curses and the shifting sands of the desert.

"Can you tell the tales of all the stars?"

"Possibly." Excitement danced in his eyes. "A life such as mine, particularly crippled, gave me lots of reading time. Books seem to be the least cursed thing beneath the sun." Elerek stopped, hesitance drawing a bit of color to his pale face. "If . . . if you're not inclined to sleep, I could share some?"

Lystra drew a deep breath, the air clear and free in her lungs. "It *is* our wedding night."

He gave a sad laugh, but the curve of his lips might have been a true smile. In that glimmer of mirth, Lystra glimpsed something of Cormek—but something deeper. Tragic, and yet noble. Unbroken despite a world that had waged its worst. A man who both lived and died in the same cursed breath.

Chapter 24

Elerek

E lerek blinked, but the vision didn't fade. No, the starlight streaming in from the open window was as real as his scarred flesh and the blood and cursed water flowing in his veins. It gleamed on the blade of the star-etched dagger and in the tear-washed eyes of the girl perched on the edge of his bed.

The ghosts that had marched across her face were familiar. Her actions spoke of fear, of terror, and the twisted trails of grief. Why else would she come to his room, armed with a weapon, and threaten his life? He glanced down at the scar on his arm, reminded of what it felt like to be so desperate—shoved into a corner without escape, each steadily collapsing wall painted with another mural of misery.

But she stayed. She listened. She *saw* him.

He'd vowed to give her starlight. As it turned out, she needed it more than he could bear. If his queen was to lead Instanolde into the dawn, she needed hope enough to outshine the sun. Stars, he wanted her to win—to rule, to reign—and never feel the taint of the darkness again.

Except, she was married to *him*.

He swept aside these grim thoughts. After all, she wanted stories. She wanted the stars. His stars. "Hand me that scroll there?" He pointed to a small shelf positioned against the wall. Despite the room's sparse furniture, he needed some place to stow books and texts. Only a few had made it to these new chambers, but he'd been certain to select his favorite chart of the heavens.

Lystra rose from the bed to retrieve it. Climbing back atop the blankets, she crossed her legs and spread the scroll between her and Elerek. "I've seen this chart before."

"Its accuracy has been verified by several revered scholars." Elerek turned the scroll lengthwise, allowing the chart's contents to mirror the view from his window. Reaching across the chart, he smoothed the corner, the parchment curled from its time within the scroll.

Lystra leaned forward. "I like the illustrations. They're pretty." Her fingers brushed over a painted lizard with the spectrum of the rainbow painted across its scales—mere inches away from his hand.

Elerek jerked back, panic jolting down his spine. The bed shifted with the sudden movement.

Across the bed, Lystra blinked, her gaze flashing with concern.

"We . . . we have to be careful," he whispered. "We cannot be close."

The curse would never have her. No depths or drowning would lay claim to his queen. This was his vow, as strong as those he'd taken before his kingdom.

Lystra shrank back, a bit of rose blooming on her cheeks.

"I'm sorry." He hated how quickly the tension mounted between them. Could he tear these walls down himself? Disarm their fears and let the air be clear?

Her gaze, perfect and amber, met his. "You owe me a story, Elerek. Not an apology."

Give her starlight. Where to begin? "Well, we already know about the wrathgiver, who has traversed well across the desert by now. The north maiden holds a tambourine, in which we find the north star."

"I know this one." A soft smile caressed Lystra's lips. "She dances to the north, led by the sound of music. Hence we place musicians northward at galas when it comes time to dance."

Music and dancing. During Cormek's reign, galas were a regular occurrence at the palace. They were something of legend, according to Razhar. Elerek hated to attend, too fearful of spreading the curse, but he remembered seeing Lystra dance with his brother, joy radiating in their eyes.

The same joy dwelt in her gaze now. Even here, sitting in the dark and silver starlight, and it was contagious.

"That's right." He swallowed, banishing away the thought of their losses. "And here we have Sealin, the great horse. His is a tale of endurance. Born beneath the house of a cruel master, the horse grew in strength until he could jump the gate and earn his freedom. His master pursued, sending search parties to catch him, but Sealin was said to have a coat pure and white. It blended into the sands during the day and the starlight at night. He would run in the night, putting miles between him and captivity, thus his traverse across the skies always leads to the wilds."

Lystra pulled her long tresses over her shoulder. She smiled as she ran her fingers through her hair. "I like that story. Though if I were to take to the desert, I'd rather take a cardant. A horse would be far too fragile in the Sancen."

Elerek also smiled, thinking of the reptile down in the stables. He wondered when it would be appropriate to take her there. "I suppose you're right. Sealin's stars are one of my birth constellations. Do you know yours?"

"Mm, I haven't been asked after my birth constellations in so long. The naeva girl, the golden lion, and the racers." Lystra's shoulders gave a small shrug. "Tell me, are they fitting?"

The naeva girl. He didn't wish to tell that story. The tale of a girl who loved a soldier, forced to fight in a war that lasted decades. She stood upon the ramparts every night, watching for his return. He never did, lost to the battles. So she took up arms and took his place on the frontlines, waging war until her lover was avenged.

Yes, he feared they were fitting, and it weighed heavily upon his heart. Elerek exhaled and leaned back against the bed's headboard. Better to tell one of the other stories.

"Well, the racers each owed a debt, both to the same creditor. They decided to race in the hopes of winning enough to pay what they owed. When their creditor found out, he agreed. Their race took them along the shores of the Gungole and it was springtime, the banks swollen, and the mud made their route difficult. One racer gave up while the other succeeded and was forgiven his debt. The other became a slave to pay off what he was owed." Elerek raised an eyebrow. "Really, Lystra? A high-stakes racing competition?"

Lystra laughed and shook her head. "Perhaps fate really is written across the heavens, as some of the priests say. If the Starkindler did indeed forge the stars and gave us these stories, surely he could have orchestrated the skies of our births."

The silk fluttered at the window, bringing with it the chilled breeze of a desert night. But no chill could dispel the warmth swirling in Lystra's laughter. Elerek lifted a hand to his brow, pushing his tousled curls off his forehead. From beneath her thick lashes, he saw how her gaze trailed from his hand, down his arm, across his bare chest, to the curse mark stretched across his ribs. He quickly looked away, noting the linen shirt he'd cast aside still draped over the dresser and quite beyond his reach. He wondered what she thought, seeing him. Was he more than scars and curses?

"I think I know the lion one." Lystra dropped her gaze to the chart again, tracing the constellations' dances until she found the great maned cat drawn on an outcrop of rock. "Isn't there a hunter chasing him, his arrows poisoned?"

Elerek nodded. "Yes, that's right. The boy was an archer and he—" *Stars.* He drew a sharp breath, the air hissing through his teeth. "Oh . . . of course."

An answer, written in the stars themselves. He wondered why he was so surprised. Hope surged through his chest, driving away the curse's horrid numbness, even just temporarily. This was merely a break, a bit of light streaming through the rare cover of storm clouds, but it was *something.*

Across the bed, Lystra lifted her eyes.

"Lystra." He leaned forward until their eyes were level, close enough for him to see the reflection of the constellations across her gaze. "I need you to tell me about the attack."

A soft gasp breathed on her lips. "Why do you—?"

"The Jarkins." His mind moved quickly, assembling the pieces, gathering information, constructing a picture that might save Instanolde. Or, at the very least, buy them precious time. "How did they kill? It was an ambush. It happened quickly. How did they so swiftly overtake a host of armed men and their cardants?"

Lystra bowed her head. A quiver moved through her shoulders. As the shadows claimed her features, seemingly pulled from the black robes she wore, Elerek's heart plunged into a horror deep enough to drown in. The trance, whatever brief levity they'd manage to achieve, had shattered like a mirror, and he was the one who had broken it.

182

You idiot. Elerek shut his eyes and looked away. Shame prickled across his skin, the skin he wished he could hide. Razhar had warned him, *countless* times. His blunt, stupid, brash insensitivity would get the best of him and here he was, on their wedding night, asking for details regarding the death of the man his queen loved as well as her beloved cardants.

"Lystra, I . . . just . . ." Why was speaking so, so difficult? Much less saying the right thing. "Forgive me."

He dared to open his eyes. On the other side of the heavens-painted parchment, Lystra's eyes were filled with tears, but not with fury or disgust. No, where there ought to be scorn, compassion stirred in her gaze.

"You're the king of Instanolde," she whispered. "I don't believe you owe me apologies."

Oh, no, he owed her more than he could ever repay. "And you're the queen who is owed no more griefs, particularly not from me."

She shifted atop the blankets, her eyes turning to the room's corners. "Our world lies in pieces, Elerek." The edge of her voice sharpened, rivaling the dagger upon his nightstand. "I'm not sure we'll ever escape. Not fully. Not unscathed."

No, but that didn't mean that the pieces had to be sharp and embrittled, glass shards prying into open wounds. "I'm sorry for my inquiry. My friends have told me that I can be extraordinarily insensitive. I hope to better myself."

Lystra's arms wrapped about herself. "You are blessed to have such friends, and I hope I can extend to you that same grace as you better yourself." She tilted her head to one side, allowing the starlight to illuminate her face again, and Elerek found that he couldn't help but stare. "Why did you ask those questions?"

"It can wait. We can't solve all the world's problems tonight."

A sad sort of laugh fell from her lips. "But we've come so far, Elerek. Can we solve one more? Have you thought of a way to save our Instanolde?"

Not save. No, they hadn't the time or resources for that. He only had a bit of starlight, a bit of hope. "The archer in the story. Instanolde hasn't had a legion of bowmen in the city in ages. In my father's bloody skirmishes, whenever he needed archers, he summoned Kushan with their condor-mounted archers." Their refusal of fealty stung a second time, the full devastation of this loss revealed to him. They *needed* those archers, but he had one option left. "We're to be sieged. The Jarkins will come at us from the desert. We need every advantage we can muster from our walls. We need to train archers of our own."

Lystra blinked. "Are we sure we cannot reattempt negotiations with Kushan? Together, we might have strength enough to save us."

Might. Elerek didn't like that word in association with strategy. When he played *barjee* with Razhar, he played to win. "They've made their decision. We can't count on them. But I've a Kushite-made bow of my own, and I know we can train regiments enough to man our walls."

"Ah, you mentioned you knew archery." Lystra managed a small smile, and the tone of her voice told him that she was impressed. The heart he carried with its woes suddenly felt a bit lighter, a bit more manageable. He wondered what other burdens they might share.

Then, like a cloud eclipsing a constellation, sorrow again shadowed the queen. Her face grew mournful, and she looked as she did the night of the pyre, still enrobed with strength, but holding her pains tightly. "The Jarkins have archers too," she whispered. "Long, black-fletched arrows. That's how they took my cardant."

Elerek opened his mouth to speak, to stop her, but the story toppled from her lips.

"I tried to flee. Cormek told me to. The arrow missed me, hit my mount. My dear Ghira." Tears filled her eyes. "Everything spun, and it seemed like the sands flung themselves to me as I left the saddle. Out of nowhere, one of the mountain men stood over us, with an axe . . ." Twin diamond droplets fell down her face. "Then the soldiers grabbed me, pulled me from the sand, saving me."

The grieving queen of Instanolde who survived the desert. Elerek didn't want to imagine, to see the scene in his mind, but it took so little prompting. The brave soldiers rallying to their king to hold off the invaders—and to ensure that this extraordinary girl who would one day wear the crown was carried away to safety. They had protected her bodily, yes, the Starkindler be thanked for that, but she carried the scars.

Lystra wiped away her tears. "Cormek too. He—"

"Don't." Elerek lifted a hand, and then drew his fingers tight. How he wished he could give comfort, like others could. A soft touch. A reassuring squeeze. An embrace to ward away every darkness. Especially to his queen, who looked as if she needed these simple consolations just as much as she'd needed salvation in the desert.

But he was cursed. Unable to be touched. Unable to touch. Stars, it made him sick.

"It's all right." He leaned toward the nightstand, opening the drawer to withdraw a handkerchief. He placed it on the star chart, the expanse between them. "Thank you for your story. You've helped save your kingdom, you know."

She took the handkerchief, drying her tears. "I liked your stories far better." Behind the handkerchief, she stifled a yawn.

Resisting the urge to copy the contagious motion, Elerek gently rolled up the star chart. "Here." He extended it toward her. "Keep this. There are plenty more stories. If ever you cannot sleep, well, you know where to find me."

"I do." She cradled the scroll gently, as if it were the most precious parchment in the world. Was it only today that he'd heard those words from her lips the first time? When she'd given vows to become his wife?

Elerek responded with a smile.

She slipped off the bed and stepped toward the silk curtains. There, she paused, turning to glance over her shoulder. A strange, wild expression swirled in her eyes. Mingled with the starlight, he could only call it wonder.

And stars, the way his heart pounded, he imagined he felt something of the same. Something unexpected. Despite their differences, the divides between them, and the distance the curse required, perhaps they could do this, accomplish the impossible.

Chapter 25

Elerek

Thud. Thud. Thud.

The sound of knocking jolted Elerek awake. Pushing himself up from the pillows, he drew a hand through his curls and glanced toward the open window. The mountains were dark, starkly inked against the pale glow coming from beyond the horizon. An hour Elerek routinely avoided, preferring the companionship of the stars.

"Your Highness?" The march of boots accompanied the voice.

It had begun. His first day as the king of Instanolde.

"A moment." Elerek swung his legs over the side of the bed, thankful for strong arms, and pulled his chair closer. *Perhaps I ought to see about appointing an attendant.*

When he finished dressing, the first rays of light streamed over the mountains, splattering the desert in gold—and catching on the blade of the dagger with constellations on its blade.

Elerek paused, his fingers still at the fastenings on his collar. A strange shiver crept down his arms. He'd paid little attention to the weapon last night, his focus given to his queen.

But now, he took note of its rich design, the gold upon its sheath. House Arghan had riches in abundance, so this didn't seem strange to him. Lystra feared the curse—a valid cause for terror—but to think killing him was the answer?

He wheeled closer, his finger brushing the ornate golden sheath.

She'd mentioned that she'd been manipulated. Could this have been part of that? Had someone sought his death—and shamelessly used his queen?

The very thought infuriated him. Not that someone had made an attempt upon his life—his entire cursed existence stood testament to the fact. But that someone would seek to control *Lystra*? The girl who raced cardants across the desert? The bold queen of Instanolde?

No, if anyone tried such a thing, he'd put a sure end to it.

Drip. A droplet rolled off his clenched knuckle. Elerek frowned. Again? Aside from last night, the curse had never done this before, and he'd been angry then too.

Was that what caused it? Anger?

"Your Highness?" The voice belonged to Norbah.

"I'm coming." Elerek turned away from the dagger and the strange workings of the curse and wheeled his chair toward the silk curtain.

In the time it had taken him to dress, the small parlor had filled. Norbah stood tall, vigilant in his armor. Driss stood at his side, scrolls tucked beneath his arm, facing a pair of advisors that had served beneath Cormek whose names Elerek couldn't remember. Somehow, Razhar had also wandered in, already making himself at home on one of the couches like another of the room's lavish adornments.

And Lystra. Her eyes immediately found his, blazing with the light of the new day. Heat spread across his face, down his throat to the collar he'd forgotten to finish fastening.

The black robes she'd worn last night didn't suit her. No, his queen belonged to the dawn, to the glories of the shimmering sun itself. Somehow, she'd made the simplicity of a riding tunic, colored a deep purple, and tall boots meant for the stables as regal as any royal garb.

Beyond the knife and the terror, something else had happened last night. A softness, a tenderness, enshrouded in whispers and starlight. Grandeur and ceremony fell away, and Lystra had sat on the edge of his bed without fear. They'd looked into one another's eyes and seen clearly, without preconceived notions or prejudice. No longer king and queen, not warriors striving with all that they were to battle the future, but two candles lighting the dark.

The courtiers bowed at his entrance, but Norbah wasted no time. "Your Highness, an encampment is set up outside the city gates. A Loccan caravan."

Lystra frowned. "They dwell upriver, near the Kushite Canals, don't they?"

"Generally speaking, Your Highness," Norbah replied. "They've taken no lands, preferring their nomadic caravans."

Drawing his hands tight, Elerek resisted his nervous habit of tapping on his chair's armrest. "Why have they come here?"

"They're claiming sanctuary. Here, within the city walls." One of the courtiers wrung his hands. "From the impending Jarkin invasion."

At the word "Jarkin," the light fled the queen's eyes, smothered in a dark and terrible shadow. Elerek watched her, understanding her fury. They both had a vengeance to satisfy.

"Word has spread," Norbah added. "Speculation will breed fear and panic. We need to decide here and now how to handle this."

Elerek's stomach tightened. Could he possibly keep refugees safe here, within the city walls? The Loccan were a small tribe, but if the larger ones, particularly those that hadn't given him fealty, came to occupy his city, what then?

The queen's gaze shifted to him again. "Your Highness." She pushed her shoulders back, her spine straight. "Instanolde is watching. If we send them away . . ."

He gave a firm nod and turned back to their court. "General, there *is* a strategic advantage to gathering the tribes within our walls. We cannot say no to soldiers, those who are able to train and fight."

Norbah dipped his chin. "Regardless, a draft must be issued."

"It would put a strain on housing and our feed supplies, but the harvest season is over and trade is still open via the canals." The other courtier spoke up.

"If the worst should happen, the outlying tribes won't last long." Elerek's gaze swept each in turn. "They can flee downriver, but the delta will fade into desert. Upriver, the Kushan will barricade themselves in the canyons." He drew his spine up a little straighter. "I will turn none away. Mobilize the city militia to prepare for an influx of people."

"You're anticipating a siege, then?" the courtier questioned.

Doubt loomed in their eyes like a thunderhead overshadowing the horizon. Elerek drew a deep breath. They thought him inexperienced and untested. They didn't yet trust him as king.

Then, gliding forward with beauty and grace, the queen entered the circle. "It is inevitable, but our walls are strong, like the hearts of our people." As she spoke, the strength of the Gungole's current flowed through her voice. "The loss of Darcress hasn't yet been confirmed before the people. Perhaps it is time."

The first courtier sighed. "My queen, it will cause panic."

"Better bitter truths then speculation." Lystra looked at Elerek again.

He held her gaze. "We will prepare an address as soon as possible. See to the Loccan."

Norbah and the courtiers bowed and swiftly departed, but Elerek hunched his shoulders, missing the usual relief when a room emptied. Instead, the silence felt heavy, as if the very air they breathed carried the weight of the world.

Near the door, Driss lingered. "I was asked to check, you are still attending tonight?"

Ah, the wedding feast. Gathering around a table with familiar faces, a bit of merriment to look forward to. "Yes, of course."

"And?" Driss's eyes darted toward Lystra. "Your queen?"

Lystra. In a room full of cursed. Elerek's stomach twisted.

His thoughts again returned to the deep hours of the night. Even though Lystra had seen the curse in all its grotesque and damning horror, she hadn't spurned him. She'd come with a knife, ready to defend her people from its evil—and instead gave mercy.

She understood.

In their intent to preserve lives, they were of one mind. Like a rare night's frost, Elerek's fear melted away. He wanted Lystra to attend, to meet his tribe of the forgotten, and to know the names of his family.

"Attending—?" Lystra appeared confused.

"I hadn't mentioned it yet." He offered an apologetic smile. "My companions are determined to prepare us a wedding feast."

From the couch, Razhar laughed. Elerek startled. *Stars, I'd forgotten he was there.* "Since when are you so quiet?"

"It was a sober occasion." Razhar rose to his feet and straightened his vest. "I hope I'm invited." He turned to Lystra with a wide smile. "You'll find, Your Highness, that El and his little tribe are always preparing some celebration involving all sorts of delectable treats. Very exclusive, you know."

Elerek shook his head. "Your membership is purely honorary."

Razhar only laughed.

Glancing between them with blinking eyes, Lystra appeared as if she wasn't quite sure what to do with them. Then she turned to Driss, her every movement as graceful as a dancer's. "I would be glad to attend, thank you for your thoughtful consideration."

The scribe bowed but couldn't hide his smile.

Elerek cleared his throat. "I only ask that . . . we exercise caution."

"Oh, of course, El." Driss's face turned a deep crimson. "We'll be careful."

"And I'll be there, quite uncursed with my *honorary membership*." Razhar folded his arms. "We'll watch after your queen, El."

The slightest of shadows passed Lystra's face. Elerek's skin began to prickle, as if the curse could somehow sense that its foul name had found a foothold in their conversation.

But with the strength of the summer sun, the darkness in her eyes dispelled as a smile lifted her lips. "I'm eager to meet your little family."

A strange warmth scattered across his cold, cursed skin.

"Tell me." Lystra tilted her head to one side, her long hair falling over her shoulders. "Do you all so freely give such endearing nicknames to your king?"

Stars. Elerek's face burned.

Razhar only smiled a smug smile. "That, my queen, is the *exclusive* part of the tribe. An honor of the loftiest order."

192

Lystra gave a soft chortle, the sound ringing like the merriest of silver bells.

This is her. The true her. Without grief's silken cocoon. Silkworms, brought from the canyonlands in tiny, gilded cages, spun the finest of threads. But upon metamorphosis, they became something else entirely, spreading gossamer wings and taking flight. Elerek wondered what Lystra knew of metamorphosis—and if these fleeting smiles and the burning of her eyes, were only the faintest gossamer glimpses of her wingspan.

Elerek's fingers gave themselves over to their nervous tapping, the sound matching the steadily rising beat of his heart. Grief had stricken his life since the first moment the curse entered his skin, in an era beyond memory. *Who am I underneath?*

For now, he'd taken vows as king, and giving his queen wings was his goal. "If you're quite finished, I believe we have business to attend."

"Right." Driss took the scrolls out from beneath his arm. "I have several objects to bring to your attention. Would you like to see them now?"

Elerek swept past them, toward the door. "The Loccan are the most pressing. We'll see to that address, but first—" He glanced over his shoulder, toward his queen. Radiance still poured from her gaze and he didn't want to see it leave. "Lystra, were you venturing to the stables?"

A faint bit of color took up residence in her cheeks. "We have more important duties."

"This will only take a moment." Elerek gestured for them to follow.

Chapter 26

Lystra

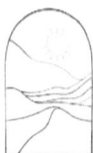

The stables? Curiosity brewed strong in Lystra's soul, like the most perfect cup of mint tea, but she followed Elerek down the palace corridors without question.

Everything appeared different in the light of a new dawn, streaming in horizontal shafts through the windows and lattice shades. Full of promise, full of opportunity, and the issue of the Loccan refugees and unifying her people in defense against the Jarkins only solidified what Lystra had always known: she'd prepared for this, to serve her people, and she was exactly where she was needed.

And for now, that mural, painted in the light of the stars, included Elerek.

She spared him a glance. His head crownless and the collar of his tunic unfastened, he lacked the poise of regality he'd worn yesterday, but the gleam in his eyes wouldn't be called anything less than noble.

We can do this. We can work together.

As they turned a corner, Lystra stole a quick glance over her shoulder.

Razhar. The stranger from the market who danced beneath the stars—and tried to kiss her. Would he have made the attempt if he'd known who she was? And while his comradeship with Elerek was amusing, had Razhar mentioned the adventure?

"How long have you two known each other?"

Razhar gave a subtle wink. "Something like forever. Another tragic tale of Instanolde's fight for survival, certainly worthy of a melancholy song or three." He used the exaggerated voice of a storyteller vying for attention. "Warring tribes, bitter battles, blood spilled upon the sands, you know, the usual."

Elerek stopped his chair at a door and leaned forward to push it open. "He was an orphan from Kushan, brought back by a soldier and raised here."

Heaving a dramatic sigh, Razhar let his well-muscled shoulders drop. "The way you tell it, El, nobody would want to listen."

A smile emerged on Elerek's face. Lystra wondered if he knew how greatly the expression improved his features. "That's why I'm not a dramatic like you."

"Come now, you have your moments."

The glare the king gave him could've stopped the most fearsome lion in its tracks. Lystra stifled a laugh. Their banter reminded her of her cousins, though their battles of wit typically ended in insults sharp enough to skin a mountain goat. She marveled at the familiar comfort warming her heart even while both these men had been strangers yesterday. Perhaps she could make this new world her home.

A home they would fight to save.

Passing beneath a graceful arch, morning sunlight streamed

into the stable courtyard. Lystra blinked, welcoming the scent of warmed straw and pungent reptiles.

A place in which she and Cormek had spent hours. She stopped, closing her eyes. Another swallow. Another steady breath. The memories hovered so near, as if they inhabited the dust dancing on each radiant shaft. She could almost *feel* Cormek's hand caressing the small of her back, the brush of his strong shoulder against hers.

But when she opened her eyes, she stood alone.

"What are we doing here?" A few of the visible pens were occupied, the reptiles busy sunning themselves, warming their blood. Lystra spotted Sama asleep with her tail curled about her body like a great cat.

"You'll see." Elerek had a bit of difficulty with his chair, the gravel soft from the charge of cardant's claws. Lystra briefly wondered if he would ask for assistance as he leaned forward, straining to spin the wheels through the dust, but he didn't. Perhaps he preferred to take care of himself.

A high-pitched scratching arrested her attention, sending a shiver down her spine. The sound of long talons being drawn over rock.

Lystra spun on her heels, her gaze drawn toward a large corner pen set apart from the others. Her eyes widened. "Oh, look at *you*."

The restless reptile hunched its back and lowered its magnificently horned head. Each long, white talon scratched deep into the packed soil at the base of her pen's gate, as if seeking to dig her way out. Yellow scales encircled her eyes and green and orange stripes ran the length of her back and streaked up each spine.

Easily the most beautiful cardant Lystra had ever seen.

Approaching the gate, cast in iron and mounted to stone, Lystra watched with transfixed fascination. She reached through the bars, her fingers near the cardant's snout, a common greeting to a docile, trained cardant.

But the reptile bared its teeth and gave a low growl.

Lystra drew her hand back and smiled. "Oh, we've got work to do, haven't we?"

Hot air blew from its nostrils, as if in prompt disagreement.

"She's yours."

Lystra looked over her shoulder. Elerek, Razhar, and the scribe all stared, watching with rapt attention, but the voice belonged to the king.

"I know . . ." Elerek paused, averting his gaze and wringing his hands in an anxious gesture. "Your cardants were killed in the attack. When I saw this one . . . she's meant for you."

An ache formed in her heart. "You bought her *for me?*" The gesture was so kind, so thoughtful, so unexpected. "I hardly know what to say."

Elerek smiled, and his eyes glimmered like starlight.

Behind him, Razhar cocked an eyebrow. "So romantic, El. You want to keep your queen whole and intact and you bought her a monster."

While Elerek's face turned a violent shade of purple, Lystra laughed. "She's not a monster." To prove her point, she ducked through the gate and into the pen.

The cardant recoiled like a cobra, keeping its head low to the ground, watching Lystra with its large, orb-like eyes. Lystra crouched down, their eyes leveled with one another's.

"Now, now," she cooed. She transitioned her speech to *Uirna,* a language from the tribes downriver who perpetuated an effective training regimen for bonding cardants, speaking soft words of peace. The cardant recoiled, hissing and snapping its jaws aggressively.

Her spectators responded with panic in their voices.

"Lystra . . ."

197

"Your Highness, maybe you ought to—"

"Hush!" she commanded.

Lystra felt no fear, only the pounding of her heart, thrilled by the challenge. While others looked on in terror, seeing only vicious claws and sharp teeth, she saw strength. A creature of survival, fast as the wind and as bold as a sunrise.

"She's meant for you." Lystra wholeheartedly agreed.

She scooted forward, her boots scraping along the packed clay. The reptile hissed.

"Shh, *et hass stel.*" Lystra reached out, her hand flat. Be still.

Her fingers brushed the scales, warmed from the sun. She smiled.

The cardant jerked its head away. Arching her back, limbs coiled, she held her tail high. A defensive position.

Lystra rose to her feet, slowly backing toward the gate. Without turning her back on the reptile, she slipped outside the pen.

"A good start." She smiled and wiped the dirt from her hands.

Three pairs of wide eyes stared at her. Elerek, still quite purple, moved a hand to his chest. Only Razhar managed to find his tongue. "If you say so."

Lystra pushed her hair behind her ear as a hot gust of wind blew through the courtyard. The air smelled of the desert, of freedom. Perhaps there would be time for a ride later. "If I may inquire, where did you purchase her?"

"House Quilam." Recovering, Elerek resumed a demeanor of collected regality. "They had their hands full."

Lystra laughed. "Stars, I offered them my assistance a few weeks back but that must have been before they purchased this one. Has she a name?"

"Not to my knowledge."

He bought her a cardant. Lystra blinked, quite unable to turn away from him, from the king who had shown her such kindness. "I'll call her Tiniah." One of endurance. She stepped closer, standing before him, and bowed her head. "Elerek . . . *thank you.*"

Crimson blossomed on his face. "You . . . you're welcome." He cleared his throat, his hands moving to the rims of his chair's wheels. "I must speak with Norbah about what we discussed last night. When you're ready, I'll be waiting . . . in the council chambers." Then he wheeled away, the scribe following close behind.

Lystra watched him go, marveling that this was the same man she'd met at the pyre. No, now she imagined him as she'd seen him last night, lying with his eyes softly closed, his chest rising and falling with even breaths.

Elerek had endured the curse, the deaths of so many friends, and had taken upon himself the task of saving Instanolde. She marveled at his tenacity—the tenacity that he had *chosen.*

Behind her, Razhar laughed. "Congratulations, Your Highness, I've never seen El so off-kilter. I do believe he's going well out of his way to please you."

Now her face took its turn, growing warm with a heat not from the sun. "That's quite unnecessary." Their duty belonged to their kingdom. Elerek had been right; they complemented each other better as allies than enemies.

Coming up alongside her, Razhar folded his arms. "Aw, let him. It's rather endearing." The mirth faded from his lips. "It's quite an obligation, pulling him out of his dark moods. I do believe you might do him some good."

Elerek isn't the only one who's seen the darkness. It loomed upon all their horizons, like a gathering storm. Yet in a matter of hours, Lystra had glimpsed a thin stripe of silver lining.

Razhar shuffled on his feet, stirring up small clouds of dust. "Your Highness, uh, about the other night." His dark complexion flushed. "My recklessness may have landed me in a bit of trouble."

"There was no harm done." Lystra waved her hand. "It was only a dance."

"For which I hope I need not apologize." A sly expression lifted his features, quite like a child attempting to talk his way out of a petty crime. "Really, I had no idea that I might be dancing with the queen of Instanolde."

"At the time, I was nothing more than a friendly dancer."

"A wonderful dancer." Razhar chuckled, adjusting his lopsided turban. "An impressive feat for a queen."

Something contagious hung in the air surrounding Razhar, like sunlight streaming through a latticed window. His smile ebbed warmth. His eyes danced with life. His optimism spoke of hope, a hope none of them felt but craved with their whole souls. No wonder everyone here seemed so taken with him— perhaps *too* taken, even if his games of flattery verged on the flirtatious, much like his dancing.

I'd best keep him in line. Turning to face him, Lystra lifted her chin, aloof and astute. "I trust that I'll have no reason to worry in the future?"

His head bobbed in a quick bow. "Of course not, Your Highness."

Satisfied, she huffed. "Good. Now, I want to make an inquiry. You seem to know His Highness better than anyone."

"A compliment of the highest order." Razhar grinned.

Then, he was useful. Lystra folded her arms. "Tell me, what has been done by way of breaking his curse?"

All at once, the light fled Razhar's face. The dancer from the marketplace vanished, replaced by a man who looked as if he'd just heard the impossible.

But it couldn't be. All curses could be broken—couldn't they? "I want—if I can—to free him."

The impossible had thrust them together, the responsibility of the throne, the fight for Instanolde, and forging a future in a world where death lay in wait and they wore grief like a well-worn tunic. She vowed to preserve life—and that included Elerek, a man cursed to drown along with his thirty cursed companions.

The thought filled her with purpose, with a hope that flowed like a stream through the desert canyons, a miracle in and of itself. A strange and impossible hope.

"Your Highness." A breath of a whisper riding the wind. "Do you know what you are asking?"

Lystra's fingers stroked the curve of her forearm, as if warding away a chill that hadn't quite manifested. How had asking for a life marked for death to be spared become such a monumental thing?

Razhar heaved a long sigh. "Curses can only be broken beneath strict statutes, usually by ridiculous provisions put forth by the curse binder or at the cost of the curse binder, or their family's blood. His father, King Lorkin, spent years hunting curse binders and never found the one who cursed El. What makes you think we've a chance now?"

Nothing. Nothing at all. Only the hope of a candle burning in the night. Lystra gritted her teeth. "He deserves a chance, doesn't he?" She met his gaze. "Will you help me?"

A shadow hung on Razhar's brow, the creation of a complete eclipse over the jovial ray of optimism he portrayed moments ago. Still, he gave a grim nod. "I'm afraid I can't share your hope for a happy ending, Torra. But yes, in this, I'm at your disposal."

Lystra replied with a smile.

And then what? Some dark, cynical portion of her mind

inquired. It reeked of Grandmother. If Elerek did live, he would remain king, a husband not of her own choosing. Till death parted them, their marriage stood.

But Lystra wouldn't be dissuaded. Not now, with her heart set aflame. If they made it that far, they would have overcome much. Perhaps it would be enough.

Be careful. This time, Grandmother's warnings held merit. If she couldn't break the curse, then Elerek would die, and she would mourn a king a second time. No, her heart needed walls, ramparts within which to hide, no matter how dire the siege.

Chapter 27

Elerek

By the time Elerek caught up with Norbah, his lungs strained for breath and his arms burned. The general had swiftly set to work, delegating tasks to his soldiers and mandates regarding the city militia in the organization of refugees. And he never stopped moving.

"For a moment there, I wondered if you'd send me searching for you all over the palace." Elerek parked his chair at the edge of one of the palace's many courtyards. Beyond the double lobed arch, edged in scarlet tiles, lay the guardkeep where the palace guard took residence.

Norbah offered him a small smile. "My apologies, Your Highness. One doesn't know what the day will bring. Best to work before the sun sets to scorching."

Indeed, the temperatures were already rising. Elerek pitied the soldiers who would be forced to train during the heat of the day. "Do you think it will work? Fortifying the city for a siege?"

Stepping closer, the general's cascading orange cape flowed with his movements, followed by the *clink* of his armor. He stood over Elerek, but not in a demeaning way, rather, his shadow promised safety. "Doubting ourselves, are we? El, you're brilliant and this kingdom knows no scholar your equal. Nothing in war is predictable. We've got the resources we have, and we can only do our best with them."

Despite his soft words, an edge emerged, one Elerek's heart quickly barricaded itself against. Cormek had said something similar once. Upon his coronation, his brother had all but begged Elerek to become his chief advisor. Elerek refused, the wound of his lost title still raw and bleeding. Cormek had considered *him* a resource, and a valuable one.

What sort of world might they have created if they could've built it together—as brothers?

"I hope you didn't find me just for reassurance." Norbah set his gloved hand on the hilt of his scimitar, a soldier set on alert. "Surely you have more plans cooking in that mind of yours?"

Elerek leaned back in his chair. "I do. If we are to fall under siege, the Jarkins will come from the desert. We ought to expect them as soon as high summer ends. We must fortify the walls as best we can. Build extra fortifications. Strengthen the stonework. Dig a trench if we must. Defend the outer wall."

The general nodded thoughtfully. "The east side of the city. Let the river defend the west?"

"An army trekking across the desert has no boats nor access to the river." The Gungole had always been their source of life, the reason their civilization had survived this long at the edge of the terrible Sancen. Elerek saw no reason for that truth to fail now. "But yes, our focus must stay on the east city. Most of that sector is markets and businesses, easier to relocate and defend with soldiers."

"The wall is the key part." Norbah huffed. "And the season's doing us no favors. Labor will be slow, difficult, and dangerous. We need to save our men for combat, but I agree with you about fortifying the walls. I'll contact the stonemasons and see if we can still quarry stone."

"The quarries are upriver. Stones are sent on barges." Connecting the pieces, like stars in a constellation, excited Elerek. A puzzle for his mind to decipher. If the situation weren't so dire, and the threat to his kingdom so immense, he might have found the task utterly enjoyable. "We keep the river open, as a means of escape and transport."

Norbah narrowed his eyes. "And on the chance that Kushan changes their minds."

They wouldn't. Elerek scowled and made no comment on the fact. "Whatever we can do must be done. As the refugees pour in, make sure every able-bodied man has the chance to enlist. We need as many soldiers as we can muster. I especially want a large regiment of those willing to learn, set apart from drills in order to be taught archery."

"Bowmen," Norbah said thoughtfully. "Instanolde hasn't possessed such a regiment in likely decades."

Kushan had filled that void quite nicely, their soldiers untouchable in the skies. Elerek wondered if they knew what a gap they'd left in Instanolde's defenses by refusing him fealty. Did they intend to punish him, recompense for the sins of his father?

The tragedy of it was that the punishment was justly deserved. Lorkin paid for his conquests with the blood of Kushites, summoning their warriors to fight in wars that didn't need to be waged. Lorkin had ascended to the throne on blood and kept it by blood.

But it would soon be over, Elerek thought morosely. When the curse took him, House Karim would be ended, the curse's intentions carried out.

"Yes, if we are going to survive this siege, we need our walls not only defensible but also able to serve on the offense. As many archers as we have time to train, we must do so."

Doubt clouded Norbah's face. "Training archers is simple. It's procuring the bows themselves that will prove difficult, particularly Kushite-made ones."

But the task was not impossible. Elerek thought of his own bow, its sleek wood carved in the canyonlands themselves. On one of his rare visits to his homeland, Razhar had brought it back for him as a gift. "Surely over the years some may have come downriver by way of trade or purchase. Meanwhile, we can make do with what we can manufacture."

"Indeed." Norbah exhaled, his great shoulders dropping. "Now, El, on the subject of training these archers. We've few men equipped for such a thing, and my time is already stretched thin. If it can be managed, I propose that you train this regiment."

Elerek raised his eyebrows, already the protests crowding his throat. "Me? But—"

"Stars, El. You're one of the best marksmen I've ever seen. Teach them the slingshot too, while you're at it. We already know you've the best aim in all of Instanolde." Norbah cracked a grin. "Must I remind you of the time you won that slingshot competition?"

Ah yes, the one that his father had forbidden him from entering. He'd been hardly fourteen. Why was the contest forbidden? Well, in Lorkin's skewed perspective, because he knew that Elerek would win, and that meant that Cormek would lose. Such a thing simply couldn't happen, not when his second son was declared as his heir and his firstborn was cursed.

Lifting his gaze, Elerek met Norbah's eyes. Despite the man's great height, his strength, and military prowess, his eyes were soft and kind. Elerek never needed Lorkin, the man who'd earned the curse's wrath and whose son carried its weight, but he did need Norbah, a man who taught him kindness, compassion, and archery.

"Won't it seem strange, if *I* teach them?" Elerek shrugged. "I don't exactly look like a soldier, now do I?"

Norbah shook his head. "That hardly matters, El. You said any man who is able. You're quite able and more than capable of leading a regiment of archers to defend our city walls." He stepped closer, giving his shoulder a slap of camaraderie. "You are their king, after all."

He used his hand that wasn't gloved, the one that didn't bear the curse mark. As always, the touch of another human being sent a jolt straight to his heart, the constant fear of being touched. Even among the cursed, it seemed that initial, primal fear would never go away.

"While we're on the subject, there's another draft you might consider."

"Yes?" Elerek folded his arms.

The general's eyes evaded his, staring off through the open arch, the summer sunlight catching in his gaze. "A sore spot, to be sure, but our soldiers also need cardants. Trained cardants. Ones that give our soldiers an advantage."

Elerek's heart dropped straight down to his shoes. Norbah was right, of course. No one would argue that the fearsome reptiles didn't make formidable mounts for warriors and nothing beneath the scorching sun could match their speed.

Speed. Yes, that was the key. "Most of the city's cardants are in the hands of the racing committee. We'll have to go to them." All the great houses. Old names and older money. The same that had come to either swear fealty to him or spurn his name. And after what had happened at Darcress, he doubted they would prove accommodating, even in the face of disaster.

Stars, was he doomed to spend this one summer to live trying to *explain* to everyone that their destruction was imminent?

"They won't be pleased about it."

"Agreed." Norbah huffed. "What about your queen? Surely her influence may win them over?"

The opposite, but Elerek wasn't about to tell his general that. Lystra would despise this idea. In fact, it may break her heart, and that was something he couldn't bear.

"I'll discuss it with her." But not now, not after his triumphant gifting of that reptilian monster. He never expected that she'd simply vault over the rail, into that pen, and approach the cardant, but she had. Unarmed, small and lithe, just a girl with enough courage to stop a nightmare in its tracks. Even now, Elerek found his heart beating wildly.

"Ah, speaking of your queen." Norbah's jovial nature returned, bringing with it a grin that looked as if it had been borrowed from Razhar's cheeky mannerisms. "You two seem to be getting along."

"And if we are?" The words tumbled out of his mouth before he could even think to stop them. Elerek's shoulders grew rigid, planted against the back of his chair.

She was his heir, the sun meant to rise out of his night. A queen to protect his kingdom. The glorious future he hoped that others would live to see—because he would not.

I should know better. He'd fallen once before, given his affections to a girl. That should have been all the lesson he needed. Breaking Myra's heart was bad enough; he couldn't break Lystra's too—or his own, for that matter.

Norbah blinked with a scowl. "That's good, El. You two need to work together, else we're doomed before the Jarkins have even besieged us."

"Yes, yes, you're right." Elerek cleared his throat and rolled his chair backwards. He wanted out of this conversation, lest Norbah get any ideas from his strange behavior. "I'm supposed to meet her—for the council."

"Right, right." If Norbah suspected, he made no indication of it. "Well, lead the way."

Chapter 28

Lystra

Lystra sighed with relief as a scribe finally opened a window. The first day of her rule proved the hottest yet and the crowded, noisy council room left little room to breathe. Scribes, advisors, and soldiers buzzed along the long table like bees. Parchments covered its top, bearing everything from crop reports to city maps. Any possible location to house the influx of refugees and defense locations to stage soldiers took preeminence, marked with tiny stone figures.

She pulled her hair over her shoulder, tying off the thick braid she'd woven. Twisting it up over her head like a tiara, she pinned it in place, relieved to have it off her neck. Before her, a scroll lay open, half filled with script.

One summer to live. Wasn't that what Elerek had said last night? Lystra dipped her quill back in the inkwell and returned to the address. She would stand before her people to deliver the blow as the queen who had witnessed the Jarkins' ambush first-hand. The survivor who returned to save them. It was all so . . . fragile.

A world that hinged upon a careful set of balances. As the

spice merchants carefully weighed their wares on their tiny bronze scales, their life in the desert carefully weighed their civilization. One tip, and everything could topple.

Disinterested in the soldiers' talk and the advisors' complaints about housing, Lystra's gaze strayed back to the open window as she yearned for a gust of fresh air to touch her skin. If only someone would send for tea.

The window lay directly behind Elerek and, more than once, his gaze had found hers.

I'm not staring. At least she could blame the flush in her cheeks on the heat of the room. She wondered if he knew the happiness his gift had brought her.

She hadn't changed from her tunic and dusty boots, a promise to herself that she'd return to the stables and her glorious new cardant. Nothing could replace what she'd lost, but she loved the reptiles enough to try again, to rebuild her stable, and to let herself be happy doing it.

As for Cormek, nothing would fill the void his presence had left behind. She would live the rest of her days with a gaping hole in her heart.

A guard entered. He bowed, his orange cape billowing. "Your Highnesses, the noble houses, as requested."

Lystra sat a little straighter and rolled up the scroll. More than an hour ago, the decision had been made to assemble as many of the heads of the houses as possible. Most owned land and sprawling estates with room to spare for refugees.

Elerek's features grew stern. "Thank you, send them in."

As if the room weren't crowded enough, eight more persons were added to the number. They remained standing, facing the table with solemn expressions. Lystra rose to her feet, bestowing gracious nods on each in turn. House Quilam. House Yissal. House Pana.

And House Arghan. Dalmah stood in elegant black silk

and glittered with jewelry. Her eyes made quick work of the room, surveying the scene like a general taking stock of her army.

When her eyes fell on Lystra's, they turned dark and bitter, like strong coffee.

Lystra swallowed. No doubt every loose hair, the dust on her tunic, and every bit of clay caked to her boots stood out. Lystra half expected Dalmah to lash out in front of everyone, rebuking her for her lack of decorum. Well, if royal robes and jewels were a statement, why couldn't her riding clothes be one too?

But in a flash, the strike of a lightning bolt, her storm dissolved. Dalmah crossed the room and threw her arms open wide, her sleeves draping gracefully, and pulled Lystra into an embrace. "Dearest granddaughter."

Lystra stiffened in her grandmother's arms. When had she last received any hint of warmth or familial affection from her grandmother? Why now?

Lystra steeled her jaw. Because she had an audience.

When Dalmah released her, their gazes held. The council room faded away. If Lystra closed her eyes, she could almost envision her grandmother's dark chambers, sitting with her spine straight upon her pupil's cushion enduring lessons in diplomacy. Perhaps this was all only a scenario in Dalmah's playbook. A chance for Lystra's every word and action to fall beneath her scrutiny and critique. Maybe the nobles, the soldiers, the king himself, were only puppets held by her strings.

No. Lystra drew a deep breath and looked away. She'd been anointed and crowned. Dalmah hadn't any control over Lystra here.

Her grandmother didn't stand with the rest of the nobles, lingering at Lystra's side.

"Is this it?" Her breath was hot on Lystra's neck. "Your boy king is to acknowledge the gravity of the situation?"

Slowly drawing her hands into fists, Lystra didn't reply. They hadn't even yet been crowned for a single day. Still, she knew that nothing would be enough. Not for Grandmother.

"Welcome, I appreciate your responding to my summons." Elerek shifted in his chair, his fingers restlessly tapping on his chair's armrest. "Especially with such short notice."

Lystra performed a quick survey of the nobles. Less than half had sworn fealty to Elerek, and now, they stood like towers, staring down at him with burning eyes.

She drew away from Dalmah, softly gliding to stand beside the king's chair.

Elerek's hands closed, silencing the sound of his nails on wood. His overview of their plan was brief, but succinct, ending with a formal request for the cooperation of the noble houses. His words were strict, severe, and blunt, lacking the finesse and grace which came so naturally to Lystra, but she saw this not as weakness. No, this was opportunity, a chance to let their combined skills shine like a gemstone in a skilled jeweler's hand.

"For how long?" a noble of House Yissal demanded.

Elerek's voice hardened. "Until the threat of Jarkin invasion is past."

"High summer's end?" another countered.

"Ah." The word spilled from Dalmah's velvet lips like warm milk. "Have we come to it at last? The unspoken? Is indeed Darcress under Jarkin occupation?"

The nobles exchanged nervous glances.

Lystra no longer felt the scourge of summer's intensity. Instead, she felt as if she'd been submerged in ice. The houses had been contemplating this, the great unspoken horror.

Dalmah again cast her words over Lystra's shoulder.

"Surely it wasn't your intention to keep your people in the dark? I thought I taught you better."

Lystra's thoughts turned to the dagger, safe in Elerek's chamber. Her grandmother's teachings had sunk deep, deeper than the unnamed slots and canyons of the Sancen where even cardants dared not venture. Dalmah's hold on her nearly had her commit a treacherous murder out of fear and ignorance. She wouldn't sway her. Not again.

"Darcress was meant to be impregnable," one of the nobles grunted. "Without it, we won't last. Instanolde has been sentenced to death."

"We ought to flee while we still can."

Elerek leaned forward, laying his hands on the table. "As ever, the safety of Instanolde and the preservation of its people remain our highest priority. Though Darcress has been lost to us, hope has not."

Too little too late. Lystra could see on their faces that the damage was done. Everything began to unravel. The seeds Dalmah planted took sprout and grew.

"We will not panic. We will not fear. It isn't over yet." Elerek turned his gaze toward Norbah, his face set with an iron-clad determination. "My general and I have already decided upon a plan of action. If we stand committed to her survival, we *can* defend Instanolde."

A shiver crept up Lystra's spine, prompted by the strength girding his voice. As for their spectators, doubt lingered on their faces, like the long shadows cast by the mountains, obscuring the last of the light. Something ignited within her, the fierce determination to uphold this display of strength, to convince them.

Sweeping into the circle, she made a slow orbit around the table, looking each noble in the eye.

"As you know, I was there, in the desert." She spoke firm

but allowed a hint of sorrow to soften the edges of her words. "When Cormek and so many loyal, courageous hearts lost their lives. Survival is our story. We have mastered the Gungole, the Kushan rein in the winds, and we have made peace with the Sancen. Our knowledge would declare it folly to wage an attack on summer's doorstep and yet that is exactly what the Jarkins have done. I believe that they wanted us to have this summer, to wallow in our fear, and wait with trembling hearts for the end to come." She narrowed her eyes. "Shall we so easily play into their hands?"

The tension fled the air. Unspoken protests retreated to the shadows. A smile curled onto Dalmah's face, but Lystra decided instead to look into the blazing eyes of the king—her king. The man who had faced and fought death each and every day of his life.

Well, he would no longer fight alone. His fight had become Instanolde's and she believed the impossible. That, together, they might just win.

Chapter 29

Elerek

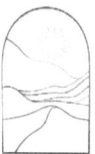

E lerek had to look away, the fire of accomplishment in Lystra's eyes enough to scorch. He hardly listened as the houses pledged their aid to the cause. Norbah gave a formal call for a draft of able soldiers and then the council adjourned.

Sitting here, face-to-face with the houses, some of whom had already spurned his rule—his birthright—he felt as crippled as they saw him. Despite his confidence in the plans that he and his queen had made, he feared that his every word sounded immature, like a child crying for help.

Nothing like Cormek.

Cormek could command a room with all the flair of power, grace, and just a hint of flamboyance. His voice carried authority as if it were made of clouds. His every asset—his physical prowess, winning smile, towering figure—all contributed to his success, whether amassing followers or securing the most beautiful girl in Instanolde on his arm. Except, that girl was now Elerek's wife, and her impressive speech had done its work, inspiring the council of nobles.

Stop it. Elerek exhaled, attempting to dispel the bitter, noxious thoughts amassing in his head. These thoughts were just that, thoughts. That didn't mean they were real, or accurate. He *knew* his plans were sound, his ability sufficient, and that would have to be enough.

His gaze returned to Lystra as she rolled the parchment that contained her address, the movement of her fingers soft and delicate. The light from the open window caught in the loose strands of hair that had escaped the careful work of the braid she wore like a crown, turning them to molten gold. He wondered if she'd noticed his confidence, and if she would call it strength.

The bold queen who returned from the Sancen to stand at the pyre of her beloved. Now, she'd risen like a phoenix from the ashes to become all that Instanolde deserved in its hour of need. He'd given only a certificate of a political marriage. Would she ever look at him—just once—as she had Cormek? Or was that merely a dream of fantastical proportions?

". . . Tomorrow morning? Your Highness?"

He blinked, returning to the world of reality. Lystra watched him with an intense expression, clutching the scroll.

The address. "Um, yes. You will deliver it at dawn."

She gave a satisfied nod.

"Granddaughter." The countess of House Arghan swept to Lystra's side, laying a claw-like hand on her shoulder and hovering like some desert vulture. "Well done. I'm glad to see that not all my training fell on deaf ears."

Elerek blinked. So quick, so subtle, he'd almost missed it.

Lystra, the queen of the shifting sands of the Sancen, *flinched.*

Leaning back in his chair, he studied the pair, the two Arghan queens. Lystra had broken in his presence before, suffocating beneath her grief and the rawness of her pain, but never out of fear. What hold could the countess have on her?

"You will inform the kingdom of your decisions?" The countess's lips tightened. "I trust that they will hear it from *you*. Yours is a voice the people will heed."

Hmph. Elerek began to tap his fingers on his chair's armrest. Whispers of the manipulations Lystra had mentioned wormed their way back into his mind. Could she have meant her grandmother?

The queen his own tyrannical father had forced off the throne . . .

He wheeled his chair closer, circling the table.

"Yes, Grandmother." Lystra's hands tightened on the roll of parchments.

"Do let me glimpse your proclamation, make sure that all is in order?" Dalmah reached for the parchment. "You are very new at this."

You old viper . . . Fury simmering in his skin, Elerek cleared his throat. "The houses will hear it from her, as they should."

Lystra's eyes went wide, staring at him in astonishment.

He spoke loud enough for his voice to travel. "They've already become accustomed to her voice, and there is no one better than the queen who has crossed the desert herself."

The countess lifted her head, her hand freezing in its reach. Her eyes, cold as the steel of a blade, fell upon him. Elerek scowled, leaving no doubt in his mind about the countess's hold on her granddaughter. Did this woman truly believe she could influence the throne—through Lystra?

And what of the dagger? The footsteps of his queen moving in the dead of night armed with a blade? Had Dalmah of House Arghan proposed this? His death?

"Indeed." Dalmah's voice clipped with ice.

With one last aloof look at her granddaughter, the countess glided from the room.

A slight shudder quivered in Lystra's shoulders and then, like a blossom after the short-lived spring rains, she reverted into her regal posture.

Elerek frowned. No, he couldn't jump to conclusions. The countess might be a bitter old snake, but that didn't mean she was planning to murder a king. Particularly one that she'd arranged for her granddaughter to marry. The picture didn't add up. "Are you all right?"

Lystra pushed a stray lock behind her ear and nodded. She didn't look at him.

Elerek leaned forward. Before his very eyes, Lystra transformed. The queen who stepped into the pen of a wild cardant vanished. Now she looked as cornered as the reptile. "Your grandmother, she—"

"—Is of no consequence," Lystra snapped.

If possible, the room grew hotter. Slowly, Elerek backed his chair away from the table. Behind him, Norbah spoke to the courtiers of training new soldiers and setting up patrols.

Lystra dropped her shoulders in an exhale. "I apologize." Somehow, even as the words slipped from her lips, the queen returned. Whatever coils the countess held on Lystra loosened and slithered away. "Thank you . . . for standing up for me."

She was real. Flesh and blood alive as anything. The only mask she wore was the fear, a suit of armor to protect herself from her grandmother. Elerek vowed that the woman wouldn't enter their palace again. "You're welcome. Thank you for your speech to the houses. Our survival may depend on such boldness."

Her lips smiled, and her eyes brightened in the glittering afternoon light.

Elerek arrived early to the courtyard where the wedding feast would take place. His gaze swept the pergolas, draped with blooming evells and surrounded by ponds populated by graceful fish and lilies. A handful of servants worked to stage the space with low tables and cushions tasseled in gold, preparing for a celebration at which they would be the guests.

There. Elerek made a wide orbit of the waterways. As the sun sank, leaving the western sky streaked with orange, torches and lamps were lit and Myra swept from one circle of light to the next, like a *pari* nymph from the old tales, dusting a bit of mineral powder upon the flames, turning each tongue a pale blue.

Elerek cleared his throat.

She looked over her shoulder. He knew from her eyes that she had been smiling, perhaps laughing with her companions. But when she saw him, her face grew as pale and sober as the stone pillars of the pergolas.

And on her arm, the curse mark continued to spread across her skin.

Starkindler, please. A soft breeze kicked up from the desert, finding its path through windows and open corridors and whistled with a sound as lonely as the cries in his heart. He didn't want to watch the curse take anyone else.

But the ways of the curse didn't belong to the Starkindler, nor was he to blame for the mark of death upon Myra.

"I need to speak with you." Elerek folded his arms, his limbs numb from the lingering deadness of the curse. He drew his thoughts away from the guilt, the self-loathing, remembering that he came to deliver rebuke.

Myra handed the tin of mineral powder off to one of her companions and stepped closer.

"What were you thinking?" He spoke through clenched teeth, every muscle set on edge.

Shame bloomed like the most delicate of rose petals upon her cheeks, as red as the kaftan she had worn to his chambers last night.

"It wasn't my intention to embarrass you." She spoke softly. "I just . . . you *wed*, and I couldn't bear the thought of you . . ."

Me—and Lystra. He leaned forward. "Myra, you know that's impossible."

"Is it?" She brushed a bit of the powder from the back of her hand, sending a small blue cloud into the shadows. "Your queen would be a fool not to see what I see in you." Her eyes flashed. "No one believes her foolish in the least. No one in all of Instanolde."

Elerek closed his eyes, his lungs expanding. The image of Lystra leaping without hesitation into the cardant's pen filled his mind. She didn't fear the reptile's sharp teeth, clawed limbs, or the thought of being trampled. This queen had already survived the impossible, the attack of the Jarkins amidst the Sancen's desolation. And she would continue to survive, to see Instanolde through this night and into the dawn.

"The queen would indeed be foolish," he replied. "Considering her understanding of the curse."

Myra tilted her head to one side, the rebuke that Elerek had come to deliver turned back threefold upon him. "El . . . consider to whom you speak. Would you call me foolish?"

Stars. Elerek looked away, air hissing through his teeth. This wasn't what he'd come to discuss. "What's done is done. I cannot turn back time any more than I can hold back the curse or halt the constellations in their dance."

Tears gathered in the corners of her eyes, tiny diamonds filled with stars. "I ask not for time undone, El. You know that."

The softness of her voice broke him, the same softness that whispered in his ear beneath the fall of darkness. "Then let me do the asking. Do you understand, Myra? What I've done? What I'm doing? I need to save Instanolde." He looked at her. "And that means I need to save Lystra."

Myra blinked, releasing the tears to run freely down her face. Her fingers reached for her scarf, adjusting it about her shoulders, veiling the curse mark. "You've changed, El."

"I had to." Had this really come as such a surprise? "My brother died. The Jarkins attacked. I became king."

She bowed her head, the shadows claiming her gaze. "Perhaps this was the way things were meant to be—and perhaps you will become a better man for it."

I'm cursed. There was no breaking it, no one striving to save him. No sunrise awaited him, and even the stars seemed dark amid his endless night. "I have only this breath in my lungs. That is all."

Myra drew a shuddered breath, her entire frame trembling with it. Pushing her hair back from her face, she turned away. "The feast is beginning. We should enjoy it. All of us, together."

Elerek nodded. Behind them, their cursed family began to gather, summoned by the loud commands of Bushra as she orchestrated plates of food to be arranged upon the tables. Laughter rang through the air, clear as tambourines.

"Yes," he whispered. "Together."

Chapter 30

Elerek

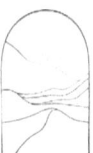

E ven after Elerek entered the circle, surrounded by the merry voices of his friends, sorrow still burdened his shoulders. He watched as Myra faded into the assembly; another face bathed in the sapphire torchlight like a star burning against the blackness. A story that had ended, the last chapter read. Its words lingered, a sorrow in his mind, but there was no more.

He turned his attention to the feast, drinking in its every detail.

They all wore their finest, exquisite silks and colors vibrant enough to complement even Razhar's wildest attire. They stood about the table, sharing jokes over goblets of mint tea and rich wines.

Elerek backed his chair away from the table as Bushra and a young stable lad named Fin approached, several platters of baklava between them.

Bushra surveyed the table, a smile on her lips, and then looked at him. "The queen *is* coming, isn't she?"

"She gave her word." Elerek blinked at the table, the sharp

scent of spices enough to make him dizzy with hunger. Great clay bowls were heated and filled with simmering tagine and flanked with baskets of karahz topped with garlic. "I believe you went overboard."

"Nonsense," the baker said with a sniff. She adjusted a garland of greenery surrounding a platter of roast chicken topped with toasted almonds. "We wanted everything to be perfect."

"And quite the sight it is! Most impressive." Razhar's voice rang through the courtyard.

Hearty cheers and raised goblets welcomed Razhar into the circle. He laughed and smiled, at ease as he slipped through the assembly, beckoning greetings and taunts to his friends and conspirators.

Elerek watched as Ishtal filled a goblet with wine and handed it to Razhar, their fingers avoiding one another. Razhar held no fear of the curse, but then again, Razhar feared nothing.

Could it be that they'd really been so careful? All these years? The Kushite orphan who dwelt in the palace without a care in the world who found his friends among the cursed. Not one stray nudge or bump?

Elerek narrowed his eyes. Their companionship ought to be dangerous, a teeter along the edge of a cliff. But he couldn't get along without Razhar. And strangely enough, it didn't feel like a risk. A laughable thought, but perhaps Razhar really was as invincible as he believed himself to be.

"All right, El?" Razhar sauntered beside his chair, the torchlight dancing in his eyes.

"Mm, yes." Elerek forced a small smile. The expression always made his face feel odd. "Long day."

Razhar wrinkled his nose. "I suppose they're all to be long now, yes? And I don't mean because it's summer."

Elerek shook his head. "I'm glad you're here, Razhar."

"Me too." He hid his smile behind his goblet as he took a sip.

"Now, don't laugh at me, but—"

"Nonsense, El. You're always worth laughing at."

Stars, someday I may punch you. Elerek tilted his head back to glare at him. "Shut up a moment, will you? Now, I know we've arranged that you'll watch over the queen tonight, but please, watch over yourself too—with the curse."

Razhar waved him off. "Don't worry about me, El."

"I will if I want to." Elerek lowered his voice. "I don't think I could stand it if you were also cursed."

Staring into his wine, Razhar stirred the glass a bit. For a moment, it looked as if he wanted to speak, but didn't. But then, something else caught his attention. "Oh, stars above."

As Elerek followed his gaze, the assembly grew silent. Reverent.

The queen had arrived.

Each torch sparking with blue powder seemed to pay homage to her. Lystra wore a striking kaftan of a blue the color of the deepest desert sky. Gold adorned the collar, the belt, and spread like wings across her shoulders. Her hair, loose and long, cascaded behind her.

Once again, Elerek remembered keenly why his brother loved her, why the kingdom had called her *Malikaa*. And here she came as the exalted queen of Instanolde to share a feast with those doomed to die.

"Welcome, Your Highness," Elerek said as the members of his cursed tribe all bowed.

A smile spread across Lystra's face with a radiance all its own. "Thank you. I am honored to be a guest among you."

The cursed still living. The dying still breathing. Heavy thoughts weighed in his mind, but somehow, Elerek felt as if his soul had been given wings, Lystra's smile disarming his every doubt. She would see them not as the cursed, but as people—her people.

Elerek signaled Razhar with his eyes. His friend immediately lowered his goblet and fell in step beside the queen.

"I'm to be your escort tonight." He offered her his arm.

"Of course." Another gracious smile appeared on her lips as she surveyed the crowd. "You can assist me with names. And if it pleases His Highness, I would enjoy it if we forgo all formalities."

Elerek didn't hold back the smile forced from his own face. "I think, Lystra, we can manage that. I doubt anyone here could suffer a formal feast anyways."

As one, the assembly seemed to relax, again filling their goblets and speaking in cordial tones about the table. Somewhere, someone took an oud and began to strum, a soft, pleasant melody.

"Ah, but I can do more than recite names." Razhar's voice took on a whimsical feel, like a storyteller in the market. "I can tell you who is the best player at *chemis*, who is the worst dancer, and who owes me money." He gave an exaggerated cough. "Actually, Cole there fits all three of those."

Cole sent a nasty expression in Razhar's direction. "It's because I'm the best at *chemis* that *you* owe me, Razhar."

A chorus of laughter followed.

"Now come! Everything is ready," Bushra announced, removing the lid from a large, rounded dish of bastille, smelling of orange blossoms and saffron. "El, will you see to the blessing?"

Elerek wheeled his chair just to the left of the only couch in the circle, reserved for Lystra and Razhar to sit slightly distanced from the closely clustered cushions.

He waited till everyone had seated themselves. Lystra perched on the edge of the couch, a bird with blue silk feathers. Then, he bowed his head and gave a short blessing, thanking the Starkindler for the nourishment of both sustenance and company.

As the blessing concluded, the gathering lifted their eyes and began to partake. Elerek surveyed the opulent table, feeling almost guilty for having even agreed to this feast. Food may become scarce, with the overabundance of people crowding the city and trade with the river lodged in such a precarious position.

Yet he wondered if he'd have another chance like this, to gather and enjoy the company of the people he'd come to love? Before the bitter end, drowned in sorrow and curses?

Dishes were passed and plates filled. Razhar doted on Lystra, offering her the best of each plate and never letting her touch even a serving spoon. At first, Elerek kept an eye on his friend, but soon enough, Razhar's attention to detail put him at ease.

"Now, please." Lystra glanced about the circle once the passing of dishes had slowed. "I would love to hear each of your names, and tell me your position at the palace. Driss." She looked to the scribe. "You assisted us in the council this morning."

"Yes, Your Highness. I scribed for a moneylender before being brought to the palace."

Pride burned warm in Elerek's chest. The voices that gave answer were not forgotten. Many had forsaken lives and family, but here, among the cursed, they had found a home. Companions with whom to savor the last days of lives cut short. The best penance he could offer.

"My name is Myra. I've served many roles, mostly as a handmaiden, though of late, I've done an extraordinary amount of baking." She didn't look at Lystra, instead casting a sideways glance at Bushra at the mention of baking.

The older woman smiled. "It seems an era of baking. I've heard no complaints."

"Hear, hear!" Razhar cheered, raising his wine.

Recognition flashed across Lystra's face, followed by a brief shadow. Fleeting as it was, Elerek saw it. A lump rose in his throat that no amount of sweetened mint tea could wash down. He wondered what Lystra would say, if he told her everything?

Elerek took another sip of his wine. It didn't matter. Their relationship had ended. Myra was his past. He'd taken vows, swearing his faithfulness to Lystra, to his queen. That was enough—wasn't it?

But Lystra also wasn't stupid—and Myra had just declared herself a handmaiden in a household without royal ladies the very night after she'd arrived unannounced in their chambers. If she suspected, would that drive a rift between them? As he'd explained to Myra, any and all entanglements with his queen were impossible. Forbidden. Stars, he wished Myra had kept her mouth shut.

"Your Highness, tell us about the cardant races. Have you ridden in them?" Fin's eager questions brought about a welcome distraction. As one, the whole assembly turned to Lystra with expectant gazes.

"I have." Lystra's smile returned. "Though I now spend my time overseeing and training a team of riders."

"Do you think anyone can do it?" Fin pressed, his eyes large and boyish.

"With time." Lystra's face glowed with a light that could only be lit by passion. "It requires a foolproof bond between rider and reptile. Cardants know the desert, rock and sand, but must learn to trust their rider. Likewise, a rider must make wise choices of terrain and know what his reptile is capable of without risk. They are one and the same, bent on a single goal."

Elerek imagined Instanolde, golden and glorious. Desert sands before and deep blue sky behind. A kingdom locked in a race of its own, a race against time. He looked at Lystra. She continued to speak, telling stories of endurance and bravery, but her eyes had turned to his.

Bent on a single goal.

"What of the cardant in the stables?" Fin inquired. "Isn't she something?"

"Oh, she is." Elation brightened Lystra's face. "I've named her Tiniah. She's no racer, not yet. But I know that she can be."

The conversation about cardants continued, with Lystra's expertise right at the center. Elerek refilled his wineglass and leaned back in his chair, content to listen. The light in her eyes was enthralling, captivating. Memories of the day Cormek rode out to Darcress returned to his mind—of Lystra sweeping into the courtyard atop her steed, graceful in her skill, elegant in her confidence.

Elerek lowered his gaze. Grief hung like silken shrouds about the recesses of his soul. It took so little to pull them across, to veil the world in misery. He wished he could've stopped them, kept them both safe in Instanolde. He wished that Cormek was here.

Had his brother ever attended a feast among the cursed? No, but then again, Elerek had never invited him. The thought pierced his heart.

"El." Ishtal, big and brazen, appeared beside him. "You've chosen well." He nodded toward Lystra, still animatedly talking of cardants and races.

Elerek nodded, pushing aside his grim thoughts. The stone-mason was known for being gruff and coarse, and typically didn't lend advice.

"It wouldn't kill you to be happy. I know your plan, leaving her the kingdom and all, but really, it can't hurt to get to know her better. She might do you some good."

Elerek drew a deep breath. His little tribe would bend over backwards like acrobats in the night market if they knew they were pursuing his happiness. He wondered if they knew just how difficult it was to be happy, particularly with the future as grim as it was.

He smiled. "Yes, I think I will."

Chapter 31

Lystra

Lystra glanced over her shoulder. Starlight danced overhead and the blue light of the torches burned bright in the courtyard. From here, the gathering of soldiers, bakers, servants, and king looked like a mural. A beautiful moment awash in color and waiting to be cast in stone. Those who watched might marvel and wonder what sort of story brought such an unusual gathering together.

One of the soldiers had procured an oud and began to play. Fin, the young boy, brought a drum. The music was hardly refined but held a passion that one could feel. A song of life beneath a sky full of stars.

She'd kept a watch on the time. If she were to address the kingdom at dawn, she wanted her rest.

Besides, if she left early, she wouldn't watch the magic end.

They would go on, talking, laughing, singing, and that was how she would remember it.

Before she turned to depart, Elerek glanced her way. Their eyes met, and he smiled. She'd learned to see the distinction between his and Cormek's smile. Elerek's smile went deeper, holding a cost, and she knew a battle had been won to gift it. She returned the smile, pleased that he had deemed her worthy of it.

Even as the shadows of the palace consumed her, she could hear the echoes of laughter. Sorrow pierced her heart. Every one of those beautiful souls was going to drown from the curse.

Like Azraa, standing in the temple courtyard with transparent skin, her bones exposed. A body shifting into water to be spilled upon the desert. Her final cries for help echoed still in Lystra's ears.

She paused in the corridor, her hand braced against a pillar. The palace took on a different air at night. Everywhere she looked, she saw ghosts of the bright and the bold, remembering the dances and galas thrown by Cormek. Her beloved, gone in an instant. Now, the laughter of the cursed would join the ghosts. Grief overtook her heart, like an invading army, and she hadn't the battlements to defend it. Blinking back bitter tears, a strangled sob escaped her throat.

A moment passed. And then another. Moments that felt like sinking into darkness, smothered and oppressed until her heart fought for each frantic beat.

And then, Lystra drew herself up, breathed in deep, and kept walking. *I have to keep walking.*

She understood what Elerek meant to do. He drew back the lattice, letting her see into his world—to share a meal with the people he loved. People who didn't deserve death, who were worthy of value, of understanding.

Their fight went deeper than the struggle for Instanolde, for survival. More than a strategic battle with the Jarkins or a political one with the dynamics of their kingdom.

No, they fought for life itself.

"Please?" A whisper moved through the murky hall.

Lystra paused. The hair on her neck prickled.

"Why? Why does it matter?"

"I can help."

"It's not really helping. I no longer care whether I live or drown."

The curse. Lystra turned, hurrying toward the source of the exchange, her steps light in her satin slippers.

Rounding a corner, she identified two figures. One was small, easily able to slip through the shadows. The other knew nothing of subtly, clad in garish colors meant for the night market.

"Razhar?" Lystra's voice seemed to shout back at her, filling the emptiness.

Razhar startled as he stared at her. He wore the same stunned expression that he had in the market when he'd learned Lystra's identity—when he'd tried to kiss her.

The slight figure also turned, her eyes as hard as weathered stone. Myra.

Lystra stopped. Her thoughts concerning the dark-haired handmaiden lay disconnected, like stars without a constellation. Her brazen appearance last night seemed strange enough —stranger still to discover that she shared the curse. Suspicion clawed at her thoughts like a burrowing scorpion.

The girl had worn a scarf before. Now, she'd cast it aside, exposing the snaking trail of invisible skin running down from her shoulder.

And—Razhar held her hand.

Lystra gasped.

"I . . ." Razhar immediately dropped it. "Your Highness . . ."

Lystra spun toward Myra, rage pounding in her chest. *"How dare you!"*

The maid stepped back, eyes wide, and clutched at her scarf. "I didn't . . ."

"You cursed him!" Lystra's voice choked. She covered her mouth with her hand. How could she tell Elerek? He would be heartbroken.

"Your High—Lystra, calm down," Razhar pleaded. "I'm not cursed."

Lystra glanced between them, her heart beating loud within her chest. "Elerek—the king—mentioned that sometimes it doesn't spread secondhand." She looked at Myra, who only wrapped her arms around herself and dropped her gaze.

"While true, this is different." Razhar rubbed the back of his neck, his movements anxious.

Lystra lifted her chin. "Well?"

"I'm . . . the curse has no effect on me."

What? How was such a thing possible?

Myra shook her head. "It's more than that." She turned a strict eye upon Razhar. "You'll have to tell her everything. Perhaps someone ought to know." Her eyelashes fluttered fleetingly in Lystra's direction. "After all, we cannot refuse our *queen*."

Lystra stiffened at her tone, without respect or honor.

A war clashed upon Razhar's brow, his words coming like reluctant warriors. "I . . . I can reverse its effects." He looked back at Myra. "Please?"

She stretched out her hand, the curse mark turned up. As he gripped her hand in his, black tendrils like dark veins appeared, spreading from their point of contact. Lystra stared in horror, watching the lines spin and writhe, black as tattoo ink.

Myra winced, but the mark along her shoulder receded, shrinking like a snake slithering into the grass. Razhar let go and shoved his hand into his pocket.

234

"It's no cure. He just . . . stays it." Myra sighed. "I'll survive longer."

Lystra raised her eyebrows. "But that's good."

"That wholly depends upon your motives to survive." Myra's expression turned cold, murderously so.

Careful. Myra could still possibly doom her with only a touch.

"I've always been this way." Razhar stared at the ground. "In Kushan, my homeland, there were many binders and casters. I've gone and searched the archives but have no explanation."

"Who else knows?" Lystra pressed. "The king?"

"No." Razhar's eyes flashed like a lightning bolt striking in the heart of a storm's fury. "Just us two—three. And I want to keep it that way."

"Why? You can help him. You can help *all* of them."

A snarl twisted Razhar's face. "I *have been*, Your Highness. I'm the reason why many of them have lived so long—but I operate in secret. Myra helps me manage the task."

"While they sleep," Myra whispered.

Which meant late night appearances in bedchambers was something of a regularity. Lystra didn't like the picture forming in her mind.

"You're Elerek's best friend." Lystra's voice softened. "And you keep secrets from him?"

Razhar shrugged. "What good will it do? You don't know him like we do." His eyes became awash with torment. "The curse makes El unbearably miserable. He's spent most of his life waiting to die and I'm capable of prolonging his suffering. Perhaps it's selfish of me."

The cursed king waiting to die. And yet Lystra had seen Elerek only display strength, a devotion stalwart as the Sancen itself. She shivered, wondering what would happen when his courage ran out.

"Wanting someone to live is not selfish," she protested, tossing her hair over her shoulder. "Life is precious, and we've all seen too much death."

Razhar began to unwind his vibrant orange turban, letting its swaths fall like a scarf about his neck. "Death lies beyond our control, Your Highness, no matter how tightly we hold on. In this"—he exchanged a sorrowful glance with Myra—"we are all cursed."

"Ah, now you sound like him." Lystra shook her head.

He smiled a sheepish smile. "El has his moments, doesn't he? I know you want to break the curse, but it's impossible. Our times, however long or short, have been appointed to us. Since Cormek's death, I've seen El commit to doing his best—*living*—like never before. I'd hate to sacrifice the good that he might accomplish." He stepped back, his shoes sliding along the tile and into the shadows. "Now, it's late and you've an early morning—"

"Not so fast." Lystra grabbed his sleeve, a sneer upon her face. "You promised you'd help me find a way to break the curse."

Myra's eyes widened, watching this exchange with a curious fascination.

Razhar slunk back into the torchlight, twisting his arm out of her grasp.

"And you kept this secret?" Lystra's face grew enflamed. "Did you even intend to tell me? Or simply let me be led along by a false promise?"

Lines twisted Razhar's face, like the ripples upon a dune. She couldn't tell whether he was wounded by her accusation or the weight of his own façades. In that moment, she realized that he wasn't the good-natured, jovial embodiment of sunshine and merriment he projected to the others—to Elerek. He was something more, and she couldn't trust him. Not by a long shot.

"I wish there were a way to break the curse, Lystra. I truly do. But as I told you, I can't hope for that optimism. Not after watching so many drown." He dropped his gaze. "I can only do what I can, and that's hold back the curse."

"But where did your abilities come from?" Lystra pressed. "You mentioned Kushan; does it have something to do with your homeland?"

"I truly don't know."

A lie. A boldfaced lie to the queen of Instanolde. Lystra ground her teeth. Worse, Razhar hadn't just lied to her; he'd been lying to Elerek—and doing it for a very long time.

"Your king deserves to know."

Razhar's eyes shifted. "El doesn't deserve to watch his friends die either. We don't choose the cards in our decks. Stars above, we certainly didn't choose the curse."

Myra folded her arms, making a *hmph* sound in her throat.

"I'm not disputing that." Lystra narrowed her gaze. "But the truth is more than this, and you *can* choose deception. Tell me why I shouldn't inform the king myself?"

Razhar stepped closer, his eyes growing wide, frightened even. "Don't, please, Your Highness. Hasn't he enough to deal with? Saving Instanolde and all that? It would only distract him unnecessarily. Our time beneath the stars is short, and his even shorter . . ."

Lystra blinked. His words spun in her mind, like the swirls of incense rising from the temple's altars. The mountain before them wouldn't be easy, with no guarantee that they would survive the summer. If the Starkindler appointed their days, why were some fated to be so short?

Then again, she might have asked the same of Cormek.

Perhaps these were mysteries beyond them, mysteries that even her own determination couldn't bend to her will.

But Razhar wasn't owed the satisfaction of her agreement, so she lifted her chin, folded her arms, and cast an icy eye upon him and the magnitude of his lies. "I'll make no promises. Goodnight, Razhar."

He bowed, and then slipped back into the shadows, blending into the night's ever deepening dark. A shudder crept up Lystra's arms in the stillness, but she swiftly remembered that she was not alone.

"Who are you, Lystra?"

At the sound of her name, spoken without title or veneration, Lystra turned, heat stoked in her chest.

Myra stood with her chin held primly, as if she were nobility herself. "You said at the feast that formalities might be disregarded, and we've only just left."

Lystra dipped her chin, watching the girl like a hawk tracking its prey.

"I only wish to understand." Myra took a step closer. "The heir of House Arghan. The people's *Malikaa*. The girl who caught the eye of kings. But tell me, why are you worthy of it?"

Lystra narrowed her eyes, ready to meet this challenge. "I have spent my life preparing for this role. The kingdom has always been my purpose."

"Maybe so. But everything that El has done since becoming king—as Razhar said, living like never before—he's done for *you*."

All at once, Lystra could hardly breathe. The high collar of her kaftan, draped in gold, seemed intent on choking her.

Pain, raw and familiar, entered Myra's face. A grief that Lystra understood better than most. "What makes you worthy of him?"

Him. The word hit Lystra like a punch to the gut, knocking the remaining air from her lungs. *She . . . she's in love with him.*

Lystra wondered why the idea surprised her. Even within the few short days that she'd become acquainted with him, she knew that Elerek wasn't without his amiable qualities. Especially the care and devotion he'd given to his community of cursed.

Lystra's eyes trailed on the mark, now only a silver stripe upon her bare shoulders. "Tell me." She folded her arms. "How did you become cursed?"

Replacing the scarf about her shoulders, Myra let the densely pattered fabric slip over the mark. "Razhar said that none of us chose the curse. Well, he's wrong. I chose it. Willingly."

Lystra stared at her, her royal façade unraveling like a tapestry's threads.

"To be with the man that I love." Her eyes blazed. "A man confined by a curse, cut off from humanity's touch . . ." She took a step closer, her voice lowered to a murmur, the flow of a river that appeared gentle, but its currents were strong. "And the arms of a lover."

One by one, Lystra felt her defenses fall. She had dined with the cursed upon an invitation of companionship and inclusion, but Myra had a different intention altogether. A spiteful ambush, and her aim struck true.

A lover. A mutual affection. A tryst kept secret. Lystra knew tradition as well as anyone, raised and groomed to secure an advantageous marriage herself. As prince, Elerek may have lost his birthright, but he still bore the royal blood of House Karim. Even in the shadows, in the eyes of the kingdom, this secret could only bring scorn.

As for her, it tore her heart to shreds. Lystra averted her eyes, straining to rein in her emotions, like a cardant still entrenched in its wild ways. His every kindness, every word girded with strength, every time she'd looked into Elerek's eyes and beheld something of kinship, she'd succumbed to his pull. The pull toward the light, of another soul fighting for a crumbling future. And all the while, he had loved someone else.

Did he still love her? Even now? Even while he'd taken vows and sworn himself to Lystra?

"Why are you telling me this?"

Myra's icy gaze remained unblinking. "He doesn't belong to you, Lystra. What claim does an unconsummated, political arrangement have over a love that defied a curse?"

No, he can't love me.

Lystra was only his heir, never to be anything more. Their vows served a purpose to their kingdom. And while this realization submerged her soul and made her feel as if she were also cursed—drowning—it had to be this way. Myra was right.

"Razhar tells me that you're seeking a way to break El's curse?" Myra narrowed her eyes. "A task that countless others, including kings, have tried and failed?"

Where the curse was concerned, Lystra knew only one option. One path lay ahead of her. She only hoped that she was worthy—worthy of breaking the curse. "As queen, it is my duty to preserve life." She gathered strength to her voice. "As you said, many have failed, but that is no excuse. My motivations are not self-serving. None of you deserve to drown."

"And if the curse is broken, what then?" Myra's tongue cut with bitterness, the venom of a scorpion.

Lystra's heart began to burn, sparking a flame that scorched across her soul. She hadn't a name for it, or an intended victim. Not the king who had become her husband nor the girl he loved who bore his curse.

Lystra fixed her stare upon Myra and stood a little taller in her kaftan of brilliant blue and royal gold. She gathered her fury, letting it consume her. Let this girl see that she was queen.

"*If* you love your king, I expect you to honor him and respect his choices—including *his* queen." Empowered, Lystra swept past her. Her fingers tingled, like the electrified air before a thunderstorm. Perhaps she'd become the great cloud, ready to rain and hail, full of power.

She wondered if this was how Dalmah felt when she flaunted her authority.

"Your Highness." Myra's whisper sounded hollow in the hallway, a shadow of the bravado she'd held. "One more thing. About Razhar . . ."

Lystra spun around with a scowl.

Myra kept her head down, her eyes full of darkness. "Don't fall for his lies. He most definitely knows the truth about his strange abilities."

The best friend to the most powerful man in the kingdom. A prickling scurried up her spine. She thought again of the man from the market, with his eager feet, winning smile, and the magic he seemed to weave with his laughter. Clever disguises to veil his mysteries, much the same way she'd worn a veil to conceal her identity that night.

Lystra dipped her chin. "Thank you, Myra. I will look further into this matter."

Myra bowed, her scarf draping from her shoulders. "Know this, Your Highness. Razhar loves El, closer than a brother. That, I do believe."

A far closer brother than Cormek ever was. Lystra sighed. "Then we must pray that Razhar does have the king's best interests at heart. Goodnight."

As soon as she turned the corner, Lystra broke into a run and fled to her chambers.

While the sky still lay dark, Lystra rose. A lingering chill hung in the desert air, leaving her soul numb and hollow. The address lay upon her dresser, the scroll tied with a length of twine. Words to strike fear into the heart of her kingdom, like an arrow from a deadly archer. She would wound them, yes, and then become their deliverer.

She dressed quickly, selecting a layered skirt and bodice with long, fitted sleeves. As the black silk flowed from her figure, embroidered in orange like the flames of a pyre, she thought of her grandmother and the mourning garb she'd worn to the royal wedding. Lystra perhaps thought that she'd begun to understand.

When she entered the parlor, the scroll in hand, Elerek waited, sipping tea. "Good morning."

Lystra didn't reply, thankful for the heavy paint upon her eyelids to mask the tumult of emotions clamoring inside her. She perched herself on the couch, pouring herself a cup. The steam from the samovar warmed her face, bathing her in the scent of mint and honey.

The king narrowed his eyes. "Is there something wrong?"

Lystra lowered her cup, the mint doing nothing to soothe the tumult in her stomach. She glanced at him, exposing herself to his sharp, jade-colored gaze. He'd promised her truth. He'd taken vows. *Living*—as Razhar had said—for the sake of their kingdom.

Whatever had happened, whatever burned between him and Myra, didn't matter. They were past. This was now. She'd no evidence of betrayal or unfaithfulness, no reason to doubt that Elerek had chosen to become wholly devoted to her.

Stars above, she hoped that was true, that he had chosen strength.

But Myra's words had taken a toll, and Lystra still felt their sting. Elerek didn't belong to her. They had a mighty work before them and she couldn't afford to be distracted, particularly in a situation as hopeless as this one. Without the curse's breaking, the great, impossible task, this story could have only one ending.

No, this distance, this low table between her couch and the place where his wheelchair parked, was necessary. Elerek would never love her. Lystra, his queen, would only be a bit of embellishment, gold adorning a kaftan gown.

"Tired, is all," she whispered.

Elerek nodded and said no more.

Lystra turned her gaze to the window. There, above the dark horizon, the last of the stars took the final steps of their dance before the dawn outshone them. The weaver, the stars that made up the constellations of delicate fingers at a loom falling like diamond teardrops. The wrathgiver, the assassin in the shadows. The same stars on her grandmother's dagger.

She wondered if her grandmother had ever used it—and if Elerek still kept the weapon on his nightstand. "Elerek, your curse mark." Lystra absently touched the jeweled earrings in her ear. "Does it ever change?"

Elerek scowled and blinked. "Minimally. Not yet, at least." He lowered his cup to the table with a *chink*. "Why do you ask?"

Lystra studied his face, searching for suspicion, and found none. Elerek had no idea.

Razhar, the man who bridged the gap, the gatekeeper between the curse and the victims it drowned—and he kept it a secret from a king. Although, Lystra supposed the task might have been simpler if he'd enlisted the help of the girl who was sleeping with him.

Don't think about Myra. Lystra drew a steadying breath in through her nostrils. "Curiosity, that's all."

Her kingdom needed her strength, her boldness, her fierce determination to outlive Instanolde's last summer. She stood, retrieving the scroll from the table. Her fingers tightened, creating creases in its paper. She would give them that. That was her vow, to her people, to her kingdom, and to her king.

As the first rays of dawn stretched across the desert, catching on the golden domes and spires of Instanolde, Lystra took her station upon the ramparts above the gates, flanked by Norbah and a company of guards. Elerek didn't accompany them, the narrow stairs quite beyond his abilities, but he watched and listened from the palace steps.

Below, the square filled with people. Nobles, merchants, and refugees, all would be affected by her message. Over and over, she exhorted them to not fear, to stand firm, to trust.

Word would spread. Soon the entire kingdom would be abuzz with the news, the knowledge that Darcress lay in Jarkin hands and that they anticipated a second attack.

When Lystra turned for the stairs, her task complete, her own heart quivered. Not since the desert, watching Cormek die, had she felt such trepidation, such foreboding dread. As the palace walls grew taller, stretching up toward the sky, she felt more and more like a grounded bird. She knew how to fly, but here her services were required.

Across the palace courtyard, she lifted her gaze. Elerek's eyes met hers, set aflame with pride.

Protect Instanolde. Together. An impossible task, but one they couldn't fail. Not with the lives of their people, their kingdom, their very existence upon the edge of the desert at stake.

Chapter 32

Elerek

Sunlight glittered across the courtyard. Elerek blinked against the light, staring hard at the scene before him. The scene he could hardly believe was real.

Soldiers. They stood at attention, equally spaced in perfect uniformity. Their sallet helmets were not yet adorned with orange turbans, functional for the battle ahead. Leather hauberks bulked their shoulders. An impressive sight, but it was their loyalty that inspired Elerek the most. Each and every one of them had chosen to be here, chosen to serve beneath their king, and had returned, day after day for the last two weeks to drill.

Along the wall to their left, a row of targets had been pierced and worn through. But it was the red marks painted in the center that were the focus. Closer and closer, the holes drew to the center, proving that Norbah's confidence was not wasted.

Elerek took up his bow. Its wood gleamed, close in color to the dark stain of his chair, and its curves were smooth and elegant. A quiver of arrows hung on the armrest of his chair, within easy reach. His hand hovered over the quiver.

"Draw!" His voice echoed over sand and stone.

As one, the regiment each retrieved an arrow from their own quivers and set it against their bows, drawing the strings back. Their weapons were less refined, manufactured from whatever wood could be found on hand or taken from old furniture, but most were made of tough river reeds or the rib bones of cows and river buffalo. What mattered was that their aim was true, each soldier devoted to the cause of defending their kingdom.

Elerek mirrored their actions, shoulders straining as he drew back on the string. He lined up his shot, turning slightly in his chair, watching the target's red bullseye.

"Volley."

As one, the bows sang. Arrows clattered against stone or hit the targets with a solid *thunk*. Elerek glanced away from his own arrow, solidly in the center of the target, scanning the faces of his men. It was easy enough to see who was pleased with their result and whose arrows had fallen into the sands after bouncing off the walls, well away from the intended targets. The men bowed their heads, snarled, or kicked at the dust beneath their boots.

Most were not soldiers before responding to Norbah's draft. No, these were craftsmen, shepherds, a few were scholars and scribes, and yet another group were the sons of noble houses, itching to prove their worth.

Elerek didn't mind their backgrounds. The variety actually stirred in him a fascination. These men were willing to take up a new skill and prove their worth in service to their kingdom. He didn't doubt that they would improve, believing their drive to be enough to inspire their perseverance.

"Take stance." Elerek laid his bow across his lap, rolling his chair forward.

The soldiers lifted their bows and raised their arms, taking the position of firing without an actual arrow on the string. Elerek moved across the front line, studying their posture and shouting out corrections as needed.

"Nearly there. Relax your shoulder." He nodded in approval at the boy at the end of the line. "Very good, Kimzi."

Lystra's young cousin puffed out his chest, eyes focused ahead on the target and beaming with pride.

Elerek had done his best to memorize their names. He tried not to wonder what they thought of him, the heir from the shadows, the crippled king, the one with a host of rumors swirling about him like a dust devil spinning wildly. His instruction was firm, but not without mercy, and, so far, he'd received the respect and honor due a king.

He wished all their military and fortification endeavors had gone so smoothly. Finding stonemasons willing to work on the walls proved easy, but getting the stones downriver from the quarry had become a headache. As high summer intensified and the river's level dropped, heavy barges weighed down with stone were getting snared in sandbars and most of the rivermen who worked the barges had refused to even try. Still, what stone they could get would go to strengthening the walls and enlarging the battlements and ramparts along the eastern wall.

Moving the kingdom's occupants to the west city was also simpler said than done. As the city shuffled, bursting with extra bodies, confusion ran rampant and once the markets began moving, no longer occupying their usual avenues, the people's complaints became vocal. Lystra visited the new markets yesterday, praising their efforts and calling attention to their new location. Elerek had heard numerous reports that she'd been charming and the streets were practically pink with tamarisk boughs.

Malikaa. Did they still see her as the grieving queen? The girl painted with mourning stripes? He wondered what it would take for their people to see her as the glorious dawn, everything that *he* saw in her.

Movement caught his attention. The soldier beside Kimzi rolled his shoulder and lifted his bow, displaying a poor stance.

"Lukor, shift your weight forward." Elerek rolled his chair closer. "And line your feet up with your shoulders."

The soldier frowned, muscles visibly tensing as he fought to shift into the correct posture. His eyes glanced down at his feet, his boots grinding in the gravel. A questioning expression emerged on his features, his gaze briefly darting toward Elerek's wheelchair.

"I had excellent instructors." He met the man's eyes, holding his head high with pride. "I watched them, and when you see something done with precision enough times, you'll know how to emulate it." He gestured to the young man of House Arghan. "Practice with Kimzi. Watch what he does."

Poof! Out of the corner of Elerek's eye, a projectile hurled itself through the air. Just to the left of his wheelchair, an explosion of purple smoke exploded, stinging his lungs and causing his eyes to water.

Several soldiers drew arrows, fitting their bows, and took aim.

"Don't shoot! Stars above!"

Coughing, Elerek pivoted his chair, a coat of purple dust covering the wheels, and scanned the wall for the culprit—who was most definitely getting exiled. "Razhar," he commanded, grinding the words out. "Get. Down. Here." Then he looked at his soldiers. "Stand down. Continue drilling."

He glared as Razhar jumped down from the wall, the tail of

his emerald turban flying. Somehow, he'd managed to procure a matching scarf, which draped behind him dramatically. In his hand, he clutched a leather slingshot, and a small, round object of purple.

"Do I have to ask why?" Elerek demanded.

Razhar tilted his face skyward and laughed. "I wanted to see how your reflexes were. If I were a real enemy, your soldiers were ready."

"I should've let them fire."

"You should've seen your face. Speaking of which." Razhar gestured to his own face. "Your nose is a bit purple."

Scoffing, Elerek brushed his face, his fingers coming away streaked with the colored powder. Unfortunately, this wasn't the first time Razhar had gotten his hands on large quantities of the mineral powder used to tint the torches. "Remind me again, where were your top three destination choices for when I exile you?"

"Aw, El, you wouldn't dream of it. You'd miss me far too much. I'd give you one hour before you'd send guards after me to bring me home."

Home. Elerek's eyes drifted to the golden spires of the palace. Its marble halls had never felt like home. No, it was the warmth of its hearths, the scent of coffee, and the glow in the eyes of people cursed to die who chose to smile.

All the things that Razhar could become, all the places he could go, and he chose to stay with them. Of course, one didn't simply "get rid of" someone like Razhar anyways.

"Drills going well?" Razhar stuffed the slingshot into the pockets of his linen pants. "I hardly see you anymore."

"Ample time for you to improve at *barjee*." Elerek tucked his bow beneath his arm. "There aren't enough hours in the day for the things we need to do. I fear we'll run out of time." In more ways than one.

A clouded look entered Razhar's face, a shadow that ought not to be there. He folded his arms, his gaze afar off. "One day at a time, El. That's all any of us have. Curse or no curse."

Frowning, Elerek wondered if Razhar hung around the cursed too much. Sometimes, it sounded awfully like he was one of them, also numbering his days.

"I must draw attention to the fact that you said 'we.'" Razhar cleared his throat. "Because while I was spying on your drills from atop the wall, your queen has been watching from the archway for quite some time."

Stars. Elerek's chest seized, a jolt of heat enflaming his face and driving away the curse's numbness. He resisted a glance towards the arch, keeping his posture rigid.

"Oh, now she's coming this way." Razhar chuckled. "You've still got a bit of purple powder in your hair."

"Once high summer ends, you're getting exiled somewhere where they don't serve dessert," Elerek muttered, glaring at his friend as he quickly dragged his fingers through his curls.

"Stars above, El. I had no idea you were so invested in impressing your queen." He winked, a cheeky smile on his face.

Ignoring Razhar, Elerek pivoted his chair again, attempting to block the splat of purple staining the dust. The moment Lystra left the shadows of the archway, the wind caught in her long tresses. She held them back, the sunlight turning her amber gaze to embers forged of starlight themselves.

"Your Highness." Razhar made a grand show of bowing.

As Lystra's gaze fell upon Razhar, the embers turned to ashes, smoldering. Elerek frowned, once again caught beneath the heaviness of something he didn't understand, something that had averted his attention. She looked—almost angry. What could Razhar have done to cause this disturbance?

"Razhar, I see you're also assisting in the archers' training."

Right, she'd seen the entire thing. Elerek huffed. "He

makes a splendid target." He turned a cool expression on his friend. "Would you give us a moment?"

With another bow, Razhar grinned and took a step back. "Glad to be of service!"

Once he was out of earshot, Elerek shook his head, hoping to the heavens that there remained not a speck of purple powder anywhere on his person. "He acts like an attention-starved hound. This is what happens when I don't spend enough time with him."

"Mm." Lystra eyed him from beneath her lashes. "He strikes me as one that ought to be kept a close watch on."

Her tone surprised him. Did she think Razhar's antics suspicious? Then again, precious few weeks had passed since their wedding. Each hour of sunlight and starlight held more tasks than they could handle. Little time remained for meals, much less socializing.

Elerek stared down at his hands. Was it permissible to wish for more time with his queen? Get to know her, as he'd been encouraged by his friends? They wouldn't reign long, their political marriage a short and strange thing.

But perhaps Lystra didn't want that. The closer they became, the more painful the ending would be. The shattering of the curse. His intended fate to drown. Maybe it was for the best.

"I heard your venture to the market went well."

Lystra's gaze returned to him, the light returned to her eyes. "Indeed. I passed through the masonry avenue. Your project at the wall appears to be well underway."

"For now, it seems so." Elerek exhaled. "I'm impressed by our efforts, given that it's only been weeks."

Weeks to save a kingdom. Was it wrong to be proud? Optimistic even? Though the real test awaited them at summer's end, when the invaders returned. These hours were a gift, one they could not squander.

A small smile glowed on Lystra's lips. "We have done well. Your archers are most impressive. And you are an excellent shot."

Elerek felt the heat at his throat again, and it had nothing to do with the high summer sun beating down upon his shoulders. Or perhaps it was. He glanced down at his arms, bare from his sleeveless tunic, noting that the sun didn't particularly show kindness to his paler skin. At least, if Lystra noticed his blush, he'd have a valid excuse.

"I see you managed to enlist my cousin." Lystra's gaze swept over the ranks. "I trust he's doing well?"

"Indeed, a model soldier. His house ought to be proud." Ah, the noble houses. Elerek's stomach twisted. One particular conversation remained that he had not yet discussed with his queen, and it wouldn't be nearly as pleasant as this small talk. "Lystra, we've drafted soldiers, craftsmen, stoneworkers, archers, we've only one thing we haven't yet drafted."

She stared at him, a question in her eyes.

"Cardants."

Blunt, brash, and to the point. As predicted, the queen's face fell, an army of agonies marching through her gaze.

He rolled his chair closer. Not close enough to spark the panic, the fear of touching another human being and dooming them to drown, but close enough to let his voice be soft, maybe even gentle. "I don't want to do this, Lystra. I hate the idea of the reptiles being exposed to battle, just as I know that many of the young men standing behind me are going to die when the Jarkins attack. I can't protect them. I can only teach them the skills necessary to defend our people. Because of their sacrifice, others may live. And you were right, you were always right, cardants are an advantage."

Stars, he sounded like Cormek, waxing poetically about fortifying the Darcress Kasbah. The strategic partnership of cardants and soldiers, birthed from the clever mind of Instanolde's future queen. Reptiles trained by her hand, gifted to her kingdom, taken across the desert from her own stables. And now, they might need them more than ever before.

Lystra's face became a torment. She wrung her hands, the embroidered sleeves of her kaftan fluttering in the wind. "There are so few cardants left," she whispered. "Most belong to the racing committee."

"Yes." Elerek's throat felt dry, cast in the sands of the desert.

She closed her eyes, her posture rigid, stalwart as the desert mountains themselves. "You want me to go to them."

Well, yes. These were her associates, men and women who had built a bonded community around the reptiles and the races. Who better than her to give the plea to allow the cardants to aid their country in the hope that they would race again?

However . . . "Only if you feel that you can bear it."

Opening her eyes, they became sharpened, the pain forged into steel. "I've borne much, Elerek. These burdens don't ask us permission before they're heaped onto our shoulders. I can only move forward, however slowly."

Each step that she'd taken had been brave, fierce. Elerek swallowed, wishing he could aspire to just a shimmer of her brilliance, a bit of mirage hovering above the golden sands. "Do you think that you can convince them?"

Lystra shrugged, folding her arms tight against her body. "I'm not sure they'll comply. Their reptiles are as precious to them as mine were—are—to me."

Every morning, his queen rose before dawn to spend what cherished hours she could with the monstrous cardant he'd given her. Then, as if blown in by a wild west wind, the queen would enter the council chambers in her riding clothes, her hair tousled, and her boots coated in dust. The sight always made him smile.

Elerek's hand moved to his chair's armrest, his fingers tapping upon the polished wood. "You're sure?"

"One summer to live." Lystra's eyes flashed as she spoke the mantra that pounded in his head and heart day after long, hot, summer day. "Forgive my brusqueness, Elerek, but they would hate you. They wouldn't see our desperate efforts to save our kingdom, but an oppressive king taking away that which they love."

An oppressive king like his father. Elerek's fingers stopped tapping. No, he never wanted to be anything like his father, remembered with such scorn and hatred. In fact, he wondered if his short reign would be remembered at all. If history only recalled Lystra, the bold queen, then it would be enough.

Except, she didn't appear bold right now. No, she looked as lost and lonely as the desolate canyons of the Sancen. A girl soft and vulnerable, sworn to take on a task that would bring her pain.

He didn't know how to give her starlight in this matter. How could he shoulder her burdens, attempt to align their purposes like the stars in the heavens, if she didn't let him?

Releasing an exhale, he squared his shoulders. "In that case, Your Highness, they will receive their queen."

Lystra lifted her eyes, staring afar off at the line of deep blue sky above the courtyard walls. She gave no reply, her expression resembling a noble statue, carved of marble.

Chapter 33

Lystra

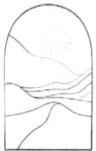

L ight spilled into the carriage, filtered through the wood lattice window. Lystra shut her eyes against the glow and turned away.

Of course the racing committee had to convene with the sunrise. Lystra despised rising in the pearly predawn to dress in a midnight-blue kaftan with swirls of flowers stitched in gold thread instead of her riding boots. She wondered if Tiniah paced her pen, muttering and stomping and scratching her talons at the dirt, waiting for her to arrive.

When the time came, would she be required to give up her cardant? Hand over the reins to a trained soldier? Would she watch as another reptile that belonged to her fell prey to the Jarkins' weapons?

Tears sparked in her eyes, but she held them back. No, she'd applied too much kohl around her eyes for tears. She wore it like a mask, as she'd worn the mourning paint, as she arrived at yet another pyre.

A pyre that the king had sent her to.

Lystra clenched a handful of her skirt. No, Elerek didn't deserve her fury, but the coals stoking in the inner chambers of her heart wanted to strike out and sear someone. Their plans were falling into place. Their city would stand fortified, ready for the Jarkins to break upon them like water upon stone. A chance existed, perhaps even more than a chance, that they might survive.

How could she tell him that this idea was folly? That those among her community who loved their cardants would rather die than give them up for soldiers to ride. Soldiers who hadn't trained with the reptiles, who had no bond. Lystra had indeed borne many things, as she had told the king, but reliving the attack, watching more cardants fall prey to slaughter was something she could not do.

Her friends and associates, racers and riders—they would blame her.

A sacrifice. Another noble sacrifice, one that a queen would make. Lystra knew these were selfish, bitter thoughts. She ought to be above this. After all, she'd already given herself in marriage for the sake of saving Instanolde.

Grief. Yes, it was only grief. A wound not yet healed. Lystra sniffled and adjusted her skirts, jostled along by the bumpy carriage. Perhaps it was the thought of the races, the cardants, and the host of memories, both the golden and the lackluster, that brought her again to this point. And stars above, how alone it made her feel.

You could have told him. And admit this weakness? That she wasn't the radiant, bold queen that he wanted her to be? Elerek believed in an idea. A queen like the one Grandmother had painted to stand before the mourning pyre. A construct, something for the people to believe in, a hope to carry them through this night. She'd already disappointed herself; she hardly wanted to disappoint Elerek too.

The carriage lumbered to a stop. Lystra watched the door, waiting for her guards.

How would he have reacted? Would he have chastised her, as he had on the day their marriage was proposed? Shown her grace, as he had on their wedding night? Did they always have to portray strength? To each other? Stalwart, without any shadow of weakness whatsoever?

The guard opened the door. Lystra gathered her skirts and disembarked.

For now, she had to face the racing committee.

They no longer assembled within the confines of a canvas tent. Not now, when training was minimal and few ventured outside the city walls with the impending threat of the Jarkins. Instead, they gathered at the estate of House Pana, in a pavilion draped with silks and trailing vines overlooking their grand grounds—including a fine stable of cardants. Members of the committee, of the great houses and those with riches and influences enough to take part in the yearly races, stood about in bright, colorful robes. They held silver cups of chilled tea or aromatic wines and the tables were laid with dried fruit and nuts. The entire scene seemed so normal, a lavish scene to be painted as the epitome of culture and affluence in Instanolde.

Unperturbed by the threat looming over their heads. In a matter of months, all this could be gone. Their way of life. Their people. The pulse of their heartbeat beneath the desert skies.

And she had come to steal it.

"Her Highness, Queen Lystra of House Karim, daughter of House Arghan, ruler of Instanolde. Fierce as the dawn. Mighty as the constellations."

Every eye in the room turned on her. Faces filled with recognition, some with smiles and some with scorn. But they all bowed before her.

Lystra kept still, waiting while they resumed their postures. She had friends, partners, rivals in this room, but the crown had cast them all beneath her. Was she worthy of this honor?

Only if I can save them.

She glided through the room, her face clear of emotion. Grandmother had taught her how to handle such interactions, and she knew to seek out her hosts first.

"Brahim of House Pana, thank you for allowing this council to take place beneath your roof." She nodded to the young man, only a few years her senior.

He gave a deep bow, graceful despite his limp and the use of a cane. A racing accident had caused his injury, and ever since, he'd spent the resources of his house devoted to serving the committee and promoting safety in the races.

"Of course, Your Highness." A slight frown settled upon his features. "Have we reason for concern, that you have called us together?"

A loaded question. Lystra allowed herself a sad smile. "We will see." She turned away, continuing her orbit of the room, making another dozen or so interactions. All bore the same ominous undertone. That she had come to take what belonged to them.

A tyrant no better than the kings of the generations before. The thought, a brief and fleeting thing, swept through her mind, that perhaps her grandmother's opinion might have served her here.

"Torra Lys—Your Highness!" Two smiling faces broke through the gloom of her thoughts.

Aham and Ikram. The two young men had ridden on her racing team—when she still had one—but had signed beneath another house when she'd become engaged to Cormek. Together, they had raised and trained many reptiles, and she counted them among her friends.

"It's good to see you two." Lystra smiled, thinking of the two reptiles the riders had bonded with. "Tell me, are Hasi and Natalia well?"

"Very well, thank you." Aham took a step closer, sympathy in his sage eyes. "We are sorry for your many losses."

She only nodded in response.

"But please." Ikram folded his arms. "You've always been honest with us. Fair and noble. Tell us that nothing has changed."

Her heart twisted. Yes, she had been all of those things. Was her purpose here fair? Noble? Perhaps in the whole, for the sake of the kingdom. But why must it be so unfair to these individuals? She thought again of Elerek's archers, the men who were learning a new form of weaponry to stand in the line of fire upon the ramparts. Her cousin was among them. They were making a sacrifice for the sake of their kingdom.

"A sacrifice is a choice, Ikram," she whispered. "I cannot make that decision for you."

"Not you, Your Highness." His tone was bitter. "But the crown well may."

The crown. The future that had sealed her fate. The fate that became a cage. Lystra knew what the crown demanded of her, and that in the end, she would see the task through.

"I must convene the council." She grasped their hands, each in turn. "Do not lose hope, my friends."

The committee officials, led by Brahim, called its members

to attention. Many took seats upon large cushions, embroidered and tasseled, gathered about low tables like herds around their shepherds. A few remained standing, stiff arms folded as they watched Lystra move to the front of the room. She kept her hands clasped, fingers interlaced to stem the shaking.

"I stand before you as a duality," she began. Stars, did they hear how her voice wavered? "Both as an associate of this committee, and as ruler of our kingdom. As you know, I witnessed the brutal attack of the Jarkins at Darcress, the slaughter of a young king, faithful soldiers, and many cardants. This loss represents a tragedy for our entire kingdom and now with this, this one summer to live, our survival depends on our resilience and our ability to come together for the sake of our life here in the desert."

"Pretty words, Your Highness." Jabir, head of House Pana and Brahim's father, cast a sneer beneath his heavy beard. He had never been keen on Lystra's involvement with the races, and she expected him to cause trouble. "But you chose to take your cardants out there and to hand them over to the royal house."

"A house, one might add, that has a bloody history of military decisions that have cost this kingdom heavily." The head of House Tikkal, a close ally of House Pana, shook his head.

Lystra bristled, their words cutting her to the bone. She'd expected this. Feared this. Here, in this room, one that she'd spent years working to earn a place within, she was not the kingdom's *Malikaa*. No, merely an ambitious girl who had married into a notorious house.

"Watch your tone." Yusef of House Himmel rose to his feet, glaring at the other two men. "She is your *queen!*"

At this rally cry, Lystra's guards each took a step closer, flanking her in a show of strength. But one look in the eyes of these men told her that her authority as queen meant nothing. No, she could only approach them as an equal.

"I am also one of you. And the Jarkins certainly won't care for our house affiliations or who has sided with whom."

"But you have sided, Your Highness," Jabir said with a hooded gaze. "That crown upon your pretty brow is proof enough. House Karim will seize our property and our sons to fight another war. Is that not why you are here? To beg our cardants from us so they may be slaughtered too?"

Lystra steadied herself with a deep breath. "To plea, my friends. Please, believe me, I wish a slaughter upon no citizen of Instanolde, man or reptile."

A stir moved through the crowd. Heads were shaken and fists formed. Armor clinked as Lystra's guards edged in even closer. The air turned noxious, churned by the whispers, the faces, and the host of terrible eyes.

"Then our fears are justified," Jabir huffed, raising his head high. "House Pana, House Tikkal, Kushan, they were right to refuse the throne fealty. Perhaps they'd no hand in the Jarkins' slaughter, but mark my words, they do not wish for peace. No, House Karim will continue as it always has—causing more violence."

Hopeless, faithless words. Words that sounded like Grandmother. Was this not the same argument she'd used when she'd pressed the star-etched dagger into Lystra's hands and spoke doom over House Karim? But there was no longer such a house. Only Elerek.

"And such shame!" Jabir's voice rose. "That a Torra who has been such an influence upon our races and become a pillar of our community, should stand here in this disgrace, allied with those who would seek to destroy us. As queen, Her Highness is no friend of ours."

Lystra opened her mouth, but terror kept back her voice.

She hadn't words, arguments, or any hope to make them believe. Worse, each syllable cut like a knife straight to her heart. Her work as queen meant nothing. Her desire to save her people meant nothing.

"Don't let the foolish girl win." How Grandmother would laugh if she could see her now, only foolish.

The patter of shoes echoed from behind. A servant dashed into the pavilion, his face crimson. Behind him, the rattle of soldiers' armor accompanied the announcement that rumbled through the air like thunder.

"His Highness, Elerek of House Karim, son of Lorkin, King of Instanolde. Fierce as the dawn. Mighty as the constellations."

Lystra turned toward the archway, eyes wide. As the guards filed in, one by one, the clatter of their boots masked the gasp upon her lips.

He came.

The king held his head high, his circlet gleaming upon his brow. The gold stitching upon his black jabador stretched across his shoulders and down his arms like the span of eagles' wings. He wheeled his chair to the front of the room, directly beside her, jade eyes flashing. He reminded her of the night they appeared before the pyre, girded in a tragic strength, the kingdom upon his shoulders.

"What are you doing here?" Lystra whispered. She could feel the committee's stares, watching them with hawkish eyes.

His eyes met hers, and in them there was austerity and kindness—balance. "Lystra, I . . ." His throat worked. "I made a mistake. I should have been here all along." Then, he turned to the assembly. "It is an honor to come before you, esteemed nobles and houses of this committee. I thank House Pana for filling the role of generous host."

Elerek couldn't know, couldn't have heard what had been

spoken about him only moments earlier. Lystra held her breath, watching to see how the committee would react to this, the king they had just denounced, now presented before them.

They bowed. Just as they had for her. Bent waists and bended knees. The respect owed a king, but Lystra knew it lay only skin deep.

Was this how it always was for him? Faced with decorum, a mirage of respect, but behind his back endured whispers and cruel words? The discarded heir of a despised ruler who had torn their kingdom apart. A new understanding dawned in her mind. He knew *exactly* how she felt here before these nobles who counted her as unworthy.

"I ought not to interrupt Her Highness's presentation." Elerek's gaze briefly turned toward her again. "But if I may be permitted a few words?"

Lystra dipped her chin. "We were *discussing*"—she drew the word out with a measure of severity—"our request of the racing committee's cardants to defend our kingdom."

Elerek's eyes narrowed, feeling perhaps a bit of the tension still clouding the air. He faced the assembly. "As your rulers, we do not lightly entertain the nature of our request. My queen holds your culture of racing and tending cardants in high regard, as I am sure goes without saying. A position I am aware that you all hold, as well, and it is a staple of our culture that has shaped our beautiful kingdom. However, we are facing a superior threat in the Jarkins' seizing of the Darcress Kasbah, and we need our every defense at the ready."

Rousing words. Words that she had already spoken. Lystra saw several of the men scowl, ready to unravel the cordial tapestry Elerek sought to weave.

Of course, it was Jabir who spoke first. "We do not believe, Your Highness, in the purity of your motives. As we informed your queen—"

"In no small words." Ikram masked his words behind a cough.

Jabir glared at the young rider. "We resent this blatant manipulation that she—"

"Her Highness is *not* a manipulation." With his jaw set like stone, Elerek leaned forward in his chair. "I will not suffer any arguments in this vein of thought. My queen and I are of one mind. Our motives are for the survival of our kingdom and we are facing a threat, perhaps the greatest of our age."

For a moment, Lystra heard only the sound of her heart pounding.

"Now, I do not say that to inspire fear." Elerek laced his fingers together, the plague scars running like veins along his knuckles. "Cooperation will be our strength and division will only be our downfall."

"We've already faced the greatest threat of our age." The head of House Tikkal took up the same refrain. "We survived the wars of a tyrant—King Lorkin. Conquest after conquest. And he never seized our cardants to fight."

Lystra clenched her teeth. The color left Elerek's face, only minimally, but she'd learned to notice the fear building behind his eyes. Now he saw the argument, the foundation stones they sought to lay.

"My father dealt many bitter wounds." The king's words were cold and sharp, like steel. "I do not claim to have the remedy. If I tell you that I am nothing like my father, I know you will not believe me. How many of you have already looked me in the eye and withheld your fealty? If I do not have your loyalty, then I do not want your cardants for my soldiers. And I will *not* seize your property. I desire your choice, given freely."

As predicted, skepticism had come to stay in the eyes of the houses. Lystra didn't think that anything could sway them at this juncture. But the wounds dealt by their words were lessened. She stood here before their glowers, and she was not alone.

"Your queen gave her cardants to the throne, to your brother, and they were slaughtered," Jabir said. "We will not follow her lead—nor the words put in her mouth."

Regality fell from the king like a curtain. Lystra watched in rapt attention as his face transformed, his expression set like flint and his eyes an avenging fire.

"I welcome your arguments, if conducted civilly. However, I refuse the blatant slander against *my queen*. This is your second offense, my lord."

My queen. Lystra forced her gaze away. How she hoped that her face hadn't blushed. No, she had to stand tall, poised, the queen that her king had given the crown.

Grandmother would call this weakness, relying upon another. She didn't feel weak but strengthened. Two pillars were stronger than one.

Except . . . he was going to die. The curse would take him, sure as the stars themselves, and she would have to face more fearsome opponents than this on her own.

Yusef stepped forward, bowing at the waist. "House Himmel will pledge their cardants, Your Highness, trusting that we will survive this conflict and live to see your word kept."

Only a few others joined in this pledge. Most refused.

They did not linger, their work complete. Lystra kept in

stride with the rhythm of Elerek's wheelchair. She waited until they returned to the courtyard before speaking.

"Did you know that that would happen in there?"

The king stopped his chair, waiting as his guards made ready his carriage. "As soon as you left, I realized what folly it was. Sending you alone would only arouse their suspicion and would not encourage unity. As predicted, they were lions and . . ." His face reddened. "I don't doubt your ability, you realize. I didn't come to . . . eclipse you."

Lystra swiftly shook her head. "Oh, no, I didn't think that at all." She wished she could embrace him, show him exactly how his appearance had made her feel. Of course, it might be awkward with his wheelchair, and she'd probably end up in his lap—*what?* She blinked, cutting her thoughts off. "Thank you, for coming."

Stars above, she wondered if her face might melt clean off. The afternoon had turned to the hour of sweltering, but it was nothing compared to the fire beneath her skin.

A moment passed, long and horrible. They stared at one another, both quite flushed.

The door to Elerek's carriage opened. The soldier standing there was familiar—one of the cursed, Lystra realized. She quickly ran down the list of names given to her at their wedding feast. "Good afternoon, Cole."

The soldier's eyes brightened at her recognition. He bowed, orange cape sweeping behind him. Another soldier appeared behind him, pulling long gloves, like those used for hawking expeditions, over his arms. They stood on either side of Elerek's wheelchair, lifting it carefully into the carriage. As they performed this task, Elerek clenched the armrests with white knuckles, probably anxious about falling.

Lystra was reminded of their conversation concerning the

riding of cardants, and her challenge that he could certainly handle a reptile. A smile spread across her lips.

"May I ride back with you?" She stepped closer to the carriage, noticing that the seat had been removed on one side to leave room for his chair.

Elerek leaned forward, grasping a wood handle set beside the carriage door. Alarm passed through his eyes.

"We cannot be close." His words from their wedding night returned. Across a bed, across a carriage, the curse demanded distance.

"Or, if you'd rather . . ." She took a step back.

"She'll be safe, Your Highness." Cole boarded the carriage, taking his place beside Elerek and placing a firm hand on the back of his chair to keep it from rolling. "Razhar rides with us all the time."

Elerek dipped his chin, leaning back as Lystra climbed inside and seated herself across from him. Once they secured the door, the guards gave the word and the carriage lurched forward, rumbling its way back to the palace.

Lystra adjusted her skirt, trying not to let the uneven roads jostle her too much. "Perhaps next time we've an appointment in the city, we ought to ride cardants."

"Hmm." Elerek's grip on the handle tightened, keeping his chair steady. She took the brooding scowl upon his face as a sign of disapproval.

A smirk pulled at her lips. Where cardants were concerned, she'd wear him down eventually.

The carriage lurched, pulling onto the main avenue. The noise of mules, carriages, and the voices of the city preparing for the night market filtered inside, along with tiny clouds of dust. Lystra almost missed the quiet words the king spoke next.

"Has the committee always treated you that way?"

She cringed. Unpleasant memories surfaced, reminding her

of races lost and won, both on and off the track. "Once. It was no small feat for me to earn my place there. I was young for them, still am, and there are few women among us. For some, like Jabir of House Pana, I'll never be enough, but that is not my concern." She sighed, her fingers tracing one of the petals stitched across the front of her kaftan.

Was it her imagination or was Elerek watching her, his eyes following the motion of her fingers? "Were they cruel?" he asked quietly. "Before I arrived?"

"It doesn't matter."

"Yes, it does."

Lystra huffed. "Well, they were cruel to you too."

Elerek's features hardened, solid as marble, but once again, Lystra could see the cracks. The broken bits that he carried with him, like the curse mark on his ribs and the scar on his arm. "Let them. I can't stop the whispers any more than I can break the curse, but I can choose not to care."

Break the curse. Lystra shifted her gaze. There'd been precious little time between fortifying Instanolde for the coming siege to even consider furthering her investigation. Maybe the task was impossible, as Razhar seemed to think. Then again, Razhar himself hid his own impossibilities, and Lystra still had no idea what to do with that information.

But if the curse wasn't broken, the king—her husband— would die.

Another death.

Sometimes, it hurt that he looked like Cormek, reminding her that grief still lingered. The circlet set amid his curls, the dark tunic trimmed in gold stretched tight across his broad shoulders, and the stare of his jade-colored eyes—the ghost seemed real, haunting her. But Elerek himself had become another sort of specter, one that, despite the necessary distance, seemed to draw closer and closer.

269

Chapter 34

Elerek

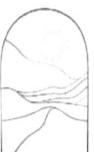

The carriage air felt suffocating and Elerek found breathing difficult. Perhaps high summer's afternoons were becoming unbearably brutal, or the stiff, embroidered jabador that clung to his arms and shoulders and draped to his knees wanted to strangle him.

Still, perhaps it was the queen, magnificent in her kaftan with its curious floral patterns, and the midnight kohl lining her eyes like a raven's inky wing, seated across from him.

He'd been an idiot—*again*. Of course the racing committee wouldn't see her as a bearer of the throne's powers. No, they only saw one of their own speaking for him, and neither of them held the authority to undo the pain his father had caused.

Elerek huffed. For all his father's endless wars and bloody conquests, he'd left the Jarkins alone across the desert. Years of infighting and they'd ignored the amassing threat upon their doorstep. Maybe the damage was too great.

No, it was too soon to lose hope. Starlight remained. Close to thirty cardants had been pledged to aid the cause and Elerek intended to keep his promises. And the way Lystra's gaze had brightened at his arrival, her joy radiating from her like the glorious dawn, was enough to fuel him forward. Their motives had aligned, their strengths balancing each other, and he marveled at how they seemed to pulse in perfect unity.

The carriage lumbered to a halt inside the palace courtyard. As soon as the guards opened the door, a gasp fell from Lystra's lips and she all but flew out of the carriage in a flurry of silk and streaming black hair.

"Is that not House Arghan's carriage?" Cole asked.

Indeed. The purple banners fluttered in the afternoon breeze and its occupants stood assembled in the shade of the palace spires. With a joyous laugh, Lystra flung herself into the arms of her father. Even from here, adoration glowed in Jethro's eyes as he embraced his daughter.

The curse's numbness returned, spreading the cold feeling of deadness over his skin. Not once had Elerek's father ever embraced him. It was easy enough to say that the curse deemed it necessary, the same requirements of all his other relationships, but that didn't mean that it didn't hurt. Even now, despite the panic, he craved the comradely gestures—a slap on the shoulder, a handshake—from Norbah, Cole, Ishtal, and the others. But this desire had also produced weakness, even if Myra's embraces had kept him from drowning.

Speaking of which, near the palace steps, Myra stood with her arms folded. Driss stood beside her, and their faces wore a grim sorrow that only the curse could conjure. His stomach twisted. A complete contrast to the joyous reunion between Lystra and her father and cousins.

Cole and the other guard lowered his chair to the paved stonework. Even on solid ground, he felt as if he were teetering. Elerek cast a glance at his queen, her and her cousins still chittering away like birds, smiles all around. He then wheeled himself toward the shade, his guards following.

"What happened?" His eyes darted between the two who shared his curse.

Myra stepped forward. She'd tied her hair back, as she often did when working with the bakers, and he could see streaks of flour on her skirt. "El, it's Fin. The curse is taking him."

Fin? The boy. Hardly more than a child, and the curse chose him next. A heaviness settled on Elerek's chest, the weight of water filling his lungs instead of air.

He swallowed and clenched his hands tight. His family needed strength. "Is someone with him?"

Driss nodded. "Razhar and Bushra. We'll keep him safe until he passes. But El, he's been asking for you."

Elerek closed his eyes. How many of his friends had he watched drown before his eyes? Their skin, everything familiar about them stripped away, until he only looked into the face of a leering skull coated in water. And they always asked for him.

Very few had spoken cruel words before their passing. Most assured him that they were all right, that the open skies of the Starkindler awaited them. Many poured out their gratitude for what he'd done for them in their final days. Elerek supposed they needed to do it, to say it.

Oh, but it hurt. Stars above, it *hurt.*

"I'll come," he choked out. "Just wait a moment, please."

Pivoting his chair, he immediately wheeled himself before House Arghan, clearing his face of turmoil and projecting what he hoped was something pleasant.

"Your Highness." Jethro bowed, the drape of his robes trailing the dust. Kimzi and his sister mirrored his motions.

Elerek dipped his chin in acknowledgment. He hadn't seen Lystra's father since the wedding and given the unusual parameters of their political marriage, he had no idea how to address the man.

Lystra looked at him with a wide smile. "We can count three more cardants among our numbers."

Jethro straightened. "Her Highness, my daughter, speaks true. I heard about your request of cardants for soldiers and I've brought three reptiles, my personal mount included, for your efforts. Your stables have already welcomed them warmly."

"Word travels swiftly," Elerek replied. "Thank you for your donation."

"Bah, the cardant circles are a gossipy lot." Jethro snorted.

Lystra grasped his hand. "Father, you must see Tiniah, my new cardant. She is a magnificent reptile and shall be the fastest I've ever trained."

"New cardant?" Her father raised his eyebrows.

"Yes! Elerek—His Highness—gifted her to me as a wedding gift."

At the mention of the wedding, Jethro looked at him with an expression of renewed scrutiny, perhaps remembering that he had become his son-in-law. "Ah, I see you've found the way to my daughter's heart. Good, good."

Not even the curse could quench the heat searing across his face.

"Father." Lystra spoke quickly, her own face quite crimson. "Please say that you'll stay for the evening meal. It's been too long."

A smile spread over Jethro's face again. "If you'll have us, of course. Your grandmother said she would also try to visit this evening."

At the mention of the countess, Lystra's eyes dimmed. The change came ever so slightly, but like the last time the former queen appeared in the palace, Elerek noticed. He wished that she could see what he saw—that Queen Lystra of Instanolde was far stronger than her manipulative grandmother could ever imagine.

"We would be honored to have you." Elerek's hand moved to the wheel of his chair. "Your Highness, I do need to speak with you a moment."

Lystra didn't seem to notice the gravity of his tone. She gave her family a fond smile, her eyes still aglow like a desert sunset. "Please, go on to the stables. Kimzi will show you. I'll be along." Once they departed, taking the passages through the courtyards, Lystra stepped closer. "Yes?"

"There's a situation." Elerek lowered his voice. "With my family—the cursed."

The queen's eyes went wide. Her painted lips parted, but she did not speak.

"Someone is drowning—dying. There's nothing I can do, but I need to be there." His heart felt as if it were a cloth, wetted, squeezed, and wrung out. "I'll come to the evening meal as soon as I can."

Lystra stared down at her hem. "Please, don't come for my sake. Go where you are needed."

Stars, he did not deserve her. "Thank you for understanding."

"Is Razhar there?" Her gaze shot up.

Elerek frowned. Why would she ask that? "I'm told so, yes."

"Good." Her eyes took on a stormfront, a swirl of contemplation in her irises.

"El!" Myra's voice. Elerek glanced over his shoulder just in time to see Driss take off running toward one of the palace's side entrances, leaving the girl standing there, her face stricken with panic. "We must hurry."

He swore beneath his breath. The curse's timeline baffled him. Why had some, like Norbah, lasted nearly a decade, while others, like Myra, had been given years, and others merely months? And at the end of it all, he lingered. Watching the curse flood out in a wave of horror.

"I'm coming, Myra." He backed his chair up a pace.

"So, you *do* know her?" Lystra's posture went rigid, arms folded, and her shoulders cut sharp. "The girl who appeared in our chambers?"

Oh. Elerek forced his hand to relax, almost frightened that his fingers might break the wheel itself. The wedding night. When he'd sent Myra away. Lystra *had* recognized her at the wedding feast. Well, of course she would. Lystra missed nothing.

"Yes, she's cursed."

"I'll have nothing but the truth from your lips." But did Lystra have to demand this truth? Did it matter? Myra no longer dwelt in his life, even his heart had closed itself off from her. He'd given his vows to Lystra.

Perhaps the stories of caution, written in the stars themselves, echoed with more truth than he realized. That even when a sin had been mourned and moved on from, consequences had their way of worming back.

"Yes, I see that." Lystra's lashes fluttered.

Stars above, does she know? Elerek didn't want this conversation. Not now. One of his tribe lay drowning and he had to see the end through. And what if Lystra was ignorant? He didn't want to bring it up unless he knew for sure. No, this could wait.

"I have to go." He rolled his chair back. "I'll try to come; I'd very much like to become better acquainted with your family." He managed a small smile. "Make sure you tell them how magnificent you were today."

But unlike his other attempts to bolster her spirit, to give her starlight, this one didn't work. A sorrow lingered in Lystra's eyes as he pivoted his chair toward the palace and followed Myra and Cole, one that he wasn't sure he could chase away.

For now, Fin lived.

But it would be soon. Perhaps even this very night. The cursed took watches, staying with him every hour. The boy would not be left alone as the waters laid claim to his body and the drowning stole away his life.

Elerek sat with him until the sun sank in the west, surrounded by the company of their tribe. The words were difficult, to speak peace and encouragement and to grieve and give sorrow. As it turned out, Elerek spoke little. Fin had never known how to keep his tongue and he used every breath left in his lungs. He held no grudge nor anger for what had happened to him. He laughed and smiled, thanking the king for his home in the palace, for the friends he'd made, and the days he'd been given.

"We all have one life, Elerek. A mighty gift from the Maker of the stars."

One life—and *this* was the sort of life they were given? Did Cormek know that his own days were up when he'd spoken those words? Did he know that his own cursed brother, doomed to die, would outlive him?

Elerek kept his emotions in check until he'd bidden his family goodnight. Then he left, barricading himself in a parlor tucked away behind the throne room. Yanking the gold circlet from his brow, he let it fall to the marble floor with a clatter. The four stone walls echoed with the howls of his rage and his sorrow.

"I didn't ask for this . . ." The words ground between his teeth. "I don't want this."

How many had died? How many had suffered? Because of *him*? Razhar told him, over and over and over, that he was not the curse. Sometimes he let himself believe it. But not now.

"Why did you let this happen? Do you despise me that much?" He buried his face in his hands, doubling over in his wheelchair.

But he knew the truth. The Starkindler hadn't done this to him. No, an ordinary human, clothed in flesh and blood, consumed by ill intent, had done this to him. He would never know who. Never fully understand why. These were truths he had to live with. None of it was fair, but fairness had no rights beneath the burning, desert sun.

"I'm doing the best I can," he seethed, clenching his eyes shut. "I'm *trying*."

He'd given everything. He'd committed himself to this kingdom, to survival, to his queen. Why did it feel like so little? Why did it feel like it wasn't enough?

It wouldn't. It would never be. But stars above, did he still have to try so *hard*? Why did it matter when his friends still died? When he would die?

Rage, feral and unfettered, rose in his chest. It ravaged his heart with the fury of a sandstorm. He slammed a fist onto the armrest of his chair. "I don't want to try anymore!"

Water surged down his arm, coated his hand, and splashed onto the marble floor. It left a dark streak along the side of his jabador, the icy cold seeping to his skin. The puddle upon the floor gathered about his circlet, a herald of the future to come.

Elerek drew a sharp breath. He lifted his hand, watching the droplets cascade from his fingertips. For a moment, he forgot that this fate would kill him, only concentrated on the deluge. He imagined that every drop held a bit of his rage, his sorrow, and he knew that stream would never run dry.

Cursed. No other title mattered. Not the weight of his kingdom or the bloody history of House Karim. Cormek had been wrong. He truly was nothing more than a cursed man waiting to die. A man who had tried—and was destined to fail.

He clenched his fist and the flow stemmed. He didn't understand why the curse was changing like this. It didn't make sense. His mark remained the same and no one else had been given this strange side effect.

With a sigh, he wiped his sleeve across his eyes and squared his shoulders. Just because he didn't want his burdens didn't mean that they would go away. In this trying, he had no choice, and he'd promised Lystra he'd spend time with her family.

Except, his circlet. Elerek scoffed at his own stupidity, and at the effort it would take him to climb from his chair, onto the floor, to retrieve it.

Before he could climb back into his chair, the door opened. Torchlight spilled in from the corridor beyond. Two figures entered, outlined in the glow.

"Why are you on the floor, El?" Razhar gave him a strange expression.

"Dropped this." Elerek lifted the circlet, replacing it on his brow.

"Dropped?" Myra questioned, lingering in the doorway.

He huffed. "Fine, I threw it." He reached for the wheelchair.

"Here, let me help you. Razhar, please steady his chair." Myra slipped her arm beneath his shoulder, assisting him back into the chair.

The scent of her hair, a musk of florals, hit him like a thunderclap. Even after the task was done, her fingers lingered on his sleeve. Her touch, her closeness, sent a resurgence of memories that he'd buried, cut off, and swore to never entertain again.

"Don't touch me." He sent her a sharp look. "Please."

Myra took a step back, avoiding his gaze.

Distance. Necessary and imperative. Between him and his kingdom, and the single touch that could curse and drown. Cut off from humanity, from all the tenderness and joy that a touch could bring. So much had been taken from him—and he *hated* it.

He hated that Myra's presence affected him so, demanding space, horizons flung as far as the east from the west. He hated that his isolation, his desperation, had driven him to her in the first place. He hated that the same distance now lay between him and the bride to whom he had sworn vows.

And stars above, he *hated* the curse.

"El? You all right?" Razhar patted the back of his chair.

Elerek glanced over his shoulder, at Razhar's dark fingers curled over the wood. "You too, back away. Please."

Razhar obeyed, a look of concern on his face.

"I'm not having a good day." Elerek rubbed his face.

A sorrowful chuckle worked itself from Razhar's lips. "Even kings have them, El. I suppose that proves you're just as human as the rest of us."

Human, and yet so many things shared by humanity had been denied him.

"Why are your clothes soaked?" Myra inquired. "And so cold?"

Elerek shook his head, not wishing to discuss how cursed water had spouted from his hands not once or twice, but *three* times now. "The curse. Some new ploy to torment me. I'm not sure yet."

"Your mark?" Razhar inquired.

"Still the same," he huffed. "Don't concern yourselves with me."

With another laugh, Razhar shook his head. The torchlight caught in his eyes, glittering in pain beneath the gleam of his emerald turban. "Whatever would I do with myself then? Surely dying a slow death of boredom doesn't suit me."

No, life suited Razhar. Death suited him. Elerek clenched his eyes shut. *Pull yourself together.* "I must go. Lystra's family is visiting."

"Are you sure you should go?" Darkness hovered in Myra's eyes at the mention of Lystra's name.

Elerek nodded, wheeling his chair past them. "No, but for the queen, I should." He didn't wait for a response, hurrying down the corridor as quickly as his arms would take him.

The evening meal would be served in the garden courtyard, where colored torches gleamed against the night and the pools were dotted with lilies. All beneath the pure white light of the stars, and the thought of watching the constellations dance made Elerek's heart a bit lighter. He pivoted his chair toward the throne room, the shortest route to the courtyard.

The two bowls of fire still burned, eternal flames each flanking the stone throne. The sight of it sent a shiver across Elerek's cold, cursed skin—as did the slender shadow standing before it.

Dalmah of House Arghan. Clothed in silver, her black hair lay twisted in braids about her head, and her bony hands were studded with jewels. The firelight flickered in her eyes, casting the perfect image of the queen who was cast from the throne by way of a relentless, bloody conquest.

Elerek stopped, his hand clenched about his wheel rim. The countess's eyes turned, falling upon him with smoldering embers. He returned the stare. His former suspicions concerning Lystra's grandmother returned to mind—including the idea that she'd given her granddaughter a dagger and poisoned her mind with murderous intent.

Why would this woman give him a bride and a death in the same night?

Dalmah turned, taking two deliberate steps toward him. She held her chin high, her blood-red lips turned down in a frown. "You look just like your father."

Elerek didn't move, didn't blink. He'd lost count of the references made to his father this day, but he'd reached his fill. "That doesn't mean that I'm anything like him."

"Hmm." Dalmah cocked her head just slightly. "No, only a monster of a different sort." Then, a smile broke across her face. "Excuse me, I'd like some time with my granddaughter."

Then she swept from the chamber, leaving Elerek alone in the marble-cast throne room, his clothes drenched in cursed water, and his heart submerged in ice.

Certainly not the king his glorious queen deserved. No, she deserved happiness, the warmth of the torches lighting the courtyard, surrounded by the smiles and laughter of her family. Perhaps her grandmother was right, and he was only a cursed monster.

He pivoted his chair, turning away from the light of the courtyard beyond, and turned back to the shadows instead.

Chapter 35

Lystra

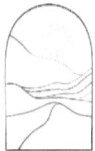

Lystra tried not to think of Elerek as she joined her family at the edge of Tiniah's pen. How he would sit at the deathbed of one whom he considered family, knowing that his touch was responsible.

Touch. Her thoughts of embracing him now seemed foolish and frivolous. She could never touch him, never close the distance. Her heart grew heavy, and it wearied her to erect barricades about it again. No, the entirety of their alliance must remain political. Hadn't she carried enough grief these past weeks? How could she even dare permit her heart into such a treacherous terrain?

But when the curse finally came to claim what it was owed, she would mourn. For Cormek, for Elerek, and the unlived days stolen from them both.

The cardant lay sleepy in the afternoon heat, sunning her scales at the edge of her pen. Lystra didn't hesitate to slip inside, embroidered kaftan and all, to rouse her enough to meet her father and cousins.

"Have you ridden her?" Kimzi inquired eagerly, leaning his lanky frame against the pen.

"Yes, just within the stable grounds." Lystra ran her hand along Tiniah's ivory horns. "She's not quite ready for the desert yet."

"Have you ridden out there?" Her father's face settled into a deep frown. "Alone?"

Lystra regarded the anxiety in his eyes. Her father had never worried about her venturing into the desert before, then again, she'd nearly not come back at all.

"Not in the wilderness, just to visit the stonemasons' efforts to fortify the outer wall." She offered Jethro a reassuring smile. "High summer will keep the invaders away, for now."

"For now," he repeated thoughtfully.

Lystra lowered her gaze, wishing that the summer months could endure longer, and give them more time to prepare. Allow Elerek to live a bit longer.

A servant had announced that the evening meal would be ready shortly, but Jethro and Kimzi lingered in the stables. Lystra, craving a few moments with Corsha, took her cousin's arm in hers and they ventured through the gardens, taking the long route to the lovely courtyard where the meal would be served.

"You've been quiet, cousin."

Corsha's green eyes seemed to deepen surrounded by the growing vegetation. "I've missed you, Lystra. The estate is so lonely, especially with Kimzi spending his days training with the archers."

Lonely and empty, exactly the sort of environment that Lystra had expected to find at the palace. Yet she'd found quite the opposite, leaving the desolation at home. "I'm sorry I haven't visited more. Everything takes so much time."

Halting on the gravel path, Corsha faced her with a stern countenance. Perhaps all the women of House Arghan were queens. "Don't apologize, Lystra. You're saving us, all of us."

Not all of us. Lystra bit her tongue and looked away. No, she was no closer to breaking the curse than she was the night she'd married a cursed king. "And Grandmother?"

Corsha huffed. "Much the same, though she's been quieter since you left, more sullen. I have been under the impression that she's dissatisfied with you for some reason."

Right, she'd chosen not to murder her husband.

"I'm sure she'll make her displeasure known tonight, if she comes." Lystra wrinkled her nose, rather hoping that Dalmah would just stay home.

Corsha gave a sympathetic nod. As they took up their stroll again, somewhere in the shade palms a bird began to sing, its voice resonating with the hot wind in the branches.

"Lystra." Her cousin's voice dropped, low as the murmur of the river. "Tell me. Are you happy here?"

The birdsong grew louder, others joining the refrain. Lystra let their notes fill the air, giving her a moment before replying. "Yes, actually. I am." Far happier than she could've hoped. "The weight of our endeavor is crushing, but I cannot think that we will fail. I have to believe we are going to succeed, and our efforts have not been in vain."

"*We.*" Corsha cast her a sideways glance from beneath her thick eyelashes.

A bundle of nerves tossed in Lystra's stomach. She couldn't meet her cousin's gaze.

"You haven't yet spoken of this marriage—of your *husband.*"

Lystra stopped, shutting her eyes. How could she possibly respond to that?

"Lystra, please. If you tell me that you are happy, I must know that you are happy with the king." She took both of Lystra's hands into hers, facing her head-on. "You've lost so much, and I couldn't bear it if you were miserable."

Opening her eyes, Lystra lifted her chin, a tactic taught by Grandmother. "I'm not miserable, Corsha. Far from it. The king and I have gotten along much better than I could've hoped."

Of course, that wouldn't be enough for Corsha. "I've asked Kimzi about him. He says that the king is strict, severe, but also fair."

"I'd agree with that assessment—and gentle." Stars, she'd begun to blush.

Corsha lifted an eyebrow. "Does he care for you as he ought?"

Surely *these* were the questions her cousin wanted to ask, the end goal of her investigation. Lystra thought again of his entrance before the racing committee, his intent to rescue her from another sort of drowning.

"Does he love you?" Corsha pressed.

No. Lystra's breath hitched. *He can't . . .* But did she want him to? And if he did, could she return the affection? Even now, with grief still lingering in her heart?

"Lystra, you're scaring me. If he—"

"Elerek and I have both lost those whom we love." She rose to her full height, as if giving an address. "He understands my pain, understands in a way that I never thought I'd find. He has shielded me, encouraged, and emboldened me. Grandmother always sought to smother me into this role. Elerek has given the opposite—wide open horizons." Tears filled her eyes. Stars above, it wasn't fair.

Corsha's eyes widened, watching with rapt attention.

"He keeps people distant because he doesn't know how to bring them close. Yes, he's severe as stone, but it's only skin deep." Deeper than the curse could touch. "Like us, he's known sorrow and cruelty, but it hasn't hardened him. It's taught him mercy, compassion."

"Stars." Corsha shook her head, bewilderment sparkling like constellations in her emerald gaze. "Lystra, you've fallen—"

"Don't say it!" Her heart beat like mad, protesting against this reality, this impossibly hopeless situation. Lystra dropped her shoulders, turning away. "I'm certain he doesn't feel the same way."

Fury rose in her chest at the remembrance of the panic thundering in his gaze when she'd cornered him about knowing the cursed girl, giving her all the confirmation she needed. Elerek couldn't be touched, embraced, or held, but he could touch Myra, the girl who had sacrificed her future to be with him.

"Are you sure?" Corsha cocked an eyebrow. "That cardant in the stables says otherwise. And if all that you say is true, I don't know how it's possible he's not taken with you."

But it wasn't possible. A deadly curse hung between them and would always separate them. Unless she found a way to break it.

Perhaps she was being foolish. If she were to fight for her kingdom, for their survival at summer's end, of course she could fight for Elerek. Even if the curse couldn't be broken, and the king was doomed to die, she would be there, right by his side, as she had vowed when she'd become his bride.

"Thank you, Corsha." She squeezed her cousin's hand. Corsha merely grinned.

Elerek didn't attend the evening meal.

Lystra hadn't expected him to. Not while one of his own lay dying. While she smiled and laughed with her family, her heart ached, as if something in their vows had opened some channel to each other's pain as the spring rains opened new washes across the desert.

She told her family nothing of the curse, of this great grief, only that a friend of his was gravely ill. They spoke no more of the king's absence, and the air soon filled with her cousins' witty banter and her father's reserved replies. Her grandmother swept into the room like a desert wraith of legend, her shrewd eyes seeing much, but for this blessed moment, she spoke little and Lystra could almost imagine that she wasn't there.

When the night had drawn nigh, watched over by the constellations dancing in the inky blackness, Lystra bade her family farewell and traversed through the palace to her bedchamber. The halls were near silent, the torches few, and the darkness immense. She wrapped her arms around herself, chilled by the absence of her family's presence.

For the first time since entering the palace, loneliness swept over her. It pounded in her chest, a fearful, vulnerable sound, and she wondered what would ease it.

Starlight—hope.

She quickened her steps, hurrying for familiar ground. The

guards stood outside her chamber, promising safety—and that meant that Elerek had retired.

No lamps were lit in the parlor and the lattice was drawn fast over the windows, veiling the light of the heavens. Lystra glanced once toward the silk covering the doorway to Elerek's room before turning for her own.

A breeze wafted through her room, warmed by the summer's heat, flowing through the open windows and teasing the canopy above her bed. She could still smell the faint perfume she'd applied before her appointment with the racing committee lingering in the air.

Lystra passed by her wardrobe and dressing screen, hurrying to her nightstand where, atop its polished wood, a single scroll lay. The scroll of the star stories, the one Elerek had given to her on their wedding night. Stories of hope, meant to inspire, and to give comfort. She clasped it to her chest, willing a bit of that hope to sink into her now.

Perhaps . . . No. She ought to go to bed, let the dawn shine its renewal across Instanolde. But some of Elerek's love of starlight had passed on to her, and she found herself returning to the parlor, the scroll in hand, and parting the silk to the king's chamber.

Her feet moved no farther, pity laying claim to her heart.

Elerek lay on his side, his even breaths telling her that he lay fast asleep. However, the way his blankets twisted about him also told her that it was a fitful sleep, one that hadn't come easy. His shoulders, bare and pale, were hunched, as if even in sleep they carried burdens that they shouldn't have, and his arm hung over the edge of the bed, his fingers dangling.

Drip.

Lystra blinked, so sure she'd imagined it.

Drip.

No, the droplet that gathered on his fingertip, glistening

288

like a diamond, was real and like the others, it fell into the small puddle amassing on the floor beside his nightstand. The same nightstand where her grandmother's dagger still lay shimmering in the starlight.

The curse. Lystra stepped closer, but she couldn't see his mark, buried beneath him in the blankets. Panic crawled across her skin and sorrow welled up in her soul. *Please, not yet.*

A soft knock sounded at the door.

Lystra glanced over her shoulder. Who would the guards permit to knock?

Leaving the king's chamber, she hurried to the door. There, in the soft torchlight beyond, stood Razhar and Myra.

"What's happened?"

Razhar huffed, folding his thick arms. "Nothing yet. May we speak with you?"

Lystra stepped outside, closing the door behind her. "It's late."

"Precisely." A bit of color appeared on Razhar's face. "Now, forgive the awkwardness of the situation but . . ." He rocked back on his heels. "You know about my abilities."

Narrowing her eyes, Lystra tilted her head back to scowl at him. "I trust you were doing all you could to keep the one who is drowning alive?"

"Fin," Myra whispered, bowing her head.

The boy? Lystra's hardness melted away. Fin was hardly more than a child. Surely he didn't deserve—no, none of them did. But for the curse to strike the youngest, a wide-eyed boy, revealed the deepest, vilest intents of the curse's twisted nature.

Starkindler, can it not be broken?

"I was." Razhar's jaw clenched. "But Fin isn't the only one who's cursed, and we're worried about El."

"It's been a long while since Razhar has used his abilities to help him." Myra's voice was quiet. "Since he married you."

Lystra wrapped her arms about herself again, staring at the stonework beneath her slippers. Their marriage prevented any late-night visitors to the king's chambers, besides her of course. Still, as she thought again of the droplets cascading from Elerek's fingers, she realized the sense in it.

"I've seen you use your abilities, Razhar." She met his gaze. "Please, help him."

Razhar nodded, slipping around her to open the door and venture inside.

"You will remain here." Lystra looked at Myra with a level gaze.

The fire returned to the girl's eyes. "You didn't know it was Fin?"

"No."

Myra scoffed, looking away. "I heard about what happened today."

Fatigue weighed itself on Lystra's shoulders. She didn't want to argue, certainly not with Myra, and wondered which part of the day she was referring to.

"El went to the racing committee. *Your* world." Torchlight flashed in Myra's gaze. "He defended you, before all those houses and stuck-up nobles."

Fine. Lystra stood a little taller, ready to play her game. "Yes, he did."

"And where were you when one of his family, one of our tribe, lay drowning?"

She struck and her mark was true. Lystra clenched her jaw, as if the sheer force of her set teeth might uphold her queenly posture. Yes, she was with her family. Myra wanted her to feel guilty, and she'd succeeded.

What would Elerek have done if she'd tried to accompany him? Would he have let her stand by him? Support him, as he had supported her? Stars, she hadn't even asked.

And neither had he.

Myra stepped closer, lifting her chin. "Do you know the cold, the numbness creeping through your skin? Do you know that every breath has been counted? Do you know what it is to look around at your companions knowing that soon they'll be nothing but spilled water upon stone?" Tears filled her eyes. "Do you know what it does to him?"

She thought of his eyes the day they were faced with the reality of their arrangement. How she had looked into another's soul and seen her own pains. And then on the night they wed, his eyes were filled with starlight. Yes, there was pain there, but Elerek was more than his pains.

Had Myra seen that? Or had Myra only seen the painful, broken parts of him?

"Our pains are different," Lystra said softly. "But I think their ache is familiar."

A tear streaked down Myra's cheek. "If not for you, I would be with him. See that he isn't suffering alone." She pinched her eyes shut. "I couldn't bear if anything happened to him."

Jealousy reared its ugly head. Lystra turned away, breathing deep to settle the heat burning in her chest. Corsha's near declaration of what precisely had happened in Lystra's heart now screamed in her mind. This was dangerous. Deadly, like a curse.

"I don't wish him harm, Myra." Lystra's voice was firm. "It is my duty to stand by his side as his queen. I am committed to that role."

Then, why did her heart yearn for more?

The door opened and Razhar returned. His brow lay furrowed, confusion swirling in his eyes. Then he bristled, glancing at the two women, and edged away from the tensions brewing between them.

"Stars above, am I interrupting something?"

Lystra wanted to strangle him. "Is he all right?"

"I hope so." Razhar shrugged. "I can only do what I can. Hold back the waters."

Did that include the waters dripping from his fingers? Lystra frowned. Was that normal? Had it happened before? Had Razhar's strange abilities stopped it?

"Keep him alive," Myra whispered.

Lystra turned away, resting her hand on the door handle. "I thank you for your concern, and your efforts. I'm sure it means nothing, for my devotion pales in comparison to what you have given, but I want him to live too."

She didn't wait for a response, too afraid of what they might think. Surely Myra would scorn her and hate her even more if she knew her heart was drawn to her king. And Razhar, well, Lystra had no idea how he would react but now was not the time for his cheeky humor.

Razhar, the man who could hold back the curse and kept such secrets from the king. Lystra shuddered, realizing that she'd become complicit in those secrets. She thought again of the curse mark, silver in the starlight, snaking across his chest. Elerek needed to live, and for that, he needed Razhar. Perhaps that's how Razhar justified his secrets . . .

But no, secrets were secrets, and Lystra needed to know them. This was her kingdom, after all. She was its queen and Razhar one of her subjects. If only there weren't so many other pressing matters weighing upon her mind.

Once the door was shut, she returned to her chambers. Before she fell asleep, she spread the scroll across her bedspread and let the starlight illuminate the chart until her eyelids grew heavy.

Chapter 36

Elerek

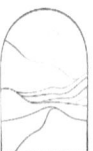

Growling, Elerek dragged his hands through his hair. Black strokes of ink swam before his eyes, muddling the maps of the Sancen into madness.

Reclining back on the couch, he tossed the map onto the pile he'd arranged on the floor and closed his eyes, blocking out the sight of the library shelves crammed with texts and scrolls. Perhaps this was a waste of time, and his efforts better spent fortifying the city rather than attempting to predict what route Gaudab Batu-Khasar would take through the desert.

Except, he'd begun to wonder just how much more fortified the city could be. Every day the soldiers trained. Militia were constantly conducting logistics work, sheltering more tribes who had entered the city as refugees. Their crop supplies had held, even with the influx of people. Forges inhabited every street corner as smiths and iron workers cast weapons and armor while tanners turned to making stout hauberks and cardant saddles.

Opening his eyes, Elerek regarded the stack of notices that Driss had left for him to sort. For the last week, he'd given himself over to this manner of work, anything to keep himself from the grief brought on by Fin's impending drowning. It hovered over him like a cloud, eclipsing the sun's brilliance, causing the light to never quite be right.

Miraculously, the boy still lived. Elerek tried not to think about the strangeness of the fact, only that another soul had not yet drowned. And how, if his curse continued to change, to drip water down his fingers, he could be next.

"El!" The door burst open, nearly flying off its hinges.

Craning his neck, Elerek scowled over the back of the couch as Razhar blustered in like a whirlwind.

His friend skidded to a halt, acutely wincing. "What, pray tell, did I ever do to deserve such a look? You'll curdle goat's milk."

Elerek only deepened his scowl.

Planting his hands on the back of the couch, Razhar shrugged. "Well, I happen to like goat's cheese. Goes lovely with dates."

"What do you want?"

"You must come down to the stables."

"Says who?"

"Me." Another of Razhar's winning smiles plastered his face. "And the queen insists, on the condition that your goat-milk-curdling face stays here. She thinks Tiniah is ready."

Oh? Lystra asked for *him*? Elerek sat up and reached to pull his chair alongside the couch. "Who is Tiniah?"

"The cardant. The one you so lovingly gifted to your equally lovely bride."

Lovely . . . Thoughts of ebony hair, sun-kissed skin, and deep, dark eyes filled his mind. He drew a hissing breath through his teeth, his gaze dropping to the swirls of ink outlining the fields of dunes on the map before him. Perhaps the danger didn't lie across the desert, but here, in his own heart.

Except, he'd barely seen her this past week beyond the interiors of their council chambers. Like the heat of high summer, the grind and toil of their work had intensified. The quarries were finally able to send enough stone to begin construction on a new battlement at the eastern gate and it seemed every day another tribe or house came to complain about something. Lystra retired early while he labored far into the night.

But that didn't account for the silence, the distance, and the fewer smiles he'd seen on her face. Was it on account of his missing the meal with her family? His sorrow over Fin? Something else?

"You're sure she asked for me?"

Razhar shook his head. "Yes, there's another *Elerek* or two around this place. Really, she's quite eager about this. She's taking Tiniah out into the desert." He nudged Elerek's chair closer, nearly crushing the pile of maps. "Now, come, we must hurry."

Elerek snatched the maps away with a growl and then climbed back into his chair. "Watch yourself, Razhar, you're far too accustomed to ordering the king around."

"I hear our king is merciful and forgiving." Razhar winked and strode toward the door.

Down among the cardant pens, chatter buzzed through the

air. A small crowd gathered about the grounds, smiling with eager anticipation. Many wore the finery of the noble houses, and Elerek recognized a few of them from the racing committee as well as Lystra's lively cousins, Corsha and Kimzi. But as Elerek drew closer, his chair bouncing and jolting through the loose gravel, he noticed many of his own tribe's faces. They stood on the sidelines —Cole, Ishtal, Bushra—watching with eager anticipation.

"His Highness, the king," Razhar announced, his tone rather too mischievous for a herald.

Elerek steeled his jaw as the crowd turned their eyes toward him and bowed. He wondered how many of the nobles' own cardants were now housed in his stable, training with soldiers to face the harrows of battle instead of training for the races. He wondered why this last summer to live had to demand everything, of everyone.

A horrid growl shattered the silence. Elerek turned toward the sound, a shiver crawling up his spine.

Inside the pen, the cardant waited in all her horrifying glory. Abdul, the stable master, tightened the girth of the saddle while Lystra held the harness, the reptile's enormous, horned head between the queen's small hands. Elerek swallowed, knowing that nothing would save her if the monster gnashed its teeth.

But Lystra looked straight into the cardant's gaze, a fire blazing in her eyes. An understanding seemed to pass between them and the cardant remained still as Abdul snapped the last of the buckles into place.

Elerek's fingernails began to tap on the wood of his chair. His mind calculated, taking in the height of the wide, leather saddle, the cardant's sharp claws, and the sheer power lurking in its muscles. Yes, a soldier would certainly gain an advantage, but not during a siege.

If it came to it, would he send men to ride out to meet the Jarkins? On the offensive?

And what of him? Would Elerek watch from the walls, armed with his bow from his chair? A cowardly thought. No, a king ought to be the first to ride out and the last to retreat, as many kings had done before. As Cormek had done. Yet the people had called Cormek a warrior, and he had fallen in his first battle. Elerek, however, had been fighting his entire life. Who else would lead his men?

He drew a steady breath, holding his head high. No, he hadn't a choice in the matter. Vows had been taken, a crown bestowed, and until his final breath, he would live as king. Even if being a king meant climbing into the saddle of a magnificent, muscled cardant.

In the pen, the cardant lifted its head, yanking it from Lystra's hands. She bared row after monstrous row of sharpened teeth.

"Oi, no!" Lystra's voice could shatter the skies themselves. She grabbed the harness, pulling the cardant's head down again. "You hold still, girl." One would think she was addressing a disobedient child, not a reptile the size of two carriages.

Elerek moved a hand to his chest, as if to reassure himself that his heart hadn't stopped beating during this exchange. What of Lystra? Where would his queen stand in the future, during the inevitable battle they would be required to fight? She may well be the most superb rider Instanolde had ever seen, but Elerek vowed that she would not ride out to battle. Not again.

No, he needed her safe.

But even as he watched his queen stand before the immense reptile with its horns, claws, teeth, and a temper to match, he began to wonder if safety belonged in the heads of the storytellers, lore to lurk in the haze and the magic. A true myth among the sands.

"Razhar." He glanced up at his friend. "Do you think I can do it?"

"Do what?"

"Learn to . . ." He slid clammy palms along his knees. "Ride a cardant?"

A roguish smile curled Razhar's lips. "Of course you could, El. What's stopping you?"

Myself.

Without prompting or permission, Razhar jogged over to the pen, waving a hand to get Lystra and Abdul's attention.

Elerek gave an inward groan.

The crowd parted as Lystra vaulted over the side of the pen with graceful agility, the tails of her scarf streaming over her shoulder.

"You came." Her lips parted in an eager smile as she strode toward him.

"Yes." His throat suddenly dried.

Lystra's gaze dimmed, her cheeks flushing. "I'm glad. Tell me." She tilted her head to the side. "Is this one of Razhar's jokes?"

"It probably should be."

A laugh burst from her lips. "Come with me."

"Right now?"

"Yes." The sunlight caught in her amber eyes, radiant as the brightest fire opals. She called over her shoulder. "Abdul, Ishtal, I'll need your help."

Sprinting across the courtyard, Lystra unlatched the gate and disappeared inside another pen. When she emerged, she grasped the horns of a cardant with yellowed scales and orange streaks in her spines. A stable hand quickly handed her a halter, which she swung over the reptile's head and tightened.

As she led the reptile toward him, Elerek imagined the ground quivering beneath his chair. And yet the lizard of the desert, with its primed claws and rows of sharp teeth, only blinked its orb-like eyes in disinterest, pulled along by the lithe frame of the queen of Instanolde.

"This is Sama. I brought her from home." Lystra lowered the reptile's head, a mere arm's length away from him. "She's as sweet and gentle as they come. I would be honored if you would ride her."

Elerek swallowed, hoping the terror in his soul hadn't surfaced on his face. Reaching out with trembling fingers, he brushed the cardant's snout. Sama sniffed, blowing hot air from her nostrils. He drew his hand back, unable to look away from the depths of the reptile's yellow-rimmed eye. Something he could touch, and not curse. He'd touched enough hounds and canaries to know it couldn't spread to animals or reptiles.

"Can we fashion a saddle for him?" Lystra glanced between Ishtal and Abdul.

"Absolutely." A smile illuminated Ishtal's bearded face. "We'd only need to devise something sturdier than stirrups. Straps of some sort? To keep your legs secure?"

Elerek scowled at the thought of toppling feebly from the back of the reptile, his bones shattered as claw and limb trampled him underfoot.

Abdul seemed to share his hesitance, his aged face wrinkling into a frown. "I'm sure that this cardant is gentle enough, but will His Highness be able to guide her?"

He makes me sound foolish. Well, Elerek felt foolish.

"Sama will be quite suitable, I promise," Lystra assured, disarming the onlookers with a smile.

Once Sama was saddled, Elerek fended off nausea as he let Ishtal and Cole help him out of his chair and onto the cardant's back. His legs ached, his muscles unable to bear his weight. Razhar stood near the cardant's head, holding her harness.

"You behave now." He spoke in low tones, as if sharing a fantastic secret. "He's not fond of your kind, and you know he's the king now. He might have you executed—or exiled somewhere without dessert. What do cardants eat for dessert?"

"Do shut up," Elerek grunted. Straightening his spine, even he had to admit that sitting atop the cardant held a rather noble appeal, rising above the heads of his attendants for once in his life. As he reached for the reins, the cardant shuffled, its powerful body moving beneath him.

Starkindler, I can't do this. Terror stole the air from his lungs, and he wondered if he might fall even before they secured his legs.

"Loosen the reins. She doesn't like them held so tightly," Lystra cautioned, watching as Ishtal used the saddle's additional straps to pin Elerek's legs in place.

Letting the blood flow back into his knuckles required several deep breaths. Sama immediately tested her new freedom, shaking her horned head and peering inquisitively at her rider. Elerek wanted to tell her that he didn't like it either.

"There," Ishtal huffed, stepping back from the cardant. "How does that feel?"

Shifting in the saddle, Elerek tested his confines, summoning what meager movement he could from his weakened limbs. "Tight. But I don't think I'll fall."

"We'll have to design something," Ishtal grumbled. "Something that'll allow you to free yourself if necessary."

Elerek cringed. He dared not tell them that he needed something battleworthy.

His eyes trailed on Lystra as she reentered the pen of the monstrous reptile. Without hesitation, without fear, she took hold of the reins and swung herself into the saddle. The cardant hissed and arched her back, a grand attempt to unseat her rider. Several spectators backed away from the pen. But Lystra only smiled, leaning forward to whisper soft, yet stern, words to her mount.

Elerek sat a little taller. If her courage was drink, it would be among the finest of wines, smooth and intoxicating.

"Oi, El." Razhar stepped closer. He pulled his scarf from his neck, its threads the color of the Gungole's aquamarine depths, and tossed it to him. "Might need this. Your fragile Karim skin doesn't see the sun much."

Elerek caught the scarf, quickly winding it into a makeshift turban.

Razhar wrinkled his nose. "Not your color, at all." He looked at Lystra. "You'll watch out for him, yes? Your Highness?"

As her cardant finally ceased its thrashing, Lystra lifted her head and pushed her braid over her shoulder. A bit of the wildness, her intensity, seemed to fade, leaving her eyes dark.

Something's wrong. Elerek watched her the way he studied his archers, looking for flaws in their stance. The shadow in her eyes taunted him, gnawing like cardant teeth on the bones of its prey.

Was she afraid—for him? Or was it something else?

But then, the murk passed, leaving clear skies and a gracious smile spread over her face, the regal look of a queen. "Of course, Razhar. I'll bring our king back in one piece." She turned to the gathering of stable hands. "Open the gate."

The creak of the old wood sent a shudder up Elerek's spine. Sama lifted her head, watching expectantly as the bigger reptile snaked forward.

Growls erupted between the two cardants. Lystra's mount bared its teeth, snapping at Sama. Elerek's hands scrambled for the reins, but he had no idea what to do with them. A string of curses slipped through his teeth.

"Tiniah!" Lystra pulled the reptile's head back. "I see we are going to be trouble today."

Elerek hoped that he didn't look as sick as he felt.

"Sama isn't one to be bullied." Lystra leaned forward, stroking her cardant's sleek neck. A smile teased at her lips. "Are you all right?"

He lifted his chin. "I'm thankful that you know what you're doing."

To that, Lystra laughed. A sound worthy of a songbird's melody. "You'll get the hang of it, don't worry."

"And if I don't?" he challenged, raising an eyebrow.

"Well." Lystra met his gaze head-on, their eyes level from the backs of their mounts. "I suggest you hold on."

Then, she gave a call and both cardants started across the courtyard.

The cardant moved in a winding gait, causing him to sway from side to side as the reptile's legs moved in tandem with one another. Every instinct told him to clutch the reins, but he forced his hands to loosen. Sama tossed her head, making clicking noises in her throat.

"She knows you're not used to her," Lystra said. "She'll take it slow."

Sparing a glance at his queen, Elerek watched as the bigger cardant hissed and thrashed, prowling forward like a cat chasing a mouse. "Is that what yours is doing?"

Lystra shook her head. "No, she's testing me. She'll do better once we're on sand."

On sand. In the desert. Outside the city. Elerek drew a steadying breath.

Twin flashes of orange caught in the corner of Elerek's eyes. The capes of royal guards, following him and the queen through the streets, mounted on cardants of their own. It seemed their presence, that flame of color, was enough for a pathway to form through the crowded city.

Everywhere Elerek looked, the eyes of his subjects stared back, peering from doorways, from market booths, from wagons full of wares. How their faces changed when they saw Lystra. Smiles of adoration and cheers of praise rose above the pounding claws of the cardants.

"Malikaa! Malikaa!" The people's queen. Elerek's chest swelled.

He cared not if they regarded him with furrowed brows, skepticism brooding in their eyes. He wondered if they saw the ghost in his face, the image of someone not quite like him. But it didn't matter what they thought of him—only what they thought of her.

Lystra glanced over her shoulder, loose hairs taking flight from her braid. "It doesn't hurt to smile."

A great many things hurt and a smile may as well be one of them. But he obliged, smiling at a group of merchants who halted their pottery wheels to give him honor with sweeping bows.

All their talk behind the doors of council chambers. All their schemes of refugees, soldiers, and the flow of supplies. All the while, Instanolde carried on, like the rotation of the constellations in the heavens. As Elerek's gaze swept from the colorful booths of the merchants to the tall gates of the great houses, he felt the pulse of a thousand heartbeats. Life flowed on these streets, as steady as the Gungole.

"We all have one life, Elerek. A mighty gift from the Maker of the stars." Cormek's words returned to him, an echo in the noise of the city.

And now, watching the colors of Instanolde pass in the haze of dust stirred by Sama's claws, Elerek understood what his brother meant. He no longer felt so different.

Blasts from rams' horns sounded at the gates. The iron portcullis rose. Lystra's cardant strained at the sight of the open road. The queen tossed her head, golden sun upon her ebony hair, her amber skin.

"We'll take the trail to the left—to the Herald Rocks."

Elerek only nodded. Maps filled his head but he knew of no such landmark. Sama seemed to need little direction from him, content to follow her own kind.

They cleared the gates, the late afternoon sun streaming into their eyes. Elerek lifted a hand, shielding his vision. Lystra's cardant pounced forward, kicking up a great cloud of dust. Sama lurched in excitement—and the race began.

I'm going to die. Not from the curse. Not from drowning. No, Ishtal's straps would give way and Elerek would fall, trampled to death by cardant claws in the sands of the Sancen.

Wind whipped at his hair and clothing, causing his eyes to smart. He steadied his breath, trying to control his panic. The speed, the passing landscape of windswept rocks, the swirl of sand caught in the golden light—Elerek had never conceived of such a thing. His scholar's life, locked away in the palace shadows, knew nothing of comparison. Fear and exhilaration took hands, a dance that sent blood racing in his ears.

No discernible trail lay before them, only haphazard piles of pale desert stone. The cardants leapt and bounded, using their claws to catch in the slightest of grooves. Elerek had no need of the reins, clutching the saddle for dear life.

At last, with one last lunge, the cardants leveled out on a long, rocky plateau. Elerek caught his breath, leaning forward in the saddle. Up ahead, Lystra's reptile slowed to a brisk walk. Sama caught up, coming alongside her. Wagging their heads and snapping their jaws, they bickered in their own reptilian fashion. Lystra, meanwhile, turned toward the sun setting across the Sancen with her head held high.

Elerek couldn't help but stare.

Thrill filled her eyes as she stared out at the desert, her face radiant with wonder. The wind whipped her hair, her scarf. This girl could wear royal robes and dazzle a roomful of nobles and win the hearts of her army and yet, out here, among the wilds, astride a cardant, she looked so natural. A queen of another sort.

Her eyes found his, a blush filling her cheeks.

Elerek quickly blinked, turning to the grand landscape before him. The parchment maps that littered the library had held his attention for hours, but this—this was *real*. The rugged terrain of sand, rock, and sky. The summer sun in all its radiance became eclipsed by the western mountains, their peaks scimitar-sharp silhouettes. Up above, the stars he loved so dearly danced in all their might, singing ancient proverbs. In a glorious exchange, the sky turned orange and the sand turned pale blue.

It's beautiful.

Something in the desert, in the stillness of its deadly beauty, far from the confines and demands of the kingdom, undid him. Burdens lifted from his shoulders. If the cardant beneath him bore wings, he was sure he would take to the skies until he could see nothing but stars.

His soul stirred like never before. It was like a memory,

something beautiful and dear, and yet something new. A freedom, like nothing he'd ever experienced. It melted the hardness in his heart and brought tears to his eyes. This beautiful world that the Starkindler had created was more than the schemes of connivers, the plans of generals, or the threat of armies. They'd been given a world in which to live, not to die, not to linger. *Live.*

Maybe they would die. Maybe the Jarkins would attack. Maybe he would spill out like water until he was no more. Maybe it was all in vain.

But today, he lived. Now, he was whole.

He wanted to remember this moment forever, to recall it when his soul grew dark, to urge him onward through the difficult days.

"Elerek?" She spoke his name softly. "Are you all right?"

He glanced at her briefly, blinking away his tears. "I . . ." It seemed a desecration to mar the Sancen's stillness with the sound of their voices. "I didn't know that the Sancen was beautiful. I can't recall ever coming out here."

"I do," Lystra whispered.

When she returned from the attack—with Cormek's body. Elerek hunched in the saddle, but he couldn't brace himself from this sort of pain. No, this arrow had pierced too deep to dislodge. "Do you regret it? Riding out with him?"

Her shoulders arched, like the gentle slope of a dune. "It was supposed to be . . . different. The Sancen, cardants, and Cormek. All that I loved. Instead . . ." A shudder sent a tremble through her body. "Those moments were all I had left with him. Moments I didn't know were going to end."

Regret clawed at Elerek's heart, its talons as sharp as his mount's. A lump rose in his throat that it would choke him to swallow. "The day before you left, Cormek and I argued. Another petty, bitter war that didn't need to be waged. I yelled terrible things at him, stormed off, told him to go." He sighed. "I'll never forget that, that the last things I ever said to my brother were fueled by rage."

Pity swirled in the amber depths of Lystra's eyes. "Cormek was quiet that morning."

Elerek lifted his gaze, watching a gust of wind blow over a nearby dune, taking glittering bits of gold sand with it. "He . . . he wanted me to live. That's all he asked, that the curse wouldn't be the sum of whatever little life I have."

The silence of the Sancen fell over them, the air heavy.

When he looked toward her again, the shadow returned to her brow. "Lystra, I . . . I was cruel, conceited. The way I treated Cormek . . ."

The queen adjusted her scarf, her eyes skirting his.

Stars. "I . . . I'm trying." He stuttered, just as he had at the pyre, when their worlds had collided. "T-to live . . . like he wished."

Trying to honor his brother, to be something more than the curse.

Lystra reached down to stroke her cardant's scales, her fingers tracing their edges. "I know you are."

Elerek held his breath.

"I don't think that Cormek would want you to hate yourself. I never knew him to clutch onto grudges."

She probably knew him better than he did, and the thought left him feeling numb.

"I believe Cormek would be proud of all that you have accomplished." Her voice grew stern, as if she spoke to a room full of advisors and courtiers. "And . . . you've done so much for me. I'm thankful."

"I wish I could do more."

Her posture stiffened, and she looked as she had at the funeral pyre, the fierce and sober queen of the desert who had survived the fires and emerged as forged steel. He could see a storm gathering in her eyes, and he wondered if she were about to unleash a terrible fury.

"As do I." She met his gaze, but only briefly. "When you came to the racing committee, you knew exactly how to help me. I fear that I've failed to accomplish the same for you."

Elerek blinked. Was that what this was about? The haze between them?

"I've been told I can't understand, what it's like to bear the curse."

"Who told you that?"

Lystra shrugged, her gaze shadowed beneath her scarf. "It doesn't matter. Perhaps it's true, but you know that I've carried sorrow. You . . . probably understand my grief better than anyone I know."

Stars, was this the first time they'd put words to the ache inside them? The collision that happened when their alliance was forged? Yes, they'd spoken of their sorrows, but not the way they'd seen it in one another.

Elerek took the reins, carefully nudging Sama forward. Lystra's vicious cardant swung its head around, baring teeth. He pulled back, realizing this was as close to her as he would get—as he would ever get. "I don't want you to know what it's like to be cursed. If I've acted distant and closed off, it's not your doing. I'm trying to spare you."

Lystra's face changed, painted with the shades of the setting sun.

Elerek's heart sank at the terrible thought that perhaps she didn't want to be spared. But she wouldn't be, the curse hadn't yet run its course.

"You will survive this, Lystra, all of this." And he would be gone.

Pain wrote harsh lines across her face. But then, in a

moment, the storm broke, leaving clear skies. Lystra looked out upon the Sancen, as if its beauty were a healing balm. "After . . . after I came back, I couldn't come out here. The memories were too sharp. It used to be that I'd come out here and my burdens would grow less heavy. I'd lose myself. The desert is large and beautiful and I could be small. Sometimes the smallness was enough."

Elerek pushed his curls from his eyes, puzzled by this change in conversation. "And how about right now?"

Wheeling her cardant in a wide circle, Lystra guided the creature back toward the edge of the plateau. Sama followed along behind, slowly snaking down a steep turnoff from the trail they'd come up.

Elerek held his breath, leaning back in the saddle as they descended, fretful that the lizards might pitch forward at any moment.

The queen's face lay obscured behind the folds of her scarf, but her voice floated up behind her. "I'm glad to be out here—and I'm thankful to not be alone. I—I wanted to share this—with you."

His stomach churned, and it wasn't the discomfort of the saddle or the powerful creature beneath him. When the trail leveled, they traversed a series of dunes where the cardants kicked up sand, glittering silver in the fading light like stars cast from the heavens.

Up ahead, his eyes fell on Instanolde, its stonework washed in the fading day's hues of purple and rose. Their kingdom, glowing in the dying light, on the distant horizon.

He feared that they'd gone too far, a steep trail like the one their cardants traversed, and there was no going back now.

He was grateful that she'd chosen to rule with him—to marry him. Though their days were full, the tasks of managing their kingdom taxing and heavy, they hadn't broken. No, together, they had forged a sort of strength.

A strength that might have been . . . something more.

Elerek looked away, blinking the dust from his eyelashes and wishing he could disperse his thoughts as easily. Before the eyes of their kingdom, he and Lystra were nothing more than a legal arrangement, a political alliance. As it should—as it *must* —be.

And yet something drew him to Lystra the way the stars were drawn in their orbit across the desert night sky. He feared it was something like the wrathgiver constellation, stalking the night, bearing a blade, a danger from which their hearts could not escape unscathed.

"Lystra." He swallowed, his throat as dry as the surrounding sand. "Thank you for bringing me out here, for allowing me to join you."

"You're welcome." She didn't look his way, her voice soft on the wind.

Chapter 37

Lystra

That night, lying amongst the pillows of her lavish bed, every time Lystra closed her eyes, she saw the desert.

The bare rock, emerging like the bones of the land from the windswept valleys. The collection of colors deeper than an artist's palette. The desolate beauty that she loved so much, a land made of strength, ancient and unchanging, outdone only by the dancing stars above.

Elerek's eyes, clear as the skies, smooth as jade.

Lystra rose from the pillows, tossing her hair over her shoulder with a sigh. No, she wouldn't be sleeping tonight.

The sight of him, mounted atop Sama with his noble head held high, startled her. He looked too much like Cormek. As the dust flew about the cardants' claws, she could almost imagine that it was the ghost of him, returned to the Sancen.

He wasn't Cormek, and never would be. Beyond his strong shoulders, rigid jaw, and dark hair—all the things that related him to his brother—she'd seen something deeper. The terror in his eyes as he climbed atop the cardant, his broken legs secured to the saddle. The way his knuckles clenched white on the reins, laced with plague scars. And how the stark beauty of the wilderness had pierced his heart. A man like any other, broken and shattered and trying to be pieced back together.

Drinking deep of the midnight air, Lystra climbed out of bed and wrapped herself in a light robe. Slipping beyond the silk curtains, she stepped out onto her balcony. A bench carved of the smooth wood of a desert tree sat near the railing and she perched herself there.

Lifting her eyes, she watched the stars. They danced, spun, wheeled—and sometimes fell, vanishing from view.

"I'm trying."

The weight of those two words could have crushed them both. Lystra could almost hear the whispers, all that Elerek had tried to say and all that he had left unsaid.

Perhaps they needed to say nothing. Let the strangeness of their marriage remain only a political arrangement, and not let whatever emotions hazed the air complicate matters. Perhaps then, their hearts wouldn't shatter.

As for the curse, in this, Lystra knew she had to remain stalwart. Death had caught her off guard, invading her life with the strength of the Jarkins. Elerek and his companions waited beside death's door, its shadow ever encroaching. How she wanted to shut that door fast and toss the key into the depths of the Gungole.

If she must stand between the threat of the Jarkins and the threat of the curse, so be it.

Starlight lit her way as she swept into the parlor. She'd heard the distinct creak of Elerek's chair an hour earlier and now all lay quiet and still.

There, upon the table, the sheen of white pottery caught her eye. Cormek's ashes.

Lystra paused, timidly approaching the jar. Her fingers brushed the painted azure swirls, the clay smooth and cold beneath her touch. The time since Cormek's death had been short, but the warmth of his presence, of his arms, now seemed a lifetime ago.

A twinge of guilt pricked her heart. The love she'd once lavished upon him had been given to other matters, forged into devotion to her kingdom, to the smiles and laughter she'd given the cursed at the feast, and—to upholding the vows she had made to the king.

What would Cormek think of all this? This new life she'd found in the held breath before summer's end? The strange arrangement with the man who had chosen her to rule at his side and yet kept her at arm's length?

Lystra closed her eyes. She wished that Cormek and Elerek could've seen eye to eye more often—and seen what *she* saw. Perhaps Cormek would be pleased, happy even, that Lystra and Elerek had chosen to trek this path together.

Taking the jar in two hands, Lystra stepped to the shelf along the back wall of the room. There, she placed it on the shelf, beside a stack of Elerek's books.

I'll always love you, Cormek, and I'll always mourn the life we never had. She closed her eyes, releasing twin sets of tears. Her kingdom needed her love, and some of her people were cursed. One of them was her king.

Turning away from the shelf, she slipped through the chamber's great carved doors. Two guards nodded in greeting, standing sentinel in the hall. One was a cursed soldier, Beoni, always prepared to come to the king's aid.

"Can we assist you, Your Highness?"

"I'm going to the library."

Beoni remained, the other escorting Lystra through the palace corridors. The library occupied one of the rounded towers of the palace and inside, Lystra found the oil lamps still lit. Her feet, clad in silk slippers, sank into the lush rugs.

Elerek often haunted this chamber. Evidence of his regular presence lay everywhere, from the scarce furnishing with wide paths between and the haphazard piles of maps and parchments.

She wrapped her arms around herself, shivering in the soft breeze blowing through the open window. The rustle of pages filled her ears with a gentle melody. She wondered what Elerek hoped to find. Then again, she wasn't sure why she'd come herself.

Passing through parchments and scrolls, she found scant information on curses scattered across the writings of scholars and poets and, like those in her father's own study, the pages had been ripped.

But Lorkin's purge knew nothing of Razhar—and his secrets.

Lystra shoved a roll of scrolls back onto the shelf, stirring up a small cloud of dust. She'd stumbled upon this information by chance. Myra didn't have to warn her of his secrets, a strange favor from the girl who considered her a rival. Lystra chewed her lower lip. If Razhar knew how to break the curse, he would've done it, wouldn't he?

She looked to the door, where the guard stood sentinel. "Bring me Razhar Emblino. I don't care if you must wake him."

When the guard returned with Razhar in tow, it didn't look like he'd been dragged from bed. Tonight, no colorful turban graced his head, leaving his hair hanging in loose waves about his shoulders. He wore a crimson vest over his bare chest, the dark edges of tattoo ink on his breast.

No jovial smile illuminated his face. A shadow hung in his eyes, as if he knew that she'd summoned him here to pry into his secrets.

Lystra asked the guard to wait outside, leaving them alone. "You said you'd help me find a way to break Elerek's curse. Well, you know more about it than anyone."

"What I know is that it can't be broken, Your Highness." Razhar moved closer, circling a couch.

Lystra primly lifted her chin. "I desire more information. Starting with how you can touch the cursed."

Annoyance flirted with his features and he made no attempt to hide it. "Why does it matter?" Then he caught her eye, lifting a wry eyebrow. "That's it, isn't it? You want that too —so you can touch him."

Do I? She wondered if the fact would change anything between them. Surely affection could thrive even without something like touch. But if they could touch, would they admit what was happening in their hearts? Would there be a way for them beneath the skies cast with stars?

She narrowed her gaze. "It matters because you can reverse an unbreakable curse."

"Only the symptoms, not the cause." Razhar hung his head, his hands braced against the back of the couch. "Fin is dead."

Lystra lifted her hands, covering her mouth.

"Drowned, spilled out on the kitchen tiles." Razhar's hands clenched, fisting about the couch's fabric. "I was there. It made no difference." He sniffled. "I haven't the heart to tell El. Not yet."

Lystra shut her eyes. Her chest heaved, as if another arrow tainted with despair had pierced her heart. If she hadn't taken Elerek out with the cardants, he would've been with Fin. Stars, she wondered why everything, every move they made, had to be so difficult.

"Don't you understand, Your Highness?" Razhar whispered, raking a hand through his hair. "There's nothing we can do. If we're going to perish, we'll go about it when the time comes. We must burn with our own spark, our own starfire. You aren't marked for death—but for life. That's why El chose you."

So many men rode with her and Cormek to Darcress. So few returned. They survived because they were saving her.

Everyone was saving her.

Grandmother for her own plans of coddling a queen. Elerek for his need of an heir. Even the people of Instanolde, praising her survival and looking to her for hope.

To them, she was freedom. She wondered if she'd ever feel free—for herself.

"Life's too short to live with regrets." Razhar circled the furniture, standing before her. "I learned this quite recently."

Tears misted her eyes. "What do you regret?"

He took a timid step closer. He lifted a finger only to trail it down her sleeve. "I regret that I didn't kiss you that night in the market."

Lystra stepped back, a breath of a gasp escaping her lips. For a moment, they stared at each other, and she had no idea how to respond. *He's saving me too.* For when this was over, if they survived.

Whoosh! The air whistled between them with the lightning-fast movement of a small and slender object. Heat burned against Lystra's arm and when she looked down at her sleeve, her robe was red with blood.

A knife, not much larger than a dart, lay embedded in the spine of a thick tome, thrown from the hand of the black-clad figure that slipped through the open window.

Razhar swore and moved in front of her, a human shield,

and reached for a squat iron sculpture that pinned down the corner of the maps on the desk. Two more knives lay poised in the fingers of the attacker, but he didn't throw, the element of surprise lost.

Lystra caught one glance before dropping to her knees behind the arm of the couch. A stocky, pale-skinned man with muscled arms and a full beard. His clothing was made of stout, dark cloth and leather.

A jackal skull capped each shoulder.

Jarkin.

Lystra couldn't breathe.

Razhar gave a grunt. A clatter followed. Peering round the couch, she saw him topple over the top of the desk and tumble to the floor, taking most of the maps and books with him. He didn't move.

A hand yanked her up by her hair. Lystra screamed and struggled, but the pain sent stars across her vision. The Jarkin threw her down, sending her sprawling over the rug. Tears sprang from her eyes and her breaths came in short gasps.

The Jarkin stood over her, a conqueror.

"Is that her?"

Lystra looked up. A second assassin stood at the window, dressed to match, brandishing his own set of knives.

A boot nudged her spine. "The little queen that escaped Darcress." His voice was hoarse and cruel, as if it came from the rocky, desert crags itself.

Darcress had brought death to Instanolde, and back to her.

Before she could react, the Jarkin planted his knee against her chest, pinning her to the library floor. She tried to yell, but his hand closed about her throat.

Her lungs screamed for air. Only the eyes of the Jarkin remained in focus, cold and evil and full of death.

At that moment, the door to the library burst open. Instan soldiers filled the room.

Black fringed the edges of Lystra's vision, but she saw the light of alarm in Norbah's gaze and glint of his scimitar.

The Jarkin released her throat and yanked her up from the floor. Lystra's lungs wheezed, fighting for breath.

An Instan soldier advanced, scimitar held high. Knives filled the air, flying from the hand of the second assassin. The soldier dropped, his blood staining the rug.

Death and dying. Men falling and meeting their end, all for the sake of protecting those whom Instanolde needed to live.

"Stay back!" The Jarkin's rough hands closed around the back of her neck, immobilizing her head. The blade of a knife cut cold and sharp against her throat. "I'll kill her."

Lystra closed her eyes, his grip sending dark stars over her vision. Their councils, their schemes, all of it was futile. They would die—cursed and uncursed alike.

Instanolde would fall.

The Jarkin slammed against her, swearing loudly. Lystra pitched forward, but the assassin kept his grip on her neck. There, at their feet, the sculpture from the desk lay. It must have hit the Jarkin after being pitched across the room.

Lystra twisted in the Jarkin's grasp. There, by the desk, Razhar had dragged himself to his feet, his eyes wide and horrified.

For one moment, long and terrible, the world went still— and then everything happened at once.

The Jarkin raised the thin blade, still dripping with Lystra's blood. But before he could drive it into her chest, Norbah's soldiers swarmed. All became chaos and movement.

Lystra fell, released from her captor's hold—and her head struck the edge of the desk. The library spun in a mass of parchments, rugs, and soldiers fighting for their kingdom.

Fighting for her.

Everything fell black.

When Lystra woke, the library still seemed to be in orbit, drifting in a constellation's dance. Except now, pain struck her eyes, throwing the room into sharp focus.

The air smelled of blood, thick and metallic.

A pillow cushioned her head, but she still lay on the floor, the stone hard against her hip.

"Keep still, Your Highness." A servant stooped over her, clutching a physician's satchel. She took a cloth, scented with the strong aroma of myrrh oil, and began to clean the cut on Lystra's neck.

How did she get here? As her eyes roamed the room, cast sideways from her position, pain throbbed in her head. She came to . . . the Jarkins. Air forced its way into her lungs.

There, several paces away, the body of the assassin stretched across the same rug as she. An Instan soldier lay dead beside him. Her attacker, the enemy who dealt her these blows, was nowhere to be seen.

Norbah's voice seemed too loud for the size of the library as he stalked into her line of vision, armor clanking as he barked orders. "Alert the city militia but keep it quiet. Let them know that no more fear is permitted in this kingdom."

"Already done." Another soldier appeared. "The king has been notified."

Lystra squeezed her eyes shut, wishing that it was only a nightmare.

But she didn't want to wake alone in her bed in the royal chambers. She wanted to wake at home, in House Arghan's estate, where her wedding gown hung unworn. Days of safety, where the Jarkins were merely the people who dwelt on the other side of the desert, not a formidable enemy staging an invasion.

The little queen who escaped Darcress.

Yes, that mocking voice spoke correctly when he'd had his hand clamped about her neck. The little queen, hardly more than a foolish girl. A queen incapable of protecting anyone. Her eyes filled with tears and she quickly shut them.

"Let me tend to your arm." The physician wasted no time, quickly binding the wound.

The march of soldiers filled the air, practically shaking the palace with the pounding of their boots, followed by the sound of creaking wooden wheels.

Lystra opened her eyes. Weakly, with the physician's aid, she sat up. She hardly wanted to be lying bleeding on the floor in her nightdress and robe when he arrived.

The room swayed with her movement, but *he* stayed in focus, the fire in his eyes hot enough to melt stone.

Elerek's gaze swept the scene, burning everything in his path. "What happened here?" Rage laced his voice, empowered with all the command of a king.

"Two assassins." Norbah spoke quickly. "We kept one alive for questioning. He's being guarded in the yard. So far, no sign of additional attacks or enemy presence."

Clenching his hands, Elerek paled with fury. Then, his eyes fell on *her*, and Lystra didn't dare look away.

He wheeled his chair closer. "Are you all right?"

With the physician's help, Lystra shakily rose to her feet.

She reached a hand to her head, feeling the tender place above her eyebrow. "For now."

Elerek's gaze followed her hand, then moved to her neck and down to her arm, where the blood already seeped through the bandage. The tortured look in his eyes twisted her soul. "Good." He spoke softly, yet stern. "I cannot lose you."

From the moment she'd met Elerek of House Karim, the cursed prince from the shadows, he'd surrounded himself with enough defenses to rival the scaled armor of a cardant. But those battlements didn't define him any more than the palace was defined by its walls. The walls had a gate, a pathway inside, and she'd been inside.

The fear in his eyes was real, and he let her see it. They were both afraid, but they both had to be so, so strong.

"I'm fine too, if anyone cares to notice."

Razhar sat hunched on the couch, his head in his hands. An empty expression haunted his eyes, and he couldn't seem to draw them away from the bodies bleeding out on the rug.

Elerek's chair pivoted, his hands clenching the wheel rims as if he meant to break them. "Why were you here? Either of you?"

Lystra's chest fluttered with panic. She cast a stern eye upon Razhar, demanding silence.

"Well, it's a good thing we were. Otherwise, they might have murdered you while you slept." He huffed, pushing a hand through his hair. "Am I needed here or . . . ?" His eyes darted toward the bodies again.

Elerek shook his head, the rage rekindled in his eyes. "No. Lystra, perhaps you should go too." He turned toward her again. "Please rest. I'll send for you if I—" He stopped, swallowing. His hands drew tight again, the skin pale across his knuckles. "If the need arises."

"If I need you."

Lystra gave a timid nod, relying on the physician's assistance to walk. As she passed Elerek, she stretched out her hand, her fingertips brushing the wood of his chair. The Jarkins attacked their palace. Tonight. She didn't know what that meant for them—or their kingdom.

She only knew that she needed him too.

Chapter 38

Lystra

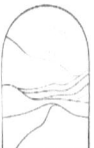

Lystra allowed herself to be led to a council chamber accompanied by the physician and a pair of guards. She asked for tea and settled shakily into a chair laden with cushions. Her head pounded and, like a whirlwind of dust kicked up across the Sancen without warning, her entire body trembled.

The physician departed to procure a mixture of herbs. Lystra sniffled, wiping unwanted tears from her eyes, and clutched her robe more closely around her.

"You didn't answer El's question."

Only then did she notice that Razhar had followed her. He took the chair opposite from her, laying his arms across the table.

Did he mean it? That he regretted not kissing me? Lystra looked away.

"Your Highness, why were you in the library?"

Glancing down at her arm, Lystra tightened the wrappings, their edges lined in red. It stung, but the pain kept her present. Here, in this moment, in the palace, in her beloved Instanolde.

Her mind wanted to wander far from here, to venture into that dreaded desert. The hell in which she'd lost everything. She felt as if it were about to happen again. She would lose everything, this new life that she'd scavenged from the wreckage. The thought made her want to sob.

"Neither did you." She regarded him with a sharp eye.

Razhar narrowed his eyes. "I came at your bidding to answer questions about breaking the curse. Stars above, I'm not about to give El any sort of false hope. Particularly at a time like now."

"Now might be the only time we have," she said softly.

Hot tea appeared before them, carried on a tray. Gratitude swelled in her chest, and she nursed the cup in her hands, its earthy scent steadying. Lifting her eyes, she saw the bearer of the tea was Myra.

Her eyes sparkled with relief as she glanced between them. Then, without a word, she drifted from the room as silently as she'd come, for once no sharp remark upon her tongue.

"I haven't yet thanked you." Lystra sipped her tea. "You saved my life."

Razhar gave a despondent sigh. "All chance, Your Highness. I'm useless."

"Don't be ridiculous." Seeing him here, as fatigued as she from the attempt upon their lives, she felt her harshness toward him soften. Her suspicions lingered, and she certainly wouldn't turn a blind eye to his actions, but she was glad that he'd been there with her in the library.

He huffed, staring into his own tea. "There's nothing to be found in the library—if you'd been researching. El would've found it decades ago if there were. Lorkin destroyed every shred of literature about the curse in the desert—except what's in the Kushite archives, of course." Bringing the cup to his lips, he downed the hot liquid. "You're serious, aren't you?"

Lystra closed her eyes. "I can't give up on them." She couldn't give up on him.

"Have you heard of the costs associated with curses?"

"I think I read something about them."

Razhar slouched, resting the base of his skull on the chair's back, and closed his eyes. "With the exception of Lorkin's purge, no one despises curses as they do in my homeland. You ought to hear the lectures of Kushite tutors with their students, they'll make your blood run cold. Heinous, unholy works of darkness, in violation of all the sacred stars and punishable by the order of kings and the laws of nature. To be caught with a binder, caster, or their articles is to be branded with unforgivable shame." His eyes cracked open. "You know about that, yes? Binders and casters?"

"Binders create the curse and casters cast them."

"Exactly. Binders can cast their own curses, but there's more money in selling them to fools idiotic enough to cast them. Now, Lorkin never found the binder of El's curse, but there's a chance someone else might have cast it. Two culprits." Razhar heaved a long sigh. "A cost is always required. I've heard it said in Kushite tradition that the more horrible the curse, the more horrible the cost. A mechanism to remind those involved of their sins, as it were. So, think about it. El has been untouchable —cut off from humanity—nearly his entire life, forced to watch those he's cursed to drown from the inside out while he languishes. Touch isn't something we realize we miss until it's taken from us."

Lystra took another sip of her tea. Her mind wandered to her father's warm embraces, Corsha's hand in hers, and Kimzi's timid hugs. The way Cormek's kisses overwhelmed her senses. The act of taking a dance partner's arm or correcting a rider's posture upon a cardant.

Elerek had lived with distance his entire life, separation

and isolation. No wonder he wanted to protect her from those horrors. No wonder he had loved Myra, someone he could touch.

Lystra closed her eyes, the nausea returning.

Razhar continued. "They might have healed his legs too, though, one must admit that he's quite a marvel with that chair."

Lystra nodded.

"But if it's true, that the cost matches the curse, something horrible must have happened to the caster. If that's the case, don't you think it might take something equally heinous to *break* the curse? And, granted we discover what that is, would you be willing to do it?"

His question hung in the air. Lystra had no answer.

The door to the council room opened, granting entrance to a soldier. He bowed low, his cape sweeping the floor. "His Highness has requested your presence. If you'll follow me."

Lystra rose from the chair with a groan, her every joint stiff as shock and terror paralyzed her muscles. Razhar circled the table, offering her his arm. As they followed the soldier, night's grip seemed to tighten, the palace corridors darker than ever.

The soldier led them to a large courtyard of drab stone. Lystra's eyes briefly lifted, following the imposing shape of the guard's keep as it vanished into the murk of the midnight skies. Even the stars seemed darker.

Elerek's chair waited just beyond the arch of the door, the wheels unsuited to the sands where the soldiers trained. His head turned at their approach, his face painted orange by the harsh torchlight.

"Norbah will be here shortly. They've finished their interrogation." He spoke softly, as if the thickness of the night suppressed his voice.

Lystra only nodded.

Slipping from her side, Razhar leaned against the archway, his arms folded. "You all right, El?"

The king shook his head, his jaw taut.

The crunch of boots on sand carried across the courtyard as the general approached, his hand on his scimitar and a fury in his eyes.

"Your Highness." He bowed to Lystra. "I'm afraid our interrogation yielded little information. It may take time to extract what we're after."

Extraction meant torture. Lystra set her jaw. Deserved repercussions. They killed Cormek. "But where did they come from?" she questioned, tugging the wrappings, stiff with dried blood, tight around her arm again. "Surely they didn't cross the desert."

Norbah grunted, tugging on the strap of the armor guarding his forearm. "I suppose that they could've already been here before high summer began."

Lystra shook her head. "No, they knew of the attack, and that I survived it."

"They recognized you?" Elerek's eyebrows knitted together, overshadowing the dark wrath in his gaze.

Little queen. Lystra shuddered. "Yes."

"That leaves us one option." Elerek's hands drew into tight fists. "The river."

"Stars above," Razhar muttered.

Oh . . . oh no. Lystra drew a shuddered breath, feeling as if this night might threaten to swallow her whole. "They might come at us by the Gungole? Through the canals?"

"The assassin kept muttering about Gaudab Batu-Khasar." Norbah spoke the name as if it were a curse itself. "If they're coming, he'll be with them."

Cormek's murderer. Lystra felt as if the blood in her veins had turned to fire.

"Not if, Norbah. *When*," Elerek breathed, and he spoke the words like passing a death sentence. "We don't have one summer to live. They'll attack us now, in the middle of summer."

There would be nowhere to flee. Nowhere they could survive. The Jarkins would come and kill them all.

Chapter 39

Elerek

Elerek swore to the Starkindler that he would never let the Jarkins touch Lystra again.

He had to force his gaze away from his queen, from the blood seeping around a clumsy bandage, the faint bruises encircling her neck, and the haunted look in her eyes. Specifics of the attack had been withheld, but he saw enough to kindle a vehement wildfire in his soul.

It wasn't enough that the mountain men had taken his brother, their defenses at Darcress, and Instanolde's hope of survival. No, now their arrows had sighted Lystra.

He couldn't protect her, he could promise no such thing, especially not when they were running out of time.

Norbah spoke quietly, assembling the puzzle that was their harsh and indomitable world. "There must be a pass, beyond the Jarkins' mountains. A wide sweep beyond the rocky crags that would take them around Kushan's canyons."

Elerek forced an exhale, consulting the maps in his head. The journey was completely possible, but time consuming. A little over a month had passed since the attack at Darcress. That was time enough, and if their suspicions were true . . .

The Jarkins could attack this very night.

His fingers frantically drummed on his chair, his hands shaking. "Norbah." His voice sounded strangled. "The east city . . ."

The fortifications they'd built. The stones they'd convinced the quarries to ship downriver. The stonemasons' work on the keeps. The markets and shops they'd vacated. The archers they'd trained. The work they'd done since his first morning as king.

Wasted.

"W-we prepared for an attack on the east city. A siege." Elerek could scarcely breathe. "But the west . . . the people . . ."

Lystra gasped. "We moved the entirety of the city, the refugees, the markets. They're all along the west end of Instanolde, along the river."

Every breathing moment, every stolen heartbeat the curse had permitted him, he'd spent on this plan. Building up their defenses, making certain the city was ready to withstand the attack. It had taken time, precious, precious time.

"We didn't fortify the river." Elerek swore. "They'll strike us where we are the most vulnerable, exposed, and where our people are gathered."

I failed.

Stars above, he had doomed them all. All their talk of his skills, his strategic mind, and he had led Instanolde straight to their doom. The numbness returned, enclosing him, suffocating him. A cold void as deep as death's embrace, the death that lay so, so close.

Elerek leaned forward, buried his face in his shaking hands.

Norbah muttered an oath. "El, we've got to move the people. Clear the docks . . ."

"There's no time, Norbah!" He didn't mean to shout. "They could attack us *tonight!* The docks are exposed. No defenses, no stout walls, no places to assemble our soldiers or stage our archers. We spent a month fortifying the *wrong* side of the city. All our plans, our tactics were focused on a different sort of warfare. Everything that we've done . . ." His throat closed, rage and fury clogging his senses.

Drip. Drip. Drip.

He didn't care. He didn't care if the curse changed, if it flung water from his fingertips. If he burst and spilled out and drowned right then and there. Meaningless. Futile. All of it.

And he'd *tried.* Stars above, he'd tried to save them all, but in the end, he would save no one.

His chair jolted, a hand grasping its back. The movement broke through the void, the numbness, however briefly. "El, don't make me smack you."

Razhar hovered in his peripheral. Always near but never close, standing in the way of the shadows.

"We can't give up." Norbah reached for his shoulder, squeezing it. Elerek could only distantly tell that he'd been touched, as if the curse heaped layers upon layers of stone surrounding his skin. "There are too many lives at stake. We are not handing the Jarkins defeat when they arrive, no, we'll not go without a struggle."

Elerek clenched his eyes shut. He wanted their faith, craved their confidence, but he didn't know how to seize hold of it. Not now, in the darkness, in the numbness.

"Norbah." Razhar's voice lowered. "I have a question."

"Yes?"

"I'm no good at this scheming, but if the Jarkins came down the Gungole, they'd use the canals, yes?"

"With an army of reasonable size? They'd have to."

Elerek's eyes shot open, realizing his friend's line of questioning. "Kushan." He turned in his chair, glancing at Razhar. "They'll sweep right through and . . ."

Norbah scowled. "They might not attack, saving their men and weapons for Instanolde, the true prize."

"But they're vulnerable, unprepared for such an attack—much like we are." Elerek wondered if it were possible for the world to simply fall apart, for existence to unravel like an old garment. If it meant knowing that the Jarkins were coming from the signal of smoke as Kushite villages burned, then he didn't want to know.

If Kushan fell . . . he dared not think of it. Kushan who hadn't sworn fealty to him. The tribe that had suffered so heavily beneath the hand of his father, leaving a generation of orphans in the chaos—and not all had fared as well as Razhar. A people wounded, who had already watched their dead bleed on the shores of the Gungole.

Perhaps Instanolde didn't deserve to survive.

Razhar's jaw tightened, and his hand slipped off Elerek's wheelchair. Behind him, Lystra covered her face with her hands, her shoulders shaking. The deepness of midnight intensified, shrouding the yard in a murk so thick that it hurt to breathe.

Norbah huffed. "The Jarkins would have to split their force. They would never abandon the Darcress Kasbah, the crown of their victory."

"Even with Darcress inaccessible until summer's end?" Lystra whispered.

"Kushan can reach Darcress, with their condors," Elerek spat. "And the Jarkins don't know that they don't stand with us. Divide and conquer."

Would it have been any different if Kushan had sworn fealty to him? United their forces against the impending invaders?

Lifting his eyes to the dark, Elerek searched for the stars but the deepness veiled their light. Would he have taken command of the sky, summoning the mounted archers to fight? Could he have possibly sacrificed the blood of Kushan, as his father had, to defend Instanolde and take back Darcress?

Brutish or strategic? Perhaps neither, perhaps both. Elerek only knew that Kushan had made its choice, content to watch the seasons turn and the skies dance. He had no blame to heap upon them, only the panic magnifying in his chest.

"Elerek." Lystra's voice. Soft, almost fearful. "Send me."

He lifted his gaze. The pain he felt in his chest she wore on her face, deep in her fatigued eyes.

"I'll go to Kushan at once. We must give them the opportunity to defend themselves. Perhaps they may reconsider and choose to stand with us."

Elerek raked a hand through his hair. "It might be too late, Lystra. And if the Jarkins are already there? I cannot send you into a war."

"War will be here, whether we like it or not, and there's a chance that I'll arrive before they will." A light caught in her eyes, like a torch in the night. "They'll listen to me. I'll make them."

Something in her voice convinced him, made him feel as if they could go on, their tasks possible. Hers was a strength that could save kingdoms.

If everything were different, what would they have become? Instanolde's beloved queen and the cursed king never meant to wear a crown.

"Please, El." The fire in her eyes burned brighter. The frightened, weary girl vanished, replaced by the bold, determined queen.

She's never called me "El" before. Elerek's fingers stilled. A deep sigh fled his lungs. "Try to rest, Lystra. You'll need it for your journey."

The queen gave a decided nod, the look of the victorious conqueror. She turned and swept back into the palace, her robe streaming behind her.

Unbidden, the image of her resting softly on the extravagant bed filled his mind. Her eyes softly closed, her dark hair splayed across the pillows as a warm wind teased the bed's canopy.

He drew a sharp breath, steeling himself back to reality, to the suffocating numbness.

"You don't have a choice," Norbah grunted. "Kushan must be warned."

Elerek's fingers began to drum again, mimicking the sound of his heart beating. On and on it went, waiting for his bones to brittle, his skin to liquidize, ready to burst, to drown, to *die.*

But not yet. Not before he saved Instanolde. He huffed and squared his shoulders, pulling the threads of himself together, the posture of a commander. "Have the assassin taken to the palace prison. We'll begin a more thorough extraction within the hour, but first, I want to interrogate him myself."

Norbah raised an eyebrow. "You think he'll speak to you?"

"No, but it's worth trying." He wanted to look a Jarkin in the eye. He wanted to tell Cormek's murderers that vengeance was coming. Justify the rage boiling in his veins. "See to the preparations. Wake the men. See that the docks are cleared, the people relocated back to the east city. We need the waters lined with soldiers by sunrise."

If they saw the sunrise.

Norbah nodded and vanished into the shadows. Only Razhar remained, dark circles beneath his eyes.

"It means little, but you have my gratitude, El." Razhar's gaze dropped to the sands. "For considering my people."

"They're a part of my kingdom, aren't they?"

Razhar nodded, a shadow in his eyes that Elerek hadn't seen before.

"You don't often regard them as 'your' people."

Shaking his head, his friend drew a hand up to rub the back of his neck. "I'm where I belong." Then he blinked, and the shadows fled. "You can do this, El."

Elerek grimaced. "I feel wretched."

A sad, rather pathetic sort of smile twitched at Razhar's lips. "I just single-handedly fought off a Jarkin assassin—and saved your lovely queen's life in the process. If I can do that, then you can face the next hour."

"Fought?" Elerek raised an eyebrow. "Bit of an exaggeration? I do thank you, though, for protecting Lystra."

Then, a true smile dawned on his face. Elerek felt he could die of jealousy to smile such a charming smile just once in his life. *That's how Razhar fights, a warrior who smiles.*

"We're still breathing, aren't we?" Razhar huffed.

Elerek's cynicism fought back tooth and nail. "We'll see what my blasted curse has to say about that." He reached for the rims of his chair's wheels. Smooth from use, stable in an unstable world. Its touch brought him comfort, something to grip, to control. He wheeled himself back into the light of the palace.

"El, you know that it's the curse that kills—not you—right?"

He stopped.

"There isn't one that you've touched with the intent to destroy. Even now, even if this is the end, you've done what you can in the interest of preserving life. It's admirable." Razhar heaved a sober sigh. "You're better than most men, you know that?"

Elerek didn't look at him. "You're a patronizing ray of sunshine, Razhar, *you* know that?"

He didn't wait to hear his friend's response.

A shudder crept over Elerek's skin as the dark stairwell of the palace prison descended into a yawning black pit built beneath the guard's keep. Cole and Norbah carried his chair down. He avoided their eyes, ashamed of requiring such assistance, but it soon grew too dark to see their faces.

Once they'd settled his chair, Norbah lit a torch, bringing the grisly cellblock into a small circle of light. Iron bars cast irregular shadows, like soldiers marching in perfect lines. Elerek blinked and drew a deep breath of the stale air belonging to the cruel, terrible place. A prison for criminals of war.

"Just ahead, on the left." Norbah's whisper seemed to shout back at them, echoing through the murk.

As he gripped the wheel rims, the rickety creak of his chair screeched in the closed space, like a sand wraith of legend. Sand covered the uneven stonework, eroded from the walls or blown through cracks and crevices, like pale lumps of sugar in haphazard piles. Elerek's gaze skimmed the empty cells, their floors covered with straw and rusty manacles. Once or twice, he heard rats scurrying about.

Then, the shadows shifted. Elerek stopped before the Jarkin's cell. The man lurched toward his bars, shackles locked on his ankles. Bruises covered his face, medals earned by his silence.

"Brought a cripple to torture me next?" His teeth gleamed in the torchlight, leering like a skull.

Norbah snarled. "Watch yourself before the king of Instanolde."

Elerek pushed his shoulders back, his chin high, and glared. The hands that gripped the bars of his cell had bruised his queen's neck.

The smirk faded from the Jarkin's mouth. "Ah, Batu-Khasar wondered if the rumors were true, if Instanolde's king had a brother hidden away somewhere."

Leaning forward, Elerek clenched the armrests of his chair. "Wonder no more." He glanced at Norbah. "You may leave us, General."

Norbah set the torch in the sconce affixed beside the cell door and retraced his steps into the darkness.

The Jarkin took a step back, kicking at the shackles. "Your *Highness.*" His eyes never left Elerek, not even to blink.

Wheeling his chair closer, Elerek allowed his eyes to adjust to the murk. How many hours, since the crown was placed on his head, had he heard nothing but talk concerning the mountain men? The invaders who brought their worst nightmares to pass by taking Darcress and murdering a king. They were a force of nature that swept down from the crags to destroy all that they loved.

But before Elerek stood a man. A man in weathered clothes and clad in human skin. A heartbeat in his chest. It seemed strange to attribute all the horrors he knew concerning the invaders to this one man behind bars.

Yet fire tingled in Elerek's veins and rage billowed hot in his lungs. This same man went after Lystra and Razhar. Scaled the walls of the palace and laid murderous hands on his queen.

"You will be executed at dawn." Elerek exhaled. "But first, my soldiers intend to make this the longest night of your life."

The Jarkin reached for his shoulder, where a patch with an insignia had been roughly sewn onto his tunic. Two interlocking diamonds stacked atop one another. "Batu-Khasar won't take that message kindly."

"I haven't taken kindly to the loss of Darcress and the murder of my brother," Elerek growled. "You and your barbarian ways have no place among my people and with every breath in my body and every beat of my heart, I will fight to keep my kingdom free and prosperous."

He meant it. Every word.

The Jarkin looked away.

"Tell me, how is that you survived while my warrior brother did not?"

Rubbing his hands, the Jarkin's knuckles cracked. "Kings die as easily as anyone. War doesn't pick favorites. It's the weak who survive. Suppose I'm one of them, since I'm here being tormented in your reeking kingdom." He scoffed. "And so are you, crippled king."

Elerek ground his teeth.

"Ah, what my people could do with this land." The shackles rattled as the Jarkin sidled to the bars again. "The whole of the desert, the mountains, the crags, and canals. All ours."

Not while he still drew breath. Not before the curse claimed him. "Consider this your chance to earn yourself a quick death. Tell me when your people will attack."

The Jarkin cursed in his own, coarse language.

"You struck Darcress and gave us something to mourn before high summer." Smothering the heat in his veins was akin to reining in a wild cardant. "You've come from the river, haven't you? Batu-Khasar will bring his armies down the canals?"

"Think you're clever, do you?"

Elerek's fingers took to tapping. That was as good an answer as any. "When?"

The Jarkin shook his head. "I'm a dead man, which means I can say what I like." He gripped the bars in both hands, peering between them with dark, sinister eyes. "You've enjoyed the river's bounties too long, dirty Instan. Your kingdom will fall, your city burn, your men will be slain before the walls, your children will toil fields for our harvests, and your women will serve us." He sneered. "Including your eyeful of a queen. A worthy prize for Batu-Khasar."

You. Dirty. Cur. Elerek took a deep breath, his blood simmering beneath his skin. This was why Instanolde needed his schemes, to save them from this. To save Lystra. "Insult my wife again," he snarled through gritted teeth. "I *dare* you."

The Jarkin gave a leering smile. "You Instans think yourselves so high and honorable, but you'll do what it takes to survive. Your tribes fight over water and fertile land, same as all beneath the sun. You think us evil on account of our desiring your river but you're no different." He cackled coldly. "When the weak survive, you pick at them, like vultures. Your father spilled much blood in lawful battle. We saw his strength and honor and didn't challenge him. But you little boys . . ." He snickered. "When we took your kasbah, we knew we would win. The river, the city, it will be no different. You think the desert protects you, but instead, it makes you vulnerable."

He's wrong. You know he's wrong. A chained prisoner shouldn't have left him so rattled.

"Easy pickings, crippled king," the Jarkin drawled, his mountain accent thick. "Your kingdom will crumble to dust. Maybe Batu-Khasar will spare you . . . so you can watch."

Terror reached with cold, iron fingers, squeezing about his heart, enveloping his rage, the poisonous wrath seething in his soul. The curse acquainted him with helplessness long ago, but now, with his kingdom slipping from his fingers, he began to fear living.

He would not live only to watch his kingdom die.

Elerek gritted his teeth, stretched out his hand, and grabbed the Jarkin by the wrist.

The prisoner's hand withered, a shrunken, strangled mass of skin. A high-pitched wail resounded in the dark. The Jarkin sank to his knees, his wrist still locked in Elerek's hold. He swore and struggled, his face twisting with pain.

Elerek didn't let go, squeezing until the man's hand turned transparent. The curse's mark dissolving skin into water. Now the man would know true helplessness—living at the mercy of the curse's damnation.

Except, it didn't stop there.

He didn't want to watch the assassin waste away here in this cell, skin and breath slowly slipping away from him. He didn't want to see the same sorrow that haunted the eyes of Norbah, Myra, and the rest of his tribe lay claim to this enemy.

No, he wanted this man to be punished.

To drown.

And by the curse's strange, dark designs, Elerek got his wish.

Pale skin and plague scars slipped from his hands, replaced by pure, transparent liquid. One by one, droplets began to fall from his fingers, followed by a steady stream straight from his cursed skin. The same element that gave life in the desert turned to death in the grip of his curse. It flowed from his palms, down his arm, spilling into the grit beneath his chair. It pulsed with power, with his own rapid heartbeat.

Elerek gasped, releasing the Jarkin. The prisoner backed away, cowering in the corner. As the water drenched his clothing, pooling about his chair, Elerek clenched his hands, attempting to quell the stream.

But when he opened his palms, its pressure intensified, matching the rage in his soul, ebb for ebb. The might of a crashing river sprayed from his hands. The force threw his chair backwards, slamming into the cell behind him.

Wh-what is this? The thought was small and terrified. Easily drowned out by the blood pounding in his ears, the primal roar of fury to drown, drown, drown.

He stretched his arms toward the Jarkin's cell, every muscle taut. Water began to fill every crevice of the uneven prison floor, swelling against the cell walls in furious waves. The Jarkin backed against the wall, cursed water lapping at his knees. His face grew white with horror.

Elerek recognized the despair in the man's eyes, the look of a damned soul coming face-to-face with his own death.

And he didn't care.

The cell filled with water but it did not pass through the bars, held in place by some invisible barrier. The Jarkin struggled, his neck stretched above the torrent. His screams muted as water poured into his lungs. Submerged by the curse, his skin turned transparent, his bones pale. He writhed, reaching for the bars, stretching a bony finger into air that he could not breathe.

Still, Elerek pushed, his shoulders straining, his palms flat against the wall of water.

Then, the Jarkin stilled. Eyeballs rolled up in invisible sockets. His body floated limp, drowned in a cell full of water.

Elerek's chest heaved. Darkness blurred the edge of his vision. The curse's power began to drain and as it did, some portion of his humanity returned.

What have I done?

His hands remained outstretched, holding the wall of water in place, but he hung his head to rid himself of the sight of the man that he'd drowned.

Razhar said that he'd never touched someone with the intent to destroy. Well, he'd just proved his friend a liar.

Then, the mass of water burst.

It surged from the cell, slamming the Jarkin's body against the bars. The wave of water hit Elerek, knocking his chair over and dousing the torch. He fell, sprawled in the stream running down the prison corridor.

Pushing himself above the flow by his elbows, Elerek gasped in the darkness. He strained for air, choked by the wretched sobs crawling up his throat. Overwhelmed by the horror, numbed from the cursed water, he wept.

"Your Highness? Are you all right?"

Elerek jerked his head up. A circle of light hovered at the end of the passage, illuminating Norbah's towering figure.

"Stay back." Elerek lifted a hand—now only dripping with water like a leaky well pump.

The general stopped, his eyes shifting from Elerek's over-turned chair to the body slumped in the cell. He marched forward, the water lapping at his ankles, soaking his sandals.

Was the water also cursed? Elerek watched as veins appeared along Norbah's bare calves, as if the curse knew its own. "No, no, don't!"

"El." Sorrow tainted his voice. "I've been cursed for years. If it hurries itself up, I won't mourn. You, my king, are my first call and priority."

Hanging his head, Elerek glimpsed the faint outline of his face in the water—the face of a murderer.

Norbah switched the doused torch with the lit one, his eyes wide at the sight of the drowned Jarkin. "You did this."

"I—I don't know h-how . . ."

"All this water—?"

"I—the curse—it came from me. I drowned him."

Norbah set his chair upright and then bent down, lifting him up by his shoulders. "Did you mean to?" Their eyes met.

Elerek settled back into his chair and shut his eyes. "Maybe —yes."

"Then the curse is getting worse?"

This was different, more. The slow transformation that had been dripping from his fingertips for weeks now turned into a torrent. Was this fate meant for him—as the curse's intended victim? Had his turn come at last? The fading light giving way to total darkness? Would there be starlight at the end of his journey for him—a murderer?

Elerek looked up. "Did . . . did you feel anything?"

The general glanced down at his legs and winced. "Nothing out of the ordinary." He pulled his glove off. The curse mark covered half his hand and three fingers. Unchanged.

Lifting his tunic, Elerek bared his side and drew a ragged breath. Like the thick coils of a snake, his mark stretched across his chest, reaching for his shoulders. A slash across his body.

Norbah's stern, soldier's countenance cracked, soft sorrow shining in his eyes.

"They're coming," Elerek whispered as he pulled down his tunic. "By the river. We need to hurry. We are out of time."

"I'll see that the west city is evacuated, and the docks fortified."

Air shuddering in his lungs, Elerek wiped his eyes on his sleeve. "I've got to get out of this place."

Chapter 40

Elerek

Over and over, the scene replayed in Elerek's mind. The suffocating darkness, the roar of crashing water echoing off the stone, the exhilarating, terrible feeling of power pulsing through his arms.

The dead man floating without breath or skin.

There, in that cell built of bedrock, Elerek knew that he would end the man's life and he didn't—couldn't—stop himself.

Starkindler, what's happening to me?

They had taken the man prisoner lawfully. The Jarkins had established their intent when they'd spilled Cormek's blood upon the red sands of Darcress. His people enslaved, their children left to die, and their kingdom wiped from the map like the renewing ripples across the sand dunes.

If the death was just, why did Elerek feel so wretched?

When Norbah and Cole brought his chair out of the prison, the midnight air swelled in his lungs. The scent of evells filled his nostrils, but up above, the sky still lay dark and starless. Perhaps each constellation had hurled itself into the Sancen's desolations. Maybe the sun wouldn't rise at all.

He hunched forward, shoulders shaking, and wept into his hands. Tears ran down his fingers, fingers that could curse—could drown. Maybe he belonged down in those cells, locked away, waiting to die.

Instanolde would wait with him, its fate sealed. Vessels loaded with warriors would dock along the Gungole, jackal skulls perched on their shoulders. It would be easy, no battlements awaited them, no blockades erected to keep them out. They wouldn't need to sully their blades with Instan blood or mar their brows with the sweat of battle, already crowned the victors.

"Norbah? El?" Footsteps pounded across the stonework. "Stars above, where are you?"

Razhar's voice—and it was tainted with fear. Terror from the man who feared nothing. Elerek looked up, blinking away his tears. There, plain as day, horror had ravaged Razhar's face, turning it the color of indigo that hit the sky just after the sun vanished.

"El . . ." His eyes went wide. "What happened?"

Elerek hung his head, rubbing the sides of his temples with trembling hands. Could he tell him? What he'd done? Razhar had seen him at his worst, in the darkest depths, and yet the shame severing his soul made him feel unworthy, even in the presence of the man he considered his best friend.

"I need to be alone," he whispered. Somewhere where the curse—where he—couldn't harm anyone else.

"Razhar." Norbah's voice was firm. "I need you to take care of His Highness. If the queen is to leave in the morning, I must see to the preparations and fortify the docks."

Stars above, what would Lystra think of him? Out in the desert, when she'd taken him to the edge of the Sancen, she'd made it clear that she wanted to be there for him. To stand by his side as more than just a figurehead, more than the queen he needed.

If he looked her in the eye, and told her that he'd murdered a man, what would she say? No, he couldn't let her see him like this. Not this, the broken wreck of a man he knew he'd always been. He'd been a fool to think he could be anything else.

"Don't tell her!" Elerek demanded. "Don't tell her what I've done."

Razhar scowled. "What have you done, El?"

Drip. Drip. Drip.

Elerek lifted his hands, watching the droplets trail down his fingertips, along his arm, dangle from his elbow, and finally plummet onto his already-soaked clothing.

"Oh." Razhar knelt in front of him, watching the display with a dark expression.

Elerek clenched his jaw to keep it from shaking. "I'm getting closer. Razhar, I'm going to die." And Instanolde would die with him.

Razhar leaned forward, gripping the armrest of his chair without fear. "No."

The word echoed within Elerek's skull, as if it held all the defiant power beneath the sun to push back the inevitable. Anything less would hardly befit Razhar and his impossible optimism.

An orphan Kushite in the palace of Instanolde and a cursed prince who'd lost his birthright, they'd both lived in worlds where they had never belonged. Cormek had never understood the curse or the brokenness in Elerek's soul.

Razhar knew. And now, staring into Razhar's eyes, gleaming like polished amber in the torchlight, Elerek could see it. Beyond his bravado, his foolish courage, an anguish dwelt there, the ghost of a mirage upon the horizon.

"Razhar, I need you to do something for me."

346

Standing, his friend gave a grim nod. "Anything. But come, let's get inside."

Everywhere Elerek looked, he saw the ghosts of the cursed inhabiting the kitchens. Both the living and the dead had gathered here, drinking spiced coffee and sweet meskouta cakes, basking in the glow of hearth and hearts still beating.

While they laughed and smiled, the sun hung low in the sky, sinking on a steady trajectory. Their hours slipping away. They lived as if it could last.

Elerek wheeled his chair close to the fire, embers glowing even at this late hour, but he didn't feel its heat. Ice ran in his veins and his skin turned numb. Alongside the crackling of tinder, he could still hear the *drip, drip, drip* of water from his fingers, his hair, and his clothes.

Razhar huffed and hung a copper kettle over the fire. "You're not dying, El. Not yet." He wiped his hands on his linen pants, leaving a trail of dust along the folds at his hip.

Elerek blinked. How had he gotten so dirty? Razhar never liked to appear in any state of filth, the value on his well-groomed appearance far too high. And his hands, the skin along his knuckles appeared strange in the firelight, as if the desert air had shriveled them like the palm dates he loved so much. "What happened to you?"

Digging into his pockets, Razhar procured a small sashe of herbs and dumped them into a cup. "Ah, another adventure." He then took the kettle from the fire, pouring steaming water over the herbs. "Here." He handed the cup to Elerek, his eyes averted.

Elerek raised an eyebrow. "What's this?"

"Just drink it. It'll help your nerves."

"Are you a tea connoisseur now?"

Razhar bowed his head. "It wouldn't profit me to give up my secrets now, El."

Elerek took a timid sip. Bitterness stung his tongue, breaking through the haze of his stalled mind. Dispelling a ragged breath, he let himself recline in his chair, releasing the tension in his shoulders.

The Jarkin. Body slack against the cell bars. Cold and lifeless. The next sip of the tea nearly gagged him.

Razhar set his arm upon the shelf above the hearth, his face set to the flames. "What was it you wanted to request of me?"

After another sip, Elerek set the tea on the table. He wasn't sure he liked feeling so at ease, particularly with his soul still tossed in the turmoil of a violent sandstorm. "I want you to go with Lystra to Kushan. Make sure that nothing happens to her."

"You have my word." Razhar's face hardened. "Though you know I've never held a scimitar in my life. I'm more suited to dancing."

Tears blurred Elerek's vision and he closed his eyes. A headache, synced to the droplets falling from his hand, pounded in his skull. Razhar the dancer with all the jokes, the life of every festival, doomed to live when kingdoms fell and kings were cursed. It wasn't fair. It never had been.

"But if that's what you want." Footsteps. Razhar moved closer. "I'll accompany your lovely queen to my homeland."

He always called Lystra lovely. Maybe if cursed water wasn't flowing from his fingers and he hadn't just murdered a man, Elerek would care about the fact. But all at once, fatigue arrested his body. His thoughts came slowly. His head lowered, his chin slowly sinking to his chest.

What did he—? The tea.

Elerek's eyes shot open. Nothing focused, and the room appeared as if the fire had spread from the hearth, consuming the kitchen. *Would burning be preferable to drowning?* he wondered.

Razhar became a shadow, a mass of darkness without any hint of his garish clothing. "Here." His voice was close. "Let me help you."

"Help—?"

Razhar grasped his wrist. Skin to skin.

"No!" Elerek gave a cry. Forcing his eyes open, he stared up at Razhar's face, somehow thrust into sharp clarity. No, not him. Not Razhar.

But Razhar only smiled his gleeful, carefree smile. "Shh, it's nothing."

"Razhar, you don't know—"

"I *do* know, El." Razhar clasped his shoulder, pushing him back in his chair. "Believe me."

He gripped Elerek's hand, their fingers entwined. The red scars along his knuckles darkened, turning as black as the vile darkness lurking inside his soul. Identical, twisting black veins crawled over Razhar's hand.

A hallucination. A drug. "Th-the tea . . ." Elerek groaned, slouching in his chair. He couldn't keep his eyes open.

"I'm sorry, El."

Everything began to fade.

"I can't let you know what I am."

Chapter 41

Lystra

Dawn came too soon. Lystra rubbed her eyes with a deep sigh, watching the faint streaks of gray shoot across the horizon above her balcony.

Pushing herself up from the pillows, Lystra's body groaned in protest. Muscles locked, stiff from the terror of the night. She looked down at her arm, peeling back the bandages that were crusty with dried blood. It needed redressing. Sharp, jolting memories of a blade, blood, and the Jarkin's hand about her neck shot through her mind. A taste of the violence to come.

The Jarkins were coming. At any moment. A vessel waited to take her to Kushan. She'd sworn to Elerek that she could rally the people of the canyonlands to come to their aid. She'd convinced him that her word would make a difference, that they could protect their people.

And already, it felt hopeless.

Lystra drew a shuddered breath, pushing her hair over her shoulder. Even if it was hopeless, she had to try.

She summoned a maid to help with her wound and dressed for travel. As she stood before her mirror, she grimaced. A ghostly face stared back at her, black circles beneath her eyes, and the faint bruises of fingerprints formed a collar about her throat.

Nothing like the bold queen, the beloved of Instanolde.

Her hands trembled as she dressed. If she couldn't feel the part of queen, at least she could dress it. A flowing skirt hung high on her hips, the color of a dark wine. A short blouse clasped at her chest, its collar high enough to hide the bruises at her throat, and a length of sheer silk cascaded from her shoulders. Jewels adorned her ears and arms, and her maid arranged her hair in intricate braids. As the thin circlet of gold rested on her brow, Lystra closed her eyes, feeling its weight and letting herself be comforted by the thought of the sun on her shoulders.

Sweeping into the parlor, her gaze lingered on the curtains of Elerek's chamber. She had to see him before she departed. If their end had come, if the Jarkins attacked before she returned, if they failed to save their kingdom, she had to tell him . . .

Tell him what?

Lystra caught her breath. The tumult of emotions raging against her ribs scarcely had names, much less a composed thought to accompany them. Could she actually mean to tell him the truth? How the gaping hole in her soul, the graves dug by grief, had begun to fill and heal? That he'd become more than the crown, more than her king?

No, something held her back. The cold distance between them, a place where the impossible had no place.

She couldn't tell Elerek that she'd dared to love a cursed man.

Shaking away these dangerous thoughts, she crossed the parlor and reached for the curtains, gently parting them. The window had been left open, and a soft breeze rippled the silk of the bed's canopy.

Her heart fell to her hem.

The room lay undisturbed. Clean and orderly. The bed made and undisturbed. Only the dagger on the nightstand appeared out of place.

A cold shiver crept down her arms. Lystra's chest pounded, and she found her fingers quivering. Elerek hadn't come back, hadn't slept here. She recalled the terrified, almost manic look in his eyes last night, and how he needed the support of his friends—desperately.

"If not for you, I would be with him. See that he isn't suffering alone."

Myra...

No, she refused to believe it. He wouldn't—would he? Unless she'd been wrong, so, so wrong. Here, upon the eve of disaster, before the end came, perhaps he'd returned to the girl he'd loved before. The one who had comforted him, eased his suffering.

The lover that he could touch.

Maybe he'd never loved Lystra at all.

Tears filled Lystra's eyes. She gulped air, the gilded walls of the palace closing in around her. This was a cage, the very prison she feared, built in the likeness of Grandmother's manipulations.

No. She spun around, turning her back on the untouched room that belonged to a cursed king. Elerek had proved himself different. He was nothing like her grandmother, she knew this to be true.

But she also knew that Myra loved him—and why shouldn't he love her back?

A soldier knocked at the door. She gave entrance with a bold command.

"Your Highness, the countess of House Arghan has arrived."

Uninvited. Lystra's heart sank. Blessed silence from the matron of House Arghan had reigned like the eerie stillness before the spring rains broke across the land. And now, a storm arrived, and she hadn't the time for it.

Lystra met her grandmother in the gardens, away from the hubbub of the palace and the preparations for war. She pushed aside the rising tide of fear inside her, thoughts of the man she'd married and the cursed girl. The less Dalmah knew, the better. Here, the hanging vines of evell blooms had begun to wither, their season past. Cultivated waterfalls ran from fountains built of rocks into ponds filled with bright, orange fish.

Dalmah wore black. Silver threads ran through her scarf, like spider's silk. Her eyelids were painted dark and her lips red as rubies. A phantom of shadow and silk.

Lystra breathed in deep. Grandmother's voice speaking strict admonitions filled her mind. Smothered her. But still, she stood tall, shoulders back, chin high, a cold, steady stare upon her features. An Arghan queen of old.

"Grandmother." Lystra dipped her head.

"Your Highness." Dalmah lowered herself to her knees. The perfect picture of humility. But when she rose, a moment later, a thin-lipped frown cast a darkness over her features.

"To what do I owe this visit? I depart to Kushan within the hour."

Dalmah narrowed her eyes. "To beg for the loyalty that they denied your foolish king?"

"It isn't your concern."

The scandalized expression on the countess's face burned hot enough to melt iron. Lystra stood a little taller.

"I told you to kill him, Lystra."

Beneath her silks, Lystra's skin prickled. Steady. She stepped closer, rounding the edge of the pond. The fish, noticing her presence, assembled at the rim. Their large mouths skimmed the surface of the water, as if breathing, but looking for a feeding.

"I'll not discuss treason within my own house."

Even if Elerek had committed treason—against her.

No, she didn't know for sure, couldn't jump to conclusions.

"And yet you entered this house on the basis of treason." Dalmah's lips curved in a cruel smirk. "You took my dagger, didn't you?"

Lystra stilled. Her chest seized.

"You must have seen the sense in my plan to have taken it. Or perhaps you feared for yourself, here in the palace among strangers? Could you possibly have considered seeing the deed done—only to change your mind?" Dalmah shook her head. "Do you think that such weakness will save you from the Jarkins? They didn't hesitate to destroy Cormek, did they?"

Lystra drew her hands into fists, steeling herself. "You will speak no dishonor upon Cormek, who stood bravely facing our enemy."

Her grandmother's eyes were carved of stone. "He stood brave only for his queen to fall."

Hot tears clouded her eyes, but Lystra pushed them back. She had no idea. She didn't know about the assassins, about their plans, about Elerek's curse, and how he'd tried so desperately to save them all.

No, she had to believe that Elerek was still trying, and she would not listen to Dalmah's critiques.

"Our chances against the Jarkins are better served in unity." She held her head aloft, thankful for her jewels, her crown, and the heavy paint upon her eyes. "My only shame is that I did consider your bloody scheme, if only for a moment. I have realized my mistake."

Honesty was a gambit, a calculated risk. Lystra didn't know if it would pay off, but whatever her grandmother thought of her would soon no longer matter. They had larger wars to wage.

Dalmah stepped closer, mere inches from the pond's edge, luring the fish to congregate at her feet. Between them, their reflections stretched downward. Women of the same family with two drastically different fates.

"I thought you had suffered enough to gain the gall to do what was necessary. I saw a queen, but you blinded me. Instead, I see now that you're only a girl. A wildly distracted girl, broken by the sight of a face that looks like Cormek's."

Lystra's face grew hot. "I'm stronger than you think I am."

Her grandmother raised a wry eyebrow. "Are you?"

Yes. Lystra knew this to be true. And it mattered. It mattered now more than ever. "I have arrangements to attend." She backed away from the pond, her eyes on its glassy surface and its careless fish below. They looked free enough, fins flared and scales sleek, but they swam in circles. She wasn't like them.

Grandmother couldn't control her any longer. She'd proved that she could rule—Elerek's trust and support at her side. Whatever happened, however short a time they had, they had done their best in these summer weeks. They had chosen to do honorably by their people. To give them hope—to give them starlight.

Even if the night had come.

Please, she begged, hoping to be wrong. Praying that Elerek had chosen strength.

But Dalmah didn't move, frozen amid the garden's splendor. Her eyes narrowed to slits, cunning and cruel. "By now, you know what your boy king is, don't you? And still, you're loyal to him?"

The warmth fled Lystra's face. The curse.

"It can't be broken, Lystra." Dalmah's voice sounded like the hiss of a poisonous viper. "It will only kill, ravage, and destroy. Just you watch, the curse will turn that boy into a monster. Anyone so tainted isn't worth preserving."

This time, when the tears filled Lystra's eyes, she couldn't hold them back.

She had seen things Dalmah's stone-cold heart couldn't even begin to fathom. How could she know of the love and devotion Elerek gave to those also inflicted with the curse? She hadn't seen the loyalty shining in their eyes as they shared a meal, laughed, and sang beneath the stars. She knew nothing of the turmoil hidden beneath Razhar's winsome exterior as he pushed back the curse, buying precious time.

Lystra counted herself privileged. Elerek *had* opened his heart, drawn back his harsh exterior, and she'd seen how he'd striven, fighting each moment to live as he'd never lived before. Surely that was worth fighting for. No matter what happened, they had to keep fighting.

El, keep fighting.

Lystra drew a sharp inhale, facing her grandmother with heat in her eyes. "How do you know about the curse?"

Dalmah only smiled. "I've lived thrice your lifetime, granddaughter. Lorkin forced me from the throne, named his second son his heir, and kept his eldest in the shadows. I had the time to watch, to listen, to learn Lorkin's secrets—and it was no secret that he attempted to purge the land of all curse binders."

The way she spoke his name—*Lorkin*—sent shivers down

Lystra's spine. Even here, the mirror of water between them, she could feel the ebb of Dalmah's hatred. A bitter poison. Elerek's death would end House Karim forever. Was that what she wanted?

Lystra crossed her arms, her chin high. "Why didn't you tell me?"

Dalmah scoffed. "I told you to kill him."

"With a dagger." Lystra shook her head. How easily she might have touched him in the act, become cursed herself.

A risk. Far too great a risk after the years spent cultivating a queen. Killing a king was an act of desperation—as desperate as the bloodlust shining in Dalmah's eyes.

"Fetch my dagger this instant, girl."

Lystra blinked, glaring at her grandmother. "I'm not some maid bound to do your bidding."

Her mind turned to the dagger—and the constellation etched in its blade. The wrathgiver. An assassin stalking the dark watches of the night. Something dangerous that moved in the shadows.

All at once, Lystra's heart stopped. Something itched in her mind, like sand caught in the folds of clothing, rubbing between skin and silk. "What does the dagger have to do with Elerek's curse?"

The look of surprise on Dalmah's face, the likes of which Lystra had never seen before, confirmed that Lystra had struck true.

Lystra turned, her gaze frantically scanning the courtyard. "Guards!"

"Don't do something you'll regret, granddaughter."

Spinning back toward her grandmother, her skirt swirling about her ankles, Lystra glared. "Answer the question."

But Dalmah only shifted her weight to one foot, her arms folded. Her eyes resembled the most perfectly cut gem, hard as diamond. "A dagger is made for killing. It might have everything to do with it . . . or nothing at all."

Soldiers swarmed the garden, standing at Lystra's bidding.

"If you intend to lock me up, go right ahead." Dalmah waved a dismissive hand. "Word will spread, you know. The longer I keep silent, the greater chance that the entire kingdom will know that its beloved queen kept her own elderly grandmother in chains."

At one time, Lystra might have cared. "The kingdom is about to be invaded by Jarkins. I doubt they'll notice." She looked at the nearest guard. "Lock this woman up until she is ready to talk." She lowered her voice as her eyes turned to her grandmother again. "My people will care when Elerek and I save them—and I break his curse and set him free."

Free to rule by her side. Free to touch without fear. Free to breathe without the terror of drowning.

Free to love her . . . or leave her heart forever.

At that, Dalmah only laughed as the soldiers took her arms and led her away.

Chapter 42

Elerek

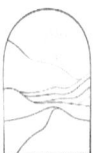

E lerek opened his eyes with a groan. Sunlight streaked across his vision, searing straight through his skull where a headache pounded without clemency. He shifted onto his side, turning back toward the shadows. His body felt heavy, and his clothes plastered to his skin. Utterly drenched.

Drenched, like the Jarkin in the prison. The one he'd drowned.

He pushed himself upright, gasping air as the memories rushed like a river through his mind. Leaning forward, he held his head in his hands, fingers trembling.

A bit of bright red thread caught his eye, a row of tiny birds embroidered along the edge of the blanket covering his legs. He knew every stitch.

He jerked his gaze up, glancing about the space, familiarizing himself with all of its ghosts. A gentle wind, already scorching, blew past the window, rattling the open lattice. Beyond, a pair of date palms swayed, giving shade to a corner of the palace gardens where he'd often parked his chair to read.

Inside, the sparse furniture had faded, its fabric worn from the sunlight.

He'd lived most of his life in these rooms. A remote corner of the palace without stairs. A host of memories marched across his mind with the discipline of a well-organized army. Memories that wouldn't serve him now. Had Razhar brought him here?

After he'd done the unthinkable, murdered a man.

Snuffed out a light kindled in the darkness.

The shock of what he'd done made everything hazy, stunning him to his core. His chest felt as if it were collapsing, crushed beneath the weight of cursed water. He yanked his shirt over his head, staring down at the curse mark, that horrid, thick line moving up along his ribs and slashing over his heart.

Maybe he'd earned this fate, a punishment for his sins.

Movement stirred across the room. The creak of a rickety chair. The light caught on the faded pattern of a scarf, seemingly pulled from the threads of the furniture. As if she belonged there.

Myra startled awake, lifting her head from the crook of her arm. Her eyes fell on him—upon the curse mark reaching across his chest.

"What are you doing here?" Elerek demanded. Heat flared across his skin, breaking the numbness. He quickly donned his shirt again.

What was *he* doing here?

Myra grimaced as she unfolded herself from the chair. "You . . . weren't well."

No, no he wasn't. Elerek clenched his jaw and shoved the blanket with red birds away, hauling his legs over the side of the bed. That bit of heat dwindled, the curse raging back with an unfeeling deadness. Stars, he wanted to *feel*. So, so badly.

"But why here?"

Lowering her gaze, Myra pushed the length of her hair over her shoulder. "Razhar thought it best. He said that the queen departs for Kushan this morning and he didn't wish to cause a disturbance." She gave him a pointed look. "You needed looking after."

The queen. Lystra. Shame sank his heart like an anchor of a ship in the depths of the Gungole. No, he didn't want her to know what he'd done. Elerek bowed his head, dragging a hand through his hair, droplets catching on his curls. "Lystra will notice that I didn't come to our chambers."

And what would she think then? Maybe she already thought him a monster—like the cursed man who drowned prisoners in shackles behind bars.

Myra blinked, watching him with eyes full of sorrow.

Elerek shook his head. His chair stood at the foot of the bed and he reached for the nearest wheel, pulling it toward him. Had Lystra already left? Had Norbah fortified the docks? Had the Jarkins come in the night?

"El . . . What happened?" Myra's voice dropped to a whisper. She stepped closer. "What has the curse done?"

Made him a murderer. Elerek's shoulders tensed as he lifted himself into his chair, his heart lodged in his throat. The weight of water pouring into the prison cell pushed against his chest. Depths deep enough to destroy—to drown.

With a shaky breath, he extended a scarred hand. It took so little prompting. Just a bit of concentration. Droplets fell from his fingertips, puddling on the polished floor.

Myra went pale. "How . . . how long has this been happening?"

Elerek closed his fist, stemming the flow. "I . . ." Stars. Could it be? "Since the coronation. Since the wedding." What correlation could there possibly be? An ache formed on his forehead. "Has yours . . . ?"

361

She discarded her scarf, revealing soft, bare skin. The curse mark snaking its way up her shoulder had become a narrow stream compared to the river slashing his body.

Elerek scowled. "It looks smaller."

Shrugging, Myra tossed her scarf aside. Her hands free, he noticed that they were trembling. "El, do you think . . . ? If the curse has gotten worse . . ."

Elerek bowed his head. "I—I don't know what to think. If I'm close—close to the end—which means it's close for all of us."

When the curse came to collect, it wouldn't only take him. Perhaps the kingdom would mourn the loss of a king—it'd had its share of practice by now—but its losses would be so much greater. Instanolde would lose its general, mighty soldiers, stalwart bakers, expert scribes, efficient stable hands, the extraordinary among the ordinary. The true might of the kingdom—its simple, beautiful people.

Myra wrapped her arms around herself, her eyes clenched shut. "The end . . ." She sounded afraid. "Why must it come so fast?"

It always did. No matter how hard they tried to uphold the sun. Elerek's chest ached. A million thoughts raced through his mind, a thousand tasks he could do. But all that he'd devoted himself to the last month had led to nowhere, only failure.

He had tried—and he had failed.

He didn't want to be king. Stars, he didn't even want to exist anymore.

Staring down at his hands, damp hands that had blood on them, he begged for a bit of feeling, a bit of warmth, anything to remind him that he was still human. That a heart still beat in his chest.

"Should I say anything? To the others?"

The others. His little tribe lived on the fringe of death's

shadow. "I don't know." Would the knowledge that it had come change anything? Would it take them all together? One deluge of cursed water broken upon the desert stone? Worse, pitted against the Jarkin invasion, the attack that would come sooner than they expected. A race grander than any cardant race. He wondered who would win?

Elerek's gaze drifted to the window. The sunlight had shifted, traveling across the wood floors. Time slipping away. "I should go."

They would ask for him. Want him to answer ridiculous questions. Look to him for starlight, for a hope that had snuffed itself out with the bleakness of night.

Numbness consumed him. Both body and soul. His chair took him down paved paths that he could barely discern, the usually familiar movement of his chair subdued. He passed through the gardens, but he could smell none of their fragrance. Skirting the kitchens, passing the bread ovens lined up in a row like great, mounded beehives, he saw the smoke rising from their stacks. It was early enough that the bakers would be preparing bread, stoking the embers. He couldn't smell their aroma.

Once back amongst the marbled corridors of the palace, he rolled to a stop. His hands shook like mad. Even the touch of his chair was dulled. It made him want to scream.

A numb, cold void. This was hell. This was drowning.

A pair of footsteps followed.

"El, wait." Myra overtook him. She reached for his arm, his sleeve locked in her fingertips. "Please."

Desperation frayed her voice, mirroring the unraveling happening within his soul.

Drip. Drip. Drip.

Elerek clenched his hands, as if his fingertips had the power to hold back the waters. But no, his hands only held death.

But Myra's touch, that sliver of contact. A bit of warmth seeped into his arm.

"You're cold . . . so cold." Her voice drowned in sorrow.

We won't survive.

No, he'd tried to fight. He'd built a façade, replacing Cormek's face with his own, giving the people a unified banner beneath his queen, and preparing the kingdom to meet its threats. A glimmer amongst the starlight, the slimmest of chances that they might survive beyond summer's end.

Meanwhile, his own cursed tribe, his family, would die.

The only hope, the only starlight, that he could grasp right now was that of the touch on his arm. A lifeline.

"If . . . if this is the end, if we are to die . . ." Myra's whisper sounded strangled. "El, please, let me help you."

If they were to die, did it matter? Did anything matter? One endless, futile battle after another. Did he have to fight them all?

Elerek reached for her hand, her fingers fitting into his. Her touch was warm, a hearth with soft, yet vibrant flames. Suddenly he didn't know how to fight anymore. He was worn, ragged, and stars, he wanted to feel again.

He didn't want to feel the curse anymore.

He turned his chair toward her. Tears glittered in her eyes. Those were the eyes that had never looked upon him with scorn. Eyes that had seen another human being, the girl who chose to love him despite the curse.

Stop.

He'd been here before. So many times. The edge of a cliff, a plummet beneath. The stars knew it was so much easier to fall than to fight. Something inside him told him to flee, but it was smothered, buried deep in the ice of his numb soul.

Concern wrinkled Myra's brow. She leaned forward,

brushing her fingers over his cheek, along his jaw. Her touch felt like fire, slowly melting him.

Leave. You can't do this.

They were going to die. The world would crumble today. He wanted to stay. Wanted it more than anything.

Myra tilted her forehead against his, her hair touching his face. "Can you feel me?"

Suddenly, he didn't know what to do. What to say. Why did everything feel like suffocating? Drowning?

He closed his eyes. There, in the darkness, he saw only water. A flood rising swiftly.

And he couldn't escape it.

Chapter 43

Lystra

Lystra flew down the palace corridors in a flurry of silk and fierce determination. In her hands, she clutched her grandmother's dagger. The dagger that hadn't killed the king on their wedding night.

Dalmah had stolen far too much of her time. As the sun marched on its journey into the deep azure sky, hours slipped through her fingers. Her boat waited to ferry her away to Kushan to make her desperate plea. She wouldn't have the time to find Elerek and say goodbye. These were the minutes upon which Instanolde's survival depended.

Then, she turned a corner—and stopped dead in her tracks. Her heart sank right down to the stonework and for a moment, she couldn't breathe—as if she too were cursed.

Elerek—and Myra.

The girl's fingers were entwined in his hair, caressing his cheek—and between them, a kiss burned.

A betrayal as sharp as the star-etched dagger in her hands.

She opened her mouth to speak, but nothing came out. She

didn't know what to say, how to protest. Pain blossomed in her chest, sharp as cardant's talons, shredding her soul, the heart she'd failed to protect. She'd been foolish, so, so foolish.

Elerek lifted his hand, cursed and untouchable. His fingers brushed her shoulder, where her curse mark shimmered in the light.

And he pushed Myra back, severing their contact. "No." The whisper hissed through his teeth. A storm gathered upon his brow and his hands slowly clenched.

They both looked straight at her.

The air practically crackled, heat setting spark to dry kindling. Ready to burn. Lystra again felt the flames of the funeral pyre, grief glowing like hot coals in her chest. But emotion wouldn't serve her here. What good were her tears? What worth was this wretched feeling in her soul? She'd wanted to believe—and she was wrong.

He doesn't love me.

Clearing her features, Lystra pushed her shoulders back, donning a stone-cold regality that would have made Dalmah smile with pride. "I'm leaving for Kushan."

Elerek's eyes grew wide. "Lystra, wait."

"You don't have to say anything." She gave a prim tilt of her head, feigning indifference.

Oh, but she wished he would.

He rolled his chair forward, but not close enough to cross the gaping canyon between them, the plummet where their vows lay in shattered shards. "Lystra, I . . ."

His voice trailed off, and for the first time, Lystra noticed the trace of water dripping from his chair, the drenched state of his clothing, and the frightful, frantic look in his eyes. The look of a man drowning from the inside out.

But Lystra hardened her heart. Myra was right, she'd no

way of helping him, comforting him, bringing him out of the darkness of the curse. She only had her crown, her power. The prestige that her king had chosen to give her.

That was all he could give her.

"I pray that there's hope—starlight." Her stoic tone knew nothing of hope. "That maybe we'll live to see Instanolde survive."

Starlight. The hope he'd given her turned to falling embers, streaking across the horizon.

Another horrible moment of silence passed. Lystra couldn't bear it. She swept past them, her knuckles pale as she gripped the dagger. "Goodbye."

Somewhere out in the city, the bells began to ring. A clear call, a warning for the people to take shelter. They filled Lystra's ears with dread as she strode out into the sunlight to the courtyard where her carriage waited. Once the people were relocated, the soldiers would prepare the defenses.

The thought ran her blood cold. Her city, with its paved streets and ornate arches, prepared for battle. The markets cleared to make way for barricades. Where wine and spices once flowed, blood would run over flagstone. One summer to live had faded into hours.

But the Jarkins would not find her kingdom strong and unyielding. They were weak, crumbled from the inside out, like her heart. Perhaps every word of hope, promising a sunrise beyond this night, was only a falsehood.

Elerek had sworn to give her the truth, without manipulation. He'd promised that he wouldn't hurt her, to give her starlight.

She stopped at the door to the carriage, unable to move. Breath shuddered in her lungs.

You told me that you needed me.

The memory struck her soul with a crack, shattering it like glass into a thousand fractured pieces. Whispers spoken in the dark, illuminated by soft starlight and the embers of purpose. If she had seen clearly that night, when their souls had lain bare to one another, that path was now veiled.

She crumbled. Her royal façade shattered. Bowing her head, Lystra clutched the dagger against her chest. Hot tears streamed down her face. Grandmother was right to call her foolish, a girl distracted. How could she possibly even think to protect her beloved Instanolde when she couldn't even protect her own heart?

Her heart that had already been ripped apart, stitched back together, and molded like clay upon a potter's wheel. Doomed to love two kings that were both destined to die.

"Oh . . . Lystra."

A soft gasp. Footsteps in silken slippers, drawing steadily nearer.

Lystra startled and spun around, skirts swirling. Here, even in the glitter of the midmorning light, Myra still seemed shrouded in shadows. Her face paled in astonishment, her eyes wide, as if she'd never seen such a thing as a grieving queen before.

Lystra hastily wiped her face, set her jaw, and drew herself tall. "I have nothing to say to you." She turned her gaze forward to focus on the carriage. Two soldiers in palace orange stood at the door and the mules shuffled anxiously.

Myra slowly stepped in a wide orbit, circling Lystra much

the same way a cardant would another cardant. Careful but not timid, testing one another's defenses.

"I didn't know . . . about you . . ."

Beneath her skin, Lystra's blood began to boil like water prepared for tea. A bitter draught that reeked of poison. She thrust open the carriage's door and tossed the dagger onto the seat before she could use it the way that it was intended. "You know plenty."

"You *do* love him." Myra exhaled; wind lost in the desert. "Of course you would."

Of course. As if it were fated, a story written in the stars themselves. A current as sure as the Gungole as it flowed down from the canals. Lystra didn't even dare admit the truth to herself, and the tragic, impossible sound of it coming from the mouth of the girl whom Elerek loved filled her eyes with traitorous tears.

"Does he know?"

Breathe. The air from her lungs escaped in hot exhales, like smoke from a bonfire. "You summarized it yourself quite nicely." Lystra turned on her, hands clenched. "An unconsummated, political arrangement. I haven't a claim to him, and never shall. You got exactly what you wanted while my duty belongs to my kingdom and my vows seek to uphold it."

Myra blinked, staring back at her. "I care about him, Lystra. I care about what the curse is doing to him."

Why did this girl keep using her name? As if they were equals? "The curse is no excuse!" Flames blazed hot in her soul, bold as the fire opals set in their ceremonial crowns, the seal of their vows sworn before the priests, their people, and the shimmering skies above. "It's a vile, horrid thing, but it isn't a reason to shut me out. I . . ."

She loved a cursed man, doomed to drown. But admitting it

to herself brought no release, no great epiphany. Instead, something inside her tortured soul *snapped*.

"And if he didn't love *you* . . ." She raised a hand, her heart aflame with fury.

"Lystra, don't!" Myra swiftly backed away, beyond the reach of her rage. "I know I deserve it, but the curse . . ."

Dropping her hand, a strangled sob broke free from her throat. Lystra thought of the night of Cormek's burning when the mourning paint spilled from the hands of a clumsy maid who received Dalmah's wrath. Was she so tainted by her grandmother's cruelty?

No, she couldn't be cruel. Not even now, with her heart broken by betrayal.

A muffled sob broke from Myra's throat. The tense, guarded look about her crumbled, and what remained was soft and fragile. "I misjudged you, Your Highness. And . . ." She drew a deep inhale. "I'm sorry."

Lystra looked away. She didn't want Myra's apologies. The girl had given her honesty from the beginning, freely admitting the truth of her and Elerek's relationship. No, his silence festered in Lystra's soul like a splintered shard.

Maybe Elerek also didn't know. How could he? Perhaps she didn't know how to love him. Their griefs mirrored one another, and yet the image that bounced back was reversed. Perhaps they could only manage to breathe as king and queen, and nothing more.

Lystra sniffled and shook her head, looking away. "I cannot send you away, but I do not want to see you. Especially not with him."

"I understand." Myra spoke softly. Her fingers ran through the frayed end of her dress's sash, its threads unraveling. "But I think you ought to tell him what you feel."

She scoffed, pushing an exterior of marble over her features. Such a declaration had no place here in her kingdom built of sands swept by the winds of war and chaos. "It's impossible."

Tears filled Myra's eyes, washing them in an empathy as soft as the rarest silk. "Impossible or not . . . it's real."

It ought to remain impossible. Let this betrayal be the spark to set fire to the pyre and let her never mourn a king again. Grief cast a host of mirages, and she couldn't be led astray, despite how she felt about Elerek. Could she still love him, even now? Amidst this betrayal?

She didn't know.

"I will stay out of the way," Myra whispered.

"What good will that do?" Lystra bit back, her voice clipped with ice. "What need have we for more grief?" No, grief was a weapon, one she would seize. The warrior queen. "Instanolde stands upon the edge. Only the survival of my people matters."

Myra's fingertips brushed the exposed curse mark on her shoulder. "Are we not your people too?" Her voice dropped to a whisper. "You should know, something's happened with the curse."

She thought of Azraa, of Fin. "Has someone else . . . ?"

"Oh, no." Myra blinked. "Not like that. It's done something to El, and I'm afraid. You ought to ask Razhar to explain."

Horror added its shard to her pierced heart. She thought of Elerek's worn, haggard appearance, the water dripping from his wheelchair. For a moment, she forgot the wound of watching him kiss Myra, and she feared for him.

No. She shook her head and gathered her skirt. "I haven't time. I must go to Kushan." She swept into the carriage, shutting herself in and allowing the wood walls to act as her battlements. Her king wasn't the only one who could surround himself with walls.

And yet she wept the entire way to the dock, to her vessel, prepared to ferry her away.

Chapter 44

Elerek

Somewhere, out in the city, the evacuation bells had begun to chime. Their rings were distant, as if Elerek listened from underwater, submerged.

Already drowning.

But it wasn't the curse that stole his breath, numbed his skin, and stole away his ability to feel. No, this time, he drowned of his own accord, beneath the weight of his own, crushing choices.

"Alert the king! Assemble the ranks!"

Would the soldiers find him here? Lingering in the shadows, as if he'd never left? Would they think him a coward? Well, he felt like one. No, he *was* a coward.

Grinding his teeth, Elerek covered his face with his hands. Shame doused his skin as the taste of Myra lingered on his lips. The bitter, familiar root of loathing ate away at the soil of his heart. He shouldn't have done it. Stars above, why had he done it?

"The bells have been rung. All soldiers report to the docks."

He'd never heard these bells before, rung on Norbah's

command to clear the city and let the soldiers pour into the streets.

They needed him. The soldiers. The people. His generals. Lystra.

The scene replayed over and over in his mind. Lystra, dressed in magnificence, glittering in all the glory of Instanolde's queen. His queen. In her hands she clutched the dagger, the one that hadn't pierced his flesh. No, he was responsible for the backstabbing.

Fire blazed in her eyes, hot enough to singe over the uncrossable distance between them. But as quickly as the water had filled the cell of the Jarkin he had drowned, sorrow staked its claim on her. The mourning queen rose from the ashes of Cormek's pyre, crushed by grief.

Her eyes—what he'd seen was impossible. A shadow, a remnant, a piece of Lystra's soul that belonged to his brother. Not to him.

The march of soldiers' boots filled the palace. Elerek pushed the wheels of his chair, arms straining as he took steep passages and sharp turns. Droplets squeezed between his fingers, causing the wheel rims to become slippery. A reminder that all that was left of him belonged to the curse's wrath and the strength of his own exertion. Feeble, broken things.

Did Lystra—did he dare think it? She couldn't, it was futile. Utterly futile. They'd taken vows made of paper and destined to burn for the sake of their kingdom. Instanolde had become a part of them, etched an identity as king and queen upon them like the stonemasons carving stories in intricate images upon the arches of the byways.

And if Lystra loved him, he'd taken her love and destroyed it, just as he had murdered the Jarkin in the cell.

When he entered the throne room, the soldiers bowed low. The captain removed his helm, speaking quickly.

"The general waits for further orders. He's evacuated the docks and ports."

Elerek inhaled deeply, his chest expanding. "Alert the archers and ready a carriage. I'll meet him at once." Strategy and soldiers and battlements and defenses took control in his mind, what the kingdom needed of him.

"You want the entire regiment of archers staged at the docks?" the captain asked.

"Every single one of them." Elerek closed his fists, hoping that the soldiers didn't notice the water gathered along his skin, soaking his sleeves, and staining the wood of his chair. "Has the queen departed for Kushan?"

"Yes, Your Highness, the last vessel."

The noise of the room faded, but it wasn't due to the curse. His heart pounded in his ears, aching with a pain he couldn't describe.

She's gone.

A void emerged in his soul, one different from the feeling of nonexistence caused by the curse's numbness. No, this was a gaping hole, one that he could feel. Something like loss.

Lystra was fire and fury and all the radiance of a glorious desert sunrise—and he had done nothing to deserve her.

Whispering a prayer for her protection, Elerek fell in pace with his wheelchair among the soldiers as they marched the length of the throne room. None of them bore the curse and their closeness put him on edge.

A shadow passed between the throne room's marble pillars, just in the corner of his eye. Elerek glanced to the side, his gaze meeting Myra's.

There were tears in her eyes.

He didn't know why he kissed her. He shouldn't have. He didn't blame the pull of her fingertips, the warmth of her skin upon his, the break in the curse's numbness. No, he blamed himself. Wholly.

This time, his failures had hurt them both, the two women he had loved. And now, he'd lost them both. Maybe he deserved it.

He grabbed the wheel of his chair, bringing it to an abrupt halt. Air hissed through his teeth. A few droplets fell from his fingertips, splashing against the marbled hall.

"Your Highness?" The captain paused, glancing at him.

Elerek blinked, closing his hand tight. Had it happened? Despite his best efforts, the walls and defenses he'd built, the curse's terrors keeping him isolated, he'd done the unthinkable.

Fallen in love with Lystra.

The thought twisted his insides in knots. Behind him, the throne loomed upon its dais, flanked by the two bowls of fire. Its image seared into his mind, declaring him wretched and unworthy of the crown—and of his queen.

But it didn't matter. He'd lost her, broken his vows, all on account of his own weaknesses.

"Your Highness, are you all right?" the captain pressed.

Elerek drew a deep draught of air, life-giving air that he didn't deserve. "Yes, I . . ." Stars, he felt awful, nothing like a king. "We may proceed."

The soldier marched on. Elerek reached for the rim of his wheel again. His eyes returned to the shadows, to the place between the pillars where Myra stood. The curse mark upon her shoulder lay exposed, winding its way down to her elbow again. Soon, it would steal away all of her skin. Maybe the end was indeed coming for them all.

She blinked, and the tears ran down her cheeks.

Did she know? That his heart had fallen, like a star in the heavens, for Lystra?

Then, she drew her shoulders back and held her head high.

An understanding seemed to pass between them, like the scent of afar-off incense. She turned, blending in amongst the shadows and splendor of the palace.

And he followed the soldiers toward the door. He didn't know what awaited him at the docks, but Instanolde demanded his loyalty, his duty, here at the end. Perhaps he'd been a king who had failed a thousand times over, but when the enemy appeared at the gate, he would be there.

Chapter 45

Lystra

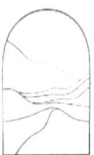

S oldiers lined the docks. Gooseflesh covered Lystra's bare arms as she boarded the ship that would take her to Kushan. She bowed her head as she passed, granting her approval to the soldiers who would stand at the frontlines. The first to fall when the Jarkins attacked.

A contingent of soldiers followed her, taking their stance along the deck. Protectors. Men in service to the crown that they hoped could save them.

Lystra felt no courage. Only numbness.

Once the vessel surged away from the docks, sailors took positions with the oars. Lystra stepped near the prow, well out of their way, and let the sun warm her arms. They rowed against the current, upriver, toward the dark haze of the cliffs and crags that defined Kushan's borders.

An attendant brought her chilled tea, shining like amber in its glass, but Lystra shook her head. She craved only the smell of the river, the spray of its waves, and the kiss of air on her skin. A soothing distraction to hold back the end of all that she held dear.

Still, the thoughts crowded her mind, repeating on an endless cycle. Arresting her own grandmother. Elerek's betrayal. Myra's confrontation. The curse, its clear and constant peril. A world in turmoil, swirling in tandem with the chaos brewing in her heart.

Lystra inhaled, a single tear running down her face. Perhaps she'd been wrong. She wasn't a strong queen, not like her grandmother envisioned. Certainly not one that could save her people, much less break a horrible curse.

Cages came in many forms; some she'd fled and some she'd freed herself from. But remaining trapped as a queen who loved a king who would never return her love—that was something she knew she couldn't endure. Not for the world.

Maybe Razhar was right. Let him live as never before and let the curse run its course.

The sound of laughter broke through her thoughts. Lystra looked up.

Razhar stood near the mast, his verdant turban on his head and an arm on the rigging. The sunlight gleamed on his bronze skin and laughter danced in his eyes as he cracked a joke with one of the sailors.

Why was he here? Lystra scowled, remembering Myra's suggestion to seek the palace trickster out. Stepping away from the rail, she marched across the deck, silks fluttering behind her.

Razhar caught her eye, and his smile faded. As she approached, he offered a swift bow. "My queen, you picked a fine day for sailing."

Lystra folded her arms. "I didn't know you were coming."

He stepped closer, turning toward the waters and resting his toned arms on the rail. The glitter of light on the water illuminated the shadows swirling in his amber eyes. "Ah, a chance to visit home. That, and El asked me to come. To look after you."

"Of course he did."

Razhar bowed his head, his gaze dropping to his hands. Lystra hadn't noticed at first, but he'd wrapped his palms in strips of bandages, leaving his fingers free.

"What happened to you?"

He shrugged, tucking his hands beneath his arms. "Bit of a skin condition." Then he looked at her, cocking one eyebrow. "What happened to you?" His low voice murmured with the water. "No offense to you, lovely queen, but you do look as if you've been crying."

Lystra sniffed, wondering if she knew how to lie as fluently as he did. She busied herself watching as the docks, waterfronts, and shipping ports passed by in a whirl of the brightly colored sails of merchant ships.

"Is . . . is it El?"

Stars, just the mention of his name made her feel as if she would unravel all over again. Lystra huffed, but didn't look at Razhar. "How long have you known Myra?"

"Oh, ages. She's been a tremendous help and a fierce protector of our little tribe." But even as he spoke, a shadow hung in his eyes, as if he'd guessed the situation.

Lystra felt her cheeks flush again. Did the entire cursed tribe know about Elerek and Myra? "I suppose that fierce protection extends to Elerek?"

Now Razhar's gaze became occupied with the riverfront. Past the ports, the buildings became stone, rising in the height and the lavishness of grand, waterfront estates. "Yes," he said softly.

Lystra looked to the horizon, a scowl tightening her face. She'd broken once and didn't intend to do it again. "I'd rather not discuss it."

Grandmother's voice blasted in her head, waxing eloquently of queens made of mountains, lofty, grand, and—and untouchable.

"Mm." Razhar turned around, staring up at the vessel's sails. "Ah, well, good. I want to talk about the curse."

"What about it?"

"I want to help you break it."

Lystra jerked her head back to look at him. No deceit or the glimmer of a joke shone in his eyes. Only stark seriousness. "What do you know?"

Razhar looked away, the shadow of his turban darkening his gaze. A prickling itched at her scalp, the unspoken hanging in the air like a noxious scent.

"I know where to start." Razhar lowered his voice to a whisper. "The Kushite archives."

A library. A grand one, if what Lystra had been told remained true. "Ah, then you're right where you want to be."

Then, Razhar grinned. "As always, yes?"

Lystra frowned, the cloud of suspicion surrounding Razhar growing thicker. A Kushite orphan living in the palace, an uncursed man among the tribe doomed to drown, and only he could hold back the curse—all the while standing at the king's side as his friend.

But she didn't call out the convenience of it, not yet. "Hmm. Why the library?"

Shrugging, the deep skin of his shoulders gleamed. "Kushan documents everything. It's quite exhausting. Research is something sacred to them. You won't find any ripped pages or altered texts there. Another war would've erupted if Lorkin wanted to purge it."

Lystra regarded him with a lift of her eyebrows. "For all your talk of curse breaking being impossible, you seem to think we'll find the information we need waiting for us."

Razhar didn't reply.

And if it was? She hardly wanted to think of it—if breaking the curse was possible. If Elerek were free.

"Why hasn't Elerek looked there before?"

"Would you rather have the official answer to that or the truth?" A sly smile curled his lips. "We both know stubborn Kushan and its overbearing mother Instanolde have had a strained relationship for its last three kings. But here's the secret." He leaned close, his breath hot on her ear. "El hates boats."

Of course. Water. Lystra gave a somber sigh. She wondered when a king had last visited Kushan without the intent to shed blood. How would they respond when a queen set foot in the canyons?

Briefly closing her eyes, the weight of her mission settled upon her shoulders. If the Jarkins invaded, they might never have the chance to break the curse. She forced herself to breathe, to focus. In this moment, she could still choose to hope. When she opened her eyes, the land before her had turned wild. A land of rolling hills and swaying grasses, life clinging to the Gungole's waters. A place without the barren stain of death. The sight steadied her, filling her soul with courage.

Beside her, Razhar shifted his weight, his eyes on the river's depths. "You inquired after my change of heart. I'll tell you because you ought to know. El's getting worse."

A shiver crept up Lystra's spine. She remembered his soaked clothes and the droplets on his fingers. "Worse how?"

"The Jarkin assassin, the one that threatened you? El drowned him last night. Cursed him—and drowned him."

Lystra stared. Did Razhar say *drowned*?

"I've known El since we were children. His curse is steady. Deadly, but steady. And what he did . . ." Razhar shook his head.

Lystra put a hand to her stomach. Nausea churned her insides, matching the rolling waves beneath the ship's hull. As her head spun, she braced herself against the prow. Death cast a shadow that she couldn't outrun, even across the desert sands. And the fear, the fear required to grasp the horror of each new turn of this unending cycle left her breathless.

"Something like murder—it taints and infects." Elerek's words spoken in the darkness. Had he been tainted? Pushed beyond his control? The king of Instanolde had killed a man, chose not to tell her—and went to Myra instead.

Pinching her eyes shut, she thought of salt, mined from the canyons, pulled by donkeys in great sleds across the sand. The crystals were cracked from the rock and sifted until only the fine, white crumbles remained. The sellers would sit in the market beneath the canopies of their booth, sifting and sifting, its rhythm a song all its own. Sorrow sang a similar song, sifting her over and over again, taking bits of her away each and every time.

Lystra's eyes filled with unwanted tears. Elerek was destined to die. His betrayal only confirmed that nothing had changed. He'd crowned her queen for a world beyond his own lifetime. Starlight for their kingdom when hope was lost.

Her hands clenched, her fractured heart striving to beat. To give up on him, to regard him as claimed for death already, raged against everything inside her. Perhaps she was meant to become the dawn, but that hadn't meant that the sun had set.

"I'm so weary of death."

Razhar smiled, but no merriment glimmered in his bronze face. "Let's not become weary of life."

Upriver, the land changed.

After miles and miles of yellowed grass and rocky shore, soft sandstone gave way to dark slate and vibrant redstone, rising elegantly in pointed buttes and dazzling cliffs. As the ship entered a narrow gorge, the Gungole rolled and boiled. The oarsmen strained, fighting the current. Lystra kept her eyes on the blue ribbon of sky above them. After a lifetime lived beneath open skies, this passage between rock felt suffocating.

"Are we almost there?"

"Almost." Razhar clung to the rigging. "I believe the main checkpoint is approaching."

Lystra held her breath, the ship pitching over a swell. "You don't visit often, do you?"

He shook his head. "No. We—my baba and I—had little. He served as a condor archer in the Kushite ranks." A shadow eclipsed his brow. "He was called to fight Lorkin's warmongering."

"Oh." She'd never heard Razhar speak of his past before. It struck her with fascination, thinking that Instanolde's blood-thirsty king and an archer of the opposing force might have sons who had somehow become akin to brothers. "What happened to him?"

Razhar set his jaw, his face tight and rigid. "Chief Wuhaz executed him. Insubordination. My baba was something of a radical when it came to Kushan opposing Lorkin." He drew a sharp inhale. "When you see the chief, don't mention my family name."

Lystra dipped her chin. "You have my word." Stars, they all had bloody histories, didn't they? Secrets and regrettable sorrows? And here, she'd sailed across the desert in the hopes of righting wrongs, of accomplishing something better. "Thank you for coming with me."

"Nonsense." Razhar offered her another small smile. "King's orders."

The gorge lowered itself again, transitioning to open plains speckled with boulders and rough-cut stone. Lystra caught her breath.

A lake stretched before them. A wide mirror of water. At its far end, the three canals emerged from a sharp rise of canyons dominating the horizon.

They docked along the lakeside, at a trade settlement called Varkei. Lystra kept to the upper deck, her face veiled, watching the waterfront. Unlike Instanolde with its golden domes and estates of stone and lobed arches, Varkei's common houses, merchant shops, and lounges were constructed of wood from imported timber. They were built high to accommodate the ebb and flow of the river, thick logs holding them above the water.

Her soldiers took great clay jars, their water supply, to have them filled. Such was travel in the desert.

Razhar slipped onshore with them. His bronzed skin blended in well among the array of colors—from dark Kushites, amber Instans, and fair easterners—but his palace clothing was terribly bright amid the dull-toned travelers. When he returned, he clutched a small bag.

"You *must* try these." He handed her a round, flat pastry.

Lystra swept her veil to the side. The pastry crumbled in her mouth, but its center was soft and chewy.

"Date and naom berry." Razhar sighed contentedly. "If there's any blight in your fair kingdom, it's that nobody in Instanolde can make these right."

At the edge of the Varkei waterfront, they docked at a squat building that appeared as if it had been shaped by the river itself. Dark slits and rounded windows looked like eyes, through which Lystra suspected that archers were stationed. Her soldiers made contact and a messenger condor immediately departed with a flap of its great, black wings. Ready to announce the queen's arrival to Kushan.

Beyond Varkei, the waters were deep and the current swift. Before them, great red cliffs striped with greenery rose like the sail of some great ship. They took the easternmost passage, again entering narrow channels of rock.

"Three passages," Lystra mused. "The Jarkins could choose any of them."

Razhar nodded. "Trade runs down all three. It isn't the season, so we won't catch wind of their arrival by merchant."

The Jarkins really did seek to outsmart them. The weight of hopelessness dragged at Lystra's heart like an anchor dredging the depths of the canal.

Finally, the canyon widened, giving way to sandy shores and deep inlets of land beyond the water's reach. Lush greenery filled the space, backed by red walls, half cast in afternoon shadow. Lystra leaned over the railing, peering at the clusters of low mound-shaped buildings flanked by corrals and orderly rows of gardens. Herds of alpaca grazed alongside long-haired tui sheep. She had to smile at the simplicity, the quaint beauty of this humble, colorful life.

Up above, a shadow eclipsed the sun. Lystra lifted her eyes as a screech filled the air. The condors wheeled in massive circles. They flew like the predatory Sancen vultures, but Lystra knew they served also as protectors. And in the cliffsides themselves, ledges supported dwellings connected by stairways, ladders, and ramps.

Their ship entered a small harbor inside a horseshoe-shaped inlet.

Razhar watched the line of docks with a mild scowl. "We're here."

Lystra glanced at him, noticing that the light had fled his eyes. She hadn't seen this side of him. A man haunted by a past he'd learned to live without. She wondered if Elerek would've sent him here if he'd known it would cause his friend such pain.

"Would you rather wait on the ship?"

Razhar shook his head. "I'll not fear anything here."

A choice rang in his words. Behind her veil, Lystra's lips curved in a slight smile.

On the dock, a company of Kushite warriors waited, armed with long spears and decked in elegant capes of glistening condor feathers. They bowed low before her.

"Lead me to your chief," Lystra commanded.

As they approached the village, people began to gather along the side of the road, watching. Their brows shone with sweat and many carried water vessels or led livestock. Their robes were simple, earth toned, and spun for practical work.

Beautiful people. Part of her kingdom. Lystra removed her veil, granting smiles to the children who peered from around their parents' legs. A façade, for surely the people knew that the queen of Instanolde wouldn't arrive so suddenly if there weren't a storm hazing the horizon.

In the center of the village, a low, arena-like circle had been dug into the red earth. Great stone condors stood on either side of its entrance, like sentries. Lystra's sandals made no sound on the clay steps, passing row after row of stone benches. A few soldiers and men in long robes sat near the front.

The chief waited at the base of the stairs, flanked by four guards in yellow turbans. He watched Lystra with sharp, hawkish eyes, as proud as the sky-born mounts of his warriors.

Fierce as the dawn. Mighty as the constellations. Lystra pushed aside any whispers of Grandmother's voice. This time, the voice of courage in her head belonged to her.

Wuhaz bowed his head, his silver hair draping in braids over his shoulder. "Your Highness."

"Chieftain." She dipped her chin. "It pleases me to behold the beauty of your fair land."

Age lined harsh creases across the chief's bronze face. "We've not had such a visitor in many years. Not since the reign of your grandparents in the name of House Arghan."

Lystra's scalp prickled. Not one of three Karim kings had breathed the deep air of the canyons. Wuhaz had seen it all, from the eruption of the tribal skirmishes in the days of her grandmother to the bloody conquests of Lorkin. She almost couldn't blame him for distrusting the throne of Instanolde.

"I have come in friendship and good faith." Lystra took another step closer. "And to give caution. In the hours of the night, we apprehended two Jarkin assassins in the palace. We believe that more are coming."

The chief's expression remained stern, but something in his eyes began to burn. "Of course more are coming. Without Darcress, little hinders them."

Lystra breathed in deep. "We believe they are coming by the river. Gaudab Batu-Khasar and at least half his force. They will strike Kushan first."

"And Instanolde is content to watch? You will use our forces to soften their blow. It matters not how many Kushites bleed into the canals, only that there will be fewer Jarkins to break upon your gates."

Lystra's heart seized. "Instanolde does not intend to be a spectator. It is in both our interests to subdue the Jarkins, and to build a bond between our peoples."

Scoffing, the chief shook his head. "You cannot protect us

from the Jarkins. Even if you hold back the tide of their wrath, they still possess the Darcress Kasbah and would be fools to leave it unarmed. Besides." He adjusted his grip upon his staff, his wrinkled hands clenching. "We've withheld allegiance to your king and owe him none of our blood."

"If we could look outside our differences to the defense and benefit of our people, the kasbah might be retaken with the aid of your warriors," Lystra insisted, her insides churning. "The Jarkins will give no regard to your allegiances when they sweep through your canals."

A quiver swept through the ranks, tension crackling like kindling.

The chief heaved a deep sigh. "This rhetoric rings with a familiarity, oh queen. You speak with borrowed words from House Karim who regard Kushite life worth so little."

Lystra bowed her head, wishing that she still wore her veil and could hide the emotions breaking her royal front. How could Wuhaz have lived so long and yet have seen so little? But he had never met Elerek. He couldn't know that the king's best friend had Kushite blood and that he esteemed even the lives of those cursed to die as worth saving.

Lystra also realized that there was nothing she could say that would change the chief's mind.

"We will evacuate and hide in the canyons," Wuhaz continued. "Let them pass on to you." He tilted his head to one side, scrutinizing Lystra with a gaze that reminded her far too much of Dalmah. "As you've come to warn us of impending doom, I would hope that you bring a solution. Instanolde hasn't taken an interest in preserving Kushite lives since other stars danced in the heavens. Will your captains and your cardants stand watch over our canals?"

Lystra felt her heart sink, burdened by the weight of a world that she couldn't hold together. Kushan had lived in a world built by the blood of others. Yesterday's death tainted the hope of tomorrow. Some injustices couldn't be forgotten. Some pains remained unforgiven.

Grandmother had taught her power, strength, and the might of the throne. She had learned to be fierce and bold as the dawn. None of that would serve her here. Dalmah's lessons had granted her nothing of healing the broken and creating the whole from the shattered.

I wish Elerek were here.

Elerek who only had a stolen birthright, who couldn't intimidate, coerce, or flaunt his power. The prince who had spent his time among the lowly, the cursed, rather than being groomed to follow in his father's war-torn footsteps. She wished that they could again appear side by side, as they had before the racing committee, and face this challenge together.

I can't do this alone. Lystra drew the softest of breaths, the pain and the sorrow heaving in her soul. But she must.

"Let me prove it to you." She drew herself to her full height, meeting the gaze of the chief who had held his tribe in place since before she'd drawn her first breath. "I'll have soldiers here by dawn, but we cannot fight alone."

Wuhaz bowed, touching his forehead with a curled fist, a sign of an oath taken. "If indeed your warriors come to our defense, so be it." His eyes turned to stone, the color of deep slate. "But if your word proves contrary, my archers will defend our own."

The air sizzled with the heat of this threat. Lystra pushed her panic deep in her soul and gave a firm nod. "I'll see it done. Let there be no more death."

"No ruler can promise such a thing, not to anyone."

Chapter 46

Lystra

A scribe led them beneath a stone arch and into a dark passageway. Lystra caught her breath, the smell of dust and paper and time filling her nostrils. Here, within the caves of the cliffs, the air hung still and cool, isolated from the wind and summer heat.

Blinking, she followed the glow of a strange stone held in the scribe's outstretched hand. It produced a pale sort of light, rather like starlight. The scribe claimed it came from an ore mined from the canyons and refined until it glowed in darkness.

The hall sloped downward, deeper into the mountain. Sand scraped beneath their shoes. Lystra peered over her shoulder, the light from the entrance small and distant. Dread twisted in her stomach with each step they took farther from the light of the sun, as if they were being buried alive.

Razhar flashed her a comforting smile in the dimness. "Courage, now."

Some of her anxiety dissipated as they entered a large cavern. Great oil lamps hung from the ceilings, casting a warm glow upon mountains of scrolls. Rolled up like pastries, they covered the shelves built into the walls. More words than one could read in a thousand lifetimes.

She breathed in deep, the dust stinging her lungs. Elerek would love it here.

"What is it that you're looking for?" the scribe inquired.

Lystra squared her shoulders. "Curses and their binders."

The scribe's lips turned down, but he nodded and led them through another dark corridor and into a chamber with ceilings that stretched farther than light could reach. The room had the jagged look of a cave, its shelves fit crudely into the natural edges of the stone. Texts lay in baskets, in piles, and in boxes. Lystra's heart sank at the thought of poring through it all, hoping for a miracle, while they waited for the Jarkins to invade and destroy all that they held dear.

Tears sparked in her eyes. Her devotion was owed to the living as her kingdom awaited its destruction, not in the hopelessness of a king doomed to die. A king who had betrayed her and certainly would never love her.

She blinked, scattering away the moisture in her eyes. If she didn't want to carry on alone, she had only one choice. Break the curse.

"Stars above." Razhar put his hands on his hips. "This is impressive. I crave pardon, but I must also make an inquiry of the archive's secrets. I understand the personal documentation of Kushite families is kept nearby?"

The scribe nodded. "Yes, do you require assistance?"

Razhar pulled a small key from his pocket. "No, please assist our queen."

Lystra scowled, wanting no more of his tricks. "I thought you were helping me?"

The mirth swept from Razhar's face. Bowing his head, he fidgeted with the key between his fingers. "I'll be along, Your

Highness." Then he turned and vanished into the darkness, taking one of those strange stones from a basket near the hall.

Lystra huffed and stalked farther into the room, glancing hopelessly about the piles of texts. She hardly knew where to begin. "Don't mind him. He's ridiculous."

"Hmm." The scribe raised an eyebrow. "He has Kushite blood."

Lystra folded her arms, eyeing the scribe. She could play Razhar's tricks too. "Are you familiar with the name Emblino?"

A troubled look passed across the scribe's face.

"Tell me their story."

"Little to tell, my queen. Fahwal Emblino was an archer during the tribal wars, executed for treasonous acts."

"What sort of acts?"

The scribe's eyes scanned the shelves. "Perhaps I should show you the records myself."

"Here." The scribe laid a thick tome on a rickety wooden table, sending up a cloud of dust. He flipped to a passage and pointed.

Lystra leaned over the table, the dust causing her eyes to water.

Fahwal Emblino, second regiment beneath Commander Guta, convicted of crimes against Kushite ordinance, nature below and the Starkindler above, and sentenced to death. Artifacts and evidence relating to previously condemned ritual site of curse binding and casting found in the home of Emblino. Artifacts including human blood and bone.

Sky readings: Weaver constellation. North maiden constellation. Wrathgiver constellation.

The wrathgiver.

Lystra's hand moved to the small woven satchel hanging from her shoulder, where the dagger lay tucked away. Somehow, the walls of the archives felt closer, as if the mountains themselves intended to crush her.

"What does it mean, sky readings?" She looked at the scribe.

The man heaved a sigh. "Many curses are tied to the stars. The requirement of human blood simmered beneath starlight is a perversion of two most holy things, the light of the Starkindler and the lifeblood through which we breathe out his intentions. Our research indicates that often the breaking of the curse must be conducted beneath the same constellation."

The pieces fell together like amber grains of sand kicked up by a sandstorm. Lystra could hardly breathe, as if her lungs had filled with the drowning weight of Elerek's curse.

"What curse did Fahwal bind?"

The scribe shrugged. "We never discovered."

But I did. Lystra shut her eyes tight.

A twisted, strange path lay behind her, a trail through dunes, deserts, and dust. She thought of that night, that horrible night, when Cormek's body burned. When her skin ran with mourning paint. When a prince emerged from the shadows and a girl drowned in the courtyard. A highway paved with death and destruction, shifting like the ever-changing desert sands.

And she had been led *here* where the answer lay to a

mystery that kings hadn't the knowledge to solve. Lystra crumpled to her knees, holding her head in her hands.

"I'm back!" Razhar's voice rang through the cavern.

Lystra didn't understand. She didn't see the whole of it. But the curse had everything to do with Razhar.

When his eyes fell on her, his face grew dark. His eyes turned to obsidian, closed off passages deep enough to hide a myriad of secrets.

"Leave us." Lystra glared at the scribe, who promptly obeyed.

Rising on shaky legs, she steadied herself against the table. "You."

Razhar stuttered, his hand rubbing the back of his neck. "Lystra . . ."

"It was your father, wasn't it? He cursed Elerek."

Razhar drew closer, leaning over the table to glimpse the open text. Beneath his arm, he carried a rolled scroll. His face contorted, bending like an acrobat from the optimistic adventurer into a man who had been crushed by agony. He looked like Elerek.

"He *cast* the curse, yes."

Lystra's hands tightened into fists that wanted to pummel him. She wanted to scream, to hear her protests echo through this cavernous labyrinth. "Why?" Tears streamed down her face. "Why didn't you tell us? Why didn't you tell him?"

Razhar shook his head. "I hadn't anything to do with it. I was a *child*. I was born here, in these canyons, to a mother who abandoned me and a baba who was forced to fight to satisfy a bloody king's battles. Do you know what it is to be a child left alone in the dark while your baba goes away to fight? Not knowing if he would come back? When Kushite ordinances executed my baba, he made sure an Instan soldier smuggled me away, hoping that

I'd see a better life. And didn't I? I grew up in Instanolde, in the *palace*. I jumped over the wall to go dance in the market. I stole sweets from the kitchens. I had a prince for a best friend." His eyes flickered with the rage of a wildfire. "I am *not* the enemy."

"But Elerek—"

"—Didn't need to know." He glared at her. "It would have destroyed everything. I've lost too, Your Highness, but I refuse to lose my best friend over events neither of us had control over."

Lystra couldn't speak. Her eyes returned to the list of executed criminals, their names blurring amidst her tears. Fahwal met his justice swiftly, by the will of Kushite ordinances. All the while, Elerek had languished, watching those whom he loved die and awaiting his turn.

Her hand moved to her bag. She withdrew the dagger, sliding it from its sheath, and tilted its blade toward the lamps. The etched stars burned. "Tell me what this is."

Razhar took a step back, a gasp hissing through his teeth. "Where did you—?" His chest heaved. He reached out, sliding his fingers over the etched constellation, a faraway look in his eyes. "My baba would've held this to . . . complete the ritual. It's a curse binder's dagger."

A curse binder's dagger. Stolen from Dalmah, who was *desperate* to get it back.

The dagger clattered to the stonework, the din amplified tenfold in the underground chamber. Lystra stared at it, the ringing screaming in her ears.

"Your Highness . . ." Razhar tentatively took her arm and guided her toward a writing desk with a stool. "I'm sorry."

Lystra pushed him away, bracing herself against the desk. A strangled sort of sound escaped her throat. Her mind felt raw, overrun by scorpions. "You . . ."

"My baba cast the curse, but your grandmother, Dalmah of House Arghan, bound it."

Her grandmother.

Bound the curse.

Razhar's words felt like the deadly arrows of mounted archers, piercing her to her core. Even now, miles and miles down the Gungole, Dalmah waited in the palace prisons. Had she actually apprehended the culprit? The binder responsible for cursing the king of Instanolde?

Lystra doubled over and wept.

Razhar procured a handkerchief.

The embers that perpetually burned in Dalmah's eyes had a purpose, driven by a vile hatred for House Karim. It must have torn her apart to see Lystra in love with Cormek, but *Elerek*, the one that she cursed . . . she wanted him dead.

"Lorkin forced her from the throne after my grandfather died." Lystra's lungs ached for air, strangled by sobs. "She did this . . . all of this . . ."

Razhar nodded grimly. "That's how she evaded Lorkin's purge. The former queen, a highly ranked noble from a revered house. She contacted my baba for his obscurity, just another soldier abused by Lorkin's wars and burning with the desire of revenge. I remember the day she came to our home, a hovel no more than a cave in the side of the Kushite cliffs. She knew he'd do it, manipulated him into the desperate act."

"I imprisoned her this morning." Lystra smeared the tears from her cheeks with trembling fingers. "Sh-she will tell us how to break it. She must."

She'd force her. Torture her. Give her a taste of the poison she'd perpetuated. At another time, Lystra might have recoiled at the vile thoughts raging through her, but not now. She'd heard all her grandmother's prattles of wisdom, honor, grace, dignity, and yet the dagger in Lystra's possession stood as a testimony that it had taken so little to sweep her into Dalmah's heinous schemes. Kill a king and take back her kingdom.

Razhar moved closer, standing so close that their shoulders brushed. He took the scroll from beneath his arm and spread it over across the tabletop.

A whisper escaped his breath, words so impossible that Lystra might have imagined them. "I already know how to break it."

Lystra turned toward him. Slowly. For one, terrible moment, the world stood still, frozen.

Razhar braced his hands against the table, his head bowed. "I saw them sign this. I didn't understand at the time, but I saw it." The scroll had frayed edges and had been torn and slashed, but its words were still legible. Written in red ink. Ink like blood.

A curse for a legacy, for kings. A curse to inflict the pain our lives have seen. A curse to take what was stolen. A curse to drown as Kushite screams did drown. Wrought beneath a wrathful star, only in final death, by blade and starlight, will this curse meet its bitter end.

Let its cost be death. Let no touch bring comfort. Let none escape the end which all men meet.

Sworn in blood. House of Arghan and House of Emblino.

The words swam before Lystra's gaze. "Wh-what does this mean?"

Razhar's hand, still wrapped in strips of cloth, brushed over the words, words penned by a father executed for treason. Tremors quaked through his voice. "'Only in final death, by blade and starlight, will this curse meet its bitter end.'" He looked at Lystra with tears in his eyes, as another descended of blood and hatred. "El must die, Lystra. Beneath the wrathgiver constellation with that dagger in his chest. Only then, will the curse be broken."

El must die.

Beneath the wrathgiver.

That dagger in his chest.

"That's not breaking the curse!" Lystra's shoulders shook. "He'll die anyways."

Razhar took the scroll and hastily rolled it up, sealing the hideous, blood-red words back in the shadows. "What about the others? Driss, Norbah, Bushra, Myra, they would all be set free. Are they not as innocent as you and me?"

Innocent. Thirty men and women who had taken no part in Lorkin's warmongering, in Dalmah's manipulations, or Fahwal's vengeance. Beautiful people who belonged to her kingdom and were loved by its king—the king who wanted her to love them too.

His tribe of chosen family didn't deserve to die, Lystra knew that for certain. She also knew that she couldn't trade their lives for Elerek's. The king would readily give his life if he knew he would set them free.

Lystra spun around, pacing the length of the room. Desperate energy sizzled in her blood. "We've only one who deserves punishment, and that's my grandmother."

Razhar shrugged. "Punishing her won't undo the damage. Violence isn't the answer to violence."

Lystra's eyes skimmed the cavern floor, finding the dagger. If she had done as Dalmah asked, she would've ended the curse for good. This cycle of blood and drowning would be forever broken. Wasn't that what they wanted?

And now, it only cost one life.

Elerek's life.

"It might take something equally heinous to undo the curse. And, granted we discover what that is, would you be willing to do it?" Razhar's words, spoken only last night.

No, she wasn't willing.

Lystra covered her face with her hands, fighting back tears. "What . . . what am I to do?" The tempest within her heart rose to her throat, strangling her voice.

Razhar leaned against the table, the scroll held tight in his wrapped hands. "I asked that same question, Your Highness. Right here, within this ghastly hole. I knew what my baba had done, and when I met El, the pieces fell together. I came back here looking for clues, for this scroll. I found the truth, the very truth I didn't want, and I chose to leave it here, buried." The fire danced in his eyes with careful steps. "I cannot answer for you, queen of Instanolde."

Heavy, suffocating words. Lystra turned away, letting her tears fall in the darkness. She wondered if it had been easy for Razhar. His chosen silence bought him exactly what he wanted. A world in balance, pushing back the curse's death for the sake of a pleasant life. Likewise, Myra had also chosen what she wanted, fewer days in exchange for longer nights.

What Lystra wanted was impossible.

She lifted her finger, brushing the gold circlet at her brow. Thin and simple, yet its weight threatened to crush and bury her. The years she had spent craving its power now seemed futile, tainted by Dalmah's poison. But she'd never wanted it only because of Grandmother. No, she loved Instanolde. She loved the Sancen with all its terrible beauty. She loved her people, and their fiercely beating hearts.

And she loved its king, despite his lies and broken vows.

Yet her vows lay to Instanolde. She wore this crown in service to them, for their security, their prosperity, and the hope of seeing the next sunrise. If Instanolde needed a curse broken, then she would have to see it through. And Elerek would have to die.

The pounding of heavy boots echoed through the archive caverns. More light added to the darkness. The scribe appeared, his face pale with anxiety, in the company of several soldiers.

"Your Highness." The captain dropped to his knee, the condor feathers draping from his shoulders. "The Jarkins have been sighted in the eastern canal in longboats. One outpost was attacked, and a small village was burned." His voice turned bitter. "Pillaged for supplies. It happened quickly, too quickly for us to act."

Lystra closed her eyes. More death.

She had failed. Her mission to Kushan hadn't protected the people of the canyons or won their allegiance. Instead, defenseless, innocent people had been burned and slaughtered. No number of soldiers or warriors, Instan or Kushite, could bring them back.

"I must go." Lystra swept past them, marching up the passageway, hoping to see the light of the sun.

"The Jarkins will reach Instanolde before nightfall."

Lystra shook her head, wondering why the Kushite soldier cared to give voice to this fact. Wuhaz and his tribe would not reach out their hand to their aid, content to let Instanolde suffer. And now, she hardly blamed them.

"We won't get there on time," Razhar huffed, falling in stride beside her.

No, but if she were to fail, wholly and completely, she would do so in Instanolde. Her home. Her kingdom. Side by side with her king.

Breaking the curse seemed so inconsequential now, when Lystra wasn't so sure they would survive sundown.

Chapter 47

Elerek

The waters of the Gungole swirled beneath the waterfront, their vibrations sending a tremor through Elerek's chair. He cast his gaze downward, watching the ripple of movement beneath the wood, hoping they wouldn't give and toss him prematurely into waters he couldn't survive.

And he only had to survive a little bit longer.

Norbah stood beside him, arrayed in full battle gear, facing a contingent of captains assembled along the boarded-up waterfront. Gone were the merchants' tents where prices were recorded, their haggling replaced with the general's clear voice, giving orders.

Elerek forced his gaze up, his head high. These were his soldiers, men sworn to the throne who were ready to die in defense of Instanolde.

A lie, a manipulation. Their king was nothing more than a weak, cursed coward. Elerek cringed at the condemnation ringing in his head like the evacuation bells. Would they have followed him if they knew that he'd murdered a man in cold blood last night? That he'd kissed a woman who wasn't his wife?

Norbah raised a fist. "For Instanolde!" He clasped it to his breast.

"For Instanolde!" the men responded, mirroring his actions.

Elerek's jaw tightened, holding his expression in place. He gave a single nod. The captains dispersed, delegated to their posts.

They weren't ready. The hastily evacuated docks were hardly an advantageous place of defense. The exposure to the water put them on display, easy pickings. Elerek kept thinking of the fortified keeps, reinforced battlements, the eastern wall of the city that his men had spent over a month preparing.

They might have had a chance. Now, there would be no prolonged siege, only a desperate fight as their blood spilled into the river's depths. Elerek no longer believed in starlight, that they might withstand this attack.

"Your Highness." Norbah turned toward him, his gloved hand on the hilt of his scimitar. "Where shall we position your archers?"

Elerek's gaze swept the waterfront. The rooftops were low, still, any height would give them a decent vantage point. But if Lystra's information concerning the Jarkins' archers were correct, it would also leave them exposed.

"The courtyards beyond, are they barricaded?"

"Best we can." Norbah's voice was grim.

Elerek shook his head. This was not how he imagined this invasion would go. "Split the regiment. Take our best and station them along the rooftops, windows, anywhere that they can take a shot at the water. The rest will take the courtyard."

"Which lieutenants shall I appoint?"

"Kimzi and Lukor." The two young men worked well

together, and Lystra's cousin had quickly become one of Elerek's best students.

Norbah nodded. "And where would you like to position yourself?"

Elerek craned his neck, eyeing the stretch of soldiers in orange turbans standing at attention, girded with spear and scimitar. "Where do you suggest? You'd know better than I."

"I am in favor of visibility. It does soldiers good to see their king."

"I've never fought in a battle." But he did know how to kill. Elerek swallowed the urge to scoff. The thought made him sick.

Norbah narrowed his eyes. Elerek wondered if he were also thinking of the lifeless Jarkin drowned in his chains. "El, are you all right?"

No. The sound of his fingers on his armrest fell in rhythm with the river. He ignored Norbah's question. "If I wait behind the gate, I could be mounted."

"We have a small force of mounted soldiers. I've kept them in reserve for pursuing fleeing enemy and guarding the city avenues." Norbah huffed. "Despite your efforts with the racing committee, there aren't enough cardants trained for battle."

There wasn't enough of anything. Elerek took a deep breath. "The cardant the queen brought to the palace, the one I rode before, I'll use her. She's not trained, but she's the only one I trust."

The general nodded. "I'll see it done."

The blast of rams' horns filled the air, ringing from the twin watchtowers at the edge of the waterfront. The sound filled Elerek's chest, shuddering against his ribs with a sickening din of dread and terror.

Norbah's eyes caught fire. "That's the alert."

Elerek's hands curled into fists, cold, cursed droplets squeezing between his fingers. "They're here."

The Jarkins.

A pair of guards escorted Elerek back through the maze of barricades and battlements to a guardhouse stationed on the other side of the wall. The passages felt tight, threatening to close in on him. One by one, reports echoed from the rooftop sentries, their echoes rattling against Elerek's skull.

"Five longboats approaching, two more sighted. No oars."

"Bulwarks lined with shields, don't waste arrows."

"They'll be on the docks in ten minutes."

"We're outnumbered."

The nightmare had come.

Elerek's mouth tasted of bile. His ears rang with a dull buzz. Outnumbered. Their defenses lacking. Was this how Cormek felt when he realized that he was under attack? When he called his men to fight? Told his guards to make sure Lystra escaped to safety?

Inside the guardhouse, a set of armor waited—for him. A leather hauberk, made to fit over his chest, lay across a chair. The image of the sun, the mountains, and the river blazed across it, gleaming with new oil. Beside it sat a helmet, its own orange turban neatly folded, stout boots, and a pair of metal gauntlets with leather bracers.

The sight twisted Elerek's gut, his thoughts turned once again to Cormek. He'd heard all the stories that he could stomach, of how his brother fought bravely, died nobly. An image he hadn't a hope of matching.

Elerek shut his eyes, the bracers' straps tight about his fore-arms. He'd promised Cormek, given his word. The crown, the kingdom, even his brother's betrothed, all left in his hands. But now, even Cormek's memory had been dishonored by his failures.

"Your Highness." Cole appeared in the doorway. "The cardant has arrived."

Elerek nodded. He placed the helmet atop his head and wrapped his turban. The gauntlets were left behind, his hands needed for his bow, and he followed Cole into the courtyard. The reptile waited, saddled and harnessed, its eyes blinking lazily despite the flurry of the soldiers assembling along the walls and barricades.

The sight struck his heart with the memory of the ride he'd shared with Lystra out into the desert. The gleam of passion in Lystra's eyes as she sat atop the ferocious cardant he'd given her, her beauty stark against the setting sun.

"Cole." Elerek glanced at the soldier, his friend. "Has there been any word? From Kushan? From the queen?"

He shook his head. "No, none. Razhar was with her, wasn't he?"

Elerek's mind spun. Had they made it to the canyonlands? Were they safe among Razhar's brethren? What might have happened if they met the Jarkins along the river?

If Lystra were dead . . .

No. His breath caught. She was alive. She had to be. If Lystra didn't return to Instanolde, then it didn't matter if the sun rose tomorrow. Their kingdom would fall into a night without stars.

Cole assisted him onto the cardant's back. Taking the reins in his hands, he centered his weight, his posture straight as an arrow. This time, they didn't tie down his legs. Panic sizzled in his blood as the cardant lumbered beneath him. He wished he'd had more time to train.

Time had run out. One summer to live had become one night to die.

The call for archers filled his ears, followed by the thundering of boots upon the courtyard walls. Captains gave orders for arrows, followed by a deathly silence. In Elerek's heart, a numbness set in, cold as stone and hard as steel. It was time.

He urged the cardant forward, out of the shadows and into the torchlight. He wanted to hear Norbah's emboldening voice, to be near his men, and see the fire in their eyes.

In the square, all lay still. The streets were cleared, the merchants' houses vacated. Soldiers waited, rigid and tense. They faced the wall, and the great lobed arch adorned with mosaics that flickered in the firelight. Elerek gritted his teeth, eyeing the barricade built of crates, barrels, steel poles, and two carts that stood in the gap.

The Jarkins would break through; it was only a matter of time. If the reports were correct, nearly a thousand Jarkin soldiers would pour into the city. Too many for them to withstand like this, without proper protection or the anticipation of a siege. Instanolde would be overrun.

But still, they would fight.

Elerek lifted his gaze to the walls and rooftops, where his archers waited with their bowstrings taut. Norbah stood among them, his eyes toward the river. He turned, his eyes meeting Elerek's.

Elerek took his bow, his polished, Kushite-made bow, and drew an arrow from his quiver. He looked to his men, the archers he knew by name, and, as one, they readied their own bows and aimed their arrows to the sky.

The air tingled. Elerek drew back on his string, willing his fingertips to remain dry. "Volley."

The twang of the bows, singing in unison, sent a snapping jolt through him. The sounds beyond the wall were muddled, hazed by chaos. He wondered how many of his men had struck true.

And then, the Jarkins returned fire. Black-fletched arrows sailed up and over the wall, finding their mark in Instan soldiers. When the first archer toppled from the wall, his body limp and broken in the square, Elerek felt the darkness, like the creeping cover of night, smother his soul. Grief and rage sifted and stirred, and it tasted like poison on his tongue.

"Hold the wall!" Norbah shouted, drawing his scimitar.

Elerek signaled his men. "Another volley."

Thus, it began. Time had no place here. There was only the song of bowstrings, the calls of the captains, and the pull of their shoulders as volley after volley pelted the invaders. As Elerek fired arrow after arrow alongside his men, he knew each shaft was another moment won, another moment where they still fought.

Thud. An arrow stuck fast in the wood of the merchants' booth on Elerek's left. The cardant stamped its claws, shuffling its footing.

Elerek lowered his bow, grabbing the saddle for stability. "Steady."

When he looked up, movement beyond the barricade caught his eye. A spark, and then a flame. The barricade went up like kindling, scattering embers across sand and stone.

"They've broken through!" he shouted, pulling the cardant closer along the wall. Ash burned in his nostrils.

The flames didn't stop them. Unhindered, the Jarkins poured into the square.

They were tall and broad, as if built of the mountains themselves. Their skin was fair, untouched by the sun, but hardened like leather. Heavily clothed, many wore the skins of animals and stout armor and black leathers. Knives, battle-axes, and spears gleamed in the last light of the dying day, not yet tainted with Instan blood.

But it didn't take long.

Elerek scanned the square, frantic as the two forces clashed like the waves of opposing tides. Steel and shouts rang through the air, choking sound itself. The heat of the burning barricade swept over Elerek's skin. The sight of bodies, of the brave soldiers who fought in his name, sickened him, their polished armor marred with grime.

The cardant thrashed, spinning around, searching for a route of escape from this awful place. Elerek hardly blamed her, but as he strained at the reins, he knew that if he didn't maintain control of the reptile, he'd certainly fall and be trampled.

"El!"

He looked over his shoulder, catching sight of Norbah upon the wall. The general leapt into the fray, fighting like an animal with his scimitar. He pulled off his glove, his cursed skin gleaming in the orange glow of the fire. A Jarkin warrior met him, sword raised. In the split second before the weapon slashed down, Norbah caught the man by the bare skin of his forearm.

The Jarkin screamed.

Using the man's pain as a distraction, Norbah quickly hewed him down. The fallen Jarkin bled blood and cursed water.

Elerek's throat tightened. His curse. The image of the drowning Jarkin in the cell commanded his mental image. A sight he wouldn't—couldn't—forget.

Drip. Drip. Drip. The battle's din faded, replaced by the small, singular sound of one drop after another from his cursed hands. Water in the desert, the extraordinary that made all the difference.

The dripping faded, becoming a roar in his ears.

Norbah approached him, his chest heaving. "We're losing ground. I've sent for reinforcements. Make for the market avenue, we'll cut them off there."

"I'm not leaving."

As he stepped closer, the general's face lost its fury. Beneath, his expression was worn. "Instanolde needs its king, El. Let us protect you."

Elerek turned his eyes to the fray, the Jarkins ploughing through the regiments. The air choked with screams. His men —those whom he knew by name—cut down, bleeding on the stone streets of their city. Norbah was right; they ought to pull back to the next defensible spot without more loss of life. What would happen when it was no longer soldiers caught in their place? Sons and daughters, the elderly, the simple craftsmen who had never held a weapon?

And *he* was a weapon. Everything he touched shriveled, twisted, writhed in bitter death. Even the best of his intentions, the vows he'd sworn to uphold, all of it crumbled away to dust. The cursed king of Instanolde who carried death wherever he went.

Instan soldiers already fell back, following Norbah's plan. Elerek watched as the next wave of Jarkins entered the square, a foothold gained. These, without the strain of battle upon them, carried themselves like victors. Conquerors.

None more so than the man who emerged from the shadow of the arch. He stood a head taller than all his warriors. Two battle-axes were strapped across his back and his shoulders were capped in the skulls of jackals. A thick beard hung down his chest, broken only by the jagged scar that dragged across his jaw.

Gaudab Batu-Khasar.

Elerek's hands tensed. Water stained his arms, sliding over his bracers. As he looked upon the man who had slain his brother, hot rage billowed in his soul. These men had invaded and crossed their borders, but they were not yet victors.

He urged the cardant forward, into the square, directly toward the Jarkin warlord.

Behind him, Norbah swore. "El . . . don't."

"Stand down, General." Elerek spoke softly. "The men need you."

The Jarkins stared at him, but none took up weapons. He was a curiosity, an oddity, an Instan with only a quiver half full of arrows.

"Batu-Khasar." His voice rang across the square, the name of his brother's killer foul on his lips.

Gaudab turned, his eyes gleaming obsidian. A cruel smirk twisted the scar across his jaw. "Ah, is this the so-called king I've heard about?" he growled in the thick accent of the mountains. "I thought you dirty river rats had run out of heirs."

Not yet. Elerek tied the cardant's reins to the saddle. He needed his hands.

"Form lines," Norbah growled to the remaining soldiers.

Glancing briefly at the men in formation behind the cardant, Elerek could feel their apprehension, their confusion. They thought their general was asking them to die for their king.

Gaudab laughed. "A more pathetic stand than we met at the kasbah. I see it now, the resemblance to your dead king. But he was a warrior. You are nothing."

Elerek glared. "You'll pay for my brother's blood."

The warlord drew a scimitar from his belt and cast it onto the stones before the cardant's claws. "Pick it up, boy." He swung one of his axes from his shoulder, its blade still glistening with blood. "Fight for your life. Then you can die just like him."

Elerek looked into the gaping faces of his soldiers. "Give me space, men."

Their movements were confused, reluctant, terrified. But then, at last, Norbah seemed to understand. "Fall back."

"Pick. It. Up," Gaudab growled.

Elerek gazed at the scimitar lying out of reach. The gold adorning its hilt bore a likeness to the craftsmanship of Instan artisans. It was probably taken from Darcress, perhaps from among the fallen. Could it have been Cormek's?

I wanted to be like you, Cormek. The warrior. The heir. The king who dreamt of peace and prosperity for their kingdom upon the sands. But sand shifted, cut from rock, moved by wind—and consumed by water.

Instanolde didn't need Cormek. Not anymore. No, now she needed a king of wrath, of vengeance, a destroyer.

Mounted upon the back of the cardant, Elerek sat eye level with the warlord. His fingers brushed the warm scales of the reptile's neck, willing her not to spook.

"The sword was my brother's weapon. I am not my brother."

He lifted his hands, his palms up. Water poured from his skin. First a stream, and then a torrent.

Chapter 48

Lystra

A s soon as the gangway lowered to the waterfront, Lystra gathered her skirts into her fist and ran.

They docked at the first available berth. Most were full of empty trade ships clustered together, like the innocent huddling to keep away from the conflict—from the massive Jarkin vessels whose masts they could see even now, above the city spires.

The port. Lystra heard the sounds of battle. Smoke rose to the stars, streaked orange with the last light of a long, horrible day.

"Your Highness, wait!"

Razhar's call went unheeded. She knew the streets and she ran with reckless abandon. Her silks streamed behind her and anyone who peeked out from their shelters would perhaps think her a lost princess fleeing some evil. But no, she was their queen—and she ran toward the danger.

She'd no hope to give, no plan to execute. She only knew that she had to be there, to stand for her kingdom and her cursed king.

Lystra skidded to a stop at an avenue corner. She could smell the blood. A shadow of foreboding filled the air, a surreal nightmare that then materialized in the shapes of men. Soldiers unlike their own stood with Instan blood on their weapons. Jarkins. *The* Jarkins. The ones who'd come to kill two kings.

She stood on tiptoe, attempting to peer over the crowd. No one was fighting. They all stood at attention, Instan soldiers among them, watching the center of the port square.

Razhar panted behind her, his hand closing on her arm. "Your Highness, we can't . . ." He lifted his eyes, awe and horror filling his voice. *"It's him."*

Lystra skirted the edge of the square, moving around the soldiers until she found an opening. There in the center stood a man.

Gaudab Batu-Khasar. No other warrior stood tall enough, broad enough, to fill in the fantastical images the stories had painted. Armored and weaponed, a man built to fight, to slaughter.

The last time she'd seen him, he'd emerged as a mirage upon the red sands of Darcress with one purpose: to kill the king of Instanolde. Now, he faced off with Elerek.

Lystra stared. Elerek sat tall upon a cardant—Sama, she realized. Clad in armor, his shoulders were broad beneath the hauberk. His eyes blazed with wrath, with fire, with a consuming vengeance. A king to execute the justice the invaders deserved.

She caught her breath. Razhar was right—about the curse.

Elerek's arms were raised and taut. He didn't cower before the warlord who had slain his brother.

And water.

Unnatural.

Cursed.

It flowed from Elerek's fingers, from transparent skin, with the force of a mountain spring. It hit Gaudab with a mighty spray, enough to make him stumble back.

Never had Lystra imagined such a thing. Water from the hands of the cursed. A strange, twisted, deadly thing in the hands of a man bent on protecting his kingdom.

Maybe . . . they needed his curse. She thought of the dagger, heavy in her satchel.

Sama reared, stunned by the wet display, but the king kept his seat. Sidestepping the spray, Gaudab loudly swore and brandished his axe. He roared and lunged forward. Elerek gripped the reins with one hand, desperate to right Sama, and with the other released another torrent. It wasn't enough. Gaudab swung his axe and found its mark in the cardant's side.

Sama! Lystra yelped. The last of her own cardants. A lone survivor, like her. Dark blood spilled over the stones. Recovering, Sama snapped her jaws, identifying her attacker, and pounced on the warrior.

The axe also severed the saddle strap. Lystra gasped as Elerek toppled in a tangle of leather and withered legs. His helmet clattered to the dirt, the turban unwound. Water pooled about him, soaking his clothes.

Footsteps. An echo. Lystra glanced over her shoulder. A shadow moved along the wall, but she didn't have time to investigate.

Gaudab roared as the cardant pinned him against the stone. Her claws slashed at the warrior, digging deep trenches into his armor. His axe hacked at air, searching for its quarry.

Fight, Sama! Lystra held her breath, hoping that the old girl would hold out.

Elerek, the king, wasn't finished. With a yell, he planted his palms on the ground. Water surged about his hands, whipped into a terrible frenzy, and surged along the stonework toward the fallen Jarkin. His chest heaved with effort, his face a terrible snarl. The water amassed around the Jarkin's head, bound without borders, and covered Gaudab's face.

The sight was terrible, but Lystra couldn't look away. Her heart turned cold. Elerek would kill him. Right here. Right now.

An eye for a kingly eye. Revenge, just and fair.

Gaudab thrashed, fighting for air. His axe fell from his hand. Sama backed away, hissing and nursing her wounds. Beneath the swirling water bearing down on his face, Gaudab's skin paled.

But the warlord wouldn't be left to die. His warriors surged forward, their eyes ablaze. They hauled Gaudab upright, above the water. Others surrounded Elerek, prompting the remaining archers to raise their bows.

"Hold!" Norbah yelled, knowing as Lystra knew what would happen to the Jarkins who grabbed the king's arms, touched his skin, and diverted the stream from his hands.

Their cries reached the stars above.

The curse had become a weapon. Lystra's insides twisted. She despised the curse and all its vile designs, the suffering it had caused Elerek and its victims. But now, she hated the Jarkins enough to desire their suffering. To see justice done and peace be restored to her people.

The Jarkins backed away from the king, watching him like a cornered animal, clutching transparent, cursed hands.

Shoulders hunched, Elerek growled. The water beneath him swirled, rushing in ripples to the Jarkins, pooling like deadly mirrors about their ankles. Tendrils encircled their legs. The men screamed in pain. Elerek's chest heaved and his bloodshot eyes bulged.

Lystra caught her breath, watching with awe and terror as Elerek *single-handedly* defended all of Instanolde. The man who showed kindness to the lowly, who had given compassion in her grief, who had striven to live while his body died, now fought for them—using the curse.

Gaudab hauled himself to his knees, gasping and gagging. Beads of cursed water dripped down his beard. He marched forward, into the circle, standing before Elerek.

Elerek balled his hands into fists, the water halting. The Jarkin soldiers stumbled backward, eager to flee. He looked up at the warlord with venom in his eyes.

"What are you? A *borneju?*" *The damned.* Gaudab spat into the water pooled at his feet. "Did you do the same to my spies?"

Elerek glowered. "The same will happen to you."

His voice sent shivers down Lystra's arms.

Gaudab reached down, grabbing him by the throat. His hand turned transparent where it contacted the king's flesh.

Even while choking, Elerek smiled.

Gaudab's face twisted first with pain, and then with rage. He let go. Elerek crumpled. The Jarkin's hand remained marked, transparent skin spreading up his muscled arm. Cursed.

A pale figure streaked past Lystra. Lithe and nimble, the figure of a young woman snaked through the warriors, into the center of the circle.

Myra.

She knelt in the cursed water, helping Elerek sit up. Transparency had spread across her shoulders like a pair of pale silk moth wings, the mark that proved she had loved beyond the fear of death.

Foolish girl. Lystra marched forward, closer to the conflict. Why was she here?

And yet she knew. The same reason why Lystra herself was here. Because of him—the man they both loved.

Elerek blinked, staring at Myra with burning eyes. The

same rage with which he attacked the invaders. But Myra only shook her head.

A restlessness stirred through the two armies. They looked to their leaders, their kings, holding their breath and waiting for command.

Incensed, Gaudab stalked closer. "What is this?" He lifted his cursed hand, water streaming down his fingers.

Myra moved behind Elerek. The king glared up at the Jarkin, his voice like venom. "You're cursed. And you will *die*."

A prickle ran down Lystra's arms. How many times had Elerek repeated those words to confused, terrified faces? Brought frightened souls into the fold of his cursed tribe? But here, to the Jarkin warlord, he spoke those words like a taunt, a sneer. A curse.

"You've nowhere to seek solace. No cure to be found." Elerek lifted his hands, slick with water. "Let's both die here. Finish this."

Lystra felt Razhar's grip on her arm. She looked at him. His face had turned purple, terror lining his amber eyes.

"Lystra, if he dies here . . ."

All the cursed would die. The curse wouldn't be broken, only satisfied with the lives of kings, Instans, and Jarkins. Her eyes turned toward Elerek once more, striving with all that he had. *Only one must die.*

But it was the curse that had the advantage over the invaders—and could lay Gaudab Batu-Khasar low.

"Myra." Elerek's eyes never left the warlord. "Help me stand."

"El, you can't—"

"Help. Me. Stand."

Myra wrapped her arms around his waist, heaving him up. Elerek's weakened legs tried to hold their weight but desperately failed. Norbah rushed to join them, sheathing his scimitar and sliding his arms beneath his king's shoulders. Supported by his companions, the humanity returned to Elerek's face. Lystra watched, her heart straining inside her chest, wishing that there were some way that she could help him.

Her hand moved to her satchel, where she kept the dagger. She had only death to offer him, death to save her people.

Gaudab met the challenge, holding his axe aloft. He stood in the water before the cursed king of Instanolde and waited.

Water surged from Elerek's hands in tight ropes. Gaudab sidestepped, but the water followed him, drenching the transparent hand holding the axe. Gaudab spun around, cruelty in his gaze. A dagger sailed from his hand, glinting in the starlight —and found its mark, thrust to the hilt in Myra's side.

The girl screamed. Her white linen dress grew red.

Lystra covered her mouth with her hand. Beside her, Razhar swore. But Elerek, his face painted white with a haunted horror, the look in his eyes was one Lystra had seen before.

In the mirror, when she returned from the desert, faced with the reality that Cormek was dead. That she had watched him die.

He didn't falter, not even for a moment. His despair turned to rage. His shoulders arched, arms outstretched, and he shot a stream of deadly water toward the Jarkin's head.

Gaudab fell to his knees, once again submerged in a deadly bubble. His axe clattered. The water surged from Elerek's hands, an intensified force of pure will.

This time, his men wouldn't let him stand alone. Three warriors attacked from the side, targeting Norbah. The general, forced to draw his scimitar, stepped away from the king. Myra buried her face in Elerek's shoulder. She held on—but she wavered.

Lystra took a step closer, and then another. Behind her, Razhar shouted her name, but she didn't heed him.

Myra's skin turned as pale as her dress. Her arms trembled. She twisted, scanning the scene, searching the crowd of warriors.

Somehow, in the torchlight, in the shadows, her gaze found Lystra's.

The whole of the world seemed to stop, frozen in that moment. Lystra caught her breath. She wondered if she would ever become accustomed to staring into the face of death.

Myra didn't blink, her eyes ablaze with starlight and secrets. No other knew the truth, the ache Lystra carried deep in her heart. An ache that they both shared.

No fear veiled Myra's face. Not for herself—and not for Elerek.

Lystra kept walking, her silks streaming behind her. No, Myra didn't fear for her king, because she knew that Lystra was here. The Jarkins stepped aside, as if parting a path for her.

She'd fled from death in the desert, but death had followed her home. There was nowhere to hide. Nothing beneath the stars could stay its hand. They could only choose to confront it with courage, and Lystra couldn't allow Elerek to contend with it alone.

Myra's eyes rolled back.

Breaking into a run, water splashed beneath Lystra's feet, and it felt like stepping on needles. As Myra toppled, her blood mingling with the cursed water upon the stonework, Lystra held her breath, steeled her soul, and stretched out her hand toward Elerek. Her king.

And touched him.

Elerek did not, would not, fall, held by the strength of Lystra's arms.

"*No!*" A mortified, incensed roar reverberated in the king's throat. He stared at her with eyes of molten metal, even while tears slipped down his face. Tears for Myra. Tears for her.

A cry escaped Lystra's lips in a breath. She felt it. The curse seeping into her fingers, her arms, and down her spine. It numbed her body like ice, stealing the warmth from her blood.

Did he always feel like this? Numb. Cold. Dead?

She looked up into his eyes, into his perfect and tragic face, mere inches from her own. Now she knew why he'd gathered his cursed tribe together, creating a shelter of community. She understood why he had loved Myra, yearning for the touch of her skin. If the deadness she now felt in her body he felt every waking moment, she could do nothing but pity him.

"Enough!"

The flow ceased from Elerek's hands. Across the square, Gaudab collapsed, gasping for breath as the water melted from his face.

Between them and the Jarkin warlord stood Razhar. His shirt hung open, his tattoo gleaming on his chest. A constellation, one that Lystra had learned to recognize well.

The wrathgiver.

Razhar's hands were outstretched—and covered in sand. Fine as the Sancen dunes and amber like his eyes, it poured from his hands and swallowed Elerek's water, breaking its current.

Lystra's head felt light, dizzy. What was he?

"Stop. Everyone stop," Razhar snarled, but tears ran down his face. He looked toward Gaudab, facing him head-on. "You can't kill him."

Lystra strained, a groan slipping from her lips. Elerek was heavier than she anticipated, his muscles solid beneath her touch. Unable to hold him any longer, they both sank to the ground, soaked in cursed water. Myra's lifeless body lay beside them.

"Who are you?" Gaudab stalked forward, water dripping from the blade of his axe.

Razhar pulled the strips of cloth from his hands. Beneath, his hands were *sand*. Perfectly sculpted knuckles and fingers, shedding amber grains as if they were drifting down the neck of an hourglass. "Nobody at all."

Lystra had never heard such a lie.

Her mind scrambled for answers, connecting the logical dots like stars in a constellation. Razhar knew the specifics of the curse's inception, cast by his baba and bound by Dalmah. He alone could touch the curse without harm, push back its symptoms. Sand to balance Elerek's water. And he knew how to break it—at the cost of the king's life.

Numb from the curse, Lystra began to tremble. The scene spun, wheeling like the stars overhead in their silent dance. Elerek's water. Myra's blood. Razhar's sand. How had simple, rudimentary things come to hold such significance?

Elerek panted for air, his chest heaving. "Razhar . . . you . . . you're cursed."

Their eyes met. "No, not cursed." Sorrow darkened his gaze. "Not like you." Then he turned, facing Gaudab with his chin high.

Lystra drew a hiss through her teeth. *No. No. No!*

"If you kill him now," Razhar said slowly, deliberately, "you'll die with him. There's only one way to break this curse— and I can help with that."

Chapter 49

Elerek

"How 'bout some of our cursed water?" The Jarkin spat in Elerek's face before fastening shackles about his wrists and letting him crumple to the harsh stone. Their coarse laughter echoed tenfold in the narrow cell.

Elerek waited until the invaders had locked the door and the sound of their boots had traveled down the hall before wiping his face with his still-soaked sleeve. The torch went with them, leaving him in the darkness of a night without stars.

Drip. Drip. Drip. Only the water falling from his fingers, clothing, and hair made any sound. He scooted to the wall, the chains dragging behind him. They'd taken his armor, hauberk, and boots, but it was his soul that felt bare, stripped, and hollowed out.

Myra was dead.

Lystra was cursed.

Razhar betrayed him.

Instanolde had fallen.

His losses circled his mind like desert vultures around the

corpse of his rotting world. He thought of the stunned faces of his soldiers, his archers, as they watched their king be bound, and he wished he hadn't failed them. The echo of Gaudab's voice over the conquered square, a place ill prepared to defend against an army.

"For now, he lives."

For now. As long as his people surrendered, compliant to Jarkin authority. Once Elerek had been bound, they'd grabbed Lystra next, her right palm wrapped in the mark of his curse.

"But I can kill others." The leering look in Gaudab's eyes as he seized Lystra's shoulder sent his blood to boiling with an insatiable rage.

They were taken to the palace as the spoils of war. Soldiers, captains, even Norbah, his fearless general, wore chains. As they dragged him away, they left the square covered in blood, water, and bodies. Myra lay still and alone, the knife in her side.

Myra . . . Elerek's chest seized. He hadn't the tears to weep. She had chosen the curse, chosen to love him, and now she was dead.

All the while, Elerek continued to live—he lived because Razhar said so.

Why had he intervened? Elerek hissed through his teeth. He could've taken them. Avenged Cormek. Drowned them all.

And *what* was he? The sand that fell from his fingers, a contradiction to his own cursed water—how long had he kept such a thing secret? The thought that Razhar, his dearest friend and beloved brother, had lied and kept secrets from him was incomprehensible.

Worse, he claimed to possess knowledge of how to break Elerek's curse. Such a lie wouldn't buy them time. Even the thought of such an impossibility could only lead to despair.

Besides, it wouldn't be long before the Jarkins grew weary of them. They had the kingdom, after all.

But they also had the curse. When the time came, they would drown just as quickly as those whom Elerek loved. Perhaps he might yet avenge Cormek and rid his kingdom of the invaders.

But Lystra would die with them.

It was her, the thought of his beautiful queen, that finally drew tears to his eyes. He could almost still feel her touch, her hand over his heart, her fingers brushing his chest. The curse spreading through her body, painting her face with agony, like the mourning paint she wore so long ago.

Why did she touch him? He hadn't an answer. *Starkindler, please, have mercy.*

Only lonely silence met his ears.

The clang of iron and the sounds of boots broke through the silence. Elerek lifted his head, his eyes smarting in the harsh torchlight. Jarkins with leathered skin and long beards unlocked his shackles just long enough to secure his hands behind his back.

He squinted against the light of a midday sun as they took him from the prisons. Dragged down the halls of his own palace, Elerek's shoulders strained. His legs ached and, more than once, he willed them to let him stand on his own. For one of the few times in his life, he felt incomplete, maybe even broken. He wondered if his chair had been left at the waterfront. This loss, coupled with all else, misted his eyes.

But he wouldn't cry over a chair. No, now he needed his rage.

Taken through the grand, gilded doors, the throne room in all its grandeur filled his vision—and it looked as if it belonged somewhere else. Jarkins, travel-worn, clad in animal skins, and heavily armed, stood between the polished pillars. No sign of an impeccable Instan soldier in sight. Not a scrap of orange silk.

At the edge of the dais, before his throne, Gaudab Batu-Khasar stood with his hands clenched, hands made of water.

Seeing the curse mark on the invader awoke something raw and vile inside Elerek's soul. A twisted satisfaction, knowing that justice would come to his brother's murderer.

The soldiers threw him to the marble floors in a tangle of misshapen legs and jutting elbows. He grunted, awkwardly hauling himself upright, straining at the bonds on his wrists.

Batu-Khasar watched him, glaring. "We'd heard nothing of this," he growled, raising his cursed hands. "Many seasons have passed since we've encountered a curse."

Elerek only glowered. One last surprise in Instanolde.

"Among my people, curses are wrought to be waged against your enemies. This one . . ." The warlord shook his head, turning his large hands over, observing their every angle. "Tell me how you use it."

"You're cursed. Now you will die," Elerek spat. "It's simple."

Gaudab scoffed. "Nearly drowned by a boy king, a filthy river rat. None of those cursed among my soldiers can do that. Why are you different?"

"It's *my* curse." Elerek's shoulders hunched. "I will drown you—all of you. Then my brother's blood will be avenged."

Mutters swept through the Jarkin company. A few uttered

what sounded like oaths and spat. Gaudab raised a fist, and silence swept over the room.

"Instanolde never had this fight, little king. You have lain vulnerable and exposed since your forebearer's end. He was a king worthy of battle. You, you are nothing. These lands belong to us now."

Elerek drew a deep breath. "Until the curse kills you." Until it took them all—the Jarkins, the great enemy of Instanolde; him, the last king of a dying era; and Lystra, the hope of the future.

What would remain? Would the sun really set on Instanolde? After all their striving, would the end come all the same? The thought broke his heart.

Gaudab mounted the dais, his steps deliberate, decisive. Watching Elerek with unblinking eyes, full of hatred and malice, he slowly settled onto the throne—the throne that Elerek himself had never sat upon. His great shoulders relaxed, fitting against its harsh angles. Then, a smile curled over his lips. His hands moved over the throne's arms in a long caress, making a grand show of his pleasure.

Elerek's arms twisted in his bonds. *I will watch you drown if it's the last thing I do.*

"You're only alive, little king, because we must break your curse. I'm told that if you die, we all perish. Is that true?"

Perish. The memory returned full force, unbidden, and left Elerek cleaved from the inside out. The haze, existence blurring at the edges like scorch marks. The air, scented with metal. His chair stood empty, and he couldn't remember why it was empty. A wetness gathered beneath him, and he remembered wondering if the curse had come to claim him.

No, that time he didn't bleed water. He'd bled blood—a lot of it.

Razhar had called his name, his voice sounding very far

428

away. There were sobs in his voice as he called for help, echoing across the darkening void in Elerek's mind.

Someone else came, kneeling beside him. Someone with eyes the same color, the same dark head of curls. Someone whose veins ran with the same blood. Some vague, distant part of Elerek's mind wanted to scream, to tell his brother to stay back. Not to touch him.

"Don't leave me, brother."

The memory ended. Elerek found himself gasping for breath, his lungs heaving for the life preserved by the love of his friends. He hunched forward, clenching his eyes shut. *I stayed, brother. It's you who left.*

"Well?" Gaudab leaned forward, his posture reminiscent of a prowling lion. "Speak!"

Elerek lifted his head, staring into the fury hovering in the invader's eyes. Yes, he stayed. He lived. Against all odds, even while his kingdom fell into darkness and ruin. He could mourn the loss, the broken dreams, and grieve until the stars rained down from the heavens. His days were few and cursed. The tragedies could outnumber the sands.

"One life, Elerek. A mighty gift from the Maker of the stars."

He gritted his teeth, expanding his lungs with a deep draught of air. He'd chosen to live before. Could he reforge himself? One last time? Even here, before the Jarkin who had murdered Cormek, slaughtered his people, and sat on his throne?

It mattered how he lived.

"I'll go back to that dank cell before I answer questions."

Gaudab huffed, signaling with his hand.

The door to the throne room opened with a mighty groan, as if it too strained beneath the weight of all that had gone wrong. Elerek looked over his shoulder, and his heart sank.

Lystra. She appeared small, walking between two hulking

Jarkins. Shadows encircled her eyes, dust and tears covered her once-magnificent skirt, and her hair flew in wisps about her face. They had bound her hands, but her steps were not that of a captive.

She walked like she did on their wedding day, following the same path across polished marble. Towards the throne. Towards him.

Elerek's heart twisted. Her fierce countenance, a boldness severe as the dawn, had drawn his soul to hers—and they had lost everything.

As she approached him, her steps slowed. Her carefully erected pretenses began to crumble, and when their eyes met, Elerek saw only misery.

All at once, Elerek knew exactly how the following conversation would play out, and if he found out that they'd hurt her . . .

"Unbind her," Gaudab commanded. "She isn't something to fear."

Lystra's hands fell to her sides. Skin made of water covered her fingers, stretching up across her knuckles.

"I touch you, and I'll die."

"I won't let that happen."

Elerek had caused a great many things to happen, terrible things that he knew he would regret for as long as he lived. But not this. No, Lystra had done this. She chose the curse—just like Myra. Did she . . . ? Could she . . . ?

"Bring her closer. Let's see this queen who fled our grasp across the desert." Gaudab's voice echoed over the marble.

The soldiers took her shoulders, marching her up the dais's steps to stand before the Jarkin warlord. Fear fled Lystra's gaze. Instead, she glared at Gaudab with all the fury of a raging cardant.

"So, then." The Jarkin took a long, lingering glance. A cruel smile appeared on his lips.

Elerek felt water gather in vengeful beads along his wrists and fingers, the wrath of an avenging torrent lurking just beneath his cursed skin.

"A queen to not one, but *two* weak, Instan kings?" A laugh, like the bark of a jackal, broke from his throat. "Ah, river lily, how much better you deserve."

Lystra said nothing.

"And what of that other girl? The dead one in the square?"

Elerek braced his soul, sealing away the pain, the grief, and glared up at him. "Another who will be avenged by your death."

Gaudab rose from the throne, his gaze burning. "It is not my death that interests me, river rat, but yours. Are you interested in answering my questions now?"

Lystra's head spun toward him, her face awash with horror. "El, don't—" Her voice cut off as Gaudab's hand clamped down on the back of her neck.

He pulled her toward him and then, drawing a small knife, set it against her neck. A trickle of blood, bright and red, ran down her skin. "Please, consider fairness, especially to your queen."

"Don't. Touch. Her." Water began to pool around Elerek, streaming from his bound hands. The soldiers circled nearer, like hunters cornering feral prey. But he couldn't move, not without his hands, not without his chair. Lystra lay out of reach of his protection.

Don't touch her. How tragic that, only a few short hours ago, this same measure applied to him.

"Yes. Yes, it's true." Elerek's breath shuddered. "You kill me, everyone who is cursed—you, me, your men, my queen— we all die."

The knife moved away from Lystra's neck. The queen began to tremble, her chest heaving in frantic pants.

Gaudab narrowed his eyes. "You know this, how?"

"I . . . I tried to kill myself." The words sounded far away, as if spoken from the farthest recesses of the palace, the shadows where he had once been content to hide. "Everyone else nearly died with me."

The familiar shame rose in his soul, hovering like a cloud amidst the most brilliant of skies. How well he remembered the pain, the ache of living a life he didn't wish to live. The knife and the blood did nothing to ease it.

Gaudab studied him with the slitted gaze of a viper. "Hmm." He tilted his head. "Do you wish that you'd died then, river rat?"

The flow ceased from his hands. Elerek's eyes traveled to Lystra's, her gaze filled with enough sorrow to rival his own.

But there, he also saw resolve. The strength of a thousand cardants pounding across the barren desert. The fierceness of the warrior queen who had survived so much—and still, still she fought, hoping for the dawn of a new sunrise upon a battle-field of shifting sands.

Here, at the end of his strength, it was hers that pulsed in his heart.

"No," he replied, drawing a deep breath. "No, I don't."

He promised Cormek that he'd try, and he wanted to live. Now more than ever before.

Chapter 50

Lystra

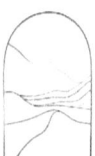

Lystra couldn't feel her hands. Numb appendages with transparent skin, evidence of the curse that now lurked in her body. The curse that she had chosen.

Dooming her to the same death as her king.

The sight of Elerek's face, haggard, worn, and set like a flint, made her want to weep. Drenched in cursed water, his tunic clung to his hunched shoulders, lining every muscle, tight with his fury.

She wished she could again help him stand, let him be the fierce, avenging warrior he'd become and help him defeat those who would have them dead. Instead, she could offer him nothing.

Behind her, Gaudab loomed close like the insurmountable mountains from which he came. Too close. She heard his knife being drawn again.

He grabbed her arm, wrenching it back. The knife's cold edge set against the flesh above her shoulder blade, letting loose a cry from her lips.

"No, *no!*" Elerek's voice roared in unison with the sound of water splashing onto the marble tile.

Silk tore, sliced from Lystra's shoulder. Blood trailed down her back, hot against the numbness of her skin. Quick slashes, each more painful than the last. She tried to break free, squirming and shrieking, but Gaudab's grip held like iron. His movements were focused and precise, far too precise.

When he released her, she collapsed to her knees. Pain dulled her ears, drowning out the sound of Elerek's roars.

Her hand moved to her shoulder, tracing the hot, sticky mess of skin. Her fingers met long lines, deep and raw. Tears dripped down her face, falling alongside great drops of blood.

Gaudab stepped past her, speaking into the whole of the throne room. "In the mountains, we claim what is ours, marking it for all to see. Our animals, our weapons, our *women.*"

Lystra didn't know what burned hotter. The wound—the mark—on her shoulder or the raging furnace of Elerek's eyes. Despite his position, planted on the ground atop crippled legs, his arms bound and useless, two Jarkins with curse marks on their arms still held his shoulders, holding him back.

Together they had striven for their kingdom, to hope beyond the bleak future. Perhaps now they would die together.

"What we have, we have fought for. Bled for. And once we have taken something for our own, we defend it—and let no one take it from us."

Across the pillared room, another door opened.

Gaudab stepped down from the dais, his shadow falling across the conquered king. "That includes a curse. So, you will tell me how to break it, and then we'll get on with it."

Lystra drew herself up, standing on legs as weak as river reeds. Elerek couldn't tell them. Elerek didn't know.

Another set of Jarkin soldiers marched down the length of the pillared hall. Between them stood Razhar. The dancer with stars in his eyes now took staggering steps. His garish clothing held no appeal, as deceitful as the lies he'd spun to carry the truth he'd hidden.

Lystra's hands clenched. She didn't see the complete picture, not yet, but this entire scene felt like a betrayal.

Elerek twisted, glancing over his shoulder. His face became cast in iron, every line hardened with an avenging fury.

Brought before the dais, Razhar glanced between Elerek and Lystra, and then his eyes fell on Gaudab. "What have you . . . ?"

"This is shameful mercy, idiot Kushite," Gaudab growled. "I'd worry about your own skin."

Razhar ground his teeth and wrung his hands, fidgeting.

Lystra's eyes darted to the edge of his tattoo, visible along his deep collar. Why the constellation? How deeply was Razhar tied to the curse? Why did his hands turn to sands the way that Elerek's turned to water?

"Now." Gaudab folded his thick arms. "I don't like Kushites. They're detestable, guarding their precious canals and fighting like cowards, out of reach atop their buzzards. If they even fight at all, more likely to bury themselves in musty parchments."

Razhar didn't speak.

"Strange to find one here, defending a cursed rat." The warlord's eyes shifted between Elerek and Razhar. "I think you're stalling, trying to save your king." He barked a hideous laugh. "Or your queen. You are a selfish bit of dust, aren't you?"

Elerek's eyes flashed, darting toward Lystra before glowering at Razhar. "You . . ." He seemed to be able to find no insult suitable.

Razhar practically shriveled.

Lystra wondered if she might simply shrivel. Surely Razhar

was only a flirt. He probably treated her no differently than any other young lady he happened to cross, to share a dance with.

If Elerek was out of the way—did he think that he stood a chance?

"I'll drown you too," Elerek growled, his voice dark and terrible.

Gaudab clenched his fists, skeletal hands surrounded by watery skin. "If what the Kushite says is true, nobody ought to drown."

"As if you can believe a word the filthy, lowly scum says." Elerek leaned forward, his neck jutting out like a viper poised to strike.

Razhar visibly shuddered. He wrung his hands, glittering grains of sand falling between his fingers. He ignored Elerek, his eyes rising to the dais, where Lystra stood before her throne with blood streaming down her back and arms. His words were a whisper, fraught with misery. The same grief that Lystra heard echoed in Elerek's voice, the same that resounded in her heart.

"Lystra, tell them."

The eyes of all the cursed fell upon her.

The blood drained from Elerek's face. His lips moved but no sound came out. The pain of a bitter betrayal poured from his eyes.

Lystra couldn't breathe, her lungs begging to drown with the curse she now also bore.

But she bore a crown, the image of the queen of Instanolde. Hers was the face of hope, the dawn of a brighter tomorrow. Hers was the voice that they would believe.

She looked at Elerek. Her king. Could she offer him anything but death? But now, he was owed the truth that Razhar didn't tell him. The truth that Elerek had promised—

that he hadn't given her—she would give, no matter how devastating.

Gaudab snarled. "Well? Shall we use the knife again, little queen?"

Lystra shook and she wondered if she might falter, right here, right now. "We . . . we have to . . ."

"Out with it!"

"He has to die." Tears poured down Lystra's cheeks. She couldn't look at Elerek. "The curse is tied to the wrathgiver constellation. There . . . and only there, the king must be killed."

"In the mountains, we've different names for the stars." Gaudab signaled his soldiers again. "Bring me a sky chart." He huffed. "If your king is slain beneath these stars, we will survive?"

"There's a dagger." The words tasted noxious, full of poison. "It belongs to the binder who bound his curse. It must be used in the . . . ritual."

Elerek gave a low growl, deep in his throat.

I'm sorry, El. I'm so sorry. Lystra summoned the courage to look at him. Her heart broke.

She'd seen hatred before, mostly in Dalmah's gaze, from the face of a curse binder who had lashed out in vengeance for the wrongs done unto her. But this was different. This was a man broken, a man who looked like her dead betrothed, who had shown her how to live beyond grief's grip. The man she loved.

The dark rage painting his face told her that he might drown her too. Maybe they all ought to drown.

"Where is this dagger?" Gaudab demanded.

Lystra shook her head.

The soldiers returned with the star chart. Gaudab unrolled it, muttering foul words about the Instans' neat, flowing script.

"There." Razhar pointed. Then, his face turned purple.

The Jarkin threw the chart aside and spun toward Razhar. Standing two heads higher than the Kushite, he looked as if he could snap him in half across his knee. "You speak of impossibilities, which can only mean that these are lies."

Razhar took a step back. "They're not."

"I'm not risking my men by dragging them across the accursed Sancen during high summer. Folly and doom."

The Sancen? Lystra's heart lodged in her throat. She scrambled to assemble the skies, to form a map from her memory.

She'd seen the wrathgiver. Framed by silk curtains. Beyond the window of Elerek's bedroom on a night when their souls were bare to one another. When tragic grief gave way to soft voices and beautiful eyes as the king told stories into the night, moments where they chose to hope with each breath. The stars had hung low on the horizon, above the mountains.

Across the Sancen. The season was wrong. All wrong.

They were water and the Sancen was sand and scorching sunlight. Death and fury and heat. Mortals fell beneath its power. They clung to the Gungole like a lifeline, choosing to survive.

Life depended on it.

Gaudab hissed a long string of foul words in his own tongue. He marched toward her and, before Lystra could react, took her by the neck and threw her down.

She hit the stonework below the dais in a tangle of silk and blood.

"Kill the girl. Slowly. I want her blood covering this room."

Lystra blinked, the tile's patterns spinning before her gaze. Blood, like red sunbursts, splattered across the marble, dripping from the mark on her shoulder.

The Jarkin screamed for blood but received water instead. Streams snaked over the tile, washing it clean. Lystra felt its touch on her feet, her knees, soaking into her skirt. She could hardly move, trembling and bleeding, but she found the strength to lift her head. The soldiers, as cursed as they were, backed away.

The cursed water settled like the surface of a mirror beneath them, reflecting the great golden dome.

Elerek glared up at Gaudab, his eyes burning. In that moment, Lystra had no doubt that the curse had changed him in a monstrous and terrible way. The same man who had fought for their lives could use the curse to inflict terrible destruction with a dark and vile power.

Maybe there was never any hope of saving him. Only a foolish thought of a broken heart. A tear fell down her cheek.

"If you want to live . . ." Each word from the king's lips was a thunderbolt thrown from the skies. "If you want to survive this curse, you will obey me. If you want to chase the stars, I can. If you want to cross the Sancen, I can cross it."

Lystra blinked. A chill crept across her skin at the fury in his voice.

"I can still drown each and every one of you." His eyes swept the room, lingering on Razhar. "Consider it mercy, for now."

Mercy from the cursed king of Instanolde who could kill with a touch and drown with a torrent. Lystra shuddered.

"But you will spare the queen. No one will harm her. Every drop of her blood that you've shed this day will be demanded of you tenfold. She. Will. Live."

Live. The word echoed down the length of the throne room. The dream of a king doomed to die. Lystra shifted, sending ripples across the water. She was cursed now. The only way for her to live was for him to die.

And she had never wanted that. Not for a moment.

Gaudab glared down at Elerek, two kings in a silent stand-off. Razhar looked stunned, almost as if he might faint. Regret swirled in his eyes, but Lystra didn't believe it.

Then, in the blink of an eye, the war ended. "So be it," Gaudab declared, his voice the jagged edge of a knife.

Soldiers stepped across the cursed water, shattering the mirror image of the marbled pillars and the great gold dome. Agony ripped through her shoulder as they hauled her to her feet. She hadn't the strength to fight them.

"El . . ." Her voice was faint, weak with the weight of all that was broken.

Another pair of soldiers took Elerek's shoulders, dragging him toward the shadows between the pillars. He craned his neck, watching her.

The rage of the cursed man had fled, taking with it the courage of Instanolde's heir, the true king.

Only bitter sorrow remained.

End of Book 1

Acknowledgments

Deserts are often referred to as a place of discovery, renewal, and also of trial and sorrow. In the little over four years from inception to publication, *Queen of Shifting Sands* has seen it all, a companion with me as I endured my own deserts. And in those dry places, I found community, support, and the love of so many people. Without them, this book would not exist, and I'm a better person for having known all of you.

Michael, my soulmate, the love of my life, my husband: through every stage of this book's crazy adventure, you were there. Every terrible draft/scene, you read it all and were there to remind me that the story was improving, that my skill had improved, and that it was a story worth telling. Thank you for the hours devoted to boring things like dishes and laundry when I needed to finish edits on time, and creating space where I could write. And thank you for loving Lystra, Elerek, and Razhar just as much as I do.

My family, mom, dad, Andrew and Blanca, Aimee and Josh (and baby Alice!), Hannah and Jake, Stephen, and Justin, for being you and being awesome. Thank you especially to my mom for making sure that I loved to read and supplying a host of fantastic books. I love you guys.

Brittany Eden, my dear friend, critique partner, and unofficial agent and marketing conspirator: so much of what this book became are things I learned from you, from your advice, sharpening, and encouraging me to dig deeper and make this book something beautiful. You have been such a steadfast supporter and I'm so thankful that Realm Makers brought us together. Every time I write a kissing scene, I think of you (and kdramas, of course).

Speaking of Realm Makers, I am beyond thankful for the support that this conference and community has given to me and so many other authors. Thank you for this space where so many wonderful relationships have blossomed. Without it, I wouldn't have met Katie Phillips and Lauren Hildebrand, the first editors who helped me get QSS into shape. Janeen Ippolito and Amy Williams and their team, who saw this story as something special worth polishing. Angela Watts who encouraged me and helped me wrangle my crazy sentences. And all the classes, workshops, mentors, and authors who have granted their wisdom and guidance.

And the people. So many people. Michelle Bruhn, Liz Koetsier, Mary Dipple, Andi Gregory, my "inner circle". You ladies mean the world to me and I'm so thankful that each of you has been placed in my life. Your encouragement and love, even when I'm at my worst, has been such a huge blessing. Your prayers and hugs and late night (and early morning, silly time zones) messages fill me with such sweetness. Also, the steady supply of memes including, but not limited to, cats and all things cosmere related. I wish we all lived closer and could drink coffee and eat ice cream together.

A few other special shoutouts, the rest of the ladies in the Iron Quill Binder critique group, Kayla and Kara. Esther Wallace, for your prayers and support. For the amazing artists that have brought the world of Instanolde to life: Hannah Rogers for your impeccable portraits of my trio that have gone with me on so many adventures, Kristen Hildebrand for painting the perfect cardant, Salome Totladze for cover art that absolutely blew me away, and Kateryna Vitkovska for bringing to life one of my favorite scenes in the book. I must also thank the National Park Service, stewards of some of my favorite places. I'm thankful to serve a God who is an artist, a creator, and the One who formed Death Valley, Zion, the Grand Canyon, and the wild places that inspired this book.

And, from the bottom of my heart, thank you to Whimsical Publishing and the incomparable Micheline. Thank you for loving this story and its characters and bringing this beautiful vision together. I didn't know what the Lord had in store for QSS when I sent off that submission, but He definitely did above and beyond what I could imagine. I'm so thankful for all the hours of hard work that have gone into this project from you, Christina, and the rest of the team. I am so blessed and eternally grateful.

All glory to God, to Jesus my Lord and Savior, the maker of the stars, the One who gave me this story to tell. I've always believed that authors are stewards of the stories we are given, and I'm thankful that this one is mine. There has never been a moment that I have walked alone, even through the deserts, and through it all, He was faithful.

-Kaitlyn Carter Brown

About the Author

Kaitlyn Carter Brown, an avid adventurer both on and off page, crafts fierce fantasy filled with high stakes, sweeping worlds, and courageous characters stories while taking inspiration from her treks across the US' National Parks. Off the page, you'll find her decorating cakes, drinking plenty of coffee, and surviving the Arizona heat much like her army of houseplants. Her work has been featured in *Bingeworthy* and *Sensational* anthologies, *Fantasea* anthology, and *Crowns* anthology.

Kailtlyn's second book, the sequel to Queen of Shifting Sands will be releasing through Whimsical Publishing in 2025.

instagram.com/mrs.carter_theauthor